The Cambion Cycle

The Cambion Cycle

Quincy Harker Year Two

John G. Hartness

Falstaff Books
Charlotte, North Carolina

Also by John G. Hartness

The Black Knight Chronicles - Omnibus Edition
Paint it Black
In the Still of the Knight
Man in Black

Scattered, Smothered, & Chunked - Bubba the Monster Hunter Season One
Grits, Guns, & Glory - Bubba the Monster Hunter Season Two
Wine, Women, & Song - Bubba the Monster Hunter Season Three

Year One: A Quincy Harker, Demon Hunter Collection

Queen of Kats Book I - Betrayal
Queen of Kats Book II - Survival

From the Stone
The Chosen

Cover Art by
www.rockingbookcovers.com

Formatting by Susan H. Roddey
www.shroddey.com

ISBN-13: 978-1543049510
ISBN-10: 1543049516

Published by Falstaff Media
Charlotte, North Carolina
Printed in U.S.A

Contents

Acknowledgements

Thanks as always to Melissa Gilbert for all her help, and for trying in vain to teach me where the commas go.

Many thanks to Adrijus at rockingbookcovers.com for the awesome cover to this and most of the Harker books.

The following people help me bring this work to you by their Patreon-age. You can join them at Patreon.com/johnhartness.

Sean Fitzpatrick	Theresa Glover
Sharon Moore	Salem Macknee
Sarah Ashburn	Trey Alexander
Wendy Taylor	Jim Ryan
Sheelagh Semper	Word of the Nerd
Charlotte Babb	Tracy Syrstad
Carol Baker	Russell Ventimeglia
Noah Sturdevant	Elizabeth Donald
Leonard Rosenthol	Samantha Dunaway Bryant
Lisa Kochurina	Shael Hawman
Patrick Dugan	Bill Schlichting
Melinda Hammy	Steven R. Yanacsek
Jeremy Snyder	Scott Furman
Emilia Agrafojo	Rebecca Ledford
Brian Tate	Ray Spitz
Michelle E. Botwinick	
Candice Carpenter	

Heaven Sent

Chapter One

I GUESS MOST PEOPLE DON'T MEET THEIR GUARDIAN ANGEL AT A MURDER scene. I guess most people don't meet their guardian angel at all, but I've never been most people. So while it didn't surprise me too much to see an angel hanging around the newly deceased body of Lincoln Baxter, Esquire, prosecuting attorney extraordinaire, it surprised me quite a bit to find out that she was there for me, not for the soul of Mr. Baxter. But I'm getting ahead of myself. I do that.

It was about seven years ago. The sky dumped rain in buckets, and there was no blood to speak of, so either Dead Lincoln had been lying there getting rained on for a while, or he'd been shot somewhere else and dropped in the parking lot of the Harris Teeter on Randolph Road. Since that strip mall was fairly high-rent, even seven years ago, I figured he hadn't been there that long. That left a body dump, and that meant trace evidence, although most of it was currently getting washed into storm drains thanks to the mid-June thunderstorm. This was before every house had streaming video, so I hadn't yet binge-watched every episode of every *CSI* franchise, but I still understood a little about fibers and transfer from a couple of cases I spent working with Scotland Yard back in the 1960s. Admittedly, the culprit in those cases had eventually turned out to be a pair of ghouls resurrected by an Oxford medical student with a talent for the occult and a moral compass that only pointed south, but the theories were sound.

I had a few advantages that Scotland Yard didn't have. I could use my Sight to take note of the fact that there was no magical trace around the body, but that didn't really mean much. Magical energy and running water don't get along very well, and it was pouring rain. What meant a lot more, although I had no friggin' idea exactly what it meant, was the pair of ethereal wings the deceased was sporting. I could only see them in the supernatural spectrum, but they glowed a pale golden yellow in my Sight, and I'd never seen them before, which made this murder pretty unique.

The blonde standing just outside the police cordon was also pretty damned unique, and the presence of a beauty like that at a murder scene at three in the morning should have been conspicuous as hell, except that no one seemed to see her but me. So I turned my Sight on her, and quickly dropped back into the normal spectrum, rubbing my temples from the glare. I'd never seen anything like her either, and that was two more new things than I typically liked in one night.

I shook my head and looked up just in time to see the rotund form of Detective Rich Sponholz lumbering toward me. Sponholz was a decent enough detective, if he wasn't winning any marathons. He was a big man, thick through the shoulders and arms, obviously an athlete who lost the drive to work out after years of paperwork and stakeouts. He didn't like me much, so it was no surprise that his face was turning red and his finger was waving wildly at me long before he covered the twenty feet between us.

"Goddammit, Harker, I told you to stay the fuck away from my crime scenes," he started in on me when he was still almost ten feet away. "I've got enough bullshit to deal with, this being that prissy fuck from the DA's office, without you coming down here talking about ghosts and devils and your hocus-pocus bullshit."

Okay, so Sponholz might have had a few blind spots in his worldview, but I usually didn't hold that against him, or anyone else for that matter. Most humans don't go through life calling the most famous vampire in history "Uncle" or throwing around magical spells from the age of sixteen. Me? Well, let's just say that when your parents are Jonathan Harker and Mina Murray, you don't come from exactly "normal" stock. So I didn't begrudge the good detective his prejudices, but I did turn to see how my ethereal visitor reacted to his diatribe. She seemed unfazed, like she either didn't hear what he was saying (yelling, really) or like she was so focused on what else was going on that she didn't notice him.

"And good morning to you, too, Detective," I said when he came near enough to converse normally. I'm not opposed to a good shouting match but only when I think it might get me something. And I've been around long enough to know that yelling at cops never gets me anything good. "What can I do to help you this fine morning?"

"You can fuck right off, that's what you can do, Harker," Sponholz replied. "It's the middle of the night, it's raining like pouring piss out of a boot, and I've got a dead city attorney lying in the grocery store parking lot. The last goddamn thing I need is you."

"Well, in that case, I'll just leave," I said, turning to go.

"Wait a minute," the detective said, grabbing my elbow. I expected him to do something like that, which is how I kept my reflexes in check. I *really* don't like people grabbing me, and it usually ends up in broken or missing body parts for the grabber. But I kinda liked Sponholz, despite his insistence that I was a fraud, and I didn't like jail, so I chose not to break his arm.

I turned back to him instead. "Yes, Detective?"

"What are you doing here?" he asked.

"What do you mean, Detective?"

"I mean, why are you in the parking lot of a closed shopping center in the middle of the night where a city attorney just happens to be lying in a pool of his own blood?"

"Actually, I think you'll find he's likely lying in a pool of rainwater, motor oil, and leaked engine coolant. I saw very little blood. But I was only able to examine things from behind the police line. You see, I arrived after your boys and girls in blue called in the body. I have a police scanner, and I like to stay abreast of what goes on in my city."

Sponholz's face turned three different shades of red as he spluttered at me. "Y-y-your city? *Your* city? You nut bar, what in the hell…oh never mind, just go home."

"Take a look at the amount of blood by the body, Detective. He wasn't killed here. Have a nice day!" I called after Sponholz as he stomped away.

"That attitude is going to get you in trouble someday, Quincy Harker," my mysterious lady said.

"It's already done that," I replied. "More times than I can count. But that's not the important thing."

"What's the important thing?" she asked, a little smile playing around the corner of her mouth.

"The important thing is what in the hell is an angel doing hanging around a dead lawyer in North Carolina? Don't you have somebody to save or a plague to call down on Egypt or something?"

"We don't do much plaguing nowadays. Just a lot less call for that kind of thing. And as for the saving thing, well, that's what I'm doing. Kinda. I'm Glory, your guardian angel."

"My guardian angel is named after a villain from *Buffy the Vampire Slayer*?"

"What can I say? Joss Whedon's a genius. Now, how did you know I wasn't just another onlooker?"

"Well, partly because you wouldn't have been 'another' onlooker, you would have been the only onlooker. It's three in the morning. There's nobody here but you, me, and the cops. Speaking of whom, let's move this conversation somewhere a little more private."

"What's wrong, Harker? Don't want to be seen talking to an angel?"

"Sweetheart, with a body like yours, talking isn't the only thing I wouldn't mind being seen doing. But since you don't seem to be visible to anybody but me, I'd rather not look like I'm completely out of my mind."

She at least had the good grace to look chagrined when she looked around and realized I was right. "Shit," she muttered under her breath. "I'm still not used to this whole walking among the mortals stuff. Let's go." Then she vanished. Because that's what angels do. They just appear and disappear whenever they feel like it, with no regard for the laws of physics or polite conversation.

Because I can't just teleport to wherever I want to be, I trudged through the rain to my battered navy Toyota Camry. Not the flashiest of cars, but almost impossible to spot on a crowded street if I needed to stake something out, and not nearly interesting enough to steal, which is probably good for the thieves given the assortment of mundane and magical weapons and accessories I keep in the trunk. I got in the car and gave myself a shake, rummaged around in the floorboards behind the passenger seat for napkins from a couple of McDonald's takeout bags, and dried off my face and hands enough to hold onto the steering wheel.

"That seems like quite a nuisance," said a voice beside me. I whipped my head around, gathering my will for a spell as I did, then relaxed and let the power flow out of me when I saw it was Glory.

"Jesus Christ, angel! You could give a guy a heart attack doing shit like that," I grumbled.

"That doesn't seem like a term of endearment when you say it like that," she said, chewing on her bottom lip in an absolutely human, and adorable, fashion. Now that water wasn't pouring into my eyes, I took a good look at my visitor from the ethereal realms. She didn't look all *that* much like Clare Kramer, the actress that played her namesake on *Buffy the Vampire Slayer*, but she did have curly blond hair, kewpie-doll cheeks, and brilliant blue eyes. She looked to be about five-eight or so, and I learned a long time ago not to guess at a woman's age or weight, and I was betting that translated into angels, too. But she was trim, and fit, and no matter how I tried to get a peek at her back, I couldn't see even a hint of wing. No halo, either. I was starting to get disappointed at the shortcomings of my guardian angel when I realized that she had just materialized in my passenger seat out of thin air, completely dry, as though raindrops didn't touch her. *Yep, she's plenty magic, halo or no.*

"They're spiritual," she said, pointing at the area over her shoulder. "The wings. I don't need them for anything while I'm here. They just help me ride the currents as I navigate the planes."

"Navigate the planes?" I repeated, having no idea what she was talking about.

"You know, Heaven, Hell, Earth, Purgatory, Valhalla…all of those." Her voice was bright and cheerful, like she talked about Valhalla like it was a real place every day. Hell, maybe she did.

"You…fly between the planes?" I asked.

"That's how we get there," she said. "You would have to use a spell, or have a spell go wrong. Or die, of course. But that shouldn't happen any time soon. Not if I have anything to say about it." With that, her expression became stern and her eyes flickered, like there was lightning behind them. Apparently she took the "guardian" part of her job description seriously.

I shook my head, then asked her the question that had been on the tip of my tongue ever since I first saw her. "What are you doing here?"

"You mean Earth, or here specifically?"

"Let's start with here specifically. If we need to broaden the scope of our conversation to include the whole planet, I'm going to need a drink. You know, now that I mention it…" I leaned over, reached across the startled angel's lap, and popped open the glove compartment. I reached in and pulled out a flask, twisted off the top, and let eighteen years of oak-barrel-aged Macallan pour down my throat. I turned the flask up and let the flavor of the Scottish moors wash over my tongue and teeth, swallowing what felt like centuries of fine craftsmanship with every drop.

After I shook the last drops from my flask, with a warm fire burning in my belly and throat from the whiskey and the slightest fuzziness at the edges of my vision, I tossed the empty flask back in the glove box, closed the door, and leaned back in my seat. "Now we can talk," I said to the angel. "I am now sufficiently fortified to hold a conversation with an angel in my economy car."

"Well, like I said, I'm Glory, and I've been assigned as your guardian angel. Not everyone gets one, but you seem to find yourself in more trouble than most, so you get me." She smiled brightly at me, and I found myself wishing desperately for more whiskey.

"And if I say no?" I asked.

"What?"

"What if I say 'thanks but no thanks'?"

"You mean refuse my protection?"

"Yup."

"I don't know if you *can*. As far as I know, no one has ever tried. Besides, why would you want to? It's not like I'm going to be watching your every move and tattling to Father whenever you sin. Trust me, the last thing I want to do is watch you and some of the women you go out with."

"Those are all perfectly nice girls, thank you very much."

"Regardless, that's not what my job is about. I'm here to take care of you, not anyone you might be sleeping with."

"And I say no thanks." I laughed a little bit, one of those short, barking laughs that almost sounds like a cough. "Sweetie, I'm pushing a hundred years old at this point. If something out there was going to kill me, it would have done it long ago."

Chapter Two

So there I was, sitting in my car with a stunned angel sitting next to me. I chuckled again and started the car. I pulled out of the parking lot and headed up Randolph into Uptown. I had a new condo, and the bed was calling me pretty loudly.

"Why were you there?" Glory asked.

"What do you mean?"

"What were you doing at the crime scene?"

"I could ask you the same thing, I suppose."

"You could, but I'd answer instead of ducking the question. I was there looking for you. I felt like it was time we met, so I followed your aura."

"You followed my aura?" I asked.

"Of course. I'm your guardian angel. Quincy, I can sense you no matter where you are."

"Don't call me Quincy."

"Why not? Your name is Quincy."

"Only my family calls me Quincy. And nowadays that list only has one name on it."

"Of course. Your 'Uncle Luke,' as you call him. But what do your friends call you, Quincy?"

"All my friends are dead, Glory."

"What about that nice policeman you spoke to back at the crime scene?"

"He hates me, in case you missed it. He threatens to put me in jail on a regular basis."

"I'm sure you deserve it. There have been some less-than-savory activities in your past, if you'll recall."

"Pretty sure I can't forget 1944. Wait a minute. Exactly how long have you been spying on me?"

"You're a fairly new assignment. I've only watched over you for the past twenty years or so. But that's plenty of time for me to understand that you have only the loosest understanding of the term 'law' as it applied to you."

"Twenty years, huh? And you decided that we need to meet tonight? What the fuck is going on?" I'd never met an angel before, so I wasn't one hundred percent sure she wasn't going to smite me for cursing, but she wasn't carrying a flaming sword, so I thought I might get away with it. Besides, I was starting to feel seriously creeped out knowing there was an angel watching my every move.

"Nothing is going on," the angel replied. "I just felt it was time we began to interact more directly, that's all."

"So angels are terrible liars. That's good to know. Now, you want to stop bullshitting me and tell me what you want with me?"

"You want to tell me why you were in that parking lot in the middle of the night?" I could feel her eyes boring into me from the passenger seat, but I kept my gaze locked on the wet street unrolling in my headlights. I passed the Mint Museum, didn't say anything. I passed Presbyterian Hospital, didn't say anything. I crossed under I-277, didn't say anything. Finally, I got caught by a red light just before my right turn onto College. I took a deep breath and let it out slow.

"I felt something." I felt something putting those words out there. Stupid. Yeah, my life hasn't exactly been a Norman Rockwell picture of normalcy, but it hasn't been all that weird, either. The occasional monster, a rogue wizard every once in a while, but nothing really heavy-duty on the psychic or mystical front. Until tonight. Tonight I'd been jolted stone sober by a sudden need to get to the parking lot of the Cotswold Mall. Whatever happened, it killed a good buzz and cost me well over two hundred bucks in top-shelf liquor.

"I was on my way home from my book club," I continued.

"They read at The Men's Club?" Glory asked, naming the strip club I'd spent most of the evening in.

"Usually the young ladies there are more interested in pictures. Pictures of Andrew Jackson, pictures of Ulysses S. Grant, you get the idea. They have a particular fondness for pictures of Benjamin Franklin."

"Not the point, Q."

"Q?" I looked at her. A playful little smile curled up one corner of her mouth, and she gave me a saucy look right back.

"Yeah, Q. You don't want me to call you Quincy, and calling you Harker all the time sounds like I'm angry with you—"

"Which you probably will be," I added.

"I will be if you interrupt me," she fired back. "But Q was the best I could come up with on short notice. Unless you'd like me to use one of your other names. Like Holmwood, maybe?"

"No thanks," I said, finally noticing my green light and turning onto College. I drove for a couple blocks and pulled left into my building's parking garage. The condo boom in the 80s and 90s had hit Charlotte with a vengeance, but the recession in the early 2000s put a lot of luxury places on the market for ridiculously low prices. With a little financial backing from Uncle Luke, I bought my condo for well under market value. Not to mention the deal I got for the rest of the building. I had the top floor to myself; was just a couple blocks from good restaurants, the library, and Spirit Square—a great place to see a play or a concert; and I had a view of the city in all directions from twenty-five floors up. As far as lairs went, I'd had worse. Northern California in the early sixties was particularly unfortunate.

I pulled my car into my reserved spot and got out. I walked around to the trunk and pulled out a black backpack, slung it over one shoulder, and walked toward the elevator. I clicked the lock button on my remote twice and got the chirp of my alarm engaging, then pulled open the door to the elevator lobby to find Glory standing there.

"That's really annoying," I said.

"So is leaving me in the car without a word."

"Fair enough." I slid my keys into the pocket of my jeans and pulled out my wallet. I withdrew a plastic key card and inserted it into a slot on the elevator panel just above the buttons. Then I pushed the "up" button and pulled out my card.

"What does that do?" Glory asked.

"It tells the elevator to ignore all other call buttons and come straight down to the garage without stopping. It does the same thing on the inside of the elevator, too."

"Isn't that kind of rude to the people waiting for the elevator?"

"There are four elevators, so only a little. And if they don't like it, they can buy their own building." I gave her my best "devil-may-care" grin and stepped through the opening elevator doors. She didn't grin back. I guess "devil-may-care" might be the wrong attitude to wear around angels. The doors slid shut with her on the other side, but I managed not to jump when her voice came from right beside me.

"Tell me more about this feeling that dragged you from the presumably warm embrace of a half-dressed twenty-something young lady out into the pouring rain in the middle of the night."

"I can't really describe it, if we're being honest."

"I'm an angel, Q. We are incapable of telling a lie. So please, feel free to be honest."

Well, that's an interesting little tidbit. Angels can't lie. But earlier she was definitely hiding something, so they don't have to tell the whole *truth.* "I just suddenly felt like something was wrong, like something in my world had shifted somehow, like there was…"

"A disturbance in the Force?" the angel supplied, somewhat less than helpfully.

"Yeah, frankly, that's pretty much exactly what it was like. There was something fucked up in the universe, and I had to go try to deal with it. And that's what got me out of the Champagne Room with Olivia and Lili and out into the cold-ass rain. Speaking of which, I should have done this a long time ago." I focused my will and muttered "*inflammo*" in a low voice. I slowly released my will into the spell, and my clothes began to steam. A few seconds and I was completely dry. I released the energy I'd taken in and looked at Glory. "That's better."

"Why didn't you do that before now?" she asked.

"Well, I probably would have, except somebody materialized out of friggin' thin air into my car and scared the shit out me!"

I stared at her for a moment, and eventually Glory blushed and said, "Oh, you mean me? I really am sorry about that. But tell me more about this compulsion. How did you know where to go?"

"Why are you so interested in how I got to the crime scene? If you're supposed to be my guardian angel, what does it matter? You just need to keep me from getting killed, right?"

"I suppose so, but it would be easier if I understood you a little more, knew why you were drawn to trouble in the first place. Maybe I could be more useful."

"It's not that I'm drawn to trouble, gorgeous, trouble sometimes finds me," I said, peeling off my t-shirt and tossing it on the floor of my bedroom. I raised my voice to yell to Glory in the living room, but I didn't need to. When I turned around, she was right in front of me, standing in the entrance to my bathroom. I pushed past her, then turned and shoved her gently out the door and closed it. I relieved myself, then opened the door.

She was sitting on my bed now. I don't care if you're some kind of monk, and I'm pretty much the furthest thing from one, but the sight of a gorgeous blonde sitting on your bed in the middle of the night is going to stir some pretty unholy thoughts, angel or not. I stood there staring at her for a few seconds, then shook my head like a disturbed Labrador or something.

"That's a little disgusting, you know. I'm an *angel*, Q."

"Yeah, but I'm not," I replied, then paused. "Wait a minute, how did you know what I was thinking?"

"I've dealt with human males for centuries. You're always thinking the same thing. Why should tonight be any different?"

"Good point," I conceded. "Now what? Are you just going to sit on my bed like some *Playboy* centerfold while I take a shower, then watch over me while I sleep?"

She thought for a moment, then nodded. "Yep, that's exactly what I'm going to do. Why are you showering, anyway? You just stood in the rain for half an hour looking at a corpse."

"Yeah, but that got me wet, it didn't get me clean. Besides I need to wash off the stripper perfume and glitter. I can't go to bed smelling like lilacs and regret. I'll never get to sleep."

Chapter Three

GLORY WAS GONE WHEN I WOKE UP, BUT I HAVE TO ADMIT, I SLEPT like a baby. I don't know if it was having an angel watching over me, or if it was getting home barely two hours before sunrise, but I woke up feeling refreshed and ready to take on the world. Or at least ready to take on whatever killed Lincoln Baxter. I made myself some coffee, grabbed a yogurt out of the fridge, and fired up the laptop. Turns out Mr. Baxter was a well-loved member of the community, which I knew, who left behind a teenage daughter from his first marriage and twin sons from his second. I wrote down "teenage daughter" and "two wives" on a legal pad by the computer.

An hour of internet searching gave me a list longer than my arm of people who wanted Baxter dead. As an assistant DA, Baxter prosecuted a lot of bad guys. Some of them, like the Mexican gang MS-13, still had friends on the outside. Some, like David Patton, aka The Park Road Strangler, managed to get their cases overturned on a technicality and got loose. And then there were the white collar guys like Bill Montgomery, who watched his net worth turn to net worthless when Baxter indicted him on a host of charges related to a Ponzi scheme he was running on North Carolina's elderly. So there were a few people who wanted our boy dead. My job was to find out who made it happen and what they did that was so powerful it jacked up the whole city's energy. There were a couple of places to find that kind of information, but only one open during mundane business hours. Good thing for me Christy made the best Bloody Marys in town.

My Camry stood out in the parking lot of Mort's Bar not because it was the best car in the lot, or the worst, but because it was the *only* car in the lot. I looked around a barren expanse of cracked asphalt, crushed beer cans, discarded cigarettes, and used fast food wrappers, but the only sign of life at the place was the tattered "OPEN" sign stuck in one window. I walked across the parking lot past the two Harley-Davidson Fatboys pulled right up to the front of the building. I banged on the door, and a panel slid open revealing a pair of yellow eyes rimmed in red.

"Password?" a gravelly voice asked. I could smell the brimstone on his breath from several feet away.

"Fuck off right back to the sixth circle, you repugnant cockweasel," I replied.

"Good to see you again, too, Harker. You know, one of these days I'm going to take offense at that and—" Doug the Door Demon started to say, but the second I heard the lock click open, I shoved the door into his face and cut him off.

"Owwww! What was that for?" The four-foot demon whined as he jumped backward off his stool and tried to keep the heavy metal-clad door from squishing him like a bug against the wall. "Come on, Harker, I thought were pals?"

"Pals?" I turned toward Doug. He was a spite demon, a prankster type that got his rocks off flattening tires and tying people's shoelaces together, but he was far from harmless. In the past he'd been known to cut brake lines, switch medications, jam up traffic signals, and otherwise do those nasty little things that can result in someone getting annoyed, or getting dead. I didn't like Doug, and never had. "You thought we were pals, you bottom-feeding little sulfur-sniffer? You're not fit to lick the dogshit off my boots, you worthless little fucktard.

"The only reason I haven't boiled your blood from the inside is that you haven't crossed the line from being an irritating little fuck to being a real threat. But if you ever do decide to move up in weight class, you worthless pile of Satan's jizz-drippings, just call me. I'll send you back to Hell so fast Lucifer himself will wonder if he installed an express elevator. Now fuck off, I'm going to see Christy."

I pushed through the inner door into Mort's, the only agreed-upon Sanctuary in the city of Charlotte. There are some places where humans are safe, and there are some places where monsters are safe, but Mort's is the only place where the two can mingle without anyone trying to eat the other. On premises, at least. What happens outside the parking lot is not something Christy is worried about.

Christy is the bartender/manager/peacekeeper/den mother of Mort's. As far as anyone can tell from a glance, she's human. She's a cute little Asian woman about five-two, curvy, with a ready smile and an ear to listen with. She's provided bartender services for me ever since I landed in Charlotte back in the 80s. Come to think of it, she hadn't changed any more than I had in the past couple decades, which spoke to something a little more than human in her DNA, too. She was pouring a scotch when I barged through the door, and as I watched her, she took one ice cube from behind the bar, deposited it into the drink, then set it on the bar in front of her.

I walked over, picked up the glass, and drained the scotch in one long swallow, then set the glass down on the bar. I waved at it in the universal sign for "Please, by all that is holy, give me more booze." Christy repeated her pour, then deposited that in my hand.

"Not much holy here, Harker," Christy said with a smile. "Now what do you want?"

"Can't I just want some company and a drink?" I put on my best "innocent" face. My innocent face looks kinda like a cross between Hannibal Lecter at a wine tasting and Uncle Luke at a Red Cross fundraiser. But it did get a chuckle out of Christy, which was all I wanted anyway.

"Sure you can. Just not at one in the afternoon. In case you missed it, we're barely open."

"Yeah, but you're never closed. Which is a little odd, if you think about it. Do you sleep, Christy?"

"You know I don't answer personal questions, Harker. It's one of the rules." She pointed to a sheet taped up behind the bar. It had a list of rules, most of them boiling down to "Don't start shit in here, or I'll fuck you up." But right there at number eight was "Bartender doesn't answer personal questions. Ever."

"Yeah, but I've gotten a lot of people to break a lot of rules in my day," I said with a grin.

"Who ever said I was a person?" She grinned right back. Dammit, she got me again. One day I'd trip her up into admitting something about herself. Or maybe I'd just actually investigate. But as long as she stayed neutral, I didn't need to go digging around in Christy's secrets.

"So, you here to meet your buddy?" Christy asked. Something in my expression must have told her I had no idea who she was talking about. Maybe it was the way my hand dropped to the butt of my Glock, riding on my hip mostly masked by my long coat. Maybe it was the way I snapped open my Sight and gathered my will, making the ring on my left middle finger glow a little. Or maybe it was the way I looked at her with one eyebrow climbing for the sky.

Her face turned sober. "There's a guy here looking for you. He's been here since early last night. He asked a few people what you looked like, then he took the corner booth by the bathroom and just waited. He orders a beer every half hour or so to keep me from throwing him out, but no food, no guests, and no interest in the girls." Christy motioned at two succubi meandering through the empty tables cleaning ashtrays and bussing drinks. In busier times, they were cocktail waitresses. With only two customers, though, they were just ambulatory furniture. Or collateral damage, if this next conversation went sideways.

I thought for a second, then held up two fingers to Christy. She stared at me for a minute, then nodded slowly. I held up one finger and pointed to the back. She nodded again.

"Well, I guess I shouldn't keep my old buddy waiting any longer, should I?" I asked. I held up one finger and pointed straight down at the bar. She nodded. So the owner of the other motorcycle wasn't waiting with his buddy in the back corner; he was crouching under the bar waiting to take a shot at my exposed back.

I pressed a hand to the front of the bar, gathered my will, and muttered "*debilitato.*" I released my will, and I heard a strangled gasp from under the bar, then a soft *thump* as my would-be assassin toppled over, paralyzed.

"*Now* I think I'll go have a conversation with my friend at the back table," I said. "Christy, is Sanctuary revoked for these guys?"

"Oh yeah," she replied. "Hide under my bar and point a gun at my belly? Fuck yeah, their Sanctuary is revoked. Paint the ceiling with their brains if you want. I've got cleaners on speed dial."

I walked back toward the restrooms, then slid into a booth just between the bathrooms and the emergency exit. I had it on good authority that emergency exit did not lead out on Wilkinson Blvd., but someplace much farther away.

"I understand you're looking for me," I said to the man in the booth. He was tall, taller than me, even, and lean to the point of being gaunt. He had deep-set eyes that looked blue, then gray, then purple, depending on how the light struck, and a trim beard along his jawline. He was dressed in biker chic, but the elbows of his leather jacket showed no signs of him ever laying a bike down. His hands were folded in front of him on the table, and they were huge. He had preternaturally long fingers, with clipped nails and no dirt or grease ground into his knuckles. This man was no biker, and we both knew it.

"Yes, Mr. Harker. I am indeed." Even without the sibilant letters, I got the impression that he was much more comfortable speaking in a hiss.

"Well, you found me. And I found your little friend up front, so let's have a private conversation, shall we?"

"Very well, I will be…succinct. You have no reason to care about Lincoln Baxter, or his death. This affair has no bearing on you, unless you wish it to.

And trust me, Mr. Harker, you do not wish it to." He leaned forward, and those shifting eyes turned the color of thunderclouds. He reached out and grabbed my wrist with his right hand, and his fingers wrapped all the way around my wrist almost twice, and I'm not a little guy. "Do you understand me?"

He gave me a hard glare, and I felt a *presence* pushing on my mind, like someone trying to control me. I tried to behave, I really did. But behaving myself has never been my strong suit, and I only respond in two ways when I'm threatened: I either break whoever is threatening me into many small pieces, or I laugh like a jackass. This time my lizard brain decided that "laugh like a jackass" was the proper response to being threatened by some mystical whatchamacallit in a dive bar barely after lunchtime. So I did. I laughed in his face. Brayed, really, just like a donkey.

He jerked back and let go of my wrist, and then my lizard brain let the switch flip to "fight." I reached out and grabbed him by the hair and pulled, slamming his face into the table. Then I shoved the table into him, effectively pinning him into the booth by his skinny midsection. I slid out of the booth and nailed him with a right cross to the jaw that spun his head around, then I put both hands on the back of his skull and slammed it into the table again.

Now that I had him disoriented, I yanked him out of the booth by the back of his collar, grabbed his belt in my other hand, and bum-rushed him out into the middle of the bar. I needed a little more room than the back hallway provided for the biblical ass-kicking I planned to unleash on this fuckwit.

"Not my affair, huh?" I punctuated that by throwing him to the floor. I'm pretty sure I heard something crack when he hit the hardwood.

"I don't wish it to, huh?" This time I capped my sentence with a kick to the ribs, and I *know* I heard something crack under the toe of my Doc Martens.

"No reason to—" I didn't get to finish that sentence because as I reached down to pick his assclown up and continue beating him bloody, he reached up with a hand and swatted me away. Yeah, he didn't punch me. He didn't throw me, toss me, or fling me. He kinda flicked one hand out, and when that hand hit me in the chest, I flew fifteen feet straight back and crashed through a table before collapsing in a pile of splinters and former restaurant furniture.

Chapter Four

ONCE I DECIDED THAT I HURT TOO MUCH TO BE DEAD, I SHOOK MY head, which was a bad idea because the room didn't stop wobbling when my head did, but I managed to clear enough cobwebs to stagger to my feet. The skinny man was standing right where I'd tossed him, perfectly still. He didn't look like I'd bounced his head off a table a couple of times, then kicked the shit out of him wearing my heaviest ass-kicking boots. He looked more like he was waiting for something.

I was that something. As soon as I locked eyes with him, a smile stretched across his face from ear to ear. Then it kept going, all the way across his face until his grin literally split his face open. He reached up with one hand, grabbed his nose, and pulled it backward over his head. He grabbed his lower jaw with the other hand and pulled down, ripping his skin-suit all the way down and revealing his true form.

"Oh, fuck," I said as I looked my first Archduke of Hell in the face. I'd fought lots of demons, everything from imps and annoying little fucks like that, all the way up to reaver demons with foot-long claws instead of fingers. But I'd never met one of the real big deal demons before. I'd never even heard of one coming anywhere close to Charlotte, and I liked it that way. But standing in front of me on cloven hooves was a legit fiend, bat wings and all. He was every bit of seven feet tall, and if his meat suit was gaunt, it was camouflaging some serious muscle because this guy was built like Hulk Hogan, only bigger. He looked mostly human, except for the cat-slit yellow eyes, the red skin, the fangs, the horns curling out of his forehead, and the hairy goat legs. Okay, so he looked pretty much nothing like a human, except for walking on two legs.

"That was a mistake, Mr. Harker," the demon grumbled. "We were content to live and let live, as it were. But no man lays hands on Duke Orobas and lives!"

Shit. Orobas was a legit badass, an archduke with twenty legions of hellspawn at his disposal. He had been through some wars in the land Way Down Under and was still standing, which didn't bode well for yours truly. He started my way, and I ran down my personal inventory looking for anything that would help. I drew my Glock and put ten rounds in the demon's chest, but he didn't even flinch. Even the fact that my bullets were blessed and dipped in holy water didn't help. I dodged right under one of his big slicing blows and looked up when I heard Christy whistle.

"Harker, use this!" she shouted, and pitched me her shotgun. I spun around and planted the barrel right into Orobas' midsection. I pulled the trigger, and the demon actually staggered back. He looked down and seemed every bit as surprised as I was when he found a bloody hole there. I racked another shell and fired again. Orobas staggered, so I ran the slide and fired again. And again, and again. I put five shells into that bastard, and he never went down. After the slide clicked empty, the demon looked down at me and did the worst possible thing I could imagine. He smiled.

"Ouch," he said, very slowly and very distinctly. "I actually *felt* that. I haven't felt pain since Michael came at me with that Satan-damned flaming sword. Good for you, little wizard. You actually put up a fight. More than I can say for—"

"Get out," came a voice from behind Orobas. I couldn't see who was speaking, but I knew. I looked over at Christy for confirmation and she nodded.

Orobas turned, and I moved over to one side so I could see Mort. Mort was the proprietor of this fine establishment, and a being of some power besides. I say "being" because up until this day, I had no idea what Mort really was. Given that what was standing at the end of the bar looked for all intents and purposes like a twelve-year-old human girl holding a very large housecat, I was pretty sure I still had no idea what Mort was.

"Mortivoid?" Orobas' voice rose, and it was obvious these two knew each other. My attacker grinned down at me, then turned to face Mort. "How many millennia has it been, old friend? You're looking well. I'm sorry, I had no idea this human was your snack. Here, have it." He gestured back at me. I scrambled to one knee and pulled a piece of chalk from a pocket. I sketched a rough circle around myself on the floor, focused my will, and with a whispered "*protego*," invoked the circle. A shimmering blue-white wall of energy sprang up around me, giving me enough protection to survive at least two, maybe three, direct hits from a demon of Orobas' power.

But Orobas seemed to have lost all interest in me. He circled Mort, or at least the girl I assumed was Mort, turning his head this way and that, checking her/him/it out from all angles. After a good minute of this, Orobas stood in front of Mort and looked down on her(?).

"Why that form, Mort? It can't be very powerful on this plane, and it's not terribly attractive," the big demon said.

"I disagree, Oro. I have a thick, glossy coat in many variations of color, and I have *very* sharp claws. Would you like me to show you?" Mort replied, and now I was even more confused because the *cat* was talking. "I've ridden many forms, Oro, you know that. This one amuses me, and it keeps the humans guessing. You wouldn't believe the things I hear from my customers while they give me lovely ear scratches. And every once in a while I let them pet my belly, and they let me scratch them in return. It's lovely, Oro! I get to shed blood in the center of a Sanctuary, and no one even thinks anything of it!"

"You always had a flair for the ironic," Orobas said.

"And you always had a flair for the overly ambitious. It's time to go home now, Oro. Or at least time to leave my bar. The human is under my protection as long as he remains here, and even you aren't brazen enough to attack him outside in broad daylight. So give him whatever warning you feel you need to give, and then leave."

"Are you throwing me out, Mortivoid? Are *you* actually daring to give *me* orders?" The big demon's voice rose with every word, until he was practically bellowing in Mort's face. Which made him look spectacularly silly, since he was basically screaming at an overweight housecat. He got right down in Mort's face, spraying hot demon spittle all over the cat's thick fur.

Mort did what cats do—he reached up and clawed Orobas right on the tender tip of his nose. The demon reared back, howling in anger and shock, and it was all I could do not to fall over laughing and break my protective circle. I somehow managed to stay upright, but my eyes went wide when Orobas struck a huge downward hammering blow with both hands at the head of the little girl holding Mort. Orobas' fists slammed into some type of force barrier just inches from the child's forehead. She never even blinked, but something told me that there was a lot more to that little girl than met the eye, too.

I gathered my will and began to open my Sight, but a whistle from Christy cut me off short. She pointed to her forehead, where the mystical third eye is usually located in art and drawings, and shook her head. I raised an eyebrow and gathered more of my will, and she shook her all the more vehemently.

"I really wish you wouldn't do that, Mr. Harker. Particularly since I am currently doing pitched battle with my cousin on your behalf." Mort's idea of pitched battle and mine obviously differed pretty wildly, since all he was doing was walking toward Orobas slowly, carried by a prepubescent girl in a pinafore dress with an honest to God bow in her hair. Orobas twirled his hands in midair, called up a ball of fire the size of a basketball, and hurled it right at Mort and the girl. Mort didn't blink, didn't try to dodge, didn't waver on his path an inch. He just walked his carrier into the ball of fire, and out the other side, none the worse for wear. The lace trim on her dress wasn't even scorched.

The cat-bearer walked right up to Orobas, who stood staring at Mort. Mort meowed at his handler, and she lifted him up to her shoulder. By standing with his front paws on the girl's head and back paws on her shoulder, Mort was able to look the larger demon more or less in the eye.

"I told you to leave, Oro," the cat said.

"I don't take orders from hijackers, Mort. Wear your own skin, or at least something properly combative. You look ridiculous in that thing."

"You know I've never cared for fashion. What I care about is peace and quiet. And you are, as they say on the television, beginning to damage my calm." Huh. Mort's a *Firefly* fan. Who knew?

"I will damage more than that if you don't scurry back into your little hidey-hole and let me at Harker. He has insulted my person, and he must suffer the consequences."

Mort turned to me. "Mr. Harker?"

"Yeah, Mort, what's up?" I asked.

"I think you should apologize to Orobas, don't you?"

"What the fuck?" I raised an eyebrow.

"His feelings were hurt, Mr. Harker. I think you should apologize. Otherwise, as his host, my feelings will be hurt. And you don't want to hurt *my* feelings, do you, Mr. Harker?" His voice never changed. There was never a hint of threat in his posture. He never even raised an eyebrow at me. But I knew that he was really saying, "Take what I'm offering you and shut the fuck up, human." So I did.

"I'm sorry, Orobas. It was not my intent to show you any disrespect, and I sincerely apologize for any distress I may have caused you." I poured on a little of the flowery language I remembered from my youth and tried to keep every hint of "go fuck yourself" out of my tone. It must have worked, at least enough to satisfy the most basic requirements of demonic courtesy, because Orobas waved his hands in the air again and was suddenly back in his human-ish form, crazy-long fingers and all.

"This isn't over, Harker. When I see you again, and I *will* see you again, you won't have Mort to hide behind." Orobas turned and swept out the front door, his long coat billowing out behind him. He paused for only the briefest of seconds to reach behind the bar and pick up his flunky, then he tossed the unconscious biker over his shoulder and continued on his merry way.

"I can never get my coat to billow," I bemoaned. "Why is that?"

"Too much Kevlar," Christy replied from the bar. "Now come over here and get some liquor in you before you fall over."

I couldn't argue, and I'd made it a policy long ago never to argue with an armed woman, especially one who hid a shotgun behind a bar. No telling what else she had back there. I collapsed my circle, scrubbed through the line in a couple of places with my toe so nobody could come after me and invoke it without at least a little bit of effort.

I sat down at the bar, and the little girl came and stood next to me. Mort climbed off her shoulder onto the bar and paced back and forth in front of me, his tail twitching. I picked my whiskey up off the bar. No need to add cat hair to my diet. Mort was currently walking around as a huge orange and white short-haired housecat, with bright green eyes and a little paunch that let me know that Mort was taking good care of this current body. He walked up and sat down right in front of me, those emerald chips locking onto my own eyes.

"What the sweet evergreen fuck were you thinking, Harker?" the cat asked, and I'll admit, it was pretty disconcerting, being cussed at by a cat sitting on a bar at barely two in the afternoon.

"Which time?" I asked. "When I sucker-punched the demon? When I decided to stand up and fight the demon fair? When I hid like a mouse in my little circle while you people, donor body and all, stared him down and ran him out of Dodge?"

"Let's start with the beginning, shall we? Why did you think it was a good idea to come in here, shit on my bar, wipe your ass with my Sanctuary, *and* put yourself in a position to get not only yourself, but any other human in a three-block radius, killed?"

"Well, it sounds bad when you say it like that," I said, knocking back the last of my drink and putting the glass down on the bar. Mort reached out with one paw and knocked it to the floor, where it shattered.

"Sorry, Christy," he said to the bartender, who wore a scowl that said it wasn't the first time he'd done something like that. "Feline instincts, I can't help it."

"God, Mort. Cats really *are* assholes," I said.

"Cats possessed by demons are even worse. I can't tell whether it's Mort being a dick, or his host. I'll be glad when this episode of 'Stupid Pet Tricks' is over," Christy said, walking over with a broom and a dustpan.

I turned back to the cat, who looked a great deal like he wanted to claw my eyes out. "I don't know, Mort. There's something strange going on, and this is the place in town to go if you want to find out about strange."

"Well, that's true enough, I guess." He licked his paw and started cleaning his head with it. "I suppose a run-in with Oro was inevitable once he started asking about you and glowering at everyone."

"It does kinda happen that way," I agreed. "People ask questions about me, and eventually I show up with answers. It's not often that I show up with answers they like, but I do bring answers."

"But you said you came here to ask about something, not looking for the guy who was asking about you. Coincidence?"

"You don't believe in that shit any more than I do. Lincoln Baxter was found dead last night. Somebody cut his throat from ear to ear, then drained his blood and dumped the body in a mall parking lot."

"What does that have to do with anything? Stupid humans kill everything anyway. Not like he was going to live very long in the first place," Mort said.

"Then why was my guardian angel at the dump site?"

I saw Mort's hackles actually raise. "What?" he asked, scouting back a little on the counter.

"What's wrong, Mort? Not a fan of the angelic host?"

"De-mon, you jackoff. Look it up. No, I am not a fan of those prissy fucks. But if one was hanging around a crime scene, then you're right, something's fucked up. And since when are you important enough to have a guardian angel?"

"I asked her the same thing," I replied.

"It," Mort corrected me absently.

"Huh?"

"Angels are neuter. They have no genitalia, thus they are neither he nor she, but properly referred to as 'it'." Mort gave me a look that was suspiciously like a cat grin.

"Whatever, dude. She looks like a chick, talks like a chick, and I'm pretty sure I'm not ever going to get a chance to inspect any closer than that."

"Yeah, Harker, if there's ever been a babe that's out of your league, I'd say anything with wings and a halo qualifies. But what was she doing at the murder scene of some human lawyer?"

"How did you know he was a lawyer?" I asked.

"The same way he knew full well that Lincoln Baxter was less human than you are, Harker. He was a regular here," Christy chimed in.

"You're speaking out of turn, Christy," Mort said, and there was a warning tone to his voice.

"Oh, like I give a fuck, Garfield." She glared at him. "Why don't you just tell him, so he can get the hell out of here and start causing a ruckus in somebody else's place of business. Then I can get started cleaning up his mess."

"Hey!" I protested. "It wasn't just me. Orobas threw me through the table, so that wasn't my fault."

"And the face-shaped dents in the back table?" Christy gave me the eyebrow. I wilted.

"Yeah, that was me. Sorry." I turned back to Mort. "So what were you going to tell me?"

He didn't meet my eye, just became very interested in licking the back of his paw. "Come on Mort, spill it," I prodded.

"Lincoln Baxter wasn't exactly human," Mort grumbled under his breath.

"Yeah, I got that. What was he? And why would anybody want to kill him?"

"Pretty sure those answers are one and the same," Christy said.

"You gonna tell him, or you gonna let me do it?" Mort snapped.

"If you'd get on with it," Christy shot back. "We don't have anyone to do a drumroll for you, so spit it out."

"Fine," Mort said. "Baxter was Nephilim." He shrank back within himself just saying the word, but it meant nothing to me.

"What's a Nephilim?" I asked. Mort looked even more uncomfortable, if that were possible for a cat. His tail was thrashing around, and his gaze kept flitting around the room.

"Abominations. Some of the nastiest beings in all the planes," Mort said.

"Not answering the question, Mort. What are Nephilim?"

"They half-human, half-angel bastards with no allegiance to anything and none of the limitations of the Host."

"So Lincoln Baxter was an angel…" I mused.

"Half angel," Mort corrected. "Half-human, half-angel, all asshole."

Chapter Five

"I THOUGHT ANGELS COULDN'T...I THOUGHT THEY DIDN'T HAVE... fuck, how do angels make babies?" Renaissance and rococo art aside, everything I'd ever learned about angels said that they were neuter. Genderless. Made it easy to refer to them as nutless wonders when they didn't help out down here as much as I wanted them to, because they really were. Nutless, that is. Except apparently not.

"Look," I started again. "I admit I've done a lot more studying of the denizens of the lower planes, mostly because angels don't usually go around killing humans, so I don't have to fight them."

"Looking at how you handled Oro, I'd say that's probably a good call on your part," Mort said.

"Look, Meow Mix, that was a friggin' Archduke of Hell. I think it's safe to say I was punching up a little in weight class."

"Whatever, meat sack," the cat demon replied. "You don't have to understand how it happens, just understand that sometimes angels and humans make babies. These babies are called Nephilim, and they live on Earth, just like you humans. Well, just like those humans you hang out with."

"Hey!" I protested. "I'm human."

"At least eighty percent," Mort agreed with a piercing look. I didn't know what kind of demon Mort was, but as cats go, he was a dick. "So most Nephilim don't have any idea that they're part divine. They just go through life, usually doing really good shit all the time, never harming a living soul, that kind of boring horseshit. Sometimes they figure out what they are, either through dreams, or noticing that they're really hard to kill, or some kind of near-death experience. These are the ones that cause trouble. They either get hyper-holy, in which case they're assholes, or they get all kinds of nihilistic, in which case they're violent assholes."

"Or they turn out like Baxter, a fucking psychopath," Christy chimed in. She was wiping down the bar and doing something with liquor bottles that looked a lot like adding water to vodka, but I decided not to ask.

"Or that," Mort agreed. "Baxter was a piece of work. He was Nephilim, all right, but he acted more like a Cambion than a lot of half-demons I've known."

"Hold up," I said. "You're saying that the Cambion are real?" I asked. I'd heard of these mythical half-human, half-succubus demonspawn, but in almost a century of traipsing all over the world and peeking in all of civilization's dark corners, I hadn't found any real proof of their existence.

"Of course they do, idiot boy." Mort actually managed to make a cat's mouth sneer at me. I never knew you could sneer without lips, but he managed. "The universe relies on balance. If there's a yin, there's gotta be a yang. If there are Nephilim, there have to be Cambion. Angels...demons. Pizza...asparagus. Beer...Zima. You get what I'm saying."

"All but that last one. You know as well as I do that Zima is not of this universe," I said.

He nodded. "Yeah, it was a sixth-circle idea that never really panned out. Like New Coke, just not quite evil enough to catch on."

"So what's the point? Baxter was a Nephilim, and he was a psycho Nephilim, and somebody punched his ticket. Sounds like the suspect list is about half a mile long at this point, but really, what's the big deal? Some asshole angel got killed, so what?" I asked.

The cat looked at Christy, who shrugged. Mort turned back to me. "Are all humans this fucking stupid, or are you just a shining example? Look, fuckwit, you're missing the point. The point is not that something killed *Baxter*; the point is that something *killed* Baxter. Killed. Made dead. Took the part-angel son of a bitch and made him not be here anymore. That takes a lot of juice. And this ain't the first time it's happened, either."

Now I was really interested. "There are more?"

"More what?" Mort asked.

"Goddammit, I can't tell which part of you is a bigger douche, the demon or the cat!" I exploded. "More dead Nephilim, you fuzzy prick!"

"There's no need for name-calling," Mort said, suddenly all prim and proper licking one paw and washing behind his ears.

"I'm pretty sure I can't kill you, but I could have you spayed," I growled.

Mort looked at me, eyes wide. "You are an asshole, Harker."

"We call these our given circumstances, Mort," I replied. "Now, about those other Nephilim?"

"Baxter is the third in the past few weeks, which is really odd. Usually the Nephilim don't hang around each other, mostly because they hate each other, and usually they don't die, like ever. So three dead Nephilim in one city in one month is way outside the realm of chance."

"Do you think it might have something to do with Big Ugly back there?" I pointed in the general direction of the booth where my mild disagreement with Orobas began.

"Oro?" Mort asked, his voice dripping with the disdain that you always knew cats would sound like if they could talk. Well, this one could, and he sounded every bit as obnoxious as I always thought a talking cat would. "Oro has way more important things on his mind than a couple of dead angels. He's one of Hell's top dogs, and he doesn't mess around with small fish."

"So why was he here waving me off the case?"

"I don't know," Mort admitted, and the cat at least had the courtesy to look embarrassed.

"So we've got something killing supposedly un-killable half-angels, a high-ranking demon telling me not to poke around in a case, and you don't think they're connected? I'm no Sherlock Holmes, but I think you might be missing the boat there, Morty."

"And what do you propose to do about it, Harker?" the cat asked.

"Now that I know there are two more dead Nephilim, I want to see if their bodies are still in the morgue. I have a couple of connections in the police department that may be useful, too."

"The bodies are long gone, but you can probably get the autopsy reports," Christy said. "Here." She slid a piece of paper across the bar with two names written on it.

"These are the other two Nephilim?"

"Those are the names you'll find their corpses under," Christy confirmed. I nodded and turned to go. "Harker?" she called.

I stopped and turned back to her. "Yeah?"

"Be careful. These things are way outside your usual weight class, and they think they're right about everything. That makes them way more dangerous."

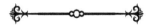

The autopsy reports were a dead end, since they don't tend to give those out to people without some official rank or, you know, job, and I had nothing like that. All my trip to the morgue got me was a distaste for the smell of formaldehyde and a lot of blank stares from paper-pushers who weren't buying any of my lies about "Freedom of Information Act" or the public having a right to know. Smart bureaucrats are something I have no superpower against.

I was just walking out the front door when my old buddy Detective Sponholz walked in. He took one look at me, scowled, and turned to leave again. I put on a little extra gas and pressed the door closed before he could pull it open.

"Where you headed, Detective?" I asked.

"Anywhere you aren't, Harker," the portly investigator replied.

"What's wrong, Detective? Scared that if you share information with a civilian, I'll show you up?"

"More like scared anything I say to you will end up on the internet," Sponholz replied. "What are you doing here? I got a call that some reporter's down here digging around in my case files, and when I show up, it's everybody's least favorite asshole—Quincy Harker."

"That's not fair, Detective. I must be *somebody's* favorite asshole," I replied.

"Nope, I checked. Called everybody on Earth. You're the winner. Asshole of the year. Now what do you want?" Sponholz suddenly turned serious.

"I want the autopsy reports for these two cases." I handed Sponholz a scrap of paper with their names on it.

He immediately looked suspicious, kinda like he did when I spoke, or show up unannounced at crime scenes. "Why do you want autopsy reports?" he asked. "Do you think these two might be somehow connected to Baxter?"

"I don't know," I replied. "But these bodies were both found in similar circumstances, rainy parking lots, early morning, not very much blood at the scene…it's not much of a stretch to think they might be connected. Have you found anything?"

"I'll be honest with you, Harker, and I don't know why I'm even giving you this much, I've just started looking myself. I wasn't on the first one of these cases, but I remembered the Brecker scene once we got everything buttoned up this morning, so I came down to get the files and check it out myself."

He didn't know why he was telling me that, but I did. It had a lot to do with a very minor truth incantation I was murmuring under my breath and the piece of quartz crystal I was channeling my will through while he spoke. The spell didn't *force* him to do anything, just made him more likely to respond to suggestions or answer questions honestly.

"How about I help you?" I offered, and focused my will on the crystal.

He started to shake his head, and I could almost feel his resistance, then his eyes glazed for a second and he said, "Alright, sure. I mean, two heads are better than one, and it's better to keep you where I can see you." He walked over to the officious woman behind the desk and filled out two forms, one for each report. He handed them in, paced around in front of the Plexiglas window for a few minutes, then reached into a slot cut under the window and pulled out two thin manila envelopes.

"Come with me," Sponholz grumbled, and I followed him down a short hallway to a small room with no windows.

"This looks like the kind of place where you guys bring out the rubber hoses," I joked.

"Not for years, Harker. Not for years," Sponholz said, and I chuckled at what I thought was his little joke. Until I saw the drain in the floor and decided he might not have been joking. Regardless of the room's former uses, it now held a small table and four chairs, with one weak fluorescent light overhead. Sponholz dropped the two envelopes on the table and sat down in one chair. I sat opposite him and reached for a file. He slapped the back of my hand, and I was impressed with myself as I didn't break any of the bones in his hand. I was hardly even tempted.

"Here's how this is going to go," Sponholz said. "I'm going to look through these autopsy reports. I'm not going to tell you shit about them. Then, when I'm done, you're going to look through these autopsy reports. You're going to tell me anything out of the ordinary that you notice. Do you understand me?"

"Sounds like this partnership is kind of a one-way street, Detective," I said, looking him in the eye.

"That's because it's not a partnership. We're not buddies, partners, pals, or friends of any sort. You are a consultant to the Charlotte-Mecklenburg Police Department, and I am the officer overseeing you. You are here because you always seem to pop up where the weird shit happens, and this case qualifies. So anything you see that's weird, you flag. Anything that you see that's unusual, you flag. Anything you see that's abnormal in any way, you—"

"Flag. I get it," I grumbled. Oh well, I got half of what I wanted. I got into the room with the files, and I was going to get access to them, even if I wasn't getting the benefit of Sponholz's expertise. I leaned back and waved at the envelopes. "You first, *partner*."

A couple hours later, I had a clearer view of the method of the murders, even if I had no idea what I all meant. I closed the last folder and slid it back into the second envelope. "Let's recap," I said.

"All three victims were killed between 10 p.m. and 4 a.m., the quietest time of night in those areas. Their bodies were dumped in areas where they would be found quickly, but where the dump itself was unlikely to be seen. Cotswold Mall, the Eastland Mall parking garage lower level, the parking lot behind Independence Arena are all public places, but also places that are unlikely to be patrolled around the clock. So our killer knows the city and knows which places are just deserted enough to make great dumping grounds," Sponholz said, his manner cool, but professional. At some point over the last two hours, he seemed to have resigned himself to working with me, at least for today.

"What else do we know?" I asked.

"Your turn, smartass." Sponholz pointed at me. "You've got my quid, now for a little pro quo."

"Fair enough," I said. "All the bodies show signs of extreme exsanguination, and not the kind that is consistent with the trauma they experienced. Each man was struck a sharp blow behind the ear, which would have rendered him unconscious, but all three men died from excessive blood loss."

"An easy call, since all their throats were slit," Sponholz said. "What have you got that's new?"

"I have agreement from the coroner that they weren't killed where the bodies were found. Like Baxter, the first two men were not found with nearly enough blood around them to explain the level to which they were drained. So they were killed elsewhere and then dumped."

"What else?"

"When is it your turn to detect, Detective? Regardless, there are ligature marks on each man's hands and feet that show he was bound, and judging by the directional marks on the ankles and the angle of the cuts on the throat, these men were hung upside down, their throats cut, and their blood drained, just like hunters do with deer."

"They weren't murdered," Sponholz said, his eyes big.

"They were butchered," I said.

Chapter Six

I LEFT SPONHOLZ AT THE MORGUE AND HEADED OVER TO LUKE'S PLACE, after a detour down Monroe to get a bowl of Lupe's chili and a little alone time to process everything I'd learned today. And hammer down a six-pack of Foster's to help my bruises fade. By the time I left the restaurant, it was close to full dark, and he'd be waking up soon. Renfield met me at the door with a smile. This Renfield was tall, thin almost to the point of gaunt, and getting way on in years. He'd been with Uncle Luke for a long time, even given the extra years hanging with the King of Vampires grants humans, and I could tell his time was coming to an end. But he still had a sparkle in his eyes and the key to the liquor cabinet on his ring, so I was always happy to see him.

"Master Quincy," he said, pulling the door open wide.

"Renfield," I replied with a nod.

"Your uncle has begun to stir. I expect him to be down for breakfast within the half hour, after he finishes his daily ablutions and newspaper." Luke is still the only person I know who reads the entire newspaper before he begins his day. He claims it's a habit he picked up from Mark Twain, but I've never found any proof he ever met the famous writer, riverboat captain, and newspaperman. Like myself, Uncle Luke has sometimes been known to embellish his proximity to some historical events and downplay his participation in others. For example, he's all too quick to bring up my poor decision-making in helping Pol Pot into power in Cambodia, a mistake I've long regretted and which set in stone my policy of never again interfering with the politics of Asia. They really are fucking inscrutable, and I hate getting bluffed. But you'll never hear him mention the St. Valentine's Day Massacre, where he got hungry and pissed off with a bunch of mobsters and ate them all. Capone took credit for the murders, shot up a bunch of corpses, and rose to power in Chicago, but if investigators ever looked around, they would see the same thing I'd seen this morning—not enough blood for all the deadness.

But anyway, Luke also had the best mystical library of anyone I had contact with. Anyone who didn't want to kill me, that is. Pesky thing about people who collect mystical texts—they either do it for nefarious reasons, or to destroy those with nefarious motives. Since my motives often are way more gray-tinged than some practitioners would like, I'm *persona non grata* in a lot of the magical circles. And let's not even mention Luke.

"Let him know I'm in the library whenever he's feeling ready for company," I said to Renfield, taking a left under the grand staircase in the foyer and heading to the large, wood-paneled room where I hoped to find more information on Nephilim and the things that killed them.

"I will do so, Master Quincy. Would you like something to eat brought in?" Renfield had a hell of a mommy instinct, always making sure I ate. I'm blessed with a hellacious metabolism, so even though I just knocked off a meal at Lupe's, my stomach rumbled at Renfield's mention of food.

"Yeah, send in a sandwich or something. Don't go to any trouble." I felt like I had to say it, no matter how useless. I know Renfield would whip up something worthy of a five-star restaurant and deny there was any trouble to it.

I was barely into my second tome when Renfield came in with a tray bearing a cold Sam Adams beer, a roast beef sandwich, chips, and a pickle spear. It looked like it had just come from a New York deli with crisp lettuce, fresh tomato, and rare roast beef almost dripping. I pushed away the book I was leafing through and dove in.

"Hey, Renfield," I said before the thin man reached the door. "What do you know about Nephilim?"

He froze and turned around very slowly. The look on his face told me I'd hit a nerve, but I didn't understand why at first. "Master Quincy, why in the world would you wish to know about those abominations?"

"Abominations? Isn't that a little strong?" I asked.

"I don't think so," he replied. "They are a mix of the earthly and the divine, creatures that were never meant to exist. I feel that abomination is a perfectly acceptable way to refer to them."

"There are those who would call me the same thing, Renfield. What would you say to them?" My uncle's voice was low, but dangerous. I could tell Renfield was choosing his next few words carefully. Uncle Luke wasn't a terribly vindictive man, but he had been known to eat employees in a fit of pique.

"I should hope that I am not put into a position to converse with such close-minded people, sir, but if I am, I am certain that you need no help from me in defending your honor or emotional well-being." The stiff-necked man then turned and continued his trek out of the room and vanished into the kitchen area.

I looked over at Luke, who stood with one eyebrow raised, his gaze locked onto the hallway where Renfield had disappeared. "What's up with Renfield, Uncle?" I asked.

"He has recently been reminded of his mortality, Quincy. I am afraid his time with us grows short."

That rang a little odd. Uncle Luke had gone through several Renfields by this point, the name becoming more of a title than anything else. But all of them had died of natural causes, as far as I was aware, and all after extremely long lives. This Renfield looked no more than sixty, but being around Luke made people's lifespans blurry, and I didn't remember how old he was when he came to the position.

"What's up with him?" I asked.

"Cancer," Uncle Luke replied. "It seems he knew about it when he took the position, but was hoping the exposure to my magic and his duties would either cure him or hold the tumor at bay indefinitely. That has not been the case."

"Bummer," I said. "Sorry about that. How long does he have? And have you started looking for a replacement?"

"As I understand it, his time can be measured in weeks, and I have not yet begun the search for his successor. That task is usually undertaken by the current Renfield, but…" His voice trailed off, and he raised a wine glass full of a rich red liquid to his lips.

"Yeah, I get it." I walked over to an antique sideboard. "Which bottle is the unleaded cabernet?" I pointed to two decanters. One held wine, I was fairly certain. The other, well, it was always better to ask before you drank anything in Uncle Luke's house. I poured myself a glass from the crystal decanter Luke indicated.

I followed my "uncle" into the parlor, where we sat opposite each other in armchairs that Luke had bought over in Europe. He said they reminded him of Louis XIV. I couldn't see anything particularly Louis XIV about the chairs, but I'd never met the man, so I just kept my mouth shut.

"What do you know about Nephilim, Uncle?" I asked as soon as we were both seated.

"I'm fine, Quincy, how are you? Yes, it has been a few weeks, but I hardly noticed, what with my own social obligations taking up all my attention lately.

I hope you've been well. You look pale. Are you getting enough sun? Vitamin D is very important for those of you who still walk among the living," Luke answered breezily.

"I get it," I said. "It's been a couple weeks since I dropped by. Sorry about that, but I've been busy."

"Doing what?"

"Excuse me?"

"You've been busy doing what, exactly? I'm interested to hear what you've been doing in the five weeks since I've last seen you, Quincy. Because that's what it's been, hasn't it? Five weeks. Over a month and not a peep from my favorite nephew. I was really starting to worry about you."

"If you were worried, you have all my numbers," I replied.

"What's wrong, son? Are you still following around that human girl like some type of dark guardian? What happened now?"

"Her college graduation was a couple days ago. I watched her walk across the stage. Because her father can't. So now she's my responsibility," I said. Luke had heard it before. He'd been hearing it for about a dozen years or more, and he bought it about as much this time as he ever did.

"Oh, good god, Quincy, sometimes you behave like that fat shite Van Helsing, with his rigid moral code and his crusading for good. He was a *human*. You made a promise to a human. We break those all the time. We have to because they die so damned fast."

"Yeah, but he was a human who didn't have to die quite so fast," I replied, and then I was back there. It was the late 90s and I was back in an alley off Seventh Street, chasing a baby vampire through the rainy streets of a deserted Uptown Charlotte. I'd spent the last six weeks hunting down a rogue, a vampire who owed allegiance to no one and followed no one's laws, not those of man or of the Shadow Council, the ruling body of the supernatural world. I took down the rogue, but not before his progeny gutted a Charlotte cop in a parking garage. He laid a promise on me as he died—to look after his daughter. I spent the next month doing just that, sitting in a tree outside a fifth-grade girl's window listening to her cry herself to sleep.

"You could have saved him, but how many more would the rogue have slaughtered while you were off saving one human? Where was he when you finally caught up to him?"

Luke was right, of course. "He was walking into the lobby of the Omni hotel. It took some quick spell-slinging, but I got him through the hotel and into the attached mall before he hurt anyone else, then convinced the witnesses that we were filming a movie after I bounced the rogue off several marble columns *en route* to crushing its skull with a giant planter."

"How many of those witnesses would be dead if you had gone off after the infant?" Luke prodded as I fell silent.

"At least a dozen," I replied.

"And do you think any of them might have a sad little girl at home crying into her pillow had you made a different decision?"

"Yeah," I admitted, albeit reluctantly. "I *know* all this, it's just..."

"It's hard. I understand."

"You do?" I raised an eyebrow.

"Of course I do," Luke said. "You're a very talented man, Quincy Harker, and you hate to lose. You feel like there should have been some way you could save both the girl's father and all the people in the hotel. But there wasn't. You made a choice. It was for the greater good. It will hurt as you fulfill your promise to the girl's father and watch her grow up half-orphaned, but you can take comfort in knowing that you did the right thing."

"Is that really going to make me feel any better?" I asked.

"Not a bit," Luke said, leaning back in his chair and crossing his legs. We sat there in silence, me studying the dregs in the bottom of my wine glass while Luke looked at me. I sat there for several minutes before I finally looked up at him and asked the question I really wanted an answer to.

"Are we, Uncle?" I asked, surprised to find my eyes moist. "Are we more than this? Are we more than anything? What's the point, Luke? Why are we doing this, year after year, decade after decade? We get a message from the Council, 'Something needs to be killed.' And we kill it.

"But for what? Why are we doing this? There's just another thing, right? I killed the rogue, he made a baby. I killed the baby, but not before it killed a cop. And now there's a new something out there, and it's killing *angels*? What the hell am I supposed to do against something that can kill an angel? I'm only human." I held up a hand as Luke cleared his throat.

"Okay, I'm mostly human. But we have no idea what that means. We know I don't get old. At least, not at any reasonable human rate. We know that I'm faster and stronger than humans, and we know that I have a predilection for magical talent. But what does that matter? Anything that can kill an angel could swat me down like a fly without even breaking a sweat. I'm supposed to hunt down something that powerful and take it out when I couldn't even hold my own against one lousy demon this morning?"

Luke raised an eyebrow at me.

"There was a demon, at Mort's—"

"I know."

My mouth snapped shut. I thought for a few seconds, couldn't remember talking to Luke earlier, then asked. "You know?"

"Mort called me. Christy, actually, since Mort doesn't have fingers right now, but let's not split hairs. He told me of your fight with Orobas, and the murder of the Nephilim."

"Why?"

"Mort and I have a long history, and he knows that it would upset me if you, as he put it, got dead. So he called me, hoping I would tell you to drop the case."

"And are you?"

"Am I what?"

"Telling me to drop the case?"

"Would you?"

"Of course not."

"Then I won't bother. Now, let's retire to the library and see what we can find about Nephilim."

Chapter Seven

WHEN SOMEONE'S BEEN COLLECTING BOOKS FOR AS LONG AS LUKE, their library is bound to be impressive, and his was about exactly what you'd expect for someone raised in European nobility. The room, easily the largest on the main floor of the house, was lined with floor-to-ceiling bookcases. There wasn't a single window, and a light-tight vestibule leading in guaranteed that Luke could spend days on end in the library without any stray sunbeams making their way inside. Comfortable reading chairs with ottomans were arranged in several loose sitting areas, and a six-foot long cherry wood table with sturdy legs and a surface scarred from decades of leather tomes marking it dominated one wall. Floor lamps dotted the room, but most of the illumination came from a giant chandelier in the center of the room. It cast a warm yellow glow all around, brightening to a brilliant white as Luke turned a dimmer on the wall.

"I'll start here with the religious texts; you work over there in the cryptozoology section." Luke waved a hand at the far right corner of the room and strode over to the left wall. He hopped up on a ladder, one of two that ringed the room on tracks mounted in the ceiling, and pushed off, gliding almost soundlessly along the room until he came to the section he wanted. I walked to the corner, passing on the ladder for the moment. Luke's bookshelves had their own organizational system, one that would baffle Dewey and the Library of Congress librarians, but made perfect sense to him. I didn't understand the genesis of it, but since I'd worked with Luke for seven or eight decades, and lived with him off and on for at least half that time, I knew where almost everything was. And if worst came to worst, I still had a map tucked into the copy of the Bible that Luke kept on a lectern at the front of the room. There was something special about that Bible although he wouldn't tell me what it was. It wasn't an expensive book, not leather-bound, or rare, or anything special really, just a battered old King James Bible. But Luke treated it like a holy relic, carrying it from home to home over the years, so I knew that anything I hid in its pages would be safe.

I spent the next six hours scouring dusty tomes for information on the Nephilim, digging through everything from an unexpurgated copy of Bullfinch's *Mythology*, still bearing the original title "Mythology and the Fantastical Creatures that Walk the Earth." Bullfinch changed the title and carved out all mention of vampires, werewolves, and magic as a real thing after a brief visit from Uncle Luke and several of his mystical pals that he never deigned to mention to me. No matter how obscure or rare the text, all I found about Nephilim was that they were half-divine, half-human, and not to be trusted. Most texts didn't mention them at all, and the ones that did treated them like fairy tales. Which was ironic because the writers were the same guys who knew fairies were real.

Finally, with Renfield asleep on a couch and even Luke starting to yawn, I hit pay-dirt with Fortner's *Zoological Fantastical*, a semi-serious tome of children's poems, cartoonish drawings, legends, and folktales written in eighteenth-century England. Fortner was a giant in the field of arcane animals, but he masqueraded as a feckless author of children's fantasy novels. That kept the more human-appearing monsters from hunting him and provided a healthy living besides. Luke had apparently visited the man late in his life, fulfilling one of the writer's lifelong dreams of actually meeting a creature generally assumed to be mythical. *Zoological Fantastical* provided a comical illustration of a Nephilim, a skeletal man with elongated arms and a narrow head with overlarge eyes set just a hair too far apart to be normal. In general, all the features of the Nephilim were just a little bit *too much*.

But what grabbed my attention was the next entry in the book. I turned the page and saw a drawing of a normal man. Just a human, a little short, maybe a little portly, holding a knife and smiling a wicked smile. The caption under the drawing read "Cambion." I scanned the description, then pulled the book closer as the words grabbed my attention.

"The Cambion," the entry read, "is the very antithesis of the Nephilim, despite the similarities in their origin. The Nephilim, while divine in origin, is completely remorseless and lacking in conscience, a feature in its personal composition that shall, over time, distance it from close relationships and may spare unwitting humans damage from proximity to the being. The Cambion, to contrast, seems perfectly human, sometimes almost alarmingly so. The Cambion moves through human society without anyone, sometimes including the creature itself, being any the wiser. Born of the unholy union of a demon and a human woman, the Cambion possesses exceptional physical prowess, beyond that of any human. The Cambion is as much a minion of chaos as the Nephilim are slaves to order, and a Cambion will thrive in positions of extreme busyness and excitement. The Cambion and Nephilim are blood enemies and will instantly hate each other violently upon introduction of the two."

I closed the book. "Hey Luke," I called.

"Yes, Quincy?" he said from my elbow. I hate when he does that, and he really only does it when he's excited about something. Whatever was going on with these dead half-angels, it had Luke ready to rumble.

"What do you know about Cambion?"

His brow knit for a moment, then he looked up and me and nodded. "It makes sense that they would be involved in this somehow. Cambion and Nephilim have a hatred for one another that goes deeper than anything we can fathom. They are internally wired to despise and destroy the other."

"So they're real?" I figured I'd start with the easy questions.

Luke chuckled. "Yes, they are real. In fact, you have encountered several although you were unaware of it at the time."

"Yeah?" I raised an eyebrow. I thought I'd know it if I'd been dealing with a demon, even half-demon. And then there was the part of me that hoped that Luke would give me a little warning if I was dealing with a demon, even a half-demon.

"Of course," Luke replied, oblivious to the concern in my voice. "There was Hans, in France in the latter stages of the Second World War. You remember Hans?"

Of course I remembered Hans. He was a nebbishy little German guy living in Paris when the Nazis invaded. Because he was German, and as white as my pillowcases, the Nazis left him and his little pub alone. They never knew that he had a little radio room built onto his wine cellar and spent his early morning hours, after last call, relaying signal intelligence for the French Resistance.

"But Hans was one of the good guys," I said. "How could he be a demon?"

"Half-demon," Luke replied. "And he never had any inkling of his heritage. He only knew that he liked being where things were exciting, and that things were very exciting in Paris."

"But you knew?"

"I knew the second I laid eyes on him. Once you know what to look for in a hellspawn, you can't miss them."

"And what exactly are we looking for?" I asked the obvious question.

"The Cambion are usually smaller than normal, short and slender, with close-set eyes and a prominent brow ridge. Narrow features, typically, they do not tend to be attractive people. Long, thin fingers, almost preternaturally long and slender. The kind of hands you'd expect on a concert pianist, or a safecracker, which they are equally likely to be. But it's the eyes that give them away," Luke said, his own eyes closing as if looking back on the demons he'd known. "Their eyes are never still, no matter how deeply they may concentrate on something. The slightest noise and they will flit around like a hummingbird."

I thought about it, and the things he was saying did describe Hans. He was perpetually nervous, with eyes always scanning the room. I chalked it up at the time to the fact that he had a radio rig in his basement that guaranteed execution if the SS found it, but it all fit.

"So if we have dead Nephilim, we probably have a Cambion involved somewhere," I suggested.

"At least one," Luke agreed.

"And the best place to find out about demonic activity is Mort's," I said.

"Where you are specifically not allowed to set foot until this business is settled," Luke replied.

"Says who?"

"Says me, as your guardian."

"Luke, you haven't needed to be my guardian for six decades."

"That notwithstanding, it is my duty to keep you safe. That is the task your mother saddled me with on her deathbed, and I intend to fulfill it. No matter how much more difficult it is since I can't bespell you."

"Yeah, well, you should have thought about the consequences before you bit my mom and threw my dad to your psycho wives. Being born of two parents who were both bitten by vampires does weird things to your DNA."

Luke actually looked a little embarrassed. "I will admit that when I first, ahem, met your mother, that I was not exactly thinking long-term." I really think that he would have blushed if his blood actually still flowed.

"Don't sweat it, Luke. I've seen the pictures. Mom was hot when she was a kid. I can't blame you for wanting to take a bite."

"You are amazingly crass, Quincy."

"I live but to amaze, Uncle." I shot him a grin, then waved at the books I had scattered across the table. "But back to the matter at hand. If going to

Mort's is out, and I'm pretty sure we're going to revisit the whole 'you giving me ultimatums' thing, then we need another way to track down a Cambion that we've never seen. So what do we have as far as evidence?"

"It seems the answer is precious little," Luke said, pacing the huge rug in the center of the library. "We know that three Nephilim have been killed, their blood drained, and their bodies left for the human authorities to find. We know nothing about a murder weapon or any connection between the victims."

"Yeah, the cops were turning over every stone in those people's personal and professional lives, and so far *nada*. So let's look at the blood. Why would someone drain the bodies? Are Cambion vampiric?"

"You mean, do they feed on human blood?" Luke shot me a look. "No. As far as I know, vampires are the only sanguivores that currently exist."

"How long have you been waiting to just casually drop the word 'sanguivores' into conversation?" I asked.

I got him again. This time I swear the tips of his ears turned just a tiny bit pink. "Quite a long time, actually. Be that as it may, vampires are the only creatures I am aware of that feed on human blood. So there must be some other quality in the blood of a Nephilim that makes it desirable."

"Or maybe a bunch of qualities," I said, reaching for a book I'd discarded several hours before.

"What have you found, my boy?" There he was, at my elbow in a blink again, all hint of muddled pacing long gone.

"Bevan's treatise on demonic possessions and exorcisms has an appendix on types of demons, and he includes Nephilim in there." I pointed. "Isn't that odd? I mean, demons are demons, and Nephilim are half-angel, so why would he put them in the same category?"

"Remember your theology, Quincy. If Lucifer was the first to fall, then all the existing demons are his progeny."

"So demons are just angels with a public relations problem?"

"A little more than that," Luke replied. "But Bevan does raise an interesting point about the basic similarities between their origins. Regardless, what does he say about the blood?"

I flipped pages to the back of the book and found the appendix I was looking for. "Apparently it has all kinds of powerful effects, depending on what species the drinker is."

"That makes sense. Inherently magical substances affect different magical beings in very unique ways. For example, the mushrooms that make up a faerie ring are completely harmless to humans, if slightly hallucinogenic, but they are very poisonous to dwarves and duergar and the like. Even brownies won't go near them."

"Right," I said, pointing back to the book. "But paying a little more attention to the possible motive for our murders—Nephilim blood is like Viagra, cocaine, and ecstasy all rolled into one for demons. It heightens all physical sensations, the more extreme the better, apparently. It allows them to 'perform as though they were human men in their early twenties,' so I guess it causes huge demon boners, and…oh fuck."

"Oh fuck what?" Luke asked. "I find the concept of demon erections as distasteful as you do, I'm sure, but that hardly accounts—"

"It opens gates," I said, pointing at a drawing on the next page of a human-looking wizard opening a portal, obviously to somewhere Very Not Nice because a huge demon was pulling himself through. I was able to be specific with the gender because I recognized the demon's manifestation—Orobas, the same demon that had kicked my ass at Mort's. "Nephilim blood is blended with Cambion and human blood to create a gate into this world. Somebody has used Nephilim blood to bring Orobas back into this world. And now it looks like our old buddy Oro is planning to create the daddy of all gates."

"Well," Uncle Luke said, pulling out a chair and sitting at the table across from me. "Oh fuck, indeed."

Chapter Eight

"That's not all," I said.

"That's enough, don't you think?" Luke said from his chair.

"Not quite. Aside from its effects on humans, which is to induce psychosis, hallucinations, paranoia, and violent tendencies, Nephilim blood has one more effect on a Cambion. Well, any extraplanar creatures, it seems."

"And what might that be?" Luke asked.

"A touch of Nephilim blood to the third eye masks the demon from Sight." The Sight was what I used to see through the illusions mystical creatures cast to hide their appearance. The third eye was a *chakra*, or focal point for energy in the body. It wasn't really a physical point, more like an energy node floating just outside the body. I'm not sure how you smear blood on a *chakra*, but probably dabbing a little on your forehead and focusing your energy on it would be close enough to get you there.

"Are you certain?"

"Well, it's one of those things that I can't really be sure of until it's way too late, so I guess I should just assume that I won't be able to use my Sight to pick out our bad guy in a crowd." Unless I found some Nephilim blood myself and figured out a way to use it to level the playing field. Probably not happening since I've never spent much time working on *chakras* or any of that deep-thinking magical stuff. I was always much more the "lob fireballs at bad guys" kind of magic-user.

"Well, that's too bad, since we're likely headed to a crowded scene," came a voice from the door of the library. I stood and spun to the door, drawing my Glock, but Luke was already on his feet and at the door, fangs out and in full vamp mode, something I hadn't seen in decades.

Not that it mattered. The leggy blonde in the doorway just stuck out her arm and stopped Luke cold. He ran into her outstretched hand and crumpled to the floor like he'd just run headlong into a Mike Tyson uppercut. She looked down at him with a cold look on her face, and I came to the quick realization that, guardian or not, this angel had a badass side to her.

"I will apologize for entering your lair uninvited, vampire, and as you are important to Quincy, who is my charge, I will ask for your forgiveness. But understand this: I am an angel of the Lord, and if you attack me again, even in misunderstanding, I will wipe you from the face of the Earth and leave not even a pile of ash behind."

Luke lay on the floor looking up at the angel, then very slowly got to his feet. "Your apology is accepted, my dear. But you should understand this: you are not the first angel I have met, and I'm still here. I make no promises about the seraph."

"If you two are done measuring things that I want to know absolutely nothing about, would you like to tell me why you're here?" I asked Glory.

"There has been another murder. Another Nephilim was found this morning, and this one was not dumped in a mall parking lot in the middle of the night. This body was found on the front steps of Trinity Presbyterian Church. The police are already on the scene, and your friend Detective Sponholz seems to be in charge."

"Great," I grumbled. "That'll make everything peaches and ice cream. Let's go." I started for the door, but Luke's voice stopped me.

"Quincy, wait."

I stopped. He sounded worried. Dracula, lord of the friggin' vampires, sounded *worried?* Now I was a little nervous. I looked at him, one eyebrow climbing.

"Be careful."

"Not a chance." I grinned and walked past Glory and out the door.

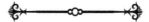

Trinity Presbyterian Church is a huge Gothic church in one of Charlotte's ritziest neighborhoods. There's a lot of stained glass and stone involved in anything that goes down there, including murder. Our Nephilim this time was a woman, sitting on the top step leaning over like she was just resting her head against the wall. Except for all the blood pooling around her. This was obviously not just a body dump; she was killed right there on the steps, or very nearby.

I walked up to the police line and a tall, thick-necked cop with flinty eyes and a scowl on his face stepped up to meet me. "Move along," he said in a voice that sounded a lot like someone rubbing two boulders together.

"I'm working with Detective Sponholz on this case. If you could call him over, he'll badge me through."

"No can do," said the cop, who looked a lot like a linebacker run a little bit toto fat. "Detective didn't tell me anything about a CI."

"CI? Do I look like a friggin' CI to you?" I asked. "Don't answer that. Just go get Sponholz. Tell him his consultant is here." Somedays I wish I had gone a little more legit with my life choices. It doesn't happen often, but sometimes. The uniform gave me a suspicious glare, but turned and walked off. I watched him go over to Sponholz, make a few dismissive gestures in my direction, then stiffen as he got a response he wasn't expecting. He turned and walked back to where I waited, as patiently as I could fake.

"Detective says you're clear," he mumbled.

I opened my mouth to say something, but a sharp pain in my ankle reminded me that I was traveling with an angel on my shoulder these days. Or at least with an angel close enough to kick me when I was about to say something smartass. I closed my mouth and ducked under the tape.

"Don't touch nothing," the gorilla muttered at me as I walked past. I bit my tongue and walked over to where Sponholz knelt by the body.

"How'd you hear about this?" Sponholz asked, not looking up.

"A little bird told me," I replied. "What do we know?"

"Why don't you give me the benefit of your expert eye and tell me what you see, then I'll think about telling you what we know."

I cocked an eyebrow at the rotund detective, who just stared back at me, blank-faced. If there was anything nefarious behind his continued testing of me, I couldn't find it. I shook my head at him and knelt on the stone steps beside the body.

The woman was fit, in her mid-thirties at the most, with auburn hair worn in a low ponytail. Her eyebrows and nails told me she took pride in her appearance, and that regular salon visits were a part of her routine. She wore an expensive-looking blouse and jacket with heels and slacks, but there wasn't much in the way of jewelry. Not an ostentatious woman, but she didn't hide her femininity, either. There was a slight smell of animal around her, and a few stray hairs on her pants, so I knew she owned a cat, and there was neither a ring nor a line where it had been removed, so she was likely single.

"No purse?" I asked. Sponholz shook his head. "Wallet?" Shake. "Any ID?" Another shake.

My physical exam finished, I closed my eyes and opened my Sight. When I looked at her again, I could see the faint outline of wings floating from her shoulders, and a rapidly dimming golden aura around her.

"She's definitely Nephilim," I muttered.

"What's that?" Sponholz asked, snapping my attention back to the mundane world.

"Nothing, just making some mental notes. Who found her?"

"Lady over there." He gestured to a woman sitting in the open back of an ambulance with two EMTs tending to her. "She's the church administrator. Showed up for work early this morning to get some laps in over at the gym and saw her sitting on the steps. She thought the victim was a new member wanting to use the workout facilities, or maybe a neighborhood jogger. The victim was non-responsive, so she gave her a little shake. That's when she realized that she was standing in a puddle of blood."

"And that explains the blanket, and the shivering, and the thousand-yard stare," I said, looking over at the witness. She was a trim fifty-something woman with a few gray roots showing among her dark brown hair, the very picture of a someone who got up early to work out. Standing next to her was a well-dressed young man with a lot of hair gel and a mostly respectable haircut, who I assumed to be the one of the pastors, or ministers, or whatever name the church had come up with for them nowadays.

"Yeah, the youth pastor found her about twenty minutes ago. She hasn't been able to pull herself together enough to make a statement, but it doesn't matter. The guy confirmed the victim wasn't a member of the choir, or the church for that matter. He doesn't know who she was." I didn't either, but I was a lot more concerned with *what* she was than *who* she was.

"Have you searched the car?" I asked.

"What car?"

I pointed off to the side of the church. "It's half past seven. Choir practice is cancelled. There aren't really many onlookers, and I assume you've got somebody photographing the crowd in case the killer come back to gloat."

"Yeah, but that doesn't—"

I pointed to the lot again. "There are ten cars in that parking lot for two churchgoers. The Camry's mine, and the shitty Ford with blackballs is probably yours. That leaves half a dozen cars to search. One of them probably has a purse in it, and that'll have the victim's ID."

Sponholz glared at me. "I don't like it when you say things I can't argue with."

"Here's another one," I said with a smile. "You're fat."

I ignored his upraised middle finger and turned back to the corpse. I opened my Sight once more and gave the dead Nephilim another look. Her aura was even thinner, but that wasn't what I was looking for. I searched the area, scanning the surroundings with my third eye, then I found it.

"Gotcha!" I said, hopefully under my breath. There, under the corpse, was the slightest trace of another aura. Human auras are strange enough, but half-angel auras were even tougher to decipher. One thing I did know was that our Cambion left a little tiny trace smeared on the steps behind our Jane Doe. I couldn't tell if that's where he stood as he killed her or what, but I knew that there was enough aura transferred that I'd know it if I saw it again.

"Got what?" Sponholz said from my elbow.

"Nothing," I replied, trying to sound depressed. "I thought I saw a piece of paper in the blood, but it was nothing." I stood up, both knees popping like rifle shots. I turned and looked at the crowd, my third eye still open to the metaphysical world. Nothing. Not a hint of demon anywhere, and I had to keep Glory in my peripheral vision or she blinded me. I'd have to talk with her about that. I did get a faint golden glow off a car in the lot, a snazzy BMW M-class convertible in cherry red. I pointed to it.

"I bet that's her car," I said.

"The Beamer? Why?" Sponholz asked.

"How many church choir directors do you know that can afford a BMW sports car? And how dumb would they have to be to drive it if they could?" I replied.

"Good point. I'll go check it out. Stay here." He lumbered off to the car, waving a uniform over as he went. I watched in the distance as the uniform roped off the area around the car with crime scene tape, then Sponholz tried the doors. Locked. I could almost *feel* the glee roll off him as he realized he was going to get to cause havoc, then I saw him reach into his pocket, pull out his fist with something I couldn't see clenched in it, then shatter the driver's side window.

"I really hope that's the right car," I said to myself, watching him work. Moments later, Sponholz had the door open and was waving me over. I was at his side in seconds, peering into the car. There were no signs of a disturbance, just a Starbucks cup in the holder and an iPhone plugged into a car charger. I reached for the phone, but the rotund detective elbowed me out of the way and reached into the car himself. He pressed a button on the phone, and the screen came to life. A picture of the victim hugging a gigantic golden retriever filled the screen.

"Well, I guess we found the right car," I said. Sponholz just grunted. I pushed the unlock button and walked around to the passenger door. I opened the door, leaned in, and popped open the glove compartment, then jerked back and hit my head on the doorframe in surprise.

"Whoa!" I said, rubbing my head. I stared at the black pistol that had fallen to the seat. "Hey Sponholz, our victim was packing."

"Yeah," he said, looking at the gun. "Glock 19. Good gun. Dependable, lightweight…good glovebox gun."

"Who brings a gun to a church?" I asked myself, reaching back into the car and fumbling around in the glove compartment. Inspection receipts, a couple maps (who carries actual paper maps anymore?), a GPS charger, and finally, buried under a roadside flare and a spare set of keys to something, I found what I was looking for—the registration.

"Terese Dover," I said.

"What's that?" Sponholz looked up at me, and it was his turn to crack his head on the doorframe.

"Our vic is very likely Terese Dover of Matthews, North Carolina," I said, passing the vehicle registration across to the grumpy detective.

"Who the hell is Terese Dover, and why did someone want her dead?" Sponholz asked.

I had no idea, but this was the second dead half-angel in as many days, and if experience was any teacher, that meant something bad was brewing, and it was going to be up to me to deal with it.

Chapter Nine

"**W**HO THE HELL IS TERESE DOVER?" DENNIS ASKED, LOOKING UP FROM the slip of paper I handed him.

"A dead woman, and I need to know everything about her," I said, sitting down in the armless chair beside Dennis' desk. Dennis Bolton was an informant I hired from time to time, a college kid I'd pulled out of a bad scene on New Year's Eve at the turn of the millennium when what he thought was a LARP turned into a dark magician's plan for ritual sacrifice. Dennis survived, but he saw a few things that made him never want to watch a horror movie again. His GM-slash-necromancer didn't survive to see the dawning of the year 2000, and after a few fire spells and an hour or two of nasty shotgun work, all the zombies were returned to their appropriate level of dead. Ever since that night, Dennis was my go-to guy for all things buried on the internet and the dark web. It's good to keep a few nerds on call for the tough ones.

"What killed her?"

"In the medical sense, a cut throat. In the perpetrator sense, I don't know yet. But I think there's something ugly brewing, and this is almost certainly tied to it."

"Makes sense, given the date," Dennis said, typing and clicking away on his souped-up Powerbook.

"What's the date?" I've never been the best in the world at keeping track of crap like dates. One of the many reasons I've never had a girlfriend of more than a few weeks. Chicks always want you to remember things like anniversaries, birthdays, and when you promised to meet them for expensive dinners. Or any dinners. Or at all. Monsters aren't real considerate of personal plans, so I've missed a lot of second dates. That means I haven't had a whole lot of third and fourth dates.

"Tomorrow is the Equinox, Harker. Isn't that something you wizard-types keep track of? Like Easter, or Christmas?"

"Nah, that's for the Wiccans. I don't really do the whole prayer thing. Now Christmas, I can keep track of. I'm oblivious, not dead. Even I can't miss all the crap in every store. But there aren't a whole lot of Vernal Equinox displays in the front of Walmart, ya know?"

"Wizards shop at Walmart?"

"One, I don't like being called a wizard. It sounds like a douche in a pointy hat and a robe, and I don't do hats. And two, everybody shops at Walmart. You can't really help it. Now what about Terese Dover?"

"She works, er…worked for AmeriBank. She was an investment banker, mostly working on financing construction projects. Office buildings, developments, that kind of thing."

"Construction, huh? Doesn't sound like the kind of thing that gets somebody killed. See if there's anything in her personal life that's out of the ordinary."

"You mean like fetish club membership, donations to the Church of Satan, subscriptions to freaky S&M magazines?" Dennis had a little bit too much of a gleam in his eyes for my comfort.

"Yeah…sure, pal. All of that, too. But I was thinking more like a relative in prison, some family or school connection to anything shady, too much money or not enough, repeated deposits or withdrawals in the same amount that don't correspond to a normal payment, that kind of thing."

His face fell beneath his close-cropped curly hair, and for a moment he looked like a really depressed Bobby Hill, from a *King of the Hill* cartoon. "Oh. Okay. I'll look into all that stuff, too. But I wouldn't ignore the work stuff, Harker. There's a lot of big money in these developments, and that's a lot of motive."

"Fair enough," I said. "I'm gonna head over to her office and talk to her co-workers. You let me know if you find anything. And keep an ear to the ground on the BlackNet about anything big going down on the Equinox. I don't think demons are much for email, but maybe some of their human pawns are using the web to communicate." I stood up and walked to the door. "And Dennis?"

"Yeah, Harker?"

"Be careful."

"Don't worry," he said, pushing his wheelchair back from the keyboard. "It's not like I'm gonna go run around in the sewers in a cape anymore."

"Yeah, well…even so, don't get dead."

"You too."

I let myself out through the front of the VCR repair shop Dennis ran as a front for his real job, which was selling information. I knew I wasn't his only client, but I'd never seen anyone else entering or leaving the shop. I didn't ask too many questions. I just took the information he gave me, paid the tab, and hoped someday he'd forgive me for cutting his legs off with a spell to save him from the grasp of a hungry demon.

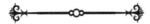

Terese Dover's office was on one of the top floors of the AmeriBank tower, a corner office furnished in sleek chrome, glass, and black leather. Her desk was huge and designed to intimidate, but it was a lot less imposing with its drawers hanging out and fingerprint dust all over it. I ducked under the crime scene tape and stepped inside. It looked like it had been tossed, but carefully. Sponholz and his boys had obviously taken a little care in the process, making a token effort not to piss off the city's biggest employer.

I stood in the center of the room, between the ego-boosting desk and a small sitting area set off at one end of the room, and opened my Sight. Traces of Nephilim energy glowed off every surface. This was certainly Dover's place, and she was one hundred percent definitely half-angel. I'd felt the same energy coming off Lincoln Baxter's body, and there was a hint of the same energy around Glory, only hers was cleaner, purer, like it was the source and Dover's energy was a diluted version. Which I guess it probably was.

I turned to the stone-faced security guard behind me. "Are any of Ms. Dover's co-workers available for me to speak to?"

"No, sir." Amazing. I never even saw his lips move. The block of granite in a rent-a-cop suit just stood in the doorway, staring at me like I was something he'd scraped off his shoe.

"What about any of her superiors?"

"No, sir."

"Her secretary?"

"Ms. Dover's assistant has taken a personal day. She was distraught at the news. We all were." He looked about as distraught as a brick wall, but since he was also built like one, I didn't challenge him. It was way too early in the day to go breaking the humans. Besides, I was on the side of the angels, literally, for once, and I was kinda liking the way it felt. I decided not to screw anything up.

"Fine, take me to HR." Sponholz had obviously beaten me to the workplace, the benefit of actually *being* the police, instead of just kinda working alongside them. But he was maybe the laziest cop I'd ever met, so I had high hopes that when he didn't find anything in her office, that he wouldn't have thought to visit Human Resources.

I followed my security golem to the elevator, and we rode down forty-something floors until the doors dinged open on the twelfth floor. I stepped out, and my shadow followed.

"I'm sure I can find it from here," I said. I pointed to the sign on the wall with an arrow pointing right and the words "Human Resources" over it.

"You are my responsibility until you leave the building," the guard replied. I took that to mean a lot more of "I'm not letting you out of my sight, jackass," than "I'm terribly concerned about your well-being."

I sighed and started down the hallway to the right. The HR office had a sizable waiting room with about ten chairs, a circular desk with a grandmotherly-looking woman seated behind it, and a wall of pamphlets with titles like "What to do if you are sexually harassed," "How to manage intra-office relationships" and "Good personal hygiene makes a happy workplace!" The last one had a cartoon figure on the cover with wavy stink lines emanating from it. I stepped up to the desk. Aunt Bea was on the phone chatting about some pound cake she had tasted at the church dinner the night before, and when I opened my mouth to ask for the personnel records on Terese Dover, she held up one finger to shush me.

I don't like being shushed. I don't know anyone who does, but there are some people who deserve it. I'm typically not the chatty type, so generally if I open my mouth to say something, it's either relevant or tied to a spell. So I don't like being shushed. And I certainly don't like being shushed, not once but *twice*, so when a glorified file clerk shushed me so she could tell Mrs. McGillicutty how many eggs to put in her pound cake, I became irritated. It's bad for technology, and sometimes people, when I become irritated.

I focused my will, flicked a finger toward the telephone, and whispered "*mortus*." I released the power, and the line indicator lights on the phone went dead. Aunt Bea looked around, puzzled, then pressed a few buttons on her phone. She looked around, puzzled, then finally seemed to notice me standing there. Directly over her desk. With a two hundred-fifty-pound security guard beside me. Because we were hard to notice.

"Huh," she said with a puzzled look up at me. "My phone's on the fritz."

"You should call tech support," I said without a hint of a smile, even when she turned and picked up the handset as if to dial. "But before you do, I need to speak with someone about Terese Dover."

"Oh, Ms. Dover? Wasn't that such a tragedy what happened to her? And right there on the steps of a church and everything. I didn't even know she went to church, do you know that? And I make it a point to know a little something about almost everybody." She beamed like being a busybody was an achievement.

"I'm sure you do," I said with what I hoped was an ingratiating smile that kept all the "I want to strangle you" off my face. "I'm working with the police investigating Ms. Dover's death. Who could I speak to about her?"

"That would be me," came a new voice from off to my right. I turned to see a trim Asian woman in her thirties standing outside the door to one of the offices. She was dressed for downtown, with a black skirt and burgundy blouse under a long jacket. She walked over to me and gave me firm handshake. "My name is Lina Flores, VP of HR. Please come this way."

She turned around and walked off in that "I know you'll follow me" way that people who are very much in charge of their environment have. I did just what she expected and followed her into a small office with a desk, two chairs, and one moderately sad-looking plant. There were a few diplomas on the walls and a couple of photos of Ms. Flores—one that looked like her college graduation, one of her with a man in ski gear in front of a snowy backdrop, one a big family photo with her face smiling in the front row. I gave her a look and a nod at the security golem.

"Gerald, please wait outside," she said. Now I knew the golem's name at least.

Gerald frowned. "I have strict instructions not to—"

She waved a hand. "Where do you think he's going to go, Gerald? I doubt he'd survive a jump from my twelfth-floor window, and you'll be right outside. Now get out. I will likely have to discuss sensitive personnel matters, and I can't do that with you here."

I didn't bother to correct the sharp little HR vice-president that a twelve-story drop would hurt like a sonofabitch, but it wouldn't even come close to killing me. I tend to leave out the "I'm not completely human" conversation until my second date. Or at least my second meeting over a murdered coworker. Tomato, to-mah-to.

Flores sat down behind her desk, so I followed her lead and took one of the armless chairs facing her. She opened a file drawer, pulled out a manila folder, and placed it on her desk.

"What can I do for you, Mr. Harker?" she asked with a little smile.

"As you know, Ms. Dover was killed this morning. While we understand the shock and grief her coworkers must be facing, time is always of the essence in these types of investigations, so we cannot allow people a typically appropriate time of mourning before we begin our investigation."

"Let me stop you right there, Mr. Harker. The police were already here, and they confiscated Ms. Dover's computer, searched her office, and interviewed several of her coworkers. And you haven't shown me a badge, or any type of official ID. You also seem to know nothing at all about the activities of the police department, and those things all add up to you not being with the police. So who are you, and why are you snooping around my dead employee?"

Fuck. I needed to think quick. *Fuck it, here goes nothing.* "Ms. Flores, do you believe in magic?" I asked, whispering *"incindare"* under my breath and sending a small gout of flame up from my palm.

The startled executive jerked back, almost toppling over in her chair. "What the hell?!?" She stood up and backed away, bumping into the bookcase behind her.

I closed my fist and the flame winked out. "Ms. Flores, there are things in the world that most people never hear of outside of children's stories. The monster under the bed, the boogeyman in the closet, the thing that goes bump in the night. They're all real, and I have spent my life fighting them. I think that Ms. Dover got mixed up in something ugly, something way outside her experience, and she paid the ultimate price for it. This is the kind of thing the local police are not very well-equipped to deal with, so I'm piggybacking on their mundane investigation with my very much not mundane one. But I need your help.

"I need to know everything about Terese Dover. Who loved her, who hated her, where she shopped, where she ate lunch, what she liked, what she disliked, where she vacationed—I need to know everything. And I need you to help me."

Now that the initial shock of seeing the world beneath her world was fading a little, Flores latched on to the only thing she still understood—rules. "I'm sorry, Mr. Harker. I can't help you. I don't know what your little magic trick was supposed to prove, but it didn't work. There are very strict regulations that cover what I can and cannot discuss with you and…"

Her words trailed off and her eyes went wide. I swept myself a clear spot about two feet in diameter on her desk, drew a quick circle with a piece of chalk I carried in a pocket, and muttered a short incantation. An imp appeared in the circle on her desk, a twelve-inch naked red man with goat hooves, bat wings, a forked tail, and short red horns curving from his skull. You know, basically every childhood nightmare of the devil? Well, that was standing on her desk.

The imp turned around, looked up at me, then started hopping up and down, shaking his fists. "Goddammit, Harker!" the tiny demon yelled, and its voice was shrill and almost comical. "I told you to stop bringing me up here if I can't eat or fuck anything!" He turned to Flores and leered at her. "Hey baby," he said, grabbing his penis, which was large out of all proportion to his size. "You want some of this? Come on sweet cheeks, you know you want to try it. You know what they say, 'Once you go red, you fuck 'til you're dead'." The horny little demonlet cackled like he'd invented the dirty limerick and turned back to me.

"Whatever you want, the answer is go fuck yourself."

"Why you gotta be like that, 'Thew?" I asked, a small smile threatening to crack my face.

"It's gotta be like that because fuck you, that's why." He turned back to Flores. "What about it, baby girl? You decided you want to come ride the crimson pony? Just reach out with your hand and erase the circle old Fuckwit McDickhead over there called me into, and I'll make you scream in ways you've never imagined."

"He's probably right there," I said. "Demons have barbed penises, kinda like cats, only with more sulfur smell. You get hooked up with 'Thew and you'll definitely scream."

"And don't worry about size, sexy," the imp chimed in. "My thundercock isn't the only thing that grows." As if to prove his point, he swelled to twice his size, almost completely filling the circle. He jerked his tail back as it grazed the chalk line, a yellow spark of magical energy arcing out from the circle to zap him.

"Ow, Lucifer damn it!" he yelled, pulling his tail around and putting the tip in his mouth. After a few seconds, he looked back up at Flores and held out the tail. "It's pretty flexible," he said, a lascivious grin splitting his crimson features. "You should see the things I can do with it. I can tickle your—"

I cut him off with a word. "*Silencio.*" The demon's lips kept moving, but no sound came out. "Now do you believe in monsters?" I asked. "If you need a little more convincing, feel free to let the little guy out. I'm sure he'd love to show you all the things he can tickle with that tail."

Flores looked up from the imp on her desk. She was very pale, and for a moment I thought she was going to faint. Then she turned to the side and vomited very quietly into a trash can next to her desk. She stayed hunched over the black Rubbermaid receptacle for several long moments before she sat up, wiped her mouth with a tissue from a desk drawer, and looked at me, her composure completely restored.

"What can I do for you, Mr. Harker? And would you please remove your demon from my office?"

I waved a hand, and the illusion of the demon winked out of existence. I reached out with my finger and scrubbed out a tiny part of the circle, making it useless for any real spellcasting. I wouldn't want anyone to actually summon a demon into the woman's office, after all. Real demons don't come in miniature sizes. The smallest ones I've ever heard of are the size of a large dog and will reduce a human being to nothing more than scraps in less than five minutes flat. But my illusionary hornball demon was pretty useful in convincing people that the supernatural is real. After all, who wouldn't get nervous at the thought of a hellspawn with a crush on them?

Chapter Ten

I SPENT ABOUT AN HOUR CHATTING WITH THE SUDDENLY COOPERATIVE HR guru and came away with the contact information for three people who filed complaints about Terese Dover within the past six months; a folder containing no fewer than seventeen letters of recommendation, promotion, and awards for productivity from her superiors; and Ms. Flores' phone number. You never know.

Loud music blared down the hall as I stepped off the elevator at 340 South, an upscale apartment building on the edge of Southend, a recently revitalized part of town that went from strip clubs to antique stores almost overnight. I checked numbers on doors against the piece of paper in my hand, my confusion rising every step I drew nearer to apartment 614. I stopped in front of the right door and raised my hand to knock, although with the level of Metallica that was screeching at me in the hallway, I knew no one in the apartment had any chance of hearing me knock.

But I knocked anyway, with the expected lack of result. I tried again, and the third time I switched over to pounding. After that, with my temper growing and the amount of time before the Equinox shrinking, I kicked it in. The frame splintered, the door crashed in, the chain holding it shut snapped, and my foot hurt.

A young woman in exercise gear was on a treadmill in the middle of the room screaming heavy metal along with the cable TV music station at the top of her lungs. She froze in mid-chorus when I came crashing in, her hand upraised in a stuck salute to the gods of rock. She looked to be in her mid-twenties, and judging by the six-pack she was sporting in her sports bra and her sweatpants, she spent a lot of time on that treadmill.

"What the fuck?" She hopped off the treadmill and took a couple of quick steps to a small table next to the couch. She pushed a button on a remote and turned off the TV, then picked up her cell phone with one hand and started rummaging around in her purse with the other.

I didn't move any closer, just closed the door behind me and stood a foot or so into the foyer. I was a good fifteen feet away from her, trying to stay as far away as the small apartment would let me so she didn't feel any more threatened by the big guy who just kicked her door in. Plus, if she tried to shoot me, the farther away I was, the better. I just focused my will in case I needed a quick spell and tried to look harmless.

"Are you Janet Hamilton?" I asked.

"That depends completely on who the fuck you are and what the fuck you're doing in my apartment." She turned to the phone. "Hello, 911? There's a—"

So much for harmless. I released my will with a whispered "*magnos*." A focused little pulse of electromagnetic energy flickered out from my fingers, and her cell phone was a paperweight. Her TV and DVR were also probably fried, as well as the remote, anything else electronic in her purse, and probably the stereo. At least this time I managed not to blow out all the power in the building.

She tossed her useless cell phone and pulled her other hand out of her purse. She held a small canister with a red button on top of it. "Don't come any closer. I've got pepper spray."

"Calm down, Ms. Hamilton. My name is Quincy Harker, and I'm working with the police." I held up the wallet containing my PI credentials, including what might or might not have been a fake badge I picked up at Morris Costumes a couple years ago. She lowered the pepper spray and her shoulders immediately relaxed. It was amazing how effective that line was. I might have to consider actually working with the cops if this kept up.

"I'm a private investigator consulting with the Homicide Division. We're looking into the death of your employer, Ms. Dover."

A sneer crossed her previously gorgeous face. Nobody's attractive when they sneer. "That bitch? Who cares? Everybody I know is glad she's dead."

This wasn't exactly what I expected to hear. "I met a woman at your office who told me you were so upset over Ms. Dover's death that you were unable to come in to work."

"That's HR-speak for 'she called in and told us to fuck off.' I figured if Satanna wasn't coming in, I'd take a little vacation, have some 'me' time, and generally chill. That keeps me from having to pretend that everybody in the world didn't hate her when people call in to give their bullshit fake condolences all day."

"So you didn't like her? But we found a ton of commendations in her personnel file."

"Yeah? And how many of them were from the bosses, and how many were from normal people?" She tossed the pepper spray back into her purse.

I thought for a moment. All of the complaints were from so-called "normal people" while all the commendations were from superiors. "So she liked to punch down, as they say?"

"Yeah, that's a good word for it." She pulled her hair back into a messy auburn ponytail and walked into the kitchen, pulling open the refrigerator and grabbing a water bottle. "I'd offer you something, but I don't want you to stay."

I barked out a short laugh. "I get it. I just need to know if you have any idea who hated Ms. Dover enough to kill her."

She leaned on the marble-topped island in her kitchen and gave me a direct look. Her green eyes were bright, but there was no mirth there. "Look, pal. I hated that bitch. She was a horrible boss, and I'm pretty sure some of the shit she did was illegal, or at least borderline illegal. But I didn't kill her, and I don't know anybody who would. We're bankers, for God's sake. It's not like we're mobsters or anything like that. Hell, we don't even handle mortgages. And in today's market, that's something that *could* get you killed. If she was a normal person, I'd say you should talk to a boyfriend or girlfriend, but as far as I know, she never dated. So I've got nothing. Except a busted door."

"Yeah, sorry about that. You couldn't hear me knock, I guess."

"Not a chance. I was rocking out, getting a good sweat on, and yelling every nasty thing I ever wanted to call Satanna and wouldn't get the chance. So now I've got to take a shower, and there's nothing to secure my door with." She leaned further over the island, giving me a pretty clear view down the front of her sports bra. A drop of sweat ran down her collarbone and into her cleavage. I watched its journey, thinking about following it all the way down that very, very flat stomach to its natural destination, then gave myself a little mental shake and looked back up at her eyes.

She was watching me watch her with a little smirk on her face. "You gonna repair my door, Mr. Detective, or you just going to stand guard outside my shower and make sure I stay safe and sound?"

Nobody's very attractive when they smirk, either, and after all my time on this planet, I'm not immune to feminine wiles, but I am pretty damned resistant. So it didn't take me too much effort to slap on a rueful expression and shake my head.

"As much as I'd love to wash, I mean watch, your back, Ms.—"

"Miss," she said, wiggling her left hand at me to show the distinct lack of rings there.

"Miss Hamilton," I continued. "I have to get back to the station and keep going on our investigation. So if there's nothing else you can think of about why someone might want to harm your boss, I'll have to be on my way."

"Your loss, Detective. I don't know any reason somebody would take out Satanna, any more than you guys know why somebody killed her two buddies."

I had been digging through my pocket for a business card, but at her mention of buddies, my head snapped around.

"What buddies?" I asked.

"Mr. Baxter and Mr. Lacey." She stared a little, like she expected me to know more of what was going on than I did.

"Ms. Dover knew them both?"

"Yeah, they were in on some big development deal a couple years ago. It was right before she came to AmeriBank. I think it was that mixed-use place out in Belmont, maybe."

I kinda knew the place she was talking about. It took a fifty-acre piece of worthless property off I-85 about half an hour outside of Charlotte and turned it into a live/work/play development with homes, condos, and apartments at multiple price points, with the condos and apartments built over street-level shops and restaurants. There was a movie theater, skate park, and small water park attached, all fronting a gated neighborhood of million-dollar homes. The lots sold quickly, thanks to the privacy and the half-acre of woods surrounding each one. The condos and apartments did pretty well, too, and the shops were some of the most high-end in the area. If Dover had anything to do with that, she should have made out pretty well.

"Where did she work before AmeriBank?" I asked.

"I don't know," she said. "Some other bank. And she was a big deal there, so AB had to really lay out some coin to get her to jump ship."

"Huh," I mumbled. That was something to think about. "Thanks, I'll look into that." Why hadn't Sponholz mentioned the connection to the earlier victims? That raised an eyebrow, at least.

"You see anything else you want to look into, Detective?" she asked, batting her eyelashes at me. That would work better if her eyelashes didn't still have treadmill sweat on them. I love getting sweaty with a woman, but I'd rather if I'm the reason she's hot and bothered, not her exercise routine. With this one, I think all I could take credit for was the "bothered" part.

"I'm sorry, Miss Hamilton, I have to get back to the investigation. But if you think of anything else…regarding the case…feel free to give me a call." I finally found a business card crumpled in the back pocket of my jeans and slid it across the countertop to her. I gave one last, slightly regretful, look at her cleavage, then turned and walked to her door.

I put my hand on the door jamb, focused my will, and whispered. "*Restoratus.*" I've found through long practice that it doesn't always matter if the words you say are really Latin, or really anything, as long as the intent is clear. The words are mostly a way to focus the mind and thus focus the magic. That's not the case with summonings or more complex spells, like healings. Those are more about asking the universe to do something for you, and you have to ask nicely and in the right languages. The universe, or God, or Allah, or Gaea, or however you want to frame it, does not respond to current Standard American English. Or maybe the complexity of carving passages between dimensions is just so complicated that you have to focus completely on the words to distract yourself from not believing that you can do what you're about to do. One of those if probably close to how it really works. I don't pretend to understand it. It's fucking magic, you're not supposed to understand.

But however it works, it worked, and Janet Hamilton's door frame, lock, and door were as good as new when I took my hand off the jamb. I turned around, gave her a wave, and headed off to figure out what else Sponholz wasn't telling me about Terese Dover, Lincoln Baxter, and the other dead half-angels.

Chapter Eleven

I GOT BACK TO MY CAR AND GRABBED MY PHONE FROM THE CHARGER. It was a new smartphone, and the battery life was for shit, but it played music and had a camera built in, so I splurged on it. Besides, it was Luke's money, and he had plenty. When you start life as a rich-ass fifteenth century mildly psychotic Count and invest wisely, or at least kill a lot of rich people over the course of a few centuries, you're never short on cash.

"Yeah?" Dennis answered on the third ring.

"Boltron, what's up?" I tried to put a cheerful tone in my voice, not an "I only call you when I want something" tone.

"What do you want?" Apparently I failed.

"What makes you think I want anything?" I tried again.

"Because you only ever call me Boltron when you want something."

Shit. Busted.

"Besides, I hate being called Boltron. You know why?"

I didn't want to ask. I didn't care why, honestly, but I had to ask or he'd never help me out. "No, why?"

"Because I know when you call me Boltron, you're not thinking of the cool lion Voltron, you're thinking of the lame as shit vehicle Voltron. And nobody wants to be the vehicle Voltron, Harker. Everybody wants to be the fucking lion Voltron. But I don't get to be the lion Voltron, do I, *Quincy*?" He said my name like it was French for "shithead."

"I guess not, bro. Sorry."

"Sorry? *Sorry?* I'm stuck in a wheelchair with no fucking legs and all I get is *sorry?* I have to be the fucking vehicle Voltron forever, and you're *sorry?* Well—"

"Well next time you decide to be a fucking idiot and dress up like Gandalf to try and get into some coed's pants, I'll just let the fucking demon eat you, okay? Does that sound like a plan, shitweasel? Now shake off your goddamn pity party, pull your shit together, and get to fucking work. We've got four dead people with only the thinnest legit connection, a high holy day of magical buggery coming up in thirty-six hours, and no fucking clue what to do about it. So get your fucking hands off your dick and let's figure this shit out so nobody else dies. Okay?"

There was silence on the line for long enough that I thought I had maybe gotten a little too verbally medieval on his ass. After a solid two minutes of nothing but background noise coming through the phone, Dennis spoke again.

"Okay."

"Okay?"

"Yeah, okay. I'm back. Now what did you find out?"

So I filled him in on everything I had learned, and after about a minute of me talking, I heard keys clicking in the background. A few seconds later, Dennis spoke. "Okay, I've got Terese Dover's employment history and banking records, as well as Lincoln Baxter's. Brecker was even easier, but this Lacey guy has his shit locked down."

"Well, what can you tell me about the others?"

"They definitely all worked on the Pinehaven development. It was one of the first multi-use developments on Lake Wylie. The most expensive houses fronted the lake, another pricing tier overlooked the golf course, and the cheapest houses, the ones that started at only a half-million, those were closer to the retail and entertainment area. And all the shops either had apartments or condos over them. It was worth a ton of money and became the model for development in the area."

"Yeah, I've been there."

"How'd you get in?"

"Part of the golf course was built over a small family cemetery, the kind people used to have in the 18th century. They called me in when a poltergeist visited one of the homes near the sand trap on the 12th hole. I showed up and noticed that the teenage daughter's bedroom window overlooked the green. I had a brief conversation with her about playing around with spells she read online, dumped a full container of salt into the sand trap, and laid the spirit to rest. They haven't had any problems since then."

"Not supernatural problems, at any rate," Dennis replied.

"What's that mean?"

"It means that there have been a lot of complaints about the building quality, and more than one lawsuit filed against the developer since the place opened up. But it turns out the developer, one Kevin Lacey, had a good lawyer.

The contracts on the homes are airtight and protect the builder against any liability past three years. The problems didn't start appearing until year five, so all those people are on the hook for their sinking foundations, substandard shingles, cracked driveway pavement, and undersized electrical wiring."

"Sounds like our dearly departed Mister Lacey had himself a hell of a lawyer."

"He did indeed," Dennis said. "A hell of a lawyer who left private practice two years after Pinehaven sold its first house and moved into public service as an assistant district attorney."

"A very tall district attorney named Lincoln Baxter?" I asked.

"One and the same."

"So how does Terese Dover tie into all this? I suppose she moved money around for the project?"

"A little, but not much. It looks a lot more like she was responsible for the cash on the back end, moving money around through shell corporations and holding companies, bouncing it to and from offshore accounts until it came back, clean and virtually untraceable, into the accounts of our 'unconnected' victims."

"And what about Brecker?" I asked.

"He was the contractor for the development. I can't find anything specific that he did that was shady, but it does look like there have been a ton of small things going wrong with the buildings ever since the project was completed."

"So Lacey sells a huge project to a bunch of rich whales, Brecker the contractor cuts corners to pad everyone's pockets, Baxter writes the contracts that protect them from lawsuits in the long term, Dover moves their money around to hide it from the tax man, and they get away with this how, exactly? Don't buildings get inspected? Isn't there some kind of oversight into all of this?"

More clicking of keys, then Bolton comes back on the line. "You called it, Q. The entire project was overseen by the same city inspector, from plan review to final certificate of occupancy. A guy by the name of Kevin Gilbert, who, as of this conversation, is still alive. And according to the records at the Government Center, is at work right now."

"That's only about a block and a half from Police Headquarters. I'll call Sponholz and get him to put a uniform on Gilbert. If he's tied into this somehow, he's either our killer, or the next target."

"Good call. I'll keep digging and see if I can figure out anything else about Gilbert."

"Like whether or not his mom was touched by an angel?"

"Something like that." Dennis chuckled and hung up the phone.

"That wasn't funny," came a voice from beside me in the car.

I jumped so high my head literally hit the ceiling and turned to Glory, pistol in hand. She looked at it and smiled a little.

"You don't think that will actually do any good, do you?" she asked.

"No, but it's the natural response when someone scares the shit out of me," I replied.

"You're very profane," my guardian angel said, her lips pursed in disapproval. I'd seen people purse their lips before, but not since the Prohibitionists. Those people were always pursing something. Serious pains in the ass.

"You're very fucking observant," I replied, emphasizing the "fucking." It was a dick move, and I knew it, but I didn't respond well to fright, especially when I wasn't allowed to kill the thing that frightened me. I didn't particularly *want* to kill my guardian angel because that seemed like a bad idea on so many levels. That's not even considering the fact that I wasn't sure I *could* kill her, even if I wanted to.

"There's no need to be childish."

"I try to stick to what I'm good at."

"Well, let's focus on something else you're good at—stirring up trouble. You're sticking your nose into some powerful matters, the kind of thing that can get even a powerful wizard destroyed. Are you sure you want to follow this road to the end?"

"Do I have a choice? It looks like whoever is killing these half-angels wants to use them to open a portal and bring a bunch of big nasties through. They've already brought Orobas through, and God only knows who or what else. I don't know if I can handle this, but I know that I probably won't survive whatever they want to bring through."

"Good point. Anyone with any magical talent will be the first ones killed if there is a demonic invasion of this plane. They wouldn't want anyone to stand against them."

"I hate it when I'm right."

"So what's the plan?"

"You are assuming I have one. I suppose I head over to Kevin Gilbert's office and make sure the cops have an eye on him. Then I kill who- or whatever comes after him, and *voila*, the day is saved."

"Because it's always that easy." I'm obviously a bad influence, even on the divine. Now my guardian angel was a smartass, and we'd only been on speaking terms for a couple of days.

"Exactly," I said. "Now let's go protect a city drone from any demonic ramifications of his being on the take ten years ago. Because this time, the angels aren't necessarily the good guys, but they're the ones I have to save."

"Probably not the last time in your life you'll say that," Glory replied, and I'll admit that I was a little frightened to see there was no humor in her eyes.

Chapter Twelve

THE DOZENS OF PEOPLE RUNNING FROM THE CHARLOTTE-MECKLENBURG Government Center when I pulled up was a dead giveaway that everything was fucked. I pulled the Camry up onto the curb and hopped out, leaving the engine running and a startled angel in the passenger seat. If she was really going to keep me alive, she was going to have to work on her reaction time.

I burst into the lobby, fighting like a salmon swimming upstream against a tide of terrified people, and stopped cold at the thing causing all the commotion. It was a demon, and by the size of it, a powerful one. It was at least ten feet tall with bat-like wings that must have been twenty feet from tip to tip. Long, curving horns stuck out from its forehead, giant black swirls slicing through the air as it whipped its crimson head from side to side, looking for more tasty morsels.

Muscles rippled across its broad chest, and thick black hair covered its torso and limbs. Its preternaturally long arms ended in three clawed fingers and a thumb, and it had cloven hooves instead of toes. A prehensile tail lashed out, piercing the chest, leg, or neck of anyone unfortunate enough to be too close. Its eyes glowed a sulfuric yellow, and scraps of fabric dangled from its mouth full of a triple row of razor-sharp teeth.

The second I burst into the room, the demon froze. It sniffed the air, its tail coming to a point, then twirling around to point its metal-clad tip directly at me. The demon turned, looked at me, and *smiled*. I've never been so frightened in my near century on this planet as I was when that monster grinned at me. I knew in that moment that I was about to die, I was going out in the most painful way imaginable, and that monster planned to laugh the whole time it devoured my soul.

Then Glory broke through the throng behind me, and I learned what a guardian angel can really do when the shit hits the fan. The gorgeous blonde in dressy casual clothes was gone, and in her place was a nearly six-foot angel of fucking righteousness in chain and plate armor with a sword made entirely of light. And not some janky red or blue lightsaber, I mean a four-foot bastard sword with a blade so bright it seared itself into your vision if you looked too closely at it. Her blond curls were tied back into a tight ponytail, and a golden helmet covered most of her face. She ran across the marble floor and launched herself into the air with enough force to crack the tile she leapt from.

Her blade flashed down as she vaulted over the demon, leaving a broad line of black blood spewing from the monster's shoulder. It whirled on her, and I pulled my will together in a hurried attack. "*Separatus!*" I shouted, thrusting both arms forward, fingers out straight and palms pointed to the floor, making a knife-edge with my hands. A glowing disc of force flew from my fingertips, slicing through one of the demon's legs just above the ankle. It began to turn back to me, but that's the moment the upper leg fell off the now-severed lower leg, and the beast crashed forward in a face-first sprawl. It crushed the information desk to splinters and plastic shrapnel, then clambered to its knees and reached for me.

I jumped back, my augmented strength helping me cover a good ten feet, and the demon's claws whistled harmlessly several feet in front of me. I looked past the creature and saw Glory charge in, sword raised high over her head. I raised my hands to cast another spell, but caught Glory's eye as she shook her head. *Fair enough*, I thought. If she wanted to handle the demon, I'd be happy to let her. I wasn't really sure I had anything stronger to call up, anyway. She slashed down with the blinding blade, then back up in a continuous loop, and both of the demon's wings flapped to the ground like giant ebon kites. Gouts of blood spurted from the monster's shoulders, and it whirled on Glory once more, but she was already on the move.

She was a ballet of holy magic and death, always striking at just the point where the demon couldn't reach her. She wove in and out and under its flailing claws like she was boneless, made of water. The thing couldn't touch her, and as it became more and more frustrated, it also grew weaker and weaker, as every stroke of her blade opened another cut, carved out another chunk of flesh, severed another limb. Finally, after long minutes of ducking and weaving, the demon stretched just a little too far and lost its balance. The gargantuan beast flopped forward, catching itself on its bloody elbows, and Glory spun around, raised her sword high overhead, and brought it flashing down in a final blow.

The demon's body collapsed, the head fell to the floor a few feet away, and the severed pieces immediately started to smoke and dissolve into extradimensional goop. Within seconds, the monster was well on its way to being nothing more than a stinky black mess all over the cracked marble floor of the Government

Center. I turned around and took in the carnage that surrounded us. At least a dozen people lay dead and dismembered around the lobby, and that many more were cowering around columns or benches, clutching wounds or simply too terrified to run. The glass doors were shattered, some from people trying to get out, and one from me and Glory charging in like the Light Brigade. Literally, in her case.

I turned to Glory, shielding my eyes from the glow of her sword. Her brow knit briefly, then she seemed to realize what was blinding me, and the sword winked out of existence. So did her armor, leaving her standing in the middle of the wreckage in jeans, tennis shoes, and a Sunnydale High t-shirt.

"What the everloving fuck was that?" I asked after I took a long pull from the flask I often carry in my back pocket.

"That was a demon, Q. I thought you'd seen them before," Glory replied.

"Not that," I said. "What the hell happened to you?"

"Oh, that. Well, you don't expect a guardian angel to be defenseless, do you? The job isn't all about making sure you don't drown in Farmer Dante's pond while running away from the hayloft he caught you in with his daughter."

I'd forgotten about that. I wondered exactly how it was that I found all those stepping stones, and why there were stepping stones in a pond in the first place. "That was you?"

"No, but I've heard stories about you. There's an entire class on you in Angel Academy."

"There's an Angel Academy?"

"No, but if there were, there would be a class on Protecting Idiot Humans Who Really Try To Get Themselves Killed. And you could fill an entire syllabus."

"Why was there a huge-ass demon in the lobby of the Government Center?" I asked. "Do you think it was here after Gilbert?"

"I doubt it. I don't think that thing could fit in the stairwell, much less an elevator. I think it was probably here as a distraction."

"Well, it was a pretty good one," I said. "Oh shit." I looked at Glory, and the look on her face mirrored what I was feeling in my gut. If the distraction was so good, what were we going to find when we located Kevin Gilbert?

Chapter Thirteen

THE ANSWER WAS A DRAINED HUSK HANGING IN THE MEN'S ROOM ON the fifth floor. Kevin Gilbert was deader than your average doornail, and paler than Uncle Luke.

"Fuck, we're too late," I said. "Can you sense anything about the killer?"

"I'm not allowed to intervene except in matters of life and death," Glory said. "While this certainly concerns death, your life is not in immediate danger, so I can't actively help you."

"Great," I muttered. "What's the point of having an angel if you can't use them to break the rules of nature?" I didn't wait for a response, just opened my Sight and looked around the bathroom.

That's not the best idea, by the way. The Second Sight utilizes all sorts of odd spectra, and there's some creepy shit in public restrooms. This one was pretty clean, mystically speaking, just a couple of smears of bad soul on the mirrors where some amazingly narcissistic executive spent too much time fixing his hair and gloating about the bad things he was going to do to his employees. And yes, people do leave that kind of psychometric fingerprint on things, if they have strong enough feelings. The strongest feeling I found in that bathroom was the abject terror centered on Kevin Gilbert's rapidly cooling body. His Nephilim nature was evident in the wing-shaped nimbus of gold that still sparkled around him, but his last moments were obviously filled with fear and knowledge of what was coming.

"That's a little odd," I said.

"What's that, Q?" I was starting to get used to Glory calling me "Q," not that I was willing to let her know that yet.

"There's no glee, or mirth, or even arousal in the room," I said. "Usually someone who kills in such a specific way, with such obvious intent, has some real hatred behind it. But I'm not picking up any emotion at all from our killer. It's almost like it was just a job for him, or he was just following orders."

"Are you sure the killer is a man?"

"As long as it's a human, it's a man. The number of women who can subdue a grown man then lift his body to be drained like a deer ready to be dressed is pretty small. Especially when you factor in that it had to be done between the time the demon first appeared and the moment we got here. Yeah, it's either a guy or some supernatural creature, so it's just easier to refer to it as male."

"That makes sense. I just wanted to make sure you weren't missing something."

"I probably am, Glory. I'm just pretty sure it isn't the gender of our killer."

"So whoever it is has Gilbert's blood—what's next?"

"Well, the Solstice is tomorrow, so maybe it has something to do with that," I said.

"Oh shit," Glory said, then clapped both hands over her mouth.

I laughed out loud. I couldn't help it. She'd known me less than two days and I already had my guardian angel swearing. A couple more weeks on the job and she'd be rolling blunts and listening to Dr. Dre.

"That's not funny," Glory said. "The solstice is a period of weakening the barriers between the realms. It's much easier to bring across much stronger beings than would normally be able to pass between dimensions."

"How big?" I asked, thinking back to Orobas and the ten-foot monstrosity that she just sliced and diced.

"Big enough to make that thing in the lobby look like an ant."

"Fuck," I said. "I guess we should probably figure out who's running this party, get ourselves invited, shit in the punchbowl, and send everybody home early before things really get rolling, huh?"

"Sometimes I don't understand human metaphor. You don't actually want to defecate in a punchbowl, do you?" the very perplexed angel asked.

"No, Glory, I just want to wipe my ass with this guy's very carefully drawn-out plans."

"Is that another metaphor? Or do you have a strange fixation with rather unpleasant bodily functions?"

"Is both an option?" I asked, opening the door and stepping out of the restroom, almost running into a rotund government functionary with a bad toupee. "You *really* don't want to go in there, bub. I just blew chunks across all three sinks after what I saw in the lobby. I'd go down a floor if I was you."

He turned away and bolted for the elevator, and I grinned at Glory. "Come on, angel. Let's go stop an apocalypse."

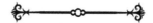

"How do you know where we're going?" Glory asked from my passenger seat. I got back to the Camry just in time to sweet-talk the tow truck driver into not hooking her up and hauling her away, so I still had wheels.

"I don't, but I know someone who will. Dennis is one of the most tech-savvy people I know, and he's got more than a little experience with things that go bump in the night. If anybody can whip up a high-tech solution for finding a low-tech beastie, it's him."

We pulled into Dennis' driveway about fifteen minutes later, a modest split-level on the east side of town. I parked behind his van and hopped out.

"Shit," I said as soon as I took a good look at the house. The front door was hanging open, and the storm door was lying in the bushes beside the front stoop.

"What's wrong?" Glory asked. It was still a little creepy that she never had to use the car doors.

"Somebody's been here, and it looks like they either killed or took Dennis."

"How do you know?"

I pointed to the front stoop and the three brick steps leading up to it. "Dennis never uses the front door. He's got motorized lifts to get from floor to floor, and a wheelchair on each floor, but he can't navigate those steps. The back door has a small ramp. Dennis uses that entrance. He says it's safer if burglars don't know the owner of the house can't run after them."

"Smart," the angel remarked.

"He's a smart dude," I replied. I hopped up the steps and looked at the door. It didn't look that out of the ordinary. It wasn't destroyed, or burned through or anything, just kicked in, like I'd done to Janet Hamilton's door that afternoon. That was only about hours before, but it felt like a lifetime.

I pushed the door open wider and drew my Glock. I slipped through the opening and swept the room with the barrel of my pistol. The front parlor was empty, as were the small dining room and kitchen. I motioned behind me to Glory, pointing her upstairs, and I went down the steps to the basement. Dennis went long days without ever leaving the bottom floor of his house, and he didn't really need to. It had a full bath, his office with all his computers, a den with a TV and every gaming system imaginable, and a small mini fridge full of sandwich meat, mayo, and sodas. A freelance web designer didn't need a whole lot more.

The stairs spilled out into a small foyer, and I passed through that quickly on the way to the den. I swept the room, then moved on to the bathroom and the office. Nothing. If Dennis was in the house, he was upstairs.

"He's not upstairs," Glory said beside me, shattering that inkling of hope.

"Whatever we're after must have taken him to slow me down."

"How? Do you think the killer came here after killing Gilbert?" Glory asked.

"No, there wasn't time. He must have subdued Dennis, then gone to the Government Center and cut the demon loose in the lobby while he murdered Gilbert."

"So Dennis was what, in the trunk of his car?"

"Or the back of his van. Dennis is brilliant, but he's not exactly a fighter. And he only lost his legs a few years ago, so he's not all that nimble moving around without his chair. All the killer would need to do is gag him and bind his hands, and Dennis would be largely helpless."

"Do we know that he's still alive?"

"No," I replied. "But I have to assume he is." Because if he wasn't, it would mean I'd failed him. Twice.

"Now what?" Glory asked.

"I don't know. Maybe there's a clue in whatever he was last working on. I know he was looking at possible locations for the ceremony." I sat down at Dennis' computer and clicked the mouse. The machine sprang to life, asking for a password.

"You know his password?" Glory asked.

"We were close," I replied. "That, and it's written on a sticky note stuck to his monitor. Dennis left it there for me in case I ever needed to get into his computer, and he always said that no one would expect a hacker to keep a password out in the open like that."

"How very meta of him."

"That's what I thought," I agreed. I clicked on the icon for a maps program still open on the desktop. A map of Charlotte popped up, with certain areas highlighted in green, yellow, and red.

"Good man, Boltron," I said with a relieved sigh.

"What is it?"

"He color-coordinated the map. The red circles are mystical hot spots, but not relevant to our case, like Luke's house and Mort's. The yellow circles are maybes, but unlikely to be the place that our main event is going down. The green circles are big magical focal points in town, exactly the kind of place that you would want to open a highway to Hell."

"Really? A hard rock reference? Now?" Glory didn't look amused at my AC/DC pun.

I just shrugged. "Seemed appropriate. Anyway, there are four focal points large enough and secure enough or remote enough for our guy to open a big hole in the universe. The big racetrack up in Concord, but I'd gonna guess no on that one. My gut says he wants to cause as much havoc right out of the gate as possible, and the speedway is pretty deserted after dark. Then there's the bandshell out behind SouthPark Mall, and I think that one's probably out as well. Same reasons—the potential for mayhem in the middle of the night is much less than the other two options."

"Why does the ritual have to be performed in the middle of the night?"

"Well, the Solstice starts at midnight tonight, and I don't think our boy wants to keep Dennis around any longer than he has to."

"That means…"

"Yeah, that means we have about six hours to find this guy, rescue Dennis, and stop this assclown from setting loose Hell on Earth. Literally."

"What are the other two options?"

"They're both pretty reasonable choices, if you think about it. The first is the Charlotte-Douglas International Airport. Tens of thousands of people go through there every day, and they all leave a little bit of their energy behind. Couple that with the anger people feel when traveling, and most folks think a busy airport is already a kind of hell. But I think it's the last one. Spirit Square Center for Arts & Education, downtown. It's the old First Baptist Church building, so the irony would appeal to a showboating demon like this one, and since it's right in the middle of downtown, as many people pass through or by it in a day as the airport. Plus, it's a lot closer to all our dump sites and the Government Center. Our killer is comfortable in the Uptown area; I'd be very surprised if it wasn't someone who knows Charlotte like the back of his hand. A realtor maybe, or postal worker—someone whose job requires them to drive all over town…mother*fucker.*" I put my elbows on Dennis' desk and dropped my head into my hands.

"He played me like a goddamned fiddle, didn't he?"

"Am I supposed to—"

"Oh cut the shit, Glory!" I snapped at the angel. "How long have you known?"

"Known what?" She was obfuscating again, but now I knew she couldn't tell me a direct lie.

I stood up and turned to face her. "How long have you known that Sponholz is the Cambion?"

"I've always known," she said, not meeting my eyes.

"And you weren't going to tell me, were you?"

"No, I wasn't. You have to understand, Quincy." No "Q" this time, I was Quincy again. That was fine. I wasn't in the mood for nicknames. "I couldn't tell you. And it's not like I didn't want to, I *couldn't*."

"The fuck you couldn't. Don't give me that shit, Glory. You could have—"

She slapped me. It was just a simple open-handed slap, but she swung my head sideways and made my ears ring.

"No, *you* don't give *me* that shit, John Abraham Quincy Holmwood Harker. I am an Angel of the Lord, and unlike all you humans walking around on Earth fighting, farting, and generally fucking everything up, I don't *have* free will. So when I tell you that I couldn't say anything about the killer's identity, it's because I *couldn't* say anything. I wanted to tell you, but when I am given an order from one of my superiors, I can't violate that directive, no matter how much I would like to."

"Oh." I didn't have anything better to say. Besides, I was a little concerned that if I said much more than that, she'd slap me again.

"So now that you've figured it out, what are you going to do about it? My ability to interfere may be limited, unless your life is in direct danger."

I gave her my best grin, which was hampered a little by the fact that I couldn't feel half my face. "Oh don't worry, darlin'. I'm going to go to an old church and try to stop a well-armed police detective who happens to be half demon from opening a portal to Hell with the blood sacrifice of one of my four friends in the world. I'm pretty sure 'life in danger' will barely scratch the surface of the shitstorm I'm about to stir up."

Chapter Fourteen

To add insult to the injuries I was almost certainly about to face, it cost me ten bucks to park downtown because of a basketball game. There were cops all over the place, so I knew if I just left the car somewhere, I'd probably never get it back before it was turned into scrap. I ran down the steps at the Seventh Street Station parking garage and hauled ass up the block to the rear entrance of Spirit Square. The thick glass doors were locked, but a side door looked to be hanging a little funny in the frame. Upon closer inspection, the lock had several suspiciously bullet-like holes in it, and the door opened freely.

I slipped into the lobby, keeping close to the walls to stay as much out of view as possible of the completely glass front of the building. Glory kept close behind me as I slid along the wall and up the short steps into the main lobby. I stepped away from the wall, less concerned about someone noticing my feet than when my full body was in view. I got through the main lobby and passed the Duke Energy Theater on my left, then opened my Sight as I started up the ramp to the main theater, once the sanctuary of the First Baptist Church, now a music and theater venue named after native musician Loonis McGlohon.

The doors to the theater stood open, and I heard screams coming from inside. Most days I would have charged right in like a kamikaze pilot, with about the same results, but since I had my third eye wide open, I saw the cat's cradle of magical threads woven across the open doors, tripwires all leading to something spectacularly unpleasant, I was sure.

Instead of running through the door and triggering whatever terrible thing Sponholz had planned for me, I turned around and walked back down the ramp.

"Where are you going?" Glory asked.

"I have a buddy who does theater around town. He was doing a couple shows in here last year, and I came over to have lunch with him. He took me all through the place, showed me how a few things work, including how the actors get to the stage from the dressing rooms downstairs."

"You don't think the Cambion has covered those entrances?"

"I think he's probably covered those, yeah. Especially since they're just open stairwells. But what I hope he hasn't covered is the door the tech staff uses to move the big cherry-picker from room to room to work on lights."

"I have no idea what you're talking about, and I'm divine in nature, Q."

"Just goes to show that there's only one omniscient being, Glory." I gave her a grin and hopped up the steps to the Duke Energy Theater. I reached the heavy glass doors, locked, of course, and drew in my will. I focused my power to needle-thin stream of force and whispered *"sesame."*

"Really? Sesame?" Glory said with a raised eyebrow.

"I just need something to focus the magic for simple stuff. If I was raising a demon, or banishing one, I'd have to actually use a spell. But just brute force bashing a lock open, I can do with 'sesame'." I pushed the door open, and we slipped into theater's tiny airlock lobby/vestibule. I repeated the process with the door to the theater, and we slipped into the small venue.

"Where is this secret door, Q?"

I led her down the right-hand wall of the theater to the tiny "backstage" area, then pressed my ear to a door painted to match the rest of the wall. I heard movement on the other side, but it was muffled by soundproofing or distance. Either way, it sounded far enough away that Sponholz wasn't going to be standing right there when I opened it, so I pushed the crash bar and flung the door open.

I managed to avoid making any noise as I slipped onto the stage and found myself behind Sponholz and what he obviously planned as his entry point for whatever he planned on bringing through to this world. Dennis lay on a makeshift altar in the middle of a summoning circle that stretched the entire width of the stage. Sponholz had an elaborate set of symbols inscribed on the floor, some Latin, some Enochian, some in languages I didn't even recognize. A huge pentagram was perfectly drawn in the center of the circle, with a smaller circle in the center surrounding Dennis and the altar. The lines of the pentagram weren't drawn with chalk, like a normal circle, or even salt, which I use when I'm working with particularly nasty critters.

Nope, the lines of the pentagram were drawn in liquid, a thick, viscous fluid that looked black in the dim light. I recognized the smell instantly—blood. Seems like I found Sponholz's use for Nephilim blood. Candles burned at each point of the star, five black pillars illuminating Sponholz standing in the center of the circle, chanting and waving a dagger over Dennis' chest.

"You go to the other side of the stage and come at him while I distract him," I whispered to Glory.

"No can do, Q," the angel whispered back. "I can't interfere in this kind of thing, even to save your life. Orders from upstairs, sorry."

What good is a guardian angel if they can't help you cheat and can't save you from the absolute worst of your decisions? I shrugged and returned to my regularly scheduled lack of faith in anything religious. With no help coming from Glory, I had to resort to the old-fashioned methods of dealing with bad guys. I drew in my will, focused on the candles, and whispered, "*cumulonimbus*." Then I blew out a breath magically amplified into a strong breeze, which immediately blew out three of the candles.

Sponholz looked up and smiled. "Why, Harker, so good of you to come. I was hoping you'd show up. So was your friend here." He brought the dagger down and drew a thin line of blood across Dennis' chest. Dennis stirred, but his eyes stayed closed.

"What's wrong with him? If you've hurt him, Sponholz, I swear to God I'll play jump-rope with your intestines."

"He's fine," the Cambion cop said. "I need him alive until the stroke of midnight, so normally I'd say you have about an hour and a half to say goodbye. But since I don't expect you to live past the next five minutes, that would be overstating the situation."

"What the hell are you doing, Sponholz? Summoning a bigger demon than Orobas and that monster you cut loose at the Government Center? Why would you even do that?"

"You think too small, Harker. I'm not planning to summon anything. My master's plans go much further than that. Too bad you won't be here to see them come to fruition."

"Yeah, because I believe you've got what it takes to kill me," I shot back.

"Oh, I don't. But he does." With that, Sponholz nodded to something behind me. I didn't bother to look around because I knew that trick. It was the oldest one in the book. I turn around, and Sponholz shoots me in the back. Or I don't turn around, and whatever is back there gets a free shot at my exposed backside.

I chose a mix of A and B, where I kept my eyes on Sponholz until the last moment, using my enhanced senses to listen for the creak of a footfall on the stage, then dove forward into a front roll. I came up in a crouch with my Glock in my hand, spun around, and put four rounds in the chest of the demon standing where I had been moments before. Four rounds out of about nine that I squeezed off, but I never claimed to be a brilliant shot. Bullets ripped through the stage curtains and buried themselves into walls and floor, but the demon didn't budge. Instead, it stood there, its image flickering between demonic and that of a really pretty blonde woman.

"Glory?" I asked, confusion making forget momentarily about the Cambion behind me trying to sacrifice one of my very few friends.

"Q? You shot me," she said. "You *shot* me! Why would you do that?"

"Because I thought you were a demon!"

"Oh, that's what that tickle was," she replied. Glory closed her eyes, and the golden glow of her aura flashed into view, burning the demonic image away in an instant.

"Again with the distraction?" I said, turning back to Sponholz, who had re-lit the candles around the circle somehow. Probably magic. "What are you now, Detective? David Copperfield?" My smartass remarks froze on my tongue as I turned fully around. Apparently tired of waiting, the half-demon cop was standing in the center circle holding Dennis Bolton's bloody heart in his hand. Sponholz resumed his incantation, and as he spoke the words, the blood of the Nephilim began to glow and smoke along the lines of the pentagram. The heart in his hand started to do the same, and Sponholz reached up with his knife and cut a long slash lengthwise along his arm. Blood flowed down his forearm to his elbow, dripping onto the floor and starting to smoke and glow like the rest of it. Sponholz began to chant in a loud voice, and a portal began to appear over the circle.

"By the mixing of the blood, Angel, Devil, and Human, I pierce the veil.
By the blood of the angels, I pierce the veil.
By the blood of this human, I pierce the veil.
By the blood of this demon, I pierce the veil.
Find the veil rent asunder, my Lord, and open the path to Glory.
Find the veil rent asunder, my Lord, and open the path to Salvation.
Find the veil rent asunder, my Lord, and—"

"Oh, for fuck's sake," I muttered under my breath. I raised my Glock and squeezed off the last six rounds. Three of them struck Sponholz in the chest, knocking him flat on his back and scrubbing out part of his inner circle with his ass. He lay there for a few seconds, then rolled over and clambered to his feet. The portal stopped growing, but it didn't close, just hung there in midair, some ten feet above the stage.

"That hurt, you asshole," he growled at me. "And I dropped my heart. I need that heart for the ritual."

"I wasn't trying to damage my friend's heart," I replied. "I was trying my best to shoot out yours."

"Well, it's a good thing the department issues us all these handy bulletproof vests, isn't it?" he said with a smile. "Now my ritual is fucked, and I've only got a couple of hours to get everything set up, and I have to kill you before I can get things started again." He shook his right arm like his shoulder hurt, then drew his service weapon from a shoulder holster and leveled it at me.

The pissed-off Cambion got off four or five shots before he realized that I had thrown up a magical shield. He holstered his gun, lowered his good shoulder, and charged me like a balding rhinoceros. My mystical shield was tuned to protect against projectiles, not people, and he was moving faster than any normal person should, so I failed my dexterity check and caught two hundred eighty pounds of half-demon right in my gut. He bulled me backwards until we crashed into the baby grand piano parked upstage, and my ribs made ugly noises on impact.

Sponholz let me go and I dropped to my knees, all my wind gone. He threw a vicious side kick to my head, and I flopped facedown like a carp on the stage. I got myself up to hands and knees, but a stomp between my shoulder blades put me back flat on my stomach. I tried to pull my will together to cast a spell, but he kept distracting me with high-level tactics like kicking the shit out of me. I finally managed to trap one foot with my right arm and twist him around until he dropped to the stage on his ass.

I rolled away from him before dragging myself to my feet, then looked back at him. "Why, Sponholz? What's in this for you?"

"I'm a creature of chaos, Harker. It's what I do."

"But you've always been a decent cop," I said. "Maybe not great, but decent. Why betray that now?"

"Have you seen what's happening all around us, Harker? These are already the end days. I'm just helping it along. The world's going to shit fast. What does it matter if a couple million more damned souls move in and help us along?"

It clicked at the mention of "damned souls." Sponholz's wife had committed suicide back in the fall, and by his faith, she went straight to Hell the instant she died. Opening a gateway to the underworld was the only way he was ever going to see his wife again. I could understand the motive, even if I couldn't condone it.

"You know Lucifer won't let her come back, right?" I asked. Sponholz's face crumpled, but he pulled it back together quickly.

"We have a deal. I give him the portal; he gives me Rachel."

"Is it in writing? Did he promise that she'd be in her right mind? With her memories? Intact?"

"Why would he betray me?"

"Oh my fucking God, Rich, how goddamn stupid are you?!?" I yelled. "He's the fucking Father of Lies, the dude singlehandedly responsible for original sin! Why *wouldn't* he betray you? It's what he does, you idiot!" I threw my hands up, and Sponholz drew his sidearm again.

"That's a good place for those hands, Harker. You keep them there, and maybe after I'm done, I'll shoot you in the head instead of throwing you to the demons that come through."

Demons? He was planning on bringing through more than one? I really had to deal with him quickly. Then I had to figure out how to close that damn portal.

"Turn around and get down on your knees," the detective said, moving toward me with his gun leveled at my chest.

"Why, Rich, I'm not that easy," I said without moving.

His eyes narrowed, and he reached for my shoulder to spin me around. Most people wouldn't move when someone points a gun at them. For most people, that's a really good idea. But, as we've discussed, I'm a little *augmented,* shall we say? The second Sponholz reached for me, I grabbed his wrist and pulled forward, stepping to one side and bringing my knee up at the same time. He shot, but I wasn't in front of his gun anymore, so the bullet buried itself in the stage floor while my knee buried itself in his gut.

His breath *whooshed* out, and I threw a left hook that caught him right behind the ear and drove him to his knees. A right to the temple, then another left, and he sprawled on his stomach on the floor. I moved over and stomped down on his right wrist with my heel, listening to a satisfying *crunch* as a lot of those little bones in his hand and wrist turned to powder. I kicked the gun across the stage, then hauled him up by his collar.

"How do I close the portal?" I hissed in his ear.

"Go fuck yourself," he said between gasps of pain.

"Nah, I think I'd rather get you fucked instead, demon-boy. Why don't I just send you home to Daddy? You think you'd like that? I hear they have all sorts of things they can do with the living down there." I stepped around in front of Sponholz, tagged him with another left to the temple, then landed an uppercut on the point of his jaw that snapped his mouth shut and made his eyes roll so far back in his head that I expected to see his optic nerve. He dropped to his knees, unconscious.

I picked up the comatose Cambion/cop and hauled him to the altar. I laid him across Dennis' lap, then reached down to pat my friend's cheek. "Sorry, buddy. You deserved a lot better than what you got, but I hope you know that this one, at least, saved a lot of people from some very bad things." I set his bloody heart on the altar next to him, then wiped my hands on his shirt.

I pulled a piece of chalk out of my pocket and repaired the circle where Sponholz had scrubbed it out with his butt when I shot him. Then I fixed the few Enochian symbols that were scuffed or askew and drew a new inner circle. I picked up the dagger Sponholz dropped, and pricked my finger with it. I shook a drop of my blood onto the circle and poured just enough of my will into it to invoke the circle. I felt the magical barrier snap into place around me, shielding me from anything that went wrong with what I was about to do.

"Q, what are you doing?" Glory asked from the stage.

"You still aren't allowed to help me, right?"

"That's unfortunately true."

"Then I think this is my best bet for closing the portal and getting rid of the bodies." With that, I began an incantation. This spell was very precise, between contacting a specific plane of existence and needing to send only specific things through, so I wanted to focus my energy very tightly to make sure nothing happened that I wasn't expecting.

"*Regna terrae, cantata Deo, psallite Cernunnos,*
Regna terrae, cantata Dea psallite Aradia.
caeli Deus, Deus terrae,
Humiliter majestati gloriae tuae supplicamus
Ut ab omni infernalium spirituum potestate,
Laqueo, and deceptione nequitia,
Omnis fallaciae, libera nos, dominates.

Exorcizamus you omnis immundus spiritus
Omnis satanica potestas, omnis incursio,
Infernalis adversarii, omnis legio,
Omnis and congregatio secta diabolica.
Ab insidiis diaboli, libera nos, dominates,
Ut coven tuam secura tibi libertate servire facias,
Te rogamus, audi nos!
Ut inimicos sanctae circulae humiliare digneris,
Te rogamus, audi nos!
Terribilis Deus Sanctuario suo,
Cernunnos ipse truderit virtutem plebi Suae,
Aradia ipse fortitudinem plebi Suae.
Benedictus Deus, Gloria Patri,
Benedictus Dea, Matri gloria!"

I poured my will into the spell, and the portal above my head opened wide for the briefest of moments. I tried to resist the temptation to look, but couldn't quite. It was a Hieronymus Bosch landscape of horrors in there—lakes of fire, imps with whips, demons rending the flesh from men and women with their bare hands—and above it all I could feel a *presence*, a malevolent overlord taking delight in the suffering of others.

I shuddered, then took a step back, careful not to disturb the circle, as the altar with Sponholz and Dennis rose into the air, then was sucked into the portal to Hell. I released my will, and the portal winked out of existence, but not before I sensed that malevolent entity's attention focus on me for the briefest of seconds, and I felt terror like I had never felt before.

I scrubbed the circle out with my toe, and the magical barrier came crashing down. I stepped intentionally on the outer circle, smearing it into nonexistence and obscuring enough of the symbols to make it unusable to anyone who didn't read Enochian. At the time I knew of two people in Charlotte who could read Enochian, and I was pretty sure Uncle Luke wasn't planning on opening any Hell-portals anytime soon.

"What was that for?" Glory asked.

"I had to get rid of the bodies, and I figured if I threw something through the Gate, I could close it. Now no one has to figure out how to hide the bodies."

"I'm sorry about your friend's death," she said.

"Thanks," I replied. "He was a good guy." I was hopeful that Renfield could help me through some of the harder points of making someone vanish in the legal sense, not just the physical sense. I looked around the theater, the bullet holes in the walls, the giant summoning circle of blood in the floor, and knew that someone was going to come looking to me for information. But not tonight. For tonight, the world was as safe as it ever was, and I had another lost friend to mourn.

Epilogue

"**N**OT THAT I'M NOT FLATTERED THAT YOU WANTED TO SHARE SOMETHING personal, Harker, but what about that story is so important that you had to drag me out of bed at three in the morning and talk 'til sunrise?" Detective Rebecca Gail Flynn asked from my sofa. I looked at the window. She was right, there was sunlight peeking in through the blinds. I'd talked nonstop for about four hours.

"I know you and Glory have been through some shit, but it's none of my business, seriously. It's not like I thought you were banging your guardian angel, and who am I to say anything if you are?"

That was a disturbing thought, but what was more disturbing was the level of emotion I felt coming through the mental link I had with Flynn. I saved her life a few months ago by letting her drink a few drops of my magical blood, and that created a bond closer than that of mother and child. I felt a flurry of things—relief, worry, confusion, jealousy, and a little…*lust*? Definitely on the list things I needed to explore later. When I had more to drink. And maybe opiates. But not now.

"A body was found last night, dumper at a strip mall in University."

"Yeah, I heard about that on the police radio."

"I went to take a look. It was a Nephilim."

"I'm sure that's just a coincidence," Flynn said, but her crinkled brow said something different.

"Yeah?" I asked, my eyebrow reaching for my hairline. "Because the story I just told you happened seven years ago. And seven is a number of power. If there was anything about that ritual that was tied to a specific time, this year is the first time that it could be attempted again."

"But you sent Sponholz to Hell. There's nobody to carry out the ritual."

"Any Cambion could do it," I said. "And I never figured out what Sponholz wanted or who put him up to it. He had a little power, but he had nowhere near the brainpower to think up something like that."

"But it could still be a coincidence, Harker. Just because a half-angel gets murdered doesn't mean…"

"Look at the calendar, Flynn." I cut her off. "The Solstice is in three days. And there was one more thing about the body that makes me sure that this is someone trying to open the portal again."

"Oh, fuck." She looked at me, eyes wide.

"Oh, fuck, indeed," I agreed. "The body's throat was cut from ear to ear, and all its blood drained. Somebody is trying to open that portal, Bex. And if we don't stop it, we're looking at Hell on Earth."

NOWHERE NEAR THE END

Heaven's Door

Chapter One

"You're trying to tell me that last night's murder is the beginning of a plot to open the gates of Hell? Real, literal, lakes of fire and little bastards with pitchforks *Hell*?" Detective Rebecca Gail Flynn sat on my couch gaping at me. I'd just spent half the night telling her the story of me and my guardian angel Glory stopping a Cambion, a half-human/half-demon/all-psychotic, from doing that exact thing seven years ago.

"Yeah, that's about it. Normally, I'd follow that up with an 'I know how crazy this sounds,' or some shit like that, but I do know how crazy this sounds, and you helped me fight the Four Horsemen of the goddamn *Apocalypse* without batting an eye, so why should a little demon mischief flip your switch?" I was tired and a little grumpy that Becks didn't seem to believe me.

"I get it, Harker, I really do. I can *feel* how much you believe this shit. And I've never seen you actually scared, so that means something, too. But…*Hell?* It's a lot, you know?" She leaned back on the couch and blew out a long breath. Without taking her eyes off my apparently very interesting ceiling, she said, "Okay, who's the new dead guy?"

"His name's Pat Dugan. He's a software engineer for Red Hat."

"What did he do?"

"I just told you, he was some kind of computer nerd."

"That's not what I meant." Now she looked at me. "I mean, how did he die? Was it like the others?"

"Kinda," I said. "His throat was cut, and his blood was partially drained, but not completely. And he was beaten before he was killed. And I mean beaten like he went five rounds with Mike Tyson, not just thumped on the head a few times."

"Tortured?" Flynn asked.

"I don't think so. There was none of the normal kinda stuff I associate with torture. His fingers weren't broken, one tooth missing, but that corresponded to a split lip, I couldn't see any electrical burns, or smell any charred flesh, no—"

"I get it," Flynn interrupted me. "There are a lot of ways to torture someone, and none of them were used on Dugan."

"Apparently not. The only reason I know he's involved in this case is because I saw the wings."

"The wings?" Becks asked.

"Yeah. When I looked at the body with my Sight, there were golden wings. He was a Nephilim, no question."

"Why were you there?"

"What?"

"Why were you at a random murder scene in the middle of the night, Harker?" Becks asked. "This is the kind of thing that I would have arrested you for two years ago. The only reason I don't suspect you now is that I know you didn't do this thing. Or if you did, you're having a psychotic break and don't know you did it. I'm not sure which of those is worse for the surrounding area."

"I'm pretty sure having a mystically enhanced wizard go batshit crazy in the middle of a city is about as 'worse' as it gets, Detective." But she was right. I didn't have anything to do with Patrick Dugan's murder, and if I did, Becks would know about it. Ever since I gave her some of my blood to save her life, we can't keep secrets from each other. It's hard enough just keeping my thoughts private, much less any impressions that come with deception. That just wasn't gonna happen with anyone as deep inside my head as Flynn was now. Truth be told, most days I didn't mind having an unbreakable mental bond with her. Kept some of the shadows at bay when the nights got real dark.

"You're avoiding the question, Harker. Why. Were. You. There?"

"I told him to go." Glory walked out of my kitchen and sat down on the couch next to Flynn. She handed her a glass of orange juice. "Good to see you, Rebecca."

"Hello, Glory," Rebecca said, accepting the glass. "We were just talking about you."

"I heard," my guardian angel replied. "He didn't even leave out any of the really bad parts. That was good, Q. A solid recounting, if uninspired."

"Oh, I was plenty inspired, Glory. Inspired by being scared out of my shorts of this shit starting up again."

"You should be. You didn't beat Orobas last time, you just beat his minion, and even that barely."

"And not without cost," I said. My friend Dennis died because I brought him into my fight. That was just one of the reasons I didn't sleep well at night.

"No battle is won without cost, Q," Glory said, then looked a little abashed at her tone. "I'm sorry. This is just scary for me, too. I don't know if we can beat Orobas. And I don't know how much I can intervene without risking..."

"Risking what, Glory?" I asked, standing up and starting to pace my living room. "What happens if you break the rules? Just this once? I mean, what's the worst thing they can do to you? You're an angel, for fuck's sake, it's not like they can—"

"They can," Glory said, her voice small. "They can, and they have before. To one of the greatest of us, one of the Father's favorites. His golden, glowing son. Remember the Lightbringer? The Morningstar?"

"Oh," I said. "Him."

"Yes, Quincy, *him*. So if you want to know what is the worst thing that the Heavenly Host can do to one of their own who rebels and causes problems, look no further than the case of God's favorite angel, Lucifer. And since I'd rather not end up condemned to never see the face of my Father again, I'm going to tread lightly. If you don't mind, of course." All the angels in Heaven and I get the sarcastic one. I guess that fits.

"So where do we go from here? We have a dead half-angel, we think we have a demon returned to rezone Charlotte as a suburb of Hell, and neither of us have slept all night," Flynn asked, downing her OJ and standing up.

"Keep talking, I can hear you!" she called out over her shoulder as she went to the kitchen and rinsed her glass. "I'm putting on some coffee. Glory, you want some?"

"No, thank you, Rebecca. Caffeine and divine power do not mix."

I looked at her, then shook my head. "Yeah, all we need is you to get jittery and inadvertently save somebody." I sat back down in my chair, leaning forward toward Glory. "So what's next? Where *do* we go from here?"

"Well, you have a detective, so I'd suggest you work on solving the murder of Mr. Dugan. And since this isn't your first run-in with Orobas, perhaps there are people who would know about it if the demon were back in town."

"That all sounds good, but first things first. I need breakfast and a shower," Flynn said, walking back into the room with a plate full of doughnuts and two mugs of coffee. She put the doughnuts on the coffee table, handed me the mug that read "World's Greatest Granny!" and kept a souvenir mug from Epcot Center for herself.

"Where the hell did you get these coffee cups, Harker?" Flynn asked, sitting on the couch beside Glory and grabbing a doughnut.

I took a sip of my coffee and reached for my own doughnut. "Where does every bachelor shop for kitchen supplies? I went to Goodwill."

"So what do we know?" Flynn asked after we each knocked back a couple of Krispy Kremes.

"We know that Patrick Dugan is dead, exsanguinated, and a half-angel. We know that likely means Orobas is back in town—"

"But we don't *know* that Orobas is back. One dead Nephilim isn't enough to prove that," Flynn countered.

"Are you willing to let another one die just to confirm my suspicions?" I asked.

"I'd rather not, but I am a homicide detective, Harker. I deal with dead people all the time. And sometimes, there has to be more than one person dead before I can be any good at my job. They don't do task forces for simple murders; for us to get the resources we need, someone else is going to have to die. But in the meantime, I'll go hit up Paul in the crime lab to see what he found at the scene. As soon as I take a shower and put on some fresh clothes. I might have to go to work on no sleep, but at least I can look like I'm well-rested." Flynn stood up and walked to the door of her bedroom. She stopped and turned to look back at me.

"Harker?"

"Yeah, Becks?"

"Is this really as bad as you're making it out to be?"

"If I'm right, it's nowhere near as bad."

"That's good, right?"

"No. Because if I'm right, it's way worse than we can even imagine."

Chapter Two

"YOU KNOW WE DON'T DO A BREAKFAST MENU, RIGHT, HARKER?" Christy asked when I walked into Mort's. Mort's was a bar owned by a demon, and Christy was his bartender, bouncer, enforcer, information merchant, and the maker of the best Bloody Mary's in Charlotte.

"You lie like a rug, you beautiful succubus," I said, leaning over the bar to kiss one cheek.

"Not even close. And not terribly original, either. Why can't you believe that I'm just a normal, run-of-the-mill human, Harker?"

"Because I'm a normal, run-of-the-mill human, and you're not even close."

"Yeah, if normal humans have vampire DNA and throw spells around like a Dr. Strange comic."

"I have never once called upon the Eye of Agamatto." I grinned as I slid onto a barstool. Christy and I had a running game going—I tried to figure out what kind of supernatural creature she was, and she didn't tell me. I don't know if she would tell me even if I got it right, but it was a cute little diversion, so I kept it going.

"Where's Mort?" I asked. "Back room?"

"Yeah, but you can't go back there right now. Seriously, Harker, don't even stand up off that stool until I tell you it's okay. I don't want to have to shoot you."

"That's good because I don't want to be shot. Let him know I'm here, and I'll just sit here and have breakfast until he's ready to see me."

Christy nodded and reached for the vodka. I don't usually drink until after lunch, but since eight a.m. Charlotte time is three p.m. Moscow time, it was after lunch in Russia. Perfect time for vodka, by my logic. As Christy tossed ingredients into a glass for my Bloody Mary, I took a look around the bar at the other inhabitants.

There was a vampire in a booth in the back, passed out face down on the table. He'd be there until after sunset, but when he woke up, he'd probably be hungry. And have a hellacious crick in his neck. A couple of lycanthropes in human form shared a table by the door, but I could smell the fox on them from where I sat, and their narrow faces and long noses were dead giveaways, along with the flaming red hair.

I couldn't see the three tables down the hallway near the bathrooms and the back door but decided it wasn't worth snooping over. A huge human sat in one corner booth with a beautiful woman who looked way out of his league. I opened my Sight just a little bit, and sure enough, she really *was* a succubus. I almost got up and went after her until I remembered two things—first, the sign over the bar declaring it Sanctuary and the vehemence with which Christy enforced the rules about not hassling the other supernatural beings, and second, the fact that she almost certainly wasn't going to kill the dude, and he might be enjoying it. Shit, for all I knew, he asked her to feed off his life force in exchange for getting off. I'd seen weirder shit on the internet, so why not? As long as his kink didn't hurt anybody but himself, he could do what he wanted.

And I really didn't want to make Christy pull out the sawed-off double-barrel she had tucked away under the bar. She nodded at me as she sat my Bloody Mary on the bar, then said, "I'll go tell Mort you're here. No promises on whether or not he'll see you, but I'll tell him."

Mort and I had a love/hate relationship. I loved the information I got out of him but hated having to consort with a demon to get it. But my job very often isn't pretty, and the pesky thing about hunting demons is that they don't often show up at Mass.

Sometimes, but not often.

Christy came back about a minute later and motioned for me to follow her. I went through a small door at the end of the bar into the back room. The last time I was there, Mort had a demon magician doing tricks for his amusement. I took exception to the tricks and killed the stage show. Mort wasn't pleased. This time I stepped through the door into a bouncy castle.

A bouncy castle. One of those big inflatable rooms that kids get for their birthday parties. Except huge, tall enough for me to stand up in. Christy stood in the doorway, hand extended palm up.

"Give me your shoes," she said.

"What?"

"Your shoes." She pointed at my feet for emphasis. "Boss doesn't want any street shoes fucking up his balloon house, so give me your shoes."

"You first." I looked at her feet and saw a pair of black leather boots with three-inch stiletto heels.

"Fuck off, Harker," Christy replied, but I heard the smile in her voice. It was mirrored on her face, but she wiped it off fast. "You're cute, but I don't date humans."

"That's fine. I think we've established that I don't qualify." I was stalling until I could get my sea legs under me. It had been decades since I was on a boat, or any other floor that moved very much, and I wanted as much balance as I could muster before I dealt with Mort. He was a naturally unnerving fucker, and I didn't want to give him any more edge than that.

"You're close enough to human for me to use the easy out. Now give me your shoes. The wind in here messes up my hair, and that makes me grouchy. You wouldn't like me when I'm grouchy."

"Angry," I corrected, sitting down to unlace and pull off my Doc Martens, not the easiest thing to do when the floor keeps moving underneath you.

"Excuse me?"

"The quote is 'you wouldn't like me when I'm angry,'" I said.

"I know what the TV show said. I also know what I meant. You wouldn't like me when I'm grouchy. You'd fucking piss yourself if you ever saw me angry."

I looked in Christy's eyes and saw the truth there. I still had no idea if she was human, demon, angel, or some other kind of monster, but I knew she had power and that I didn't want to piss her off. So I shut the fuck up and handed her my shoes.

"Thank you," she said. "I'll have these behind the bar for you. If Mort kills you, I'll send them to Goodwill."

"Seems fair. You want to send them out to be shined, too?"

"They're suede, you dick." She turned and went back into the bar, laughing.

I turned and wandered farther into the bouncy castle, which was more like a bouncy maze. Imagine wandering through a giant, squishy, red and blue tunnel, where the floor has way too much give, and the noise of the fans keeping the building inflated made hearing anything more than a few feet in front of you impossible. I walked the red-tinged halls of Mort's inflatable house for a good five minutes, traveling a lot farther than I would have been if we were in normal space, and walking through seemingly endless plastic-lined corridors.

Finally, I turned a corner and stepped out into a room the size of a basketball court. Mort sat in a recliner in the center of the room in front of a bank of televisions. On each screen was a different room, all apparently in the bouncy castle. Some screens showed people wandering aimlessly, lost as hell trying to get out. Some showed people in a bouncy arena, either dueling or wagering on duels. And some screens showed people and monsters doing what they usually do when they don't think anyone is watching them. With some monsters, and pretty much every single type of demon, that is not something you want to see with any food on your stomach. My Bloody Mary made a run for it, but I managed to keep down breakfast.

"Hello, Quincy! So good to see you again!" Mort stood up and gave a florid bow. The last time I'd seen Mort, he was possessing the body of a little boy. The time before that he was riding along inside a low-budget porn actress. This time he was an athlete. I cocked my head sideways, trying to see if I recognized him from somewhere, but I couldn't place him. He was tall, African-American, and good-looking. He had muscles on top of his muscles, and nothing on but his boxer briefs, so I could see exactly how muscular he was. And pretty much how blessed he was in other areas, too.

"Hi Mort," I replied. "New suit?"

"Yes, someone made a poor decision in wagering on the Super Bowl, so I get to wear his body during the offseason. Too bad training camp is coming up. I promised him he could have control back by then."

"And what else is he going to have when he gets his body back?"

"Oh, nothing much. A little chlamydia, but he could have gotten that anywhere. I wasn't allowed to do any permanent harm to his body, reputation, or career during my tenure in his body, but I was allowed to get laid. A lot. I missed sex, Harker. I spent *three years* wearing that kid, and you'd be amazed how few women actually want to fuck a prepubescent boy. I expected it to be a much more popular kink, but not so much."

"That's strangely encouraging, Mort. What happened to the kid?" Mort was a passenger demon, hopping from body to body pretty much whenever he felt like it. But he wasn't always very careful with his toys, and sometimes the bodies he hung out in weren't good for anything but paperweights and doorstops when he moved on to the next host.

"Coma," Mort said. "Just like when I found him. I put him back where I got him and left him hooked up to plenty of machines for breathing, feeding, shitting—all that garbage you mortals have to deal with. He'll be around if I ever need him again."

"I'm sure that's heartening to somebody," I said.

"Oh, who cares, Harker? You don't. You don't give any more of a shit about these humans than I do; you just fake it for some ungodly reason. Although I suppose by definition, *all* my reasons are ungodly." He let out a laugh that sounded like fingernails down a chalkboard, high-pitched and shrieky, all out of proportion to his Adonis-like body.

"Now what do you want, Quincy? I have important things to do, and only a few more days of using this body to do them."

"Then what, Mort? Gonna hop back inside a kitty cat?"

"That was more fun than you'd think, being a cat. It's a lot like being a demon, actually. You do what you want, you don't give a fuck about anything or anyone, and if you decide you don't like someone, you can take a shit in their shoe. But no, I have several options lined up for my ride. There's a businessman who wants to trade a year of carrying a demon around in his meat suit for a guaranteed ten years of wealth, a model who wants me to magically make her a size zero until she's fifty, and a housewife who just wants me to murder her entire family for her. She offered the rest of her life in exchange."

"That last one's a trap, Mort. Better go with the stockbroker."

"I never said he was a stockbroker," Mort said a little too quickly.

"You didn't say lawyer, and stockbrokers are the only other people willing to wager a year of having your slime inside their head for a decade of comfort. His morals are so fucked he probably wouldn't even notice you were there."

"True," the demon jock mused. "But why do you say the housewife is a trap?"

"Think about it, Morty. What's the one thing we know about people?" I mused. Mort gave me an arch look, and I answered my own question. "People don't change. So why would a housewife want to make a literal deal with the devil to kill her husband and kids that she loves? She wouldn't. So either she knows she's dying and wants to take you to Hell with her, or she knows they're all about to die and she's going to double-cross you somehow. Either way, it's going to be more effort than it's worth. And the model is just stupid. She's probably a really hot size six and wants to be skinnier, and if you ride along with her, you'll have to live in the head of a stupid person for a year. Nah, take the stockbroker. It'll feel just like home."

"You are a heartless fuck, aren't you, Harker?"

"Nah, I just don't like bankers. Now can we quit dicking around and get to it?"

"Ah yes, I was waiting for the threats. Are going to forego the empty threats this time?"

"Yeah, Mort, I thought I'd skip those this time. We both know I can't really hurt you, so why let my mouth write checks my ass can't cash? I need information."

"I didn't think you were here to enjoy the bouncy castle. But it is fun, isn't it?" He punctuated this by standing up and starting to do jumping jacks.

The floor roiled under his weight, and I started bouncing opposite him. I decided to nip that shit in the bud before I barfed in the bouncy house, so I drew in my will and said, "*Levitas!*" I thrust both palms at the floor and smiled as I floated six inches off the ground.

"You know that's not a real word, right?" Mort said, sitting back down in his recliner.

"Be glad I didn't say '*wingardium leviosa,*' you snide prick," I said.

"Fine, fine." Mort waved a hand and the bouncy castle disappeared. We were in a big room that mirrored the front of the bar. Then I looked around and realized we were actually *in* the front of the bar. Same werefoxes over there, same passed out vampire in the booth, same Christy behind the bar.

"That's impressive," I said.

"Of course it is, it was meant to be. Now what do you want, Harker?"

"Information."

"Would you care to be more specific? What brings you to my doorstep at this ridiculous hour?"

"There was a Nephilim killed last night in Charlotte. His throat was slit and his body partially drained of blood. I think Orobas is back, and I need to know if I'm right."

"You're partially right. Orobas can't be back, though."

"Why not?"

"Because he never left."

Chapter Three

I WAS ON MY FEET, ONE HAND REACHING FOR MY GUN AND THE OTHER tracing sigils in the air. "What the fuck do you mean, Orobas never left?"

Mort never moved. He didn't even look like he thought about moving. Christy, on the other hand, reached under the bar and brought out her twelve-gauge. She leaned on the bar like it was a sniper perch and pointed both barrels at me.

"I know you're tough, Harker, but I don't think you're tough enough for these slugs. They've got a little hellfire sprinkled on them, and they'll light every scarred part of your soul on fire. If you're pure, they can't even touch you. But you've lived a long time in some interesting places, and I'm willing to bet you're almost as far from pure as I am. Now sit your ass down and stop scaring my customers."

The singular would have been a better way to phrase it since the succubus and her beau were nowhere to be seen and the werefoxes shifted and bolted for the door the second I stood up. The only one in the room now except for me, Mort, and Christy was the vampire, who was still face-down on his table.

But not unconscious, as I realized when he spoke. "Oh, for shit's sake, child. Please sit down before she gets any louder. My head is splitting. Christy, would you please refrain from killing the stupid human for long enough to get me some coffee, some O-positive, and a couple Vicodin?"

Christy looked at me with narrowed eyes, then put the shotgun down on the bar. "No problem, Jacob. Harker, *behave.*"

Mort looked at me, a little smile playing around his lips. "Yes, Quincy, do sit down. Besides, what exactly did you think you could do to me? Kill me? I'm a passenger demon, remember? All you can do is kill my body, and then what happens? I go to Hell. Big deal. It's long past time I went to visit dear Mummy and Daddy anyway. But you'd have to deal with killing a potential future Hall of Famer. And I don't think that would go over well with the sports fans in this town, do you?"

He was right, of course. He'd be in Hell yukking it up with all the other pitchfork-toting fucktards, and I'd be so deep under the jail that not even Becks or our Homeland Security buddy, Agent John "There's No Fucking Way That's My Real Name But I'm Not Telling You Anything Different" Smith, could find me. And that's if I was lucky. If I was unlucky, rabid football fans would draw and quarter me at midfield and spread my intestines across both end zones. I sat down.

"What does he want?"

"Who? Orobas? I have no idea," Mort said, leaning back in his chair. "I suppose he wants to rip your heart out and eat it, but the list of people who want your internal organs for entrees is long and varied, I suppose."

"You could say that, but why does this particular asshole want to kill me?"

"You spoiled his fun a few years ago, remember?"

"Oh, I remember. He wanted to open a portal to Hell in the middle of my city. I objected, and he murdered one of my best friends in the attempt."

"Well, he's still pissed about that." Mort waved his hand and a glass appeared in it. I couldn't quite tell what was in it, and I didn't want to ask. Mort saw me looking and tipped the clear liquid in my direction. "Want some? It's the vitreous humor of Central America virgins. Belize, specifically."

I swallowed hard and said, "No thanks. Trying to cut back."

Mort threw his head back and cackled at me. "Harker, you are a treasure! It's a vodka martini, for Lucifer's sake! You can't drink vitreous humor, everybody knows that. Actually you can, but there's no point. It's mostly water and salt, no real flavor to it. And a little gooey, like thick broth. But this is vodka."

"I'm good. Had a Bloody Mary earlier. Now about Orobas?"

"Yes, Oro. What about him?"

"Where can I find him?"

"No idea."

"Who is working with him this time?"

"Not a clue."

"What is his endgame?"

"Haven't the foggiest."

"Goddammit, Mort!" I snapped, then pulled myself under control. "Do you know anything useful?"

"Useful, yes. I know many useful things. Germane to your current problem, no."

"Then what fucking good are you?"

"You know Orobas is on this plane. That's more than you knew when you walked in. And I didn't even charge you for the information, so as you humans say, quit your bitching." He was right. I knew that Orobas was in town, but nothing else.

"Where else does he hang out?" I asked.

"I've never asked. Probably because I don't care. Let me be clear, Quincy. There are several reasons people come here in particular. First, it is a Sanctuary. They know that no matter what happens, or how drunk they get, if they are in my establishment, or on its grounds, they are safe. Sanctuary is old magic, Harker, extending far past anything you understand. Older even than me and my kin, which is saying something indeed. That is the reason our patrons feel safe, and I will never jeopardize that.

"Second, they know that I will never ask questions. I don't have to. The laws of Sanctuary protect me as well, so I know that no one who comes in these doors will harm me. And third, they know that I know things and come here to get information. But everyone knows this, so if they have something to hide, most people don't talk to me. Orobas is not a stupid demon, Harker. He does not blab his business in public, and he certainly doesn't tell me anything that he doesn't want spread all over town like the clap."

"That's great, but if that's the case, why do you know so much?"

"Just because Oro is not stupid doesn't mean the rest of my customers aren't. Most of them are morons, and even worse when you add alcohol. So I add lots of alcohol and glean lots of information. Just not from Oro."

"That's somewhat less than helpful," I said. "And if the power of Sanctuary is so damn strong, how did your buddy Oro almost rip my head off seven years ago?"

"Some spells weaken with time, but old magic grows stronger. When you last met Orobas, we were a fairly new establishment, just a few years old. Since that time, the club has thrived and put down roots in the community. That gives this place spiritual weight, strengthens the bonds, that sort of thing."

It made sense. I didn't know a whole lot about the old magic, just that it was nothing I wanted to fuck with. "Fair enough, I guess. So you have no idea where I can find Orobas or who his new minion is?"

"I never said that," Mort replied. "I believe that Oro can be found in the emergency room of St. Matthew's. He is the head trauma surgeon there."

Sonofabitch. It made perfect sense. A demon feeds on fear and pain, and nowhere is that more evident than in the only hospital in the city not affiliated with some huge corporation. St. Matthew's was a small church-run hospital with an overflowing emergency room and an empty bank account. Kept afloat by church backing and a prayer, Saint Matt's was the last chance for the indigent, the addicted, and the people who needed medical treatment for gunshot wounds they weren't prepared to explain to the authorities. I'd been patched up there myself more than once.

I stood up. "Thanks, Mort. You've been more help than you probably realize or intended."

"That's me, Harker. I'm a giver. Where are you going?"

"I'm going to the hospital. I hear there's a demon there that needs banishing."

"Well, the only good part of that plan is that you'll be close to the morgue. If you go after Oro without serious backup, he's going to rip your arms off and beat you to death with them. He almost killed you last time until we interfered, and he's gotten nothing but stronger after feeding on human pain and suffering for most of the last decade."

I stood there for a minute, thinking. Then I took a deep breath and let it out. "Yeah, but that's the job. I pick the fights I can't possibly win, then I go win them. I always knew someday I'd run into the thing that's bigger and badder than me. Maybe today's that day."

Mort opened his mouth, but just then my cell phone rang. "I think you may have been literally saved by the bell, Quincy."

I knew it was Becks before I looked at the caller ID. Our mental bond was strong enough that I could feel whenever she was focused on me, no matter how far apart we were. I swiped my finger across the screen and held the phone to my ear. "Yeah, Becks?"

"Harker?" Her voice sounded funny.

"Yeah?"

"Are you okay?"

"I'm fine, why?"

There was a long pause on the line. "Never mind, it's nothing. You need to get out here."

"Where's here? You at the crime lab with Paul?"

"No, I'm in Matthews."

"Matthews? I thought they had their own department?" Matthews was a small city just outside Charlotte, but still inside Mecklenburg County.

I frequently wasn't sure whether I was in Charlotte or Matthews, even after decades.

"They do, but they found a body that sounded a lot like the one you saw last night, and they notified us. Smith was in the building when the case came in, and he laid claim to it."

"Wow, for once the government really is on our side."

"Ours, yes. Mine, not so much. Finnick and Ramos were supposed to catch this case, and Coren and Mazer had the one from last night. Now I've got both of them. So I've got two fresh homicides and half the division pissed at me. So could you please get your ass out here and do that mojo that you do? I need to know if this chick was Nephilim or just a murder victim."

"Will do. Text me the address. I'll be there in fifteen." I ended the call and turned back to Mort. "Looks like you're stuck with me for at least a day."

"The day is young, Harker. I have no doubts you can drive someone to a murderous rage before nightfall."

I thought about it for a second and figured he was probably right. I'm just a charmer that way.

Chapter Four

THE BODY WAS LIKE THE FIRST ONE, IN THE MIDDLE OF A STRIP MALL parking lot. It was just like the first dead Nephilim I saw, all those years ago. Except it was daylight instead of pouring rain in the middle of the night. And the dead half-angel was a woman, not a gangly lawyer. And this strip mall was about three times the size of the last one.

And there was a big blue tent erected over the body and the surrounding parking lot. I pondered as I walked up to the crime scene tape exactly how bad the scene could be that they couldn't just cover it with a sheet. An enthusiastic and red-faced beat cop marched over to me with his hand held up as I approached.

"I'm sorry, sir—"

"Yeah, me too," I said as I ducked under the tape. His hand went for his taser, and mine went for my badge. I was quicker on the draw, fortunately. I've been tasered a few times. It hurts, and every once in a while you piss yourself. I tossed the rookie my badge holder and never slowed as I blew past him. I pulled back a side of the tent and stepped inside, then stopped cold at what I saw.

There was a very good reason not to let the public see the body, and an even better reason not to let the press see her. Not only was this a dead woman, this was a stark naked dead woman staked to the asphalt with big-ass nails in the center of a red pentagram. Her stomach cavity was sliced open, the sides peeled back and nailed to the ground, and my fucking name was written around the perimeter of the circle. Using her intestines for letters. Whoever had done this shit took his time and wanted everyone to know exactly who he was after. And what he planned to do to me when we met. I decided in a split second that I was going to take this fucker out if it was the last thing I ever did. And there was a pretty good chance that was going to be exactly the case.

Flynn stood off to one side of the body, a sketch pad in her hands, with the crime scene photographer. He was snapping pictures and circling the body while Flynn took notes on her drawing. She didn't look up as I approached. "Glad you could make it, Harker."

"I would have come sooner if you'd mentioned that I got an invitation," I said, pointing to my name scrawled on the asphalt. "Please tell me that's really written in paint."

"Not even close, Detective," the crime scene guy replied. Becks shot him a nasty look, and he went back to snapping pictures like a pervert at a Victoria's Secret fashion show.

"You can call me Harker. You're Paul, right?"

"Yes, sir." He stuck out a gloved hand, and I shook it.

"What can you tell me, Paul?" He was a quick study, I'll give him that. He looked to Flynn before he opened his mouth again. She nodded, then looked at me with one of those little "yeah, it was petty, but fuck it, I'm the boss" smiles.

"It appears that the crime occurred sometime between midnight and four a.m. She was found this morning by the manager of the hardware store at the opposite end of the parking lot. He likes to come in before his shift and run laps."

"I suppose that's a thing," I said. "I suppose you'll tell me that there's no trace captured in the…material used to write my name on the ground?"

"Too soon to tell, sir."

"What about her clothes?" I asked.

"None were recovered."

"Interesting. Thanks, Paul." I waved him off, and he went back to taking pictures. "The other bodies were all fully clothed," I said to Flynn.

"You think this woman is special somehow?"

"I don't know, to be honest. If this is Orobas working through an intermediary, he could be doing this just to fuck with me, to throw me off the scent. If the minion is going off the reservation, then she might be important. Who is she?"

Flynn looked at me, and I would have felt the sarcasm even if we weren't tied together mentally. "I don't know yet, Harker. Let me whip out my cell phone and run her through the instant worldwide facial recognition program that all cops have in their back pockets, just like they do on TV. I have no goddamn idea who she is. There's no ID, and it'll take hours to run her prints. And if she's not in the system, we have to go wider. It could be days before we get a result. We'll have a better chance just sitting at the station waiting for someone to come in and fill out a missing person's report."

"Not a bad idea," I said. "I'd alert all the departments in nearby counties to the murder and make sure they know you want to be notified of any new missing adult female reports immediately."

"You think? Gee, Mr. Harker, is there anything else you think I should do in *my* murder investigation? The one *I* called *you* in on?" Some of the old fire was back in Becks' eyes, and she was obviously flashing back to the time when she didn't like me very much. Okay, not at all. And it wasn't really that long ago, either.

"Sorry." And I was, really. "I didn't mean to step on your dick."

She laughed at that. "You asshole. If I couldn't feel your emotions and know you were sincere, I'd think you were trying to make me laugh just so I wouldn't be as pissed at you anymore."

"I can be sincere and still want you to not be so pissed at me, can't I?"

She laughed again, then turned serious. "Have you looked at her yet?"

"Yeah, I'm looking at her right now."

"No, asshat. I mean *looked* at her."

"Oh. Yeah, not yet. Hang on." I closed my eyes and focused my energy. When I opened my eyes again, my Sight was overlaid on the image of the mundane world. People glowed with their personal auras, Flynn with the gold and blue mix that I had learned to associate with guardians or protectors. Paul, the crime scene guy, was surrounded by a light green aura, of a type that I usually saw with scientists or researchers. Most of the cops were surrounded by blue with varying levels of gold, but one working the perimeter had a cold blue light shining from within him, shot through with grey and black. He was dangerous, the kind of guy who shot first and kept a cheap pistol in his glove compartment to throw down beside the body later. They were rare, particularly in the Charlotte PD, but I tried to keep an eye on them whenever I saw them.

I turned my attention to the body and took a step back. The ethereal golden wings I expected to see in the woman's aura were there, but so was something else. I stared at her long enough for Flynn to notice something was wrong and touch my shoulder. I gave a violent shake and snapped my vision back to the "normal" world.

"What was it?" she asked.

I didn't respond. I couldn't speak yet. I stared off into space, still processing what I'd seen.

"Harker." Flynn shook me this time, and I focused on her at last. "What did you see?"

"Let's go get some coffee," I said, then turned and walked out of the tent. I had to put some distance between me and the dead woman in the parking lot before I threw up or destroyed something. I walked into a CupABucks coffee shop and cut in front of a soccer mom hemming and hawing over her latte choices.

"Hey!" the blonde woman in yoga pants squeaked.

I turned to her and held up my badge. "Homeland security, ma'am. We're investigating a possible terrorist attack in this parking lot. Now if your goddamn coffee is more important than the safety of every single American man, woman, or child, then you feel free to stand here with your thumb up your twat debating choices when we all know you're just fucking around until the National Drink of the White Girl, the Pumpkin Spice Latte, comes back in style. So go do some crunches and shut the fuck up or I'll ship your husband off to Gitmo."

I turned back to the stunned clerk, who probably called himself a barista, but was really a pimply-faced kid working his way through his first year of college. "Give me two large black coffees, no bullshit."

"Excuse me?" The kid, Bruce, if I was to believe his nametag, looked honestly confused.

I leaned forward. "Bruce, right?" He nodded. "Good. Let me be clear, Bruce. I need two cups of coffee. The strongest, blackest shit you can find. Blacker than my shriveled little heart. Blacker than the girl you picked up from your economics class last week. Blacker than...fuck it, I'm out of metaphors. Just take two of the biggest cups you have, fill them full of the strongest coffee you have, and fucking sell them to me. No lattes, no cappuccinos, no foam, no whip, no *bullshit*. Just give me a couple of goddamn coffees. You with me?"

"Yes, sir." A terrified Bruce turned away and started fixing my coffee.

I felt a tug on my sleeve. I turned around, and Soccer Mom had her pepper spray out and pointed at my face. In the other hand, she held a cell phone.

"I'm calling the cops. If you move, I'll spray your ass into oblivion."

I smiled at her. She turned pale at my smile, which was the intended result. I whispered "*reversari*" under my breath and released my will. The top of her sprayer glowed for an instant, then everything went back to normal. Except that, for the next three minutes, her pepper spray worked backwards. I snatched her cell phone with my right hand, then held it up in front of her face. A little squeeze, and the aluminum body crumpled, the screen shattered to dust, and the circuit board experienced what I believe the experts refer to as a "catastrophic failure." I dropped the devastated scraps of phone to the floor and just kept on smiling.

"Go for it," I said in my coldest "yes, I eat babies raw" voice. I first used that tone on a mugger in London around 1919, not long after my father died. I was walking along and he stepped out of the shadows with a knife. I used that exact inflection on the mugger, and he ran screaming back into the shadows. Shortly after that, rumors surfaced of a return of Jack the Ripper, claiming that the Ripper attacked an independent businessman who managed to escape with his life. Soccer Mom didn't assume I was the Ripper, at least I didn't think so, but she did back away until she was out of arm's reach then turned and bolted for the door.

She ran right into Becks, who had to talk to the other cops on the scene before following me. The tiny tornado in stretchy pants and a sports bra almost bowled Flynn over as she bolted, but Rebecca regained her footing just in time. Flynn walked over to the counter just as Bruce put two big-ass cups of coffee on the counter. I dropped a twenty in the tip jar and handed Flynn her coffee.

I led her to a corner of the shop where I had a clear line of sight on the entrance and everyone in the room. We sat down, and Becks leaned in to me. "Okay, Harker. Spill it."

I took a deep breath. "She was a Nephilim, but that's no surprise."

"Yeah, we expected that."

"But I didn't expect a personal message on the body," I said.

"What?" Flynn exclaimed, then lowered her voice and leaned in again. "What are you talking about?"

"The killer didn't just leave my name spelled out in her guts, although that was a nice touch."

"A nice touch? Are you fucking high?"

"God, I wish," I replied honestly. "Yeah, it made sure that I would find out about this killing even if you weren't involved with the case. It was effective. And so was the other message." I took a big sip of coffee, stalling.

"What was the other message."

"It was twofold. First was the message itself, which was written on her torso. It says, 'I'm coming for you.'"

"That's direct enough," Flynn said.

"Yeah, but that's not the part that worries me."

"Go on."

"It's what he wrote it in. He used her soul, Becks."

"I don't understand. How can you use a soul to write a message?"

"A soul is a person's essence. It's everything that makes them who they are, and when you die, it either goes to Heaven or Hell. In some rare cases, it's left to walk the earth. That's how we get ghosts."

"Okay, that makes sense so far. What about the writing?"

"In the Otherworld, the part of the universe that I peek into when I look at things with my Sight, souls are corporeal. They have mass and substance. Someone who knows how to step into that world can literally touch souls. This guy didn't just touch her soul, he ripped it to shreds and painted her corpse with it."

"So that means…"

"Yeah, that means she didn't go to Heaven. She didn't go to Hell. She isn't a ghost. When she died, instead of following the natural order of things, she was torn apart at an almost elemental level. She was destroyed, Becks. Destroyed more completely than anything I've ever seen. And now the thing that did that is coming for me."

"Fuck. I'd be scared, too."

I shook my head and drank more coffee. "That's not it. I'm not scared for me. I mean, seriously, I've seen the century flip twice. I know my warranty's up, and whenever somebody or something punches my ticket, so be it. But there are people I give a shit about, and I don't want them to get hurt. Luke can take care of himself, but…"

"If you say it, I might shoot you right here in the CupABucks," Flynn warned.

I didn't care. I said it anyway. "I want you to get off this case, Flynn. This one's too much for you. Too much for any human."

"Let me use small words and short sentences so you'll understand me. Fuck. You."

"Dammit, Becks, you don't—"

"No, motherfucker, *you* don't understand. I know you feel guilty because you didn't save my dad. I get it. I feel shitty that my dad died when I was a little kid, too. But that doesn't change the fact that I'm a *cop*, Harker. I stand between the bad things in this world and the innocent people in it. That's not just my job, it's a goddamn calling. And I'm not going to stop doing my job because things get scary any more than you would."

"But this thing is out of your league," I protested.

"Yeah, well, it's out of your league, too," Flynn countered. "And you don't see me asking you to sit on the sidelines, do you?"

I had to admit, she was right on all counts there. "No, you're right."

"Of course I'm right. I'm always right. Look, Harker, I get it. It's dangerous. It's a big bad, and we have barely any chance of getting out of this alive. But that's the fucking job, isn't it? You said it yourself—there are things that go bump in the night. We're the ones that bump back. So put on your fucking big boy pants and let's find this thing. And when we do, we'll bump it right back to the Hell it came from."

I'm pretty sure that was the moment I realized I was in love with Rebecca Gail Flynn. Then everything got really *fucked* up.

Chapter Five

"**I** LOVE YOU."

"What?" Not exactly the reaction a man hopes for when he professes his love for someone. But I suppose a woman doesn't usually think that a horrific demonic murder scene is the kind of thing that inspires professions of love, either.

"I said, I—"

"I heard you." Becks stared at me. I didn't look away. I looked into her brown eyes and let the walls inside me fall down. I let her feel everything I felt about her, everything I'd felt about her for years but kept bottled up and renamed and wrongly filed in the card catalog of my brain. I let it all out, let her feel the love, the joy, the abject fucking terror rolling through my every cell.

Then I felt our mental connection blink out, severed like it was cut with a machete. My eyes widened, and I stared at Flynn. "Becks..." I started, but she just stood up and stalked out of the café.

I followed her, easily keeping up with her fast walk, and grabbed her elbow. Not my best move.

She whirled around and drew her pistol in one smooth motion. She jammed the barrel of her Smith & Wesson under my chin and got almost nose-to-nose with me. "You listen to me, you sick son of a bitch. I don't know what kind of game you're playing, but you come near me again and I swear to God I will blow your fucking brains out."

"Rebecca..."

"No. You don't get to talk now. I get to talk now, and you get to listen, or I'm going to ventilate the top of your goddamn head. I don't care who your uncle is. I don't care how old you are. I don't care that you can throw magic around like we're in a fucking Dungeons & Dragons game, you don't get to fuck with me that way. You don't get to tell me to back off on a case because you *love me*. What kind of candy-ass bullshit is that? You don't love me. You barely know me. We've worked together for what, a year? A year and a half? Jesus fucking Christ, you think that gives you the right to—"

I've made a lot of bad decisions in my life. Some of them have gotten good people hurt, even killed. Many of them have caused immense property damage, and one was responsible for the extinction of an entire species of South American monkey. But I have never really expected to die from one of my bad decisions.

Until I kissed Becks right in the middle of her rant. That one I thought had a better than fifty-fifty shot of getting me killed on the spot. So I made sure it was worth every drop of blood that she was about to spill. I wrapped one arm around her waist, the other around the back of her head, and I crushed her to me. I planted my lips on hers in mid-sentence, cutting off her speech by putting my mouth on hers. I held her tight to me, tangled my fingers in her hair, and kissed her like there was no tomorrow. Because if she thought there was an ounce of deception in me right then, there wouldn't be.

She struggled for a second, and I thought I was done. Then she relaxed into it and kissed me back like we were teenagers under the bleachers at a football game. She held me tight, and I poured everything I'd ever felt about Rebecca Gail Flynn into that kiss. After well over a minute, I pulled back. She looked at me, hair coming loose a little from her ponytail and her lipstick smeared, and holstered her pistol.

"So you're not going to shoot me?" I asked.

"Not right this second." Then she hauled off and slapped the fucking taste out of my mouth. She swung from the heels and laid an open-handed slap on my face that spun my head around and made my eyes water. Not to mention made my lip bleed.

I wiped the blood off my lip with the back of my hand. "I suppose I deserve that?"

"You suppose? I could charge you with assault, you dick. Contrary to what you've seen in shitty Nicholas Sparks movies, kissing a woman is not an acceptable method to get her to stop yelling at you."

"Apparently not, since you're still yelling at me. But you did put your gun away, so I'll call that a win."

"Yeah, take 'em where you can get 'em, Harker, because you're not going to get many in the 'W' column with me around."

"So that means you're planning on sticking around?"

"Yeah, I'm not going anywhere." She gave me a lopsided little smile, shook her hair loose, then pulled it back into a neat ponytail again.

"Now do you see why I don't want you on this case?"

"Oh, I understood it before you owned up to loving me. Which was only a surprise because of the location. I mean, goddammit, Harker, you've been alive for over a hundred years. I thought you'd know something about romance by now."

"I spent at least fifty of those years traipsing all over the world with my vampire uncle who traded his humanity for the power to avenge his wife's murder. My views on romance might be a little skewed."

She thought for a moment, then nodded. "Okay, that's a valid point. But still, a CupABucks? Right beside a murder scene? You have the heart of a fucking poet."

"I do, actually. It's in a jar in my closet. He wrote a limerick in the 1930s that Luke didn't approve of." I held it for a moment, then gave her a grin. She laughed, and I felt the wall between us come down. I could *feel* her presence again, and it was like water in the desert. I didn't know how much I missed that connection until it was gone. *Shit*, this whole love thing was going to make fighting big nasties really complicated.

"So…now what?" she asked.

"You mean about the case, or about us?"

"For now, let's focus on now what about the case. At least while we're less than a hundred yards away from a murdered woman. We should talk about us later."

"Tonight? My place?"

"I'm good with that. I'll bring sushi from that place on Sardis."

"Deal. You know I love their firecracker rolls."

"Now that dinner twelve hours from now is sorted, what about the woman with her guts strewn all over the parking lot?"

"Okay, fair enough. I've already spoken to Mort this morning, and he's not being terribly forthcoming with the assistance, so probably not a ton of help coming there. How about you go back to the station and ride herd on Paul while I go talk to Renfield and maybe avail myself of his computer savvy while Uncle Luke sleeps."

We turned to head back to our cars, and of course that's when a pair of black Suburbans and a black Sprinter van pulled into the parking lot. The van backed up right to the side of the tent, and Agent John Smith hopped out of the passenger side of the lead Suburban, his coffee cup from the high-rent joint next to police HQ in one hand and his badge in the other.

Smith marched over to us. Smith marched everywhere, his military background evident in every step. Not to mention his close-cropped haircut. His steel-gray hair stuck up like bristles on a brush, and his neat goatee matched the silver atop his head. Smith walked right up to Becks, his stocky frame blocking our escape.

"Flynn. Harker." He nodded to each of us in turn. "Where are we?"

I drew a breath to respond with something like "the parking lot," but Rebecca elbowed me in the gut. The air *whooshed* out of me, and I shut up.

"We have an unidentified victim, staked to the ground inside what appears to be a pentagram, with Harker's name written in entrails around the perimeter of the circle."

"Entrails?"

"Yes, sir. The victim's intestines were used to write Harker's name on the outside of the circle."

"That's nasty, even for a demon."

"There's a reason they make lousy interior decorators, Smitty." I couldn't help it.

"Do you know her, Harker?" Smith asked, turning his blue-grey eyes on me.

"The victim? No, never seen her before. At least, not that I can remember. And there was no specific aura or signature around the circle or the body. But this is Orobas. I know it."

"How can you be sure?" Smith asked.

"I talked to Mort today. He confirmed that Orobas is still in the city, and actually never left. He's just been waiting until the right moment, with the right minion, apparently."

"You trust that hitchhiking little fuckwit?" Smith and Mort didn't get along. To the point that Mort put him on the very short list of people that the laws of Sanctuary didn't apply to. I never heard a straight answer as to why they hated each other, just that Smith didn't set foot inside Mort's, and Mort didn't step outside."

"He's never steered me wrong yet," I replied.

"So what's next?" Smith asked. I looked over his shoulder and watched as a couple of men in Tyvek suits loaded a stretcher into the back of the Sprinter van. They stepped out, closed the back doors, and pulled away.

"Well, our initial plan was for Flynn to go back and oversee the autopsy and see what the crime scene guys turned up, but since your boys just loaded the body into a van and drove off with it, I guess part of that is off the table."

"What?!?" Becks exclaimed, starting to move after the departing van.

I grabbed her arm. For the second time in one morning. At least this time, she didn't put a gun under my jaw. "Hold up, Flynn. You can't catch them on foot, and it's not like Smitty here won't tell us where he's taking the body. Right, Smith?"

"Of course I will. They're just going to the county morgue. All the ME vans were out, so I had a couple of my guys lend a hand. We grabbed a stretcher from the morgue, then came over here. The body will be waiting on you when you get downtown."

Flynn's shoulders relaxed, and she looked back to Smith. "Okay. That's fine. I just wish you would have mentioned that first."

A silence hung in the air. I figured if she was waiting for an apology from Smith, we might all be white-haired before that happened. So I stepped in. "So now what's next? I was heading over to Luke's to do some research on Orobas and see if I can come up with any other ways of identifying Cambion. Orobas has managed to stay hidden for seven years, so I bet his new half-demon lapdog is using Nephilim blood to mask its identity."

"Maybe you should come with me instead," Smith said. "We've got a pretty extensive library at my office, including a few books picked up when a certain Alexander Marlack disappeared last year. Not that you'd know anything about that, of course."

"Of course," I replied, somehow keeping the grin off my face. Marlack was an asshole lawyer whose privileged asshole son summoned a demon last fall and let it rape and impregnate a teenage girl. I had to burn down the girl's house with her in it before she gave birth to a demon that could walk both planes. Then I went after the son, which led me to the father, which led me to summoning a demon myself to deal with those assholes.

I hate demons, but sometimes when you need to pound a nail, you have to have a hammer. And sometimes you need a really big, flesh-rending, life-devouring hammer that besmirches your immortal soul just by being in the same room with it. But killing that particular dickwhistle was totally worth it.

Chapter Six

We sped along Independence Boulevard in Smith's Suburban, strip malls and car dealerships whizzing by our windows. We rode in silence for a few minutes, until Smith looked over at me.

"So, you and Flynn finally got some things sorted out, huh?"

"Not even close. But what makes you say that?" I asked.

"The way you two were being very careful not to look at each other for very long, no touching, not even accidental, that kind of thing."

"You're pretty observant, Smitty. That's a little more than the typical human would pick up on." It was kind of a game by this point—I try to figure out exactly what Smith was, and he tries to hide his real identity from me. He was just a little bit *off*. He didn't quite smell right for a full human, and he didn't quite move right, either. He wasn't a were-something, I'd figured that much out, but I couldn't get him to even admit he was more than human, much less tell me what he was. So I kept poking at it, and he kept obfuscating.

I opened my mouth for another guess, but just then Smith's cell phone rang. He pressed the screen on his dash, and a voice came over the car speakers.

"Agent Smith?"

"Speaking. I have Quincy Harker with me, so nothing classified."

"You take all the fun out of espionage, Smitty," I said with a grin. He replied with the same stoic look he always wore. Sometimes I wondered if the man knew how to smile.

"Sir, this is Sergeant Jade from Dispatch. You asked me to relay any calls that came in that I thought were odd, and this one seemed to fit."

"What is it, Sergeant?"

"We just got a call about a disturbance at Freedom Park. Some folks protesting construction or widening roads or something are raising hell out there."

Smith looked exasperated, and it showed in his voice. "That's not exactly what I was thinking about when I told you to call me with anything unusual. I'd say a bunch of hippies bitching about something is pretty normal."

"So would I, sir. Except for the reports of a giant plant monster tossing huge rocks around the park and destroying the bandshell."

"What?" The bored and frustrated look was gone from Smith's face.

"The report said something about a giant tree-thing walking around and throwing shit at people. Park benches, trash cans, boulders, that kind of thing. I've got a couple squad cars on the way. I'll let you know what they say."

"Never mind, we're on our way." He tapped the screen to end the call, then turned to me. "I'm going to drop you off at the entrance to the park, then I'll head to the station and get started on our research."

"You're not going to back me up?"

"Harker, it sounds like you're going to fight an Ent. I don't even have a can of weed killer on me, and I bet bullets won't do much to something made of wood and grass, or whatever this thing is made of."

He was right, but I wasn't ready to admit it. I drew my Glock and checked the magazine, then made sure my spare mags were in my back pocket and topped off.

"You think you're going to shoot the plant monster, Harker? I didn't hire you for your marksmanship."

"Good thing since I'm not a great shot," I replied. "No, I just want to make sure I can shoot out your tires if you really do try to leave me there."

Smith didn't respond, just flipped a switch on his steering column to turn on his flashing blue and red lights, then started passing people like they were sitting still. I suppose the giant engine is another reason the feds like their Suburbans. It can't *all* be to compensate for tiny penises, right?

Ten minutes later, Smith pulled off to the side of Princeton Avenue and looked at me. "Try not to get turned into fertilizer, Harker. I need you on this serial case. If it's anything like that mess you were in seven years ago, it's going to take everything we have to stop whatever this guy has planned."

I didn't bother asking how he knew about my run-in with Orobas seven years ago. Even if the most interesting bits weren't in any official records, Smith had good sources. Better than mine, sometimes, and one of my sources was a friggin' angel.

"Thanks, Smitty. I'm sure your only concern is for my well-being," I said as I stepped out of the SUV.

"Nah, I just don't want to deal with the paperwork if you're on one of my cases and get killed. So if you're going to die, try to do it off the clock."

I just shook my head and slammed the door, then turned to see what kind of shitstorm I was walking into. A steady stream of people cascaded out of the gates of Freedom Park, and a fair number were just hauling ass down the greenways and ungated exits, too. I didn't see any sign of a giant plant monster, so I did what every sane, well-adjusted human being does when faced with hundreds of people running in terror from something.

I ran right in.

Good thing for me I've never been accused of being sane or well-adjusted, and reports of my humanity are muddled at best. I hopped the low fence around the parking lot by the softball field with one easy bounce and ran toward the bandshell. The sergeant had mentioned destroying the bandshell, and that part of the park was popular with protestors, so it all fit. It took me a couple minutes to jog there, and when I arrived, the waterfall of escapees had slowed to a trickle.

When I crested a small hill, I got a good look at the lawn area across the small pond from the bandshell. Sure enough, what I saw fit into the category of "giant plant monster" pretty well. It was a good ten or twelve feet tall, covered in chunks of grass, flowering plants, and hunks of sod. What I could see of whatever constituted its muscles and bones looked like tree branches, roots, and thick vines. From somewhere inside its head, a reddish-orange glow emanated, like there was a pissed off fire inside the thing. Which, frankly, would piss me off, too, if I were made of sticks.

The plant-thing was chucking rocks the size of my head at a couple of Charlotte cops who were trying to take cover behind a two-wheeled ice cream cart. I guess any port in a storm, but if I were a normal human, I would have stayed right the fuck away from that thing.

As previously stated, I am far from a normal human. Step one was to get the cops to stop shooting long enough for me to get close and try to take out the beastie. It just wouldn't do to get shot in the ass trying to save the city. Or at least the park. Let's just accept the fact that I don't want to get shot in the ass and leave it at that.

I ran over to where the cops huddled behind the cart and crouched behind them. "You guys know that thing can totally see over this cart, right?" As if to prove my point, a basketball-sized rock arced high over the cart and sunk itself a foot into the ground behind us.

"We know, but we got no place else to be," one of the cops said. He was young, nowhere close to out of his twenties. A young, good-looking African-American kid who really didn't need to get his brains splattered all over the park.

"You do now. This is now officially federal government business. I'm Agent Harker from Homeland Security." I even pulled out my badge.

"We know you, dickhead. You're that moron who thinks he's a wizard that's banging Detective Flynn," the other cop, a fat guy in his forties, grumbled at me. He was white, fat, and stupid. If he wanted to put his head in the way of a falling rock, I didn't have a problem with that.

I glared at Fat Cop and said, "First, don't call me dickhead, fuckwit. Second, I don't think I'm a wizard. I do magic, that's all. No funny hat, no robes, no hobbits. And third, keep your fucking bullshit speculation about my and Detective Flynn's personal interactions to yourself, or I'll have your ass busted back down to parking lot traffic monitor at Carowinds."

"You don't have that kind of juice," Fat Cop replied.

"I have a badge that says Federal Motherfucking Government on it. You want to see how fast the department budget gets cut when I pull a few strings? Just keep annoying me, greaseball. Now if you two fine gentlemen would like to live to see tomorrow, how about you stand up, run like holy hell, and stay the fuck out of here until I get shit sorted. How does that sound?"

Black Cop nodded, then got up and ran like there was a two-for-one sale at Krispy Kreme. Fat Cop sat there glaring at me for a few more seconds, then stood up and ran to his car. Well, it was more like a fast waddle, but he still moved with some purpose at least. I stood up, then reached out and snatched the big umbrella off the top of the cart. It came free with a snap, and I folded it shut. I reared back and chunked that folded umbrella like a javelin, channeling all my former Olympian ancestors with my mighty throw.

Okay, more like I used my vampire-infused blood to hurl it like Ahab chunking a harpoon, but I'll take that, too. The umbrella expanded a little in flight, which is the excuse I'm sticking with for why I buried it into the monster's chest instead of its eye like I planned. But I hit it, which is some level of triumph. And I pissed it off, which wasn't the best idea I'd ever had.

The plant monster turned to me, the fleeing cops completely forgotten. It plucked the umbrella from its chest, snapped all the ribs and the fabric off it with a quick swipe of one hand, and hurled it back at me. The plant's aim was dead on. The spear whizzed just a little over my head and buried itself two feet into the ground. I got the distinct feeling that even if the spear went through me, it was thrown with enough force to bury itself at least a foot in the dirt.

"Okay, Plan B," I muttered, wondering to myself exactly what Plans A, C, and hopefully D were. I reached down and picked up the ice cream cart high above my head, then took a couple of running steps and chunked that at the monster.

It caught the cart in midair. It staggered back a step but didn't go down. And of course, because playing catch with a forest elemental is exactly what I want to be doing with my morning, I opened my Sight, looking for any mystical trace that meant the creature was being controlled by someone nearby, but there was nothing. No strands of magic linking it to anything around, no traces of dark magic, just the rich verdant glow of nature magic. Yup, I was about to be squished by a real-life giant flower child. My life sucks sometimes.

Chapter Seven

I COULDN'T SEE ANY TIES BETWEEN THE MONSTER AND ITS SURROUNDINGS. But I also didn't find anything tying it to another plane, either. So I was kinda at a loss about how to deal with the thing. I dodged a couple of big rocks, then hauled ass to hide in a nearby copse of trees when the giant tree came at me directly.

I hid behind a couple of small maples, and almost immediately vines crept along the ground and twined around my feet. "*Infernos!*" I shouted, pointing at the vines. A small stream of fire flew from my fingertips and burned the vines away, but more slithered toward me. I retreated to the sidewalk, but nature's assault pursued.

The giant fern-covered bastard wasn't chasing me, just sending vines, so I figured I could deal with those. I took a couple of running steps, then leapt for a nearby light pole. I scurried up the side, using speed as my leverage, then swung around so I was perched on the light fixture like a demented superhero, or a skinny gargoyle. That broke my contact with the ground and confounded the creature for a few seconds. I had to use them wisely, or I was screwed.

"*INFERNOS!*" I bellowed, pulling in power from the nearby electrical lines and converting it to magic. That hurts like a sonofabitch, by the way. A fireball bigger than my head flew from my hands and crashed into the elemental's chest, only to burst into about a bajillion pieces and scatter sparks all over the ground.

Yup. I was screwed.

By now the vines were back and climbing the pole, so I decided that moderate insanity was better than sitting there getting strangled by kudzu, so I jumped off the top of the light pole. I hit the ground rolling and was really glad for my oddball ancestry. If I were just human, I probably would have broken both legs, but since Dracula and his wives all took a bite out of my parents at different times, it left me a little more human than human, as the song goes.

I sprinted across the grass to a small concession stand and jumped up on the roof, wracking my brain for ideas. A tree-monster that was immune to fire? That was just totally unfair. A thought hit me, so I stopped, picked up one of the big-ass rocks lying around everywhere, and chunked it at the creature like a shotput. It flew true, arcing high in the air and coming down to smack into the elemental's shoulder. Kinda. Except instead of breaking off the monster's arm, like I'd expect when a basketball-sized rock hits something in the shoulder, it bounced off onto the grass. No effect. It was like I'd hit the monster with a balled-up piece of newspaper.

I opened my Sight again, this time focusing on the creature, not whether or not it was tied to another plane. Most of the creature was surrounded by green pulsating magic, the magic of life, of the earth and nature, but the core of the thing, deep in its center, glowed bright crimson red. It was like someone put a very bright light behind a pool of blood, that kind of dark, roiling red. Even for a giant tree monster, that wasn't normal. I scanned the area with my Sight, looking for anything similar, and saw a flicker of red light from the water just in front of the bandshell.

Great, I thought. *I find what I'm looking for, and of course it's underwater.* I kicked off my boots, carefully set them aside, put my pistol in one and spare ammunition in the other, and jumped off the roof. Good Doc Martens are expensive, and the last thing I wanted to do was fuck up my boots if this thing went sideways. Well, *more* sideways. My days and nights are pretty odd, but fighting an honest-to-God Ent in the middle of Charlotte is weird even for me.

About five seconds after I hit the ground running, I regretted leaving my boots on the roof. The plant-monster, obviously tired of throwing things at me, decided to take a less direct approach, this time making the entire lawn erupt in thorny root growth. I ran on because stopping would have let the razor-sharp spiked vines and roots twine around me and give me the old iron maiden treatment, but every step was excruciating. I put a foot down and brought it back bloody. I stepped again and pierced my sole on more thorns. Lather, rinse, repeat the bloody process for every step. Eventually, I sacrificed the small pains for fewer, larger agonies as I started to jump across the grass ten feet at a time, still racing for the water. I finally reached the edge of the pond, took a deep breath, and dove in headfirst.

And couldn't see shit. Not only was the water dirty and murky, but whatever I was looking for was apparently very mundane to the normal eye. I resurfaced, hung on to the lip of the artificial island where the symphony frequently performed, and focused just long enough to open my Sight. This time I could feel as well as see the flickering red whatever beneath me. And I could also see the tendrils of green magic racing across the surface of the water at me like a vanguard of pissed-off snakes. Except these snakes were vines, and they weren't there to bite me—they were there to drown me. So much better.

I gulped in air, dove again, and swam straight at the red glow. I got there in seconds, reached out, and grabbed it. As soon as I did, I let my Sight drop so I could see what the thing was in the mundane world.

It was a thermos. I'd just dashed across a field of thorns and jumped in water full of who knows what for a thermos. I surfaced and dragged myself up onto the island, then onto the concrete stage, hoping the man-made surface would give me a little barrier against the elemental's attack, at least for a few seconds. I look down at the thermos in my hand and shook my head. That's all I needed, an angry shrubbery and a magical thermos. I reared back to throw the stupid thing back into the water but felt something rattle in it and stopped.

I unscrewed the lid and held my hand under the mouth of the thermos. I gave it a little shake, and after a pint or so of pond water poured out, a small vial dropped out into my hand. I recognized the dark red substance as blood immediately since you don't drink "wine" with my uncle more than once before you learn the difference in viscosity between Cabernet and O-Positive. I blinked and focused my Sight on the object in my hand. Sure enough, the vial of blood was the source of the red glow in the thermos, and it matched exactly the shade of red emanating from the tree-dude's chest. I blinked away the Otherworld and threw the vial to the ground. I lifted my foot to grind the glass to dust under my boot heel, then remembered I wasn't wearing boots. I decided I didn't want to mix the blood coating my feet with the enchanted blood of whatever-the-hell the vial contained. That and stomping on glass with my already ripped and abused foot was just adding injury to injury. Instead, I found a nearby brick and smashed the vial to smithereens.

The tree-man let out a bellow, which was interesting since it had no visible mouth, and I watched as the red glow went out in its chest. I stood on the stage, waiting for the elemental to topple over and return to its natural state, like inanimate, but it didn't happen.

"Shit, it's always the hard way," I muttered to myself, then yelped as I felt a tickle on my leg. I looked down and hopped away, wincing with every step. The stage was covered in vines, and every one of them was reaching for me, trying to turn me into a literal hedge wizard. I took two running—well, limping—steps and dove back into the pond, swimming underwater back to the sloping hill leading to the giant tree-thing.

I pulled myself out of the water and was immediately ensnared by winding grass and weeds. It seems the elemental had decided that shoving thorns into my feet wasn't going to stop me, so it was going to mummify me in plant matter instead. Roots wrapped around my throat, cutting my air to a trickle, while super-grown grass wove itself into a blanket pinning me to the ground. I was very quickly bound up like Gulliver in Lilliput, stuck to the ground, face-down and unable to move except my lips.

Good thing my mouth is almost my deadliest weapon. I couldn't touch the life force around me, and the ley lines were all out of whack with the powerful magic used to animate a tree giant, so I reached down deep into my own soul, focused my will, and shouted, "*Incendiarus!*"

It came out more of a croak than a powerful bellow, but it had the desired, if excruciating, effect. I burst into flames. Every inch of my skin turned into living fire in an instant. I burned myself like a goddamn roman candle, but in seconds, I was free. I released the spell and got to my feet in the middle of the scorched patch of earth I was pinned to seconds before. I was buck naked, burned to a crisp, and really, really pissed off.

I wasn't exactly not on fire anymore, so when I took a step, I singed the grass beneath my feet. After a yard or so, the grass literally retreated from me, leaving me nice cool topsoil walk in. I stalked the elemental, smoke coming off my shoulders and the top of my head.

"You want to take the gloves off, motherfucker? Well, let's dance, bitch." I held up both hands and bellowed "*Infernos!*" Flames shot from my palms like water from a firehose, dousing the plant monster in fire and setting it ablaze. I let the fire die out from my hands and picked up a rock the size of a softball.

"*Infammato!*" I poured magic into the rock, and it burst into flames. The *rock* was on *fire*. I hurled the fireball at the elemental and caught it right in the head. I repeated the process with two or three other small rocks until I came to one of the boulders the thing had chucked at the cops earlier. I picked up the big stone with both hands, lofted it over my head, and screamed "*Flambeé, motherfucker!*"

I hurled the boulder, now basically just a mass of congealed lava, overhand at the now-smoldering Ent and hit it right in the center, where the old red glow used to be. Now there was a new red glow as the boulder punched a hole in the tree-beast, and it began to be consumed by flames from the inside out. The elemental teetered, then collapsed backward onto the lawn, breaking apart into just a collection of saplings, vines, twigs and leaves, all burning merrily on the grass.

I walked over to what had been the head of a ten-foot monster just seconds ago, kicked it into nothing but glowing cinders, then reached down into where its chest had been, pawing around for what I knew was in there but couldn't see anymore. After a couple seconds, I pulled free exactly what I expected to find, a glass vial just like the one I pulled out of the pond. I reached in my pocket to pull out an evidence bag and was painfully reminded of two things. One, I had burned off all my clothes when I magically set my skin on fire. Two, I had *set my skin on fire.*

Adrenaline exhausted, the searing agony of being covered in extensive burns hit me like a Mack truck. I screamed, fell to my knees, screamed again from touching the ground, and passed right the fuck out. But I didn't let go of that vial, and the goddamn plant monster was dead.

Chapter Eight

"**Y**OU'RE AN IDIOT."

Those were the first words I heard when I regained consciousness. On the bright side, they were in Becks' voice, so I had that going for me. On the less bright side, she was one hundred percent right.

"But I'm a cute idiot," I croaked. It's remarkably hard to speak when you've been choked by trees and set on fire. But I had the opportunity for a smart-assed comment, and I wasn't going to waste it.

"Not right now, you're not. You look like Deadpool. Only Deadpool if he had a skin condition that made him look even more fucked up."

"So I'm like a less cute Ryan Reynolds? I'll take that."

"You look like a stunt mannequin of Ryan Reynolds that got blown up, dragged behind a truck for a mile, then dipped in acid. I don't think there's an inch of your skin that's not burned. How are you even talking?"

"I learned some badass meditation techniques from a Buddhist monk in the sixties. And I didn't set my lungs, throat, or mouth on fire. Just my skin. Have you called Luke?"

"Yes, and *what*? Did you just say *you* did this? Like on purpose?"

"Yeah. It's a long story. That goes better with morphine. And tequila. And preferably many other narcotics."

"Well, for now you'll have to make do with a nice fresh red. While it's recently decanted, I can vouch that it's aged appropriately." The new voice was deeply cultured, the dulcet tones of a man who had seen multiple centuries pass in front of his eyes. The voice of the man I referred to as "uncle," but who had been a father to me for many years. The man, the myth, the many, many legends, Vlad Tepes. My uncle Luke, Count Dracula. He stepped to my bedside, every bit the European aristocrat even after decades in the States. Luke was tall, with dark hair and the pale skin you'd expect from a man who hadn't seen the sun since a century before Shakespeare was born. He wore a tailored suit that probably cost more than my entire hospital bill, with a pocket square perfectly matching his tie. I saw Uncle Luke ruffled once, in Europe during World War II. It wasn't pretty, and I never wanted to see it again.

"Hi, Luke," I said. I gave him a little wave.

"Hello, Quincy. You do understand that when I promised your mother I would take care of you, none of us believed that it was an endeavor that would require quite these great lengths, correct?"

"We didn't expect me to celebrate my hundred-twentieth birthday, either, did we?"

"Well, if you insist on setting yourself on fire every time you face a difficult foe, you certainly won't make it one hundred twenty-one. Oral, or intravenously?" he asked, holding up a wine bottle and an IV bag.

"Let's just go for both barrels, Unc, This shit hurts a lot more than it looks like."

"I find that hard to believe," Luke said, handing me the wine bottle and hanging the bag on the IV stand beside my head. He quickly hung the bag to drip into the IV alongside the morphine, but in trying to get the blood to flow, he set off some kind of alarm that had a nurse rushing in seconds later.

"What is going on in…" She started off ready to read Luke the riot act, but he turned his gaze on her and had her under his complete control in seconds. Her face went blank, and she stopped in her tracks.

"Come over here," Luke said to the dazed nurse. She walked over to the IV contraption. "Make this work. He needs this blood as quickly as our machines can put it into him."

She pushed buttons and tweaked tubes, and the mixed blood and morphine started to flow into my veins together. Luke looked at her nametag.

"Nurse Banks," he said. "You will disable all alarms on this equipment, then go to your station and ignore anything you see or hear from this room, or the three of us. Do you understand?"

"I understand." Her voice was flat and her eyes dull, but she pushed a bunch of buttons, then walked out.

"Holy shit, you can really do that?" Flynn asked.

"Yes," Luke replied. "I find it distasteful, but it does prove useful at times."

"So you're giving Harker blood? Why couldn't they just do that here?"

"The blood from the blood banks does not have my unique qualities, Detective."

"Wait, you're giving him *your* blood?"

I decided that there was nothing to be gained from me being part of this conversation, so I lay in my bed and drank my merlot mixed with Dracula blood and kept the fuck out of it. I felt the morphine, and I felt the wine, but most of all I felt the power and healing properties of Luke's blood coursing through my veins. My skin began to heal itself, rebuilding itself on an almost cellular level underneath the sheets and the gauze that covered me. I felt better immediately, but I knew from unfortunate past experience that it would be a while before I was back to full strength.

"So you're giving him your blood to heal him, like he did with me." Flynn's face was knit in concentration. This was all new to her. A year ago, she didn't even believe in magic. Now she was kinda dating a dude that was born in the nineteenth century and still looked in his late twenties.

"Exactly."

"And you know this will work because you've done it before?"

"My dear, I am over half a millennium old. I've done almost everything before."

"Wow." She sat down in the chair and started to stare at me. "Will I be able to see it?"

"See me heal? I don't know. I assume so, but I've never been hurt in quite this way before, so I don't know exactly how it's going to...ow *fuck*!" I knew one thing, re-growing all your skin at once hurt like a bitch. I wasn't sure which hurt worse, the burning it off or the growing it back. I was pretty sure the burning it off part. And I really wasn't looking forward to the itching as all my hair grew back.

"Are you okay?" Flynn leaned forward.

"I will be," I said. I took another long swig of wine, then followed that with a long gulp that drained the bottle to the halfway point. "I'm going to need to get in the shower soon. I think all my new skin is growing back under the old, burned skin, and I'm gonna need to get that off me."

"Like a snake shedding its skin?" Becks asked. Her eyes were bright and curious, and I could only chuckle and shake my head.

"Yeah, kinda like that. Luke, did you bring me some clothes?"

"I did. These were in your rooms at my house. I hope they are adequate." He held up a small shopping bag.

"They'll be fine. I just need to be able to walk out the door without everybody seeing my junk." I lay there for a couple minutes, alternating drinking from the wine and just letting the morphine and blood infusion take effect. I started to feel better, stronger, more whole within seconds. By the time I knocked off the bottle of wine, I was loopy as hell from the booze and morphine, as well as on a rush of healing energy. I was ready to take on the world, if not so much walk a straight line.

"Help me stand up," I said, tossing back the bloodstained sheet that covered me. "I think I'm pretty good, Luke. If you want to disconnect the IV, I should be able to go shower."

"Lay there for a few more minutes. You need all the blood you can get."

"I don't have time, Uncle. I only had three days until the solstice before I lost an entire day in here. And has anybody heard from Smith? I figured he would have blown up my phone by now."

"You didn't have a phone when you got here, Harker. I think between the swimming in the pond and the setting yourself on fire, you probably lost it, destroyed it, or melted it," Flynn said.

"I think melting it counts as destroying it," I replied with a grin.

"Oh, shut up, you drunk. Anyway, I talked with Smith. Told him what happened, and that I would be here with you until we could get you moved. He said something about research and questioning suspects. Then he asked what happened, so I told him," Becks said.

"And how did you know what happened? As far as I knew, I was alone in the park with the tree-thing."

"Oh, Harker, that's so cute. Like anybody is alone anymore. One of the cops you rescued videotaped the whole encounter with his phone and his body cam. He said he didn't think anyone would believe his report without proof, so he made sure to get it all on tape, so to speak. I told him that his burden of proof didn't include YouTube, then confiscated his phone and body camera. That was a helluva fight."

"Yeah, you should see the other guy. I flattened him." I giggled, and that's how I knew I was really high. Giggling—not my thing. "Oh, I left my boots and my gun—"

"On the roof of the concession stand. Yeah, I've got them," Flynn said.

"Good. Those are my favorite boots."

"And the gun?"

"Nah, I like my Colt 1911 better. The Glock is nice and easier to conceal, but that Colt has some sentimental value."

"Which he'll be happy to tell you about later," Luke said. "Some time when he has less alcohol and narcotics in his system. But right now, the IV is finished, so you may go bathe. If you can manage to walk to the bathroom."

"I'll be fine," I said. I swung my legs onto the floor and stood up, fresh as a daisy. Then almost fell over and had to grab the handrail on the bed because I was a very drunk daisy. Under normal circumstances, one bottle of wine will give me a good buzz, but mix it with a couple doses of morphine, and I was blotto.

I looked over at Flynn. "I could probably use a hand getting to the shower," I admitted.

She looked at Luke, who shook his head. "I brought the wine and donated blood to the cause. It is your turn to suffer for your association with our dear Quincy, Detective. It happens to us all eventually."

I wasn't sure how to take that, so I kept my mouth shut. I gave Flynn my best puppy-dog eyes, and she let out a huge sigh and took my elbow.

"I am not getting any closer to you than this, Harker. You're still oozing a little, and I really like these clothes."

"They're nice clothes," I said, trying to be the good boyfriend. "They cover almost all of you, and those pants definitely do not make your butt look big." I was being sincere because I was too drunk to lie. Her butt looked great in those pants.

"I don't think that comment had the effect you were looking for, Quincy," Luke said.

"Why not? Her ass looks great," I protested.

"Can we not talk about my ass with your five-hundred-year-old uncle?" Becks asked.

"I guess, if that's what you want," I replied. "When can we talk about your ass?"

"I'm not answering that," Becks said. She got me to the bathroom door and had me sit on the toilet while she set up the flip-down chair in the small shower.

I reached out with one foot and pushed the door closed. "Alone at last," I said, in my most romantic voice. Or at least, my most very stoned romantic voice.

Becks straightened up and said, "All set." Then she reached for the door, but I kept it closed with my foot.

"What if I need you?" I asked.

"I'll be right outside."

"I'd feel a lot safer if you were in here with me."

"I'd feel a lot safer if I weren't in a bathroom with a drunk burn victim."

I made a pouty face, and she laughed. "Okay, fine. I'll sit here while you get cleaned up."

"You just wanted to see me naked, Detective," I said, standing up and peeling off the hospital gown.

"Not like that," Flynn said with a wince at my destroyed body. The gown stuck to me in places and pulled off chunks of burned flesh. I didn't mind since I had nice, new skin underneath it, and I took great glee in yanking off the bandages and the skin attached to them.

Then I hopped in the shower, and immediately almost went down. I caught myself with the grab bar and sat down on the fold-out seat. I typically shrug off the effects of drugs and alcohol quickly, but I expended a lot of energy fighting the elemental, then even more healing, so I was staying intoxicated a lot longer than normal.

I turned on the water to a medium warm and started scrubbing off my skin. I sloughed off an entire suit of charred and destroyed epidermis, then made another pass to make sure I got everything I could reach. "Hey, Becks?" I called.

"Yeah, Harker? You need me?"

"Yeah, actually, I do."

"What's up?"

"Umm…this is gonna sound like I'm putting the moves on you, and on any other day, I would be, but…there are some places I can't reach."

Her voice sounded amused. "So you want me to come in there and wash your back?"

"Yeah, exactly."

"I thought you'd never ask," she said, opening the shower curtain. Rebecca Gail Flynn stood there, already naked with her hair tied back. Her clothes were folded in a neat pile in the far corner of the bathroom, and she looked at my fresh man-suit and smiled. "Nice. The hairless look kinda suits you, Harker. Definitely shows off some muscle definition."

"Yeah," I said, looking her up and down. "Looks good on you, too."

She stepped into the shower and pulled the curtain behind her. I stood up, kicking the seat so it folded flat to the wall.

Flynn wrapped her arms around me and pressed her head into my chest. "I thought I was going to lose you."

"I'm a lot harder to get rid of than that, Becks. You're stuck with me, for a long time to come."

"I can live with that," she said, turning her face up to mine.

I bent down, kissed those lips I'd stared at for months, and we clung to each other under the pounding water. Eventually we got around to washing my back.

Chapter Nine

AT LEAST LUKE GAVE US A LITTLE ALONE TIME BEFORE HE GOT IMPATIENT and knocked on the door. We were almost dressed, or at least Flynn was, since my clothes were still in a bag on the dresser.

"Yeah, Luke, what's up?" I called through the door.

"Are you two quite finished?"

"Yeah, I suppose. I feel pretty clean." I grinned at Becks, who was even prettier when she blushed.

"Good," Luke responded through the door. "I've hypnotized three nurses into ignoring the sounds coming from the bathroom, and Detective Flynn's phone has been ringing almost constantly. It's almost as if you were in the middle of an important investigation."

"You act like it's the end of the world, Luke."

"It may well be, Quincy."

"Oh yeah. Good point." I opened the door and walked out into the main room wearing a towel and a slight grin.

"You look better," Luke said. "Refreshed."

"Growing a brand-new skin will do that to you," I replied, stepping into my underwear and jeans.

"Is that what we're calling it?"

"Oh, leave him alone, Luke," Flynn said, stepping out of the bathroom and sitting on the bed to put her shoes on. She picked up her phone. "It's Smith, checking on you. I'll text him."

"Tell him I got burned to a crisp, but I'm all better now," I said. I laced up my Docs and clipped the holster to my belt. I threw a light jacket on to hide my gun and looked over at Becks. "We ready to roll?"

"Where are we going? What's our next move?"

"You're going to call someone in the permits department and find out what eco-friendly bunch had a protest permit for today, then I'm going to go see how they're connected to the murder of a bunch of half-angels, or if they're part of some other angle Orobas is working."

"And what am I doing in this plan?" Flynn asked.

"Making sure I don't get burned up again?"

"That could be a full-time job, the way you handle investigations."

"It's kept me busy for the better part of a century," Luke said. "Since you seem to be feeling better, I shall take my leave. I have a bit of blood to replenish, and not that many hours until sunrise to find a suitable donor. Then I shall have Renfield look into the reports your crime lab has logged and see if anything leaps out at him."

"How is he going to get our crime lab reports?" Flynn asked.

"I think it is better for all involved if you know nothing about that," Luke replied, then turned and moved quickly out of the room.

I chuckled a little. "He can't help it. He hasn't worn a cape in over eighty years, but he still kinda swoops when he walks."

"Is Renfield hacking the police department computer system?" Flynn asked.

"I don't think he's currently hacking anything. By now, I think he's got his backdoors built into anything we need access to." Somehow, that didn't seem to reassure her.

We walked out into the hall and turned toward the elevators. I froze.

"What's wrong?" Flynn asked.

"The nurses aren't going to let me leave. I need a disguise or something." I started looking around for a lab coat or a baseball cap. That always worked on TV.

"You're wearing a disguise, you big idiot," Becks said with a smile.

"What are you talking about?"

"You look a little different from anything they saw in that hospital bed, remember? Hell, you look different from any time I've ever seen you, what with the whole bald look you've got going on."

Oh yeah, new skin. I forgot about that. We walked past the nurses' station like we were just ordinary visitors, turned into the lobby, and pushed the down button on the elevator. We rode in silence down to the basement parking lot, got in Flynn's car, and pulled out onto the street.

"Where to, Harker?"

"Let's start at the scene. There's something I need to check on."

Becks pointed to the car toward Freedom Park and flipped on her lights. Then she glanced sideways at me. "Are we going to talk about this?"

"What's there to talk about?" I asked. "I told you I love you, and I'm guessing that you like me a little bit, too."

"Just because I had sex in a hospital shower with you? Maybe that's just something I'm into." She didn't look at me, but I could see a little smile.

"Oh, you were into it, alright. But don't forget, Becks, I can feel what you feel. I try not to read your thoughts, but I can't shut out strong emotions. Just like you can't shut mine out. I know you can sense what I'm feeling for you, just like I sense all the confusion running around inside you. But I can feel what's underneath all that confusion, too. And that's love, or as close to it as I know anything about. So we love each other, and we can't hide from each other, and we just had amazing sex in a hospital shower. So what else do we need to know?"

A wave of sadness and fear poured over me, and I looked over to see tears streaming down her face. "I need to know you're not going to leave me. I need to know that you're not going to get yourself killed fighting some goddamn demon, or monster, or fucking *plant monster!*" She pulled the car over to the side of the road and turned to me.

"Harker, you need to understand this. When my dad died, I was crushed. I was just a little girl, and my hero was gone. But I pulled my shit together because my mom needed me. She fell apart, crawled inside a bottle of Xanax, and never crawled back out. She drank and drugged herself to death before I graduated high school. I moved in with my boyfriend and his parents to finish out the year, then he got in a car wreck the week after graduation coming home from a party I didn't go to. He wrapped his truck around a tree, and his parents couldn't stand to look at me after that, so I moved out. I lived in my car for a couple months until I went to college and moved into the dorms. I didn't have a real boyfriend after that. For fifteen years.

"So this is a little scary for me, Harker. I haven't lived for a hundred years. I haven't watched world wars and industrial revolutions. I'm just a normal girl who's watched everyone she ever loved die, no matter how young and no matter how much I loved them. So this…thing we're doing. *This* scares the fuck out of me. Not monsters, not demons, not even the fact that I just hung out with fucking *Dracula*. But you scare me, Quincy Harker. Because if you die, if you leave me, I don't know if there'll be enough left of me to put back together again."

"Then I'll just have to keep my century-long streak of staying alive in spite of myself, right?" I tried to lighten the mood, but she was having none of it. "Look, Becks, I know you've had it rough. I've been there, remember?"

"Yeah?" she said, letting a little bitter flavor creep into her voice. "Where were you when I was sleeping in my car?"

"Sitting in my own car fifty yards away pissing into a coffee cup keeping an eye on you," I replied. Her eyes went wide, but I kept going. "You were safe, and it was warm. The only time you almost had trouble was one time a couple of MS-13 'bangers wandered by looking for trouble. They saw a little hot chick curled up in the hatchback of her Geo Metro and decided they should bash in the back window and have a little fun with her. I convinced them that was a bad idea."

"I never knew."

"You weren't supposed to. Look, Becks, I know you're scared. I am, too. This isn't the first time I've done this whole sharing a mind thing, but it is the first time I've fallen for somebody this hard, this fast. And it almost killed me when I lost Anna. So I know what it's like to lose your heart and soul. I can't promise you I'm not going to be in danger, but I will promise you that I will *never* leave you."

"That's my guy, the herpes of relationships." But she smiled when she said it, so I felt like my little pep talk had served some purpose.

"There aren't even shots for me," I quipped back. "Now let's go to the park."

Chapter Ten

Freedom Park was lit up like Christmas when we pulled into the parking lot. Firefighters still stalked hot spots and sprayed water once in a while on a smoldering chunk of elemental, and cop cars stood sentry, their blue lights strobing through the normally quiet neighborhoods around the park. We walked through a crowd of onlookers as Flynn badged us under the cordon of crime scene tape. We walked straight to the center of the activity, a cluster of cops in cheap suits standing together near where I'd knocked off the plant monster.

"Hey look, it's Mulder and Scully," a fat detective I recognized as Emrack called out as we approached.

"What happened to your hair, Harker?" another detective, whose name I didn't know, jeered.

"I got the shampoo and your wife's Nair confused when I took a shower this morning. By the way, that's a cute birthmark on her butt," I shot back. He took a step in my direction, but Emrack put a hand on his chest, holding him in place.

"Don't let those guys bother you," Flynn whispered.

"It's been a long time since a fat fuckwit like Emrack has gotten to me," I said. I knelt by the ashes of the tree-critter, bringing handfuls of the ash to my nose and sniffing deeply. I put my nose to the ground and breathed deep. "There's something here, but I can't remember where I've smelled it before."

"Would you recognize it if you smelled it again?"

"I'm pretty sure, but it's not a hundred percent," I admitted. I opened my Sight and scanned the area for any hints of magical energy. There was still a little green energy in the remains of the creature, but that was to be expected. I looked around and finally spotted something out of place. Just a glimmer over a hill, but the same green energy pulsed in the distance.

I stood up. "Come with me, and cover me," I said to Flynn.

"Cover you from what?"

"Anything that tries to kill me," I replied. I took off at a fast walk toward the glow, ignoring sidewalks, police tape, and anything that wasn't the pulsing verdant light in front of me. I crested the hill and had to shield my eyes from the glare. What I thought was one source was actually a circle of seven individual green lights all coming together, weaving together to make one big undulating mass of energy. I dropped to my belly at the top of the hill and motioned for Flynn to hit the deck with me.

"There's something down there calling up a shit ton of the same magic that animated the elemental," I whispered.

She got up on her elbows for a better look. "It looks like a bunch of hippies in a drum circle. Can't you hear them?"

I dropped my Sight and listened. "Yeah, I hear them. They're not very good. Enthusiastic, but not good."

"But they're calling magic with it?"

"Yeah," I said. "It doesn't take much if the area is predisposed to it, and there are a fuckton of ley lines running through this park. I can't tell what they're doing from here, but we need to stop them before they get ambitious and call up another monster. I'd really rather not burn myself half to death twice in one day. Hang back and shoot anybody that looks more threatening than me."

I stood up and walked over the hill. The drummers ignored me, and I pretended not to notice the unmistakable smell of marijuana floating my way. Great, because stoned wizards make the best decisions. Still twenty yards or more from the circle, I held my right hand out to my side, palm up, and whispered, "*Flambé.*"

A ball of fire appeared floating above my hand, and I snapped my wrist forward. The fireball shot toward the stoner magicians and exploded into sparks right in the center of their circle. The drumming stopped instantly, all but one scrawny white kid with dreadlocks and no shirt, who was wailing away on a djembe with his eyes closed. He was lost in the music, his kokopelli tattoo glistening with sweat, and he pounded on the drum.

I muttered "*infernum!*" and summoned up another fireball. This one I flung right at the kid, and he jumped as the ball of magical fire hit him right in the drumhead and exploded with an impressive *boom* for a ball the size of a grapefruit.

He quickly switched from beating on the drum to beating out the sparks, then took the drum off his neck and shouted up at me. "Hey man, what the hell do you think you're doing?"

"I think I'm giving you stupid fucktards a taste of what I went through earlier today, thanks to you and your fucking hippie bullshit magic," I yelled back, even though I was only five yards or so away from him now.

Shirtless Hippie came at me, flailing his fists before he ever got going. He looked like a psychotic Don Quixote who thought he was both knight and windmill, his skinny arms waving everywhere as he ran at me. I stood right in front of him and kicked him in the gut when he got close enough. It was more like I just held my foot up and let him run onto it, but it had the same effect. He went down like a pile of smelly, hairy straws, and I stepped on him a little on my way to interrogate the rest of the circle of dumbasses.

"Who's in charge here?" I asked when I got to the center of their circle. Against experienced magic-users, there's no way I would ever put myself in the middle of a circle, but these guys couldn't lock me down in Alcatraz, much less a half-invoked summoning circle.

"Dude, nobody's in charge, man. That's like a totally patriarchal monotheistic way of looking at the world, and we aren't about that, man." The idiot in front of me was wearing the official uniform of the southern stoner. He had on a tie-dyed music festival t-shirt, ripped khaki shorts one size too big held up with a braided belt, and flip-flops that cost more than my jeans. I did the only logical thing anyone could do when confronted with such obvious poseur douchebaggery—I slapped the piss out of him.

I didn't hit him because that really might have killed him. I drew back my right hand and laid an open-handed slap across his face that spun him around and sat him down on the grass holding his jaw. His eyes were a little crossed, and there were four lines on his face where my fingers struck.

"You don't even know what half those words mean, you ignorant little shit. Now keep your goddamned mouth shut unless you've got something worthwhile to say." I looked up at the rest of the circle of morons. "Now who had the bright idea to summon a plant elemental and have it go on a rampage through the park? Because if that's how you're protesting, I think you need to go back to hippie school."

"I brought the spell. I bought it from some guy I met at a concert," a waif girl with long honey-blonde hair in pigtails said. Good move, she probably figured I was less likely to punch her. She was mostly right. I was less likely to punch a girl, but I would if I needed to.

"So are you evil or stupid?" I asked.

She narrowed her eyes at me, a look that probably intimidated men that wanted to sleep with her. But since I had recently consummated a relationship with a woman who didn't use crystals for deodorant or smell like patchouli, I had a better standing offer. That, and I'm notoriously hard to intimidate. Something about my upbringing, probably.

"Answer the question, or I slap Dipshit again," I said, raising my hand to the cowering idiot on the ground. I didn't take my eyes off the girl, but directed my next remark to the boy directly behind me. "And if you even think of pulling that knife on me, I will take it away from you and break both your arms. Do you have anyone willing to wipe your ass for you for the next six weeks? Because that's the shit you need to think about right now."

I heard the him thump back down on the grass and looked back at the girl. "Well, which is it? Evil? Or stupid?"

She stuck her jaw out, and I could see her trying to hold her shit together. So it was stupid. That's good. I didn't really like killing pretty twenty-something girls, but I would if I had to.

"He told me it was a spell to make the trees and grass grow."

"Did he have a name?"

"He said his name was Jones."

"Of course he did. And he was a powerful wizard and knew you were a powerful witch, and you both wanted to make the grass grow and the earth bountiful, right?"

A single tear escaped, and she dashed it away with the back of her hand. "Yeah, that's all I wanted to do—make the trees and grass healthier. Is that so bad?"

"I think this is what we mean when we talk about unintended consequences, you moron. You made the shit grow, alright. But you also made it sentient and very, very pissed off. And then I had to come deal with it, and that meant I set a lot shit on fire, including me. I don't like being set on fire. It makes me grumpy."

"What are you going to do to me?" She was openly terrified now, so a large part of my job was done. The rest of the hippies collectively looked like they were about to crap their pants, too, so I doubted any of them were going to be playing around with magic in the foreseeable future. Still, I didn't have much success getting people to stop using magic once they started. It was usually a bell you couldn't un-ring.

Still, she didn't kill anyone. Not even me, despite my best efforts to get myself killed. And she did try to do things right. "Here's the deal, kid. You're an idiot. A kind-hearted idiot, but an idiot nonetheless. And that's often the most dangerous type because you see the best in everybody. So here's what we're going to do. You're going to give me your spell book, and I'm going to give you the name of someone to contact. She can hook you up with someone to teach you, and she'll give you the name of someone good, and mostly harmless. But if I hear of you stepping off the path of light once, just a little bit, I will find you, and I will wear your skin for a winter coat. Do you understand me?"

She went even paler and nodded. I wouldn't really make a coat out of her skin, of course. Human skin is way too thin for that. Doesn't even really keep the rain off all that well. But she didn't know that.

I turned in a circle, making myself glow a little for added effect. "And the rest of you, get haircuts. Get jobs. Fucking go sell weed at Phish concerts for all I care, but quick fucking around with magic. You're going to get somebody killed, and it's probably going to be you. Now get out of here." They all bolted, except for the girl.

I motioned to the ground, and we both sat. I waved Becks over. "This is Detective Rebecca Gail Flynn of the Charlotte-Mecklenburg Police Department and Homeland Security. What you did today could very easily be considered a supernatural terrorist event, and we could have you sent to a pocket dimension that is kinda like Gitmo, but with more monsters. But we're not going to do that. What we're going to do is take a statement from you where you describe the man who gave you the spell, and then we're going to go through your spell book. Anything in there that could be dangerous, I'm going to destroy. You can keep all your blessings, protection spells, and wards, but anything that could be used offensively is outta there. You good with that?"

"Do I have a choice?" Some of her old fire was back, and while I liked seeing it in young people, I preferred to see it from a distance. A great distance.

"Of course you have a choice," Flynn replied. "You can do this, or we can send you to the magical prison dimension Agent Harker just described."

"Or I can lobotomize the magic out of your brain. That's always an option. But it's your call, so you decide. But you need to decide right now."

She closed her eyes for a minute, obviously swallowed the part of her that wanted to call us fascist pigs, and handed me her backpack. I poked around in there and brought out a battered copy of Alexander Schictling's seminal work on magic for beginners, *Spells for Complete Idiots*. Never has a book been more truthfully advertised, or more a pain in my ass because of it. Too bad Schictling turned himself into a toad and got run over by an ice cream truck because I really wanted to strangle him every time some kid handed me a copy of his book.

I knew right where to go for the stuff she had no business screwing around with, so I set to ripping out pages with gusto. Each page I tore out, I tossed into the air, and it burst into flames. Ashes fluttered all around me as I tore out summoning spells, binding spells, love potion recipes, and battle magic spells. I left her the illusions, the astral projection stuff, and the harmless environmental manipulation stuff, although it was really a lot easier to grow tomatoes with water, fertilizer, and patience than with magic.

By the time I was done with the book, Becks had a solid description of the guy who gave her the spell. Unfortunately, it boiled down to "white guy between thirty-five and sixty wearing a baseball cap somewhere between five-six and six-two, and maybe around one-eighty to two-twenty." In other words, completely average white dude of middle age and unremarkable size. Everything I ever wanted in an eyewitness description.

I grabbed a pen out of the girl's backpack and scribbled a name in the inside front cover. I wrote a phone number underneath it. "This is the number to a woman named Christy. She's a bartender at a place called Mort's. It's owned by a demon, but Christy knows everyone in the city with an ounce of supernatural power, and she's good people. Tell her I sent you her way and that you need a light witch mentor. And if you fuck with her, have your affairs in order. She's a lot less forgiving than I am."

"Whatever got into your head to make you think this shitshow was a good idea today, get it out of there, and fast. A lot of people could have died because you believed the wrong dude. This magic stuff is serious business, and if you fuck it up, people die. Do you get that?" Flynn asked.

The girl nodded.

"Good," Becks continued. "Now we're going to go try to find this son of a bitch and keep him from destroying our city."

"That's going to be harder than it looks." I looked up, and Glory stood over us, her arms crossed and a really irritated look on her face.

"What's up, Glory?" I asked.

"While you two have been busy washing each other's backs and playing kindergarten teacher, our friendly neighborhood serial murderer has left another pair of bodies for us. He's almost at the number of dead Nephilim he needs to open the portal to Hell. So if you're quite finished being guidance counselors and playing house, come with me to the latest crime scene. That is, if you're still interested in saving the world."

Chapter Eleven

FLYNN AND **I** FOLLOWED A PISSED OFF ANGEL INTO THE CHURCH, AND
I wish that were the beginning of a bad joke. It looked like something out of a
horror movie, with blood almost literally painting the front of the sanctuary. We
were there before the crime scene techs, before the bright lights and evidence
cards, before the bustle that dulls the edge of even the most horrific scenes. The
metallic smell of blood almost bowled me over, with the horrible underlying
miasma of death and shit and puke and sweat and pain and fear that accompanies
horrific murders. I didn't need my Sight to know that the energy of this place was
corrupted, and it would take a lot of work to put the church back right.

The sanctuary was a big room, all Gothic arches and rose windows. My
rubber soles moved almost silently across the floor, and I could hear the
occasional *drip-drip* of blood falling to the stone. The only light in the place
was one chandelier over the pulpit and a rack of prayer candles on either side
of the main door, with the odd streetlight peeking in through the stained glass
and casting crazy-quilt colors all around the room. Every single candle in the
rack blazed brightly, casting a flickering yellow glow that made long dancing
shadows across the walls. It made me feel like the killer stopped on the way out
the door to light fresh candles everywhere, in a mockery of prayer.

Everything about the room felt like a message, a mocking Zodiac letter to
the cops, a nasty letter from Jack the Ripper to investigators, a blood-soaked
"you can't touch me" from the killer to me, addressed very specifically by
writing my name in blood all over the walls of the sanctuary. "HARKER"
shrieked at me from every window, a crimson-turning-brown message that I
couldn't miss if I were blind.

The room was dim, but I could make out the shape of a body lying on
the communion table as if in state. The robes marked him as a priest, and the
glimmer of golden light around him in my Sight told me he was Nephilim. He
was gutted, his body ripped open and spread across the table, with a lake of
blood pooling on the floor beneath the table.

The splintered light from the chandelier and the windows cast long shattered shadows all over the room as the light fixture swung. I looked up to see what was making it move, then stopped dead as I realized what I was looking at.

"Tell me that's not…"

"I wish I could," Glory said.

I pulled a small flashlight from my pocket and shone a light up at the grotesque display hanging from the ceiling. A young boy, no more than twelve, hung from the chandelier, wearing nothing but his white underpants splattered red with his own blood. His feet were bound at the ankles with a nail jammed through them for dramatic effect. His arms were spread wide and lashed to the curved arms of the light, then a huge nail jammed through each palm. A wicked slash marked one side, but the cause of death was obviously the fact that his throat was cut from ear to ear. Everything else was just window dressing, a message not just for us, but for Glory and her bosses, too. And the *piece de resistance* was on the boy's head, where a battered Atlanta Braves ball cap was tacked to his head with at least two dozen nails, hammered into the child's skull to make a modern-day crown of thorns. I lowered my light from the mockery of the crucifixion and looked back at Flynn.

"Becks, you shouldn't be in here."

"Why, because it's gross? Because it's an affront to everything anyone holds holy? I get it, Harker. I don't think I did until right this second, but I get it now. This motherfucker wants to send a message? Well it's received, loud and goddamn clear. He wants to mock God? He thinks using faith as the model for his butchery is going to what? Rattle me? Scare me? Fuck that. Fuck him, and if you think this is doing anything more than pissing me off and making me stronger in my faith, then fuck you, too." The vehemence in her voice was matched by the fire in her eyes, and I backed off.

"That's not really what I mean, but I'm glad that your faith is strong because you're going to need it to beat this bastard. I meant that you should go call this in before we step in something and fuck up the crime scene. I don't want to have to fight a Cambion, a demon, *and* Paul from the crime lab."

It didn't work. Didn't lighten the mood at all. Flynn just looked at me and nodded. "You're right," she said. "I'll go call it in. Look around quickly for anything magical, then meet me outside."

"Are we going to talk about that before you go?" Glory asked, pointing the walls.

"I was really trying to think of a way not to," I said. "I need to not be the focus of the police investigation, and I don't know how to do that without destroying evidence."

"So destroy the evidence," Glory said.

Flynn and I whipped our heads around. "Why not?" the angel asked. "You know the police can't do anything to stop these killings. You also know there will only be one more Nephilim murdered, then a human, then either the Cambion will sacrifice itself or kill one of its own ilk to open the portal for Orobas, and then your world is probably destroyed."

"Unless we stop it," Flynn said.

"We'll stop it," I said.

"I hope you're right. I like this world, and most days I like some of its inhabitants," Glory replied.

"Thanks." I gave her a wry look.

"You're welcome. But you need to remember that Orobas has learned a lot in seven years, and he didn't like you much to begin with. After you spoiled his plan last time, he's had nothing but time to study you and find a way to beat you. It won't be as easy this time."

"Last time cost me one of my best friends," I reminded her.

"That's going to feel like chump change when he's through with you this time, Harker. Do you not get it?" Glory's voice rose as she went on. "He doesn't just want to win, he doesn't just want to open a portal to Hell anymore, he wants to destroy you and everything you've ever cared about."

"Then he's going to have to come heavy because I've learned a lot in seven years, too. And this time I know what I'm up against, and I might not be ready, but I'm a lot more prepared than I was last time. Becks, get outside. Call this in, and I'll give the place a quick scan to see if there's anything mystical that can lead us to the Cambion."

"Done. You've got about five minutes before the first units get here. Be somewhere else before that happens." Flynn turned around and walked out the main entrance.

I turned to Glory. "You think Orobas is going to kill her, don't you?"

"It would be the best way to incapacitate you. Especially now that you've admitted your feelings about her."

"It's been a long time, Glory. I didn't think I could feel like this again. After what happened the last time…"

"I know. Luke told me."

"You talk to my uncle?" Every time I think I can't possibly be surprised anymore, the universe reminds me that it is very large and very fucking weird. By doing something like having my guardian angel casually mention that she had a conversation with my uncle, Dracula.

"Not often. He doesn't like to be reminded that there is an afterlife. I'm honestly not sure if it's because he doesn't want to believe, or if he's afraid of where he'll end up."

"Does it really work that way?" I asked.

"You know I'm not going to tell you that, not even if I could."

"I know, but it's worth a shot," I replied with a little grin. "But what did Luke say?"

"He said that when Anna died—"

"Was murdered," I corrected. I could still feel her in my arms. Seventy years gone, and I felt it like it was yesterday. Kneeling in the snow, the cold seeping through my damp pants, holding Anna's body as her blood and life poured out onto the ground around us. Then looking up at the Nazi who stood there with his pistol still smoking.

He grinned at me, then said, "You should thank me, friend. Now there's one less Jewess stinking up the city."

That particular son of a bitch learned what his own shit smelled like from the inside when I took his own knife and opened him up from bellybutton to backbone. I hacked him almost in half, then literally ripped his head off. All I remembered after that was a lot of red on a lot of snow, and a lot of black uniforms torn to pieces before me. I have a flash of me holding a leg in one hand and an arm in the other, and I'm pretty sure they didn't start the day on the same people. I spent the rest of the war racking up a body count rivaling that of the Black Plague and drinking my way through Europe.

"It was a bad time," I said. "I lost myself for a long time, and I don't know what I would have done if there hadn't been a ready supply of Nazis to kill. If anything happens to Flynn, you should probably find a way to teleport me to a nice quiet terrorist camp, or a pirate ship in the Pacific. Because I don't know if there are enough bad guys in America for me to work through my anger on."

"Why don't we just work on not letting anything happen to her?" Glory said. I looked at her, and for the first time in our relationship, I really understood what she was there for. She watched over me to keep me from getting killed, sure, but she was also a failsafe. A last resort in case I went off the deep end. It made sense. I wasn't exactly known for my restraint, and my temper was obviously a work in progress. Glory was there to take me out if she had to, and I had no doubt that she would be more than capable if push came to shove.

"Yeah, that would be better for everybody," I agreed.

Everything okay in there? I hear sirens coming. Becks sent me a message through our mental link. She didn't use that much, preferring to keep some part of her head private at least. I felt the concern resonate through our connection and sent her a quick reassuring pulse of feeling.

Bending to the task at hand, I opened my Sight again, this time spreading my net wide and peered around the room. The intensity of the residual emotion almost bowled me over, most of it centered on the bodies of the boy and the priest on the communion table. Their souls were gone, but without the tatters of energy that I saw at the parking lot murder.

"They moved on, at least," I said, continuing my look around.

"Even Orobas himself can't touch the soul of a priest and an innocent in the House of the Lord," Glory said. "No creature under Heaven is that powerful. This man, and the child with him, were with God before the monster that did this had a chance to even reach for them." The angel's voice was cold, as if she knew how little comfort she had to give.

"There's nothing here," I said. I dropped my Sight. "This son of a bitch is good. If we're going to catch him before he completes his ritual, either he's got to make a mistake, or we're going to have to get lucky."

"Both things that seem more and more unlikely with every body we find," Glory said. "The police are here. You need to get outside before they find you. I'm going to be out of contact for a few hours. Try not to do anything egregiously stupid."

"No promises," I said, then ran for a side door. I stopped by the door and turned back to look at the sanctuary. "She's right," I muttered. I pulled in my will and focused my attention on the walls, on my name splattered across the gray stone in crimson essence. "*Erasa,*" I said, releasing my energy and watching the blood vanish, breaking up into dust and falling to the floor.

I pushed out of the door into the night, ready to move around the front of the church and pretend to be surprised when I re-entered that House of God turned House of Horrors.

Chapter Twelve

I WALKED TO THE FRONT OF THE CHURCH AND STOOD WITH BECKS AS Paul and the rest of the crime scene techs arrived.

"What do we have, Detective?" Paul asked.

"Double homicide, lots of blood. Similar MO to the Matthews case. I've called Agent Smith from Homeland; I assume he's going to want to claim jurisdiction of the case."

"You're damn right I am, Flynn," Smith's voice boomed from the street as he slid out of the Suburban, his ever-present coffee clutched in one hand. "Set up a perimeter. Get some of the locals to help you man it. Anybody but me, Harker, Flynn, or a tech tries to go into that church, shoot 'em."

The stocky ex-soldier stomped up to where we stood by the bottom of the steps. "Is the scene secure?" he asked.

"We didn't see anyone else around," I replied.

"Go ahead then," Smith said to Paul. He took a photographer and another tech into the church.

"You're gonna need a ladder," I called after them. "And a rope!"

"Bad?" Smith asked.

"The worst thing I've seen in a while," I said.

"That's pretty bad," Smith agreed. "You find anything the techs won't?"

"The killer left another message for me. My name written all over the walls in blood. I wiped it out before they got here. And both our victims were Nephilim. I saw the wings," I confirmed.

"So that's four that we know of. Our guy is either close to getting his freak on or he's ready," Smith observed.

"He either needs one more Nephilim, or he's killed one we don't know about, which I think is unlikely given the amount of taunting this dickhead has been doing to me. So let's assume that four is an accurate count of dead half-angels. That means he needs a human and a Cambion to complete the summoning."

"I doubt this one plans to use himself as the sacrifice," Flynn said. "Something about all the taunting just seems way more narcissistic than what you told me about the last killer. So I think he'll have a plan to find another Cambion to serve as the sacrifice. As far as a human goes, those are pretty simple."

"Yeah, only a million and a half of those running around this town. But Cambion are pretty thin on the ground," I said. "I don't know of any central repository for birth records of half-demons, though."

"And if he knows the trick of masking his true nature with Nephilim blood, then you wouldn't have any way of knowing who he was," Smith added.

"That's what we've got Paul for," I said. "At least, I hope so. Did your research turn up anything, Smitty?"

"A great big pile of fuck-all," he grunted. "There was plenty in Marlack's books about how to summon demons and how to communicate with the Lords of Hell, but not shit on demonspawn or anything useful in this case."

"Damned inconsiderate evil necromancers, not ever having useful shit in their spell books. Where's Giles and Willow when you need them?" I quipped.

Smith turned to me with a glare. "Do you take *anything* seriously, Harker? We've got people dying here, and you're making fucking *Buffy* references?"

"There's plenty I take seriously, Smitty. I'm pretty serious about catching the demonspawn son of a bitch that's writing my name in innocent people's blood all over my city. I'm serious about keeping the people I care about safe from the aforementioned demonspawn motherfucker, and if you really want to know how serious I can get, you can ask the plant elemental that I killed this afternoon by *setting myself on fire*. So yeah, there's shit I take seriously. But there's nothing so goddamn dark I can't crack a joke about it. I've fought demons hand-to-hand, beat the ever-loving fuck out of one of the Four Horsemen of the Apocalypse, and eaten Flynn's cooking. And I've come out of all that alive, if maybe a little scarred. So if you don't like me poking shit with a stick, too goddamn bad. Because even though I talk a lot of crap, when it hits the fan, I'm not just the smartass you want by your side, I'm the smartass you've got."

"That almost inspired confidence, Harker," Smith said with a grudging smile. "Especially the bit about surviving Flynn's cooking. That's some serious stamina there."

"If you two assholes are quite finished, Paul just radioed me. He's got something inside," Flynn said.

We pushed through the big doors with Smith in the lead. Paul stood at the front of the sanctuary holding an evidence bag. There was a small piece of white material in the bag stained red, presumably with blood.

"What have you got, Paul?" Smith asked.

"It appears to be a small fragment of torn wax-treated paper," the tech replied. "I found a similar piece under the body in Matthews this morning. At the time, I chalked it up to possibly being something in the parking lot under the body, but now that I have a sample to test against, I'll see if the two scraps match."

I stared at the bag, dialing in my enhanced vision to focus on any details that were apparent. The white paper was maybe a quarter inch on each side, with a hint of a deep blue on one torn corner. "What do you think it is?" I asked.

"I have no idea, Mr. Harker," Paul said. "But I will run tests to determine whether or not the two pieces match, then I will try to extrapolate the meaning of this blue design on the corner. I believe there was also a bit of blue on the piece from the parking lot."

"Good eye, Paul. Please let us all know as soon as you have something."

"Yes, ma'am."

"Anything else?"

"We have a tentative ID on the victims."

"That was fast," I said.

"I Googled the church directory. The priest is Gaines Pence. He's the senior priest here. The…"

"Child," I supplied.

Paul looked at me, stricken. "Yes. The child is Eugene Ziban. He's an altar boy here. He's…he was twelve years old. I'm sorry, Detective. I know it's not professional, but who would *do* something like this? This is…just awful."

Flynn put a hand on the young tech's shoulder. "I know, Paul. It's terrible. But sometimes people do terrible things to each other, and that's where we come in. We figure out who did these things, and we make damn sure they don't do them again."

"Ever," Smith said, his face grim.

"Did you find the kid's clothes?" I asked, changing the subject. Every head snapped to me. I didn't flinch. I needed to know.

"They're already bagged," Paul said.

"Did the kid…did Eugene have a wallet?"

"It's in the bag."

"Detective, I need you to come with me, open the bag, and get the kid's wallet. We need to maintain chain of evidence." I knew chain of evidence was useless because this killer was only ever going to face one judgement, and that wouldn't take place on Earth. But I needed Paul to think we were still working this like a mundane case.

"What do you want with his wallet, Harker?" Smith asked.

"Either in his wallet, or in his cell phone will be his emergency contact. Somebody has to tell his parents what happened." Those words hung heavy in the air for a long, silent moment before Flynn moved.

"That's for the ME to do. After the autopsy, when they can come positively identify the body," Becks said. "Not our gig, thank God."

Just then we heard a muffled *thump* from the rear of the sanctuary. Smith, Flynn, and I whirled around and drew our weapons, each pointing in a slightly different direction. There was nothing there, but when I listened harder, I could just barely pick up the sound of someone moving near the back of the church. I motioned for the others to follow me and for Paul to stay put. He nodded and crouched between two pews. His other techs looked around, then knelt behind the first row, taking what cover they could find.

Smith moved through a pew to one wall and Flynn the other while I moved silently up the center aisle, my Glock in hand and flashlight held crossways under the pistol, just like the professionals on TV all do. I didn't count on it doing shit to improve my mediocre aim, but at least I had a light. I figured if it was anything really dangerous, I wouldn't do shit with a pistol anyway, but it was good start.

We got to the back of the church and still saw nothing. I opened my Sight and scanned the area, and jackpot! I holstered my gun and pointed at the confessionals tucked into the back corner of the sanctuary. The smaller rooms looked like four freestanding closets, and my Sight told me there was someone alive in the one nearest the back wall. Someone whose daddy lounged around on clouds and played harp all day.

There's another Nephilim in the room, and it's hiding in the confessional, I sent to Flynn. *Cover me.* She nodded, and I held up a hand, palm out, for Smith to hold his position. I wanted Flynn where she could shoot the half-angel if it came at me and Smith where he could run it down if it got past me.

I didn't need to worry about either option. I yanked open the door, and the man that greeted me was the most terrified mostly human being I'd ever seen. He was a skinny dude in his early thirties, short, with thick glasses and lank dark hair plastered to his head with sweat.

"Please don't kill me!" the man cried as he curled up even further into a little ball on the floor of the confessional. "I don't want to die, please don't kill me! I've got so much to live for!"

Personal hygiene obviously wasn't one of his motivating factors for seeing another sunrise because this dude stank to high heaven. And not just fear-sweat, either. He had that acrid stink that long-time tweakers carry like a cologne, and I knew immediately why he was in the church.

I turned to Flynn and Smith. "It's okay, just a junkie who crawled into a dark safe place to sleep it off and then heard some things he couldn't un-hear. He's still kinda fucked up, from the drugs I mean. The rest of it would fuck up anybody, no matter how well-adjusted."

Flynn walked up behind me and looked down at the twitching, babbling mass of half-angel. "What's wrong with him? Oh, never mind, I smell the meth-funk."

"BO and cat piss, that's the smell of somebody who's been on crystal a long time," I replied. I knelt down to the tweaker's side. "Hey man, be cool. Nobody's gonna hurt you. Did you see who did this?"

He looked at me, eyes wide. "What are you, man? What *are* you?"

"I'm just a guy. Just a normal guy, like you. But I work for the government, and I need to know if you saw who did this."

He shook his head, and I felt disappointment well up inside me. "Nah, man, you ain't like me. And you ain't no normal dude, either. I don't know what you are, but I ain't never seen nothing like you. Me, I'm special. I ain't normal neither, but you ain't like me. You ain't like that other dude, though. You ain't black inside. You ain't gold like me, but you ain't black neither. You ain't red like the dog-dudes, or blue like the vampires, but you ain't gold. You're like, silver. Ain't never seen silver. She's pretty. She's green, with a little pink. You got some of that pink, too. You like her, don't you? Heh. It's okay, man. She likes you, too. I can see it. You got a taste, man? I could really use a little sumpin-sumpin, if you know what I mean."

"I don't have anything on me, man. I'm sorry. But you saw the other dude, the one that was here a little while ago?" I slipped into his freaked out cadence, but couldn't quite match his lingo.

"Yeah, man, I saw him. I saw right through the walls, man. He was fucked up, that dude. All black and red inside. And I heard him, too. Heard him super-loud." *Shit.* I looked into the addict's eyes. There was nothing there. No recognition, no nothing. I waved a hand in front of his face, and he snatched his head back, but didn't track my hand with his eyes. He was blind as a bat.

I turned to Flynn and Smith. "He's blind. He sees with Sight. That's what the color bullshit is about. He reads auras. He won't be worth a fuck as a witness, but he's Nephilim, and if our guy gets anywhere near him, he's toast."

"Three Nephilim in one church? That seems like a big coincidence, Harker," Flynn said.

"It probably isn't one," I replied. "If the guy in the pulpit was half-angel, people like him would naturally be drawn to the place just because it felt right. That priest's juju was all over this sanctuary, until he died, but until that, he was probably a beacon for the partially divine all over town."

"I guess that makes sense. But what do we do with your new buddy here?"

"I'll take him," Smith said. "I know of a couple of safe houses around town. I'll take him there and sit on him while your techs process the scene. When the sun comes up, I'll put a few agents on him and we can get back to the hunt."

"How does that sound?" I turned to the blind half-angel, but he was staring up at Smith, a look of pure horror on his face. He pointed to the agent, gasped once, and passed out. But not before he pissed himself, sending a stream of urine cascading into the floor and all over my leg.

"Thanks, Smitty. I knew you were a scary fuck, but did you have to make the guy piss all over my foot?"

"Sorry," Smith said. He didn't look very sorry. Like, not at all. Asshole. "I'll get a couple of my guys to load him into the car. Call me if your techs find anything bigger than a postage stamp." He stomped out the front door.

"Smith's gonna deal with this guy, and I gotta get some dry pants," I said to Flynn.

"I'll hang here with Paul and meet up with you when they're done."

"Your car's at my place," I said in a voice low enough to keep the techs from overhearing.

"Shit, you're right. Okay, I'll come with you, but I'm not washing your back again." But she smiled when she said it, so I had a little hope. And a boot full of tweaker piss, but at least I still had hope.

Chapter Thirteen

S**HE REALLY DIDN'T WASH MY BACK, BUT WHEN** I **GOT OUT OF THE SHOWER,**
I found hard-nosed Detective Rebecca Gail Flynn, scourge of Charlotte bad
guys and badass chick, curled up on top of my bedspread, fast asleep. I looked
over at the clock on my bedside table, saw the 3:45 a.m. in glowing blue
numbers, and decided that a few hours of shuteye would do us both good. The
rush I got off Luke's blood had long since run its course, and I was feeling the
weight of all my one hundred twenty years. I grabbed a spare blanket out of the
closet, lay down next to Becks, and pulled the blanket over us both.

Sunlight was streaking in the window when I felt the body beside me stir.
I looked over at Flynn, auburn curls splayed out on the pillow like a waterfall,
and felt something twist in my gut. I was so completely fucked. I'd fallen for
this human woman, hook, line, and sinker, and if anything happened to her,
I wasn't sure I'd ever be able to get myself back. So I just had to make sure
nothing happened to her. She stirred, stretching like a very contented cat, then
I watched her snap awake as she realized she wasn't in her own bed.

"Chill out, Becks, it's okay. You fell asleep while I took a shower, so I laid
down with you and we caught a few hours of shuteye. We both needed it."

"Why are you naked?" I looked down. Yup, naked.

"I walked in here after the shower, and you looked so cute I just decided to
let you sleep. Then I realized how much yesterday took out of me, so I decided
to sleep a little, too."

"Still doesn't explain the naked part."

"I got out of the shower, dried off, and got into bed. None of that requires
clothes. So I didn't wear any."

"You sleep naked?"

"You don't?"

She let out a sigh. "I've gotta pee. This is not the time to discuss sleepwear." She
got out of bed and stretched, pulling her shirt up just enough for me to get a glimpse
of her flat belly. I liked what I saw, a fact that was obvious and exacerbated by my

own need to relieve myself. Which, of course, got a lot more difficult the more I saw of the gorgeous detective. She clumped off to the bathroom and closed the door. I walked out into my den, then across the room to the guest bathroom. I thought about baseball long enough to be able to pee, then gave my face a quick wash in the sink.

I wandered back into the bedroom just as Flynn opened the bathroom door. "Jesus, Harker! Put that thing away, will you?"

"Yeah, yeah," I muttered. "If you see anything you've seen before, feel free to shoot it." I grabbed a pair of underwear out of the dresser and stepped into them. "Happy now?"

"Yeah, not bad. Face it, Harker, guys are just way sexier in underwear than out of it. I mean, face it, you've got a decent body, and you're actually a pretty good-looking guy."

"Glad to hear you don't think I'm a troll," I quipped, digging around for a pair of jeans. I put on my pants and an undershirt, then walked over to the closet and pulled out a black dress shirt. All my dress shirts are black, long sleeve, and basically identical. I was doing the whole "wear the same thing every day" long before Mark Zuckerberg started bragging about it. I always just thought I was fashion ignorant and basically lazy. I never knew I was simplifying my decision tree, or whatever bullshit other lazy fashion ignoramuses came up with.

"Oh no, you're a definite hottie, but all guys look a little silly naked."

"I'll take your word for it. I've spent a lot more time examining the naked female form, personally. And I'm a fan."

"Took you a hundred years to figure that out, huh?" She grinned at me.

"Nah, I developed a pretty good theory in my first twenty years. The last century has just been additional research. But I'm finally ready to announce my findings—I like naked women."

"Yeah, better change that plural to singular, if you want to see *this* woman naked again." I knew I wasn't in trouble because she was still smiling. As long as I kept her laughing, I was okay.

"You've got a deal. I like naked *woman*."

"Good to hear. Now do you have a new toothbrush lying around? My mouth feels like death."

"Under the sink."

She went back into the bathroom, leaving the door open this time. I followed her in, assuming the open door was something of an invitation. I grabbed my own toothbrush and proceeded to chisel the remnants of the day before out of my mouth, then put a little gel in my hair to tame the bedhead and gave my stubble a quick glance and promise to tend to the thicket as soon as we caught the murderer.

"What's the plan?" Flynn asked, sitting on my bed to put her shoes on.

I grabbed a fresh pair of Doc Martens from the closet and sat next to her to put them on. If there's anything running around the world with Dracula for a mentor will teach you, it's to have spare clothes around. The bootful of tweaker piss I got in my boot the night before wasn't even on the top ten list of most disgusting things to ever happen to my wardrobe.

I looked over at Flynn. "We'll grab a quick breakfast, then call Smitty and see if the junkie we found at the church has told him anything."

"Do you think we can use that guy? He was pretty nuts, and he didn't actually see anything."

"Remember, Becks, we aren't looking at a burden of proof that will stand up in a court of law. We just need to figure this shit out beyond our reasonable doubt, and then put two in the Cambion's head."

"I don't like this vigilante shit, Harker. We're the good guys; we're supposed to be better than this."

I turned to her and put on my serious face. "No, *you're* the good guys. I'm the guy who gets shit done. Sometimes I work with the good guys, and my endgame is always tilted toward the side of the angels, but a lot of rules either don't apply to me or can't be applied to the things I hunt. This is one of those things. A Cambion with the knowledge to open a portal to Hell? Even if we had evidence to get an arrest and a conviction, we can't put that thing in the general population in prison. And we sure as hell can't send it to a psych ward where it will have all that disturbed mental energy to feed off of. No, Becks, this is one of those black and white times when it's kill this motherfucker or a lot of innocent people die."

"Doesn't mean I have to like it."

"You wouldn't be the woman I fell in love with if you did. We all need a moral compass, Becks. You're mine."

"Great, I'm Jiminy Cricket."

"Could be worse, you could be my fairy godmother. Now let's go grab some breakfast and then find this asshole. By my reckoning, the Cambion only needs one more Nephilim and then a couple other sacrifices for the ritual, which is probably scheduled for some time in the next three nights."

"Why the next three? I thought the Solstice was tomorrow?"

"Solstice is like the full moon. It's more a rough period of time than a specific date on the calendar. Astronomically, it's about when the sun and Earth are either at their nearest or farthest points. That's a very specific moment, but magically, there's a little gray area on either side of the exact moment, basically because ancient druids and wizards and witches didn't have much in the way of high-tech astronomical tools, but they could feel the strengthening of our connection either to the lands of light or the lands of shadow. The summer solstice is specifically better for casting lighter spells, but all magic is strengthened. The winter solstice, which we're fast approaching, is one of those times when the physical plane is in much greater contact with the shadow planes, so it's easier to cast darker magic."

"Like opening a portal to Hell," Flynn added.

"Exactly. So since we're more closely contacting the shadow planes right now, there's a period of about seventy-two hours that our Cambion has to work with."

"So how did you know when to catch him last time?"

"I got lucky. I read a bunch of Dark Ages bullshit about how the ceremony had to be done at midnight, and I bought it one hundred percent. Fortunately for me, Sponholz bought it, too. Otherwise I don't think we'd be having this conversation."

"So you saved the world just by getting lucky?"

"Happens more often than you'd think," I said. I stood up and held out my hand. "Come on, chickadee, let's go get some breakfast. This pile of sexy requires coffee to function. And bacon. Then we can go visit our ear-witness at the safe house. Smitty texted me the address while we were asleep."

"Hmmm, a man that runs on caffeine and bacon. That's my kind of guy." She stood, gave me a quick kiss, and swooped past me out the bedroom door. I stood there for a second, wondering if I'd ever get used to having a woman that ridiculously pretty, smart, and badass interested in me. I decided the answer was "probably not," and that I was completely fine with that.

Chapter Fourteen

I WAS ON MY SECOND HELPING OF BACON WHEN HE WALKED IN. HE WAS disheveled, looking like he hadn't slept in a couple days, and his eyes were red. I was sitting in IHOP with my chair facing the door, and I pegged him for trouble the second he pushed through the door. His shirt was untucked, and his socks didn't match, but that wasn't what gave it away. No, it was the air of frantic emptiness he carried with him like his own personal cross. This was a guy that had nothing left to lose, and that made him very dangerous, even if he was completely human.

I held up a hand to interrupt Flynn talking about a new DNA report that Paul just sent to her phone. "Becks." I kept my voice low but put enough force behind it that her head snapped up.

"What's wrong?" I don't know if she read my voice or felt the concern through our mental link, but her phone was instantly forgotten.

"The guy that just came in. He's trouble."

Flynn nodded, then said loudly, "Okay, honey. Let me just go wash my hands and we can go." She stood up and walked past me to the restrooms. That not only got her out of the line of fire if something went to shit, it also put her on her feet and mobile enough to deal with a threat if one arose.

Her movement caught the man's attention, and he called out to her. "Are you Detective Flynn?" I felt her freeze right behind me and turn. My attention was divided between the man and the inertia-dampening spell I was muttering under my breath.

"I'm Detective Flynn," Becks said, not moving any closer. That kept her out of my way if I needed to do something and still kept the guy's attention on her. "What can I do for you?"

"You can tell me why you're in here eating breakfast while my son is lying the morgue, for one thing."

The man's voice shook. So did his hands, and I could see that he was barely holding on. *Shit.* It hit me then. He was the altar boy's father. What the fuck was he doing here? And how the fuck did he know we were here?

"Sir, I assure you, the department is doing everything we can to find out what happened to your son, and as soon as we know anything—"

"Don't you lie to me, bitch! I see you in here, eating fucking pancakes with your asshole boyfriend instead of out there figuring out who killed my boy!"

"Sir, Mr. Harker is an investigator with Homeland Security. He is assisting in our investigation. We believe that your son's death may be connected to others in the area, and we are putting all our resources—"

"Goddammit, bitch, I said shut up!" He pulled a pistol out of his pocket, and I realized I probably wasn't getting that refill on my coffee.

I got up and held up both hands, palms toward him so he could see that I was unarmed, at least as far as he probably considered "armed." "Calm down, sir. We don't want anybody to get hurt here."

"Hurt? *HURT?!?*" he screeched. "You didn't see your little boy lying dead on a table in the morgue. No, you were here having breakfast with this idiot cop, chatting about the goddamn weather like nothing bad ever happened!"

No, I saw your little boy hanging from a chandelier with nails in his hands, but we spared you from that. That's what ran through my head. What came out of my mouth was some nonsense meant to be reassuring but really only intended to give Flynn enough time to get her hand on her service weapon.

Whatever I said, it didn't calm him down one bit. I suppose nothing could, and I didn't really blame him for that. He looked back to Rebecca. "What are you doing here, bitch?"

"Sir…Sir!" This time I shouted, and I covered most of the distance between us in two quick steps. Sometimes having Dracula's blood in your veins is really handy.

His head snapped to me, and he stepped backwards, just out of my reach. He trained the gun on me. "Stay back, asshole."

"I'll stay back, but you call Detective Flynn a bitch one more time, and one of us is going to shoot you. I don't make any promises about which one it will be, but watch your mouth."

"Fuck you," he spat at me. "My boy is dead, do you hear me? Dead!"

"I don't have to hear you," I said. "I saw. I saw it, and I'm sorry. No parent should ever have to go through that. But we are only human, and we have to eat. And we have to sleep. Because if we don't, we can't do our jobs, and then nobody finds the son of a bitch that killed your boy."

He looked like he was wavering, and I thought I had him. I thought I was reaching him, but then somebody pushed through the front door, and the door chime rang out, and his eyes went wide and paranoid again, and he lost it.

"You're just trying to distract me! You don't care about my boy! You don't care about anything!" He raised the pistol, and I went for him. I slapped the gun out of his hand, but not before he got a shot off. It was a little gun, maybe a .22. It sounded more like a loud handclap than a gunshot in the restaurant. I slapped his hand, the gun went to the floor, and I punched the distraught father in the jaw. He was out before he hit the ground, and I turned around to make sure the errant bullet hadn't hurt anyone.

"Is everyone okay?" I asked. A room full of people nodded back at me. "Was anyone hurt?" The same room full of people shook their heads. "Does anyone really have to pee right now?" Half the room got up *en masse* and bolted for the restrooms.

"Detective, will you get some uniforms in here to take this gentleman to the station? And they'll probably need to get statements from everyone here. As soon as they get here, we've got to go. As he so vehemently reminded us, we have a murderer to catch."

"Actually, I think you're going to the hospital," Flynn said, pulling out her cell phone. "Call 911," she said to the nice lady at the cash register.

"Why would I…*oowwwww!*" I looked down at my left arm and saw the shirt sleeve soaked with blood. "Did that son of a bitch *shoot* me?"

"If not, then you *really* need to see a doctor because you're bleeding out of your skin for no reason. Which might be even worse than getting shot," was Flynn's response. That's my girl, always helpful. I felt her concern, though, so I sent reassuring feelings to let her know I didn't think it was all that serious.

I moved my arm around. It hurt, but really not too bad. A lot less than any of the other times I'd been shot, even wearing a Kevlar vest. "I don't think he hit anything vital, but I'd like to get the bleeding stopped."

Flynn knelt to the unconscious man, checked his pulse and his pupils to make sure I hadn't accidentally killed him. Satisfied with what she found, she rolled the man over onto his stomach. When she was done, she waved me over to a nearby table.

"Come here," she said. "Sit." I sat. Flynn reached into her pocket and pulled out a small pocketknife. She cut the sleeve off my shirt and rolled up my t-shirt.

"I could have taken that off, you know."

"It was ruined anyway," she replied, not looking up from my arm. "Bullet holes and bloodstains are the end of most clothes."

"Some of my favorite shirts have bullet holes and bloodstains," I protested. She ignored me, which was probably safer for me anyway.

"This doesn't look too bad. The bullet just grazed you, but you should still have it cleaned and bandaged, so you don't get an infection."

"I don't get infections," I said, keeping my voice down.

"Can we skip the part where you're all macho and don't want to go to the hospital and go straight to the part where you do what I say?"

I took a second to think about it, then said, "Yeah, that's fine, but I'm driving myself."

"Take a cab. You're losing blood. But there is this nice ambulance right outside."

I looked out the big windows, and sure enough, a pair of EMTs were running for the front door. I let out a sigh and waited for them to fuss over me and eventually load me into the ambulance for the three-minute ride to the nearest hospital.

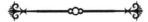

At least they didn't make me wear a stupid gown once I got to the hospital. The nurses just sat me back in an exam room with a big bandage on my arm waiting for an ER doc to get loose and deal with me. I had run through all my emails, checked my Facebook twice (doesn't take long when you only have a dozen friends and half of them are scam accounts) and read the opening of a new Rick Gualtieri novel by the time the doc came in. He was a hefty Asian dude with a big smiling round face and a lab coat that probably never met in the middle.

"Good morning!" he proclaimed, gesturing broadly with his left hand. His right was clutching a big white-and-blue cup from WhattaBean, the snazzy coffee shop a couple blocks away. Popular with bankers, WhattaBean proudly proclaimed that it had the best coffee beans anywhere, harvested by hand from Argentina. I didn't see any real difference in their coffee and the swill at the Exxon station, except for the four-dollar price tag, but coffee nerds like Smitty swore by the stuff.

"I'm Doctor Cho. What can we do for you this morning?"

"I got a little shot. I need a few stitches, then I've got to find a murderer. So can we move this along, Doc?"

The doc seemed a little offended for a moment, then I could almost see him actually process the words that came before "hurry the fuck up." He looked at my face, then at the badge I held up with my right hand, and nodded.

"Absolutely. I can get you out of here and back on the case, as it were, in just a few minutes. Let me just clean and numb the wound, then we'll get this stitched up and you can be on your way. Do you think you'll need a prescription for pain?"

"I won't ever say no to a few Vicodin," I replied.

"Not a problem. You might feel a little pinch," he said, as he turned and set his coffee cup on the table behind him. Something tickled in the back of my head, then he stabbed me in the arm with a goddamn burning railroad spike and I almost came off the exam table.

"Jesus fucking Christ, Doc, what the fucking *fuck?*" I looked down at my arm, and he was just pulling a tiny needle out of it.

"Sorry, sometimes the Novocain gives off a slight burning sensation when it goes in," the inscrutable Asian master of understatement said. I turned my head so I didn't have to watch him sew my flesh back together and thought about all the other scars littering my body and the interesting and mundane ways I'd acquired them.

A few minutes later, he slapped some Steri-strips over the wound and pronounced me done. "Keep that clean and leave the strips on until they fall off on their own. Make an appointment with your primary care physician for a follow-up in a week to ten days, and good luck catching whoever you're after," the doc said.

I thanked him, we shook hands, and he picked up his coffee cup and tilted it up, knocking back the last swallow. Then he pitched the empty cup in the trash can and walked out. I hopped off the exam table and stepped toward the door, then froze.

I stared at the coffee cup in the trash, glaring up at me like a beacon. I reached down and picked up the cup, turning it over and over in my hands. The blue-and-white swirl pattern spun in my hands, undulating as I turned the cup this way and that.

"Son of a bitch…" I whispered.

"Excuse me?" the nurse asked.

"I gotta go." I pushed past her out the door and headed down the hall toward the Emergency Room exit.

"Sir! You have to sign this paperwork before you can leave!" the little nurse called after me.

"National security, sorry!" I yelled back to her. I was in the hall and moving fast. An overweight security guard stood up off his stool and moved like he thought he was going to intercept me but sat back down when he saw the badge clipped to my belt. He slapped the automatic door opener, and I bolted through the double doors into the waiting room.

I yanked my cell phone out and dialed Paul the second I was outside and away from a hundred prying ears and coughing sick people.

"Crime lab, Paul speaking." He answered the phone like a banker, but he was as solid a tech as I'd seen.

"Paul, it's Harker. I need to ask you about the scrap of paper you found at the parking lot murder," I said.

"I've processed it. What do you need to know?"

"Were there any substances found on it?"

"I found blood from the victim, some traces of silica from the asphalt, and coffee."

"What about wax?"

"What about it?" Paul asked.

"Was the paper coated with wax?"

"Yes."

"Was it a coffee cup?"

"It certainly could be, although I suppose there are other things it could be as well."

"Was there coffee and wax on the paper you found at the church?"

"Yes, and it was an identical blend."

"What does that mean?"

"The similarities in the coffee means that the beans were harvested from the same region, specifically near Buenos Aires."

"That's in Argentina, right?" My education focused a lot more on Europe than South America. I could find Lichtenstein blindfolded from the Black Forest, but I was a little soft on Argentina.

"Yes. Why?"

"I think it may become relevant," I said, looking down at the cup in my hand. "Thanks, Paul." I hung up and dialed Flynn.

"How's the arm?"

"Come get me. I'm outside the ER on Caswell."

"Harker, I'm a little—"

"I know who it is, and we've got to move. I can't talk over the phone. Get here, *now*."

I paced in front of the Emergency Room entrance for five minutes or so before Flynn pulled up, lights and siren rolling. I opened the door and slid in.

"Drive. We've got to get to South Boulevard."

"What's on South?"

"That godawful big pink building. The safe house that's supposed to have our witness is there. But I'm willing to bet anything it's empty." I held up the coffee cup. "Look familiar?"

"Yeah, it's from WhattaBean, that hipster coffee place Smith loves so much."

"It's also the exact piece of paper that was found underneath our parking lot victim. It was also the type of scrap of paper that was by the priest's body last night. Paul matched the analysis of the coffee to the same crop in Argentina."

"They can do that?"

"Fuck if I know, but Paul says they can, and that's good enough for me."

Flynn didn't say anything for a long moment. "What are you saying, Harker?"

"I'm saying that Agent John Smith is the Cambion, and we have to find him before he kills our Nephilim eyewitness and opens a doorway to Hell."

Chapter Fifteen

I NAVIGATED WHILE FLYNN DROVE LIKE A BAT OUT OF HELL. THE "SAFE house" was actually a condo in a huge pink monstrosity of a skyscraper in Charlotte's South End, a newish neighborhood that developed from the corridor of strip clubs and local businesses. There were still a few local stalwarts, like Mr. C's diner and the Leather and Lace topless bar, but most of the place was taken over with sterile construction projects instead of cool old buildings. With the siren going, it only took us about five minutes to get there from the hospital, and we left the car in the front of the building and bolted inside.

I flashed my badge at the fat guy behind the counter and said, "Is Agent Smith here?"

The guard, whose polished name badge designated as "Marvin," hopped right up and inspected my badge. He gave it a thorough looking over before he handed it back to me and stood up. "Smith? Mean guy, crew cut going gray?"

"Yeah, that's him," I said.

"No sir, I haven't seen him in weeks. Not since we had a witness in that terrorism case in DC. They stashed one of the witnesses here for a couple days. I stood guard outside her door." I was pretty sure that his idea of "standing guard" involved a whole lot of sitting, but I didn't argue.

"Has anyone brought a witness in here today? What about last night?"

"I just came on at eight, but there's nothing in the logs about a new John or Jane Doe. That's what we call the people that want their identities hidden." He grinned like it was his original thought or something. I didn't bother correcting him.

"Let me see your log book," Rebecca asked. He handed her a blue three-ring binder open to this morning's visitor logs. We flipped pages back an extra day, but there was no entry showing Smith or any John Doe coming into the building.

"Is there another entrance?" Flynn asked.

"Yeah, there's a back stairwell, but nobody is supposed to use it. Everybody's gotta come through here and get logged right. And I don't let anybody through without signing in, unless they got a key card." He seemed very proud of his adherence to the rules, and

I started to think that he might have some slight learning disability or something. And that would make him easier for an asshole like Smith to take advantage of.

"Does Agent Smith have a key card?" I asked.

"Yeah, but only to the condo. He doesn't get one to the front door, on account of the condo not really being his and it belonging to the government. So I have to get up and let him in whenever he comes here."

"But the overnight guy might not have made Agent Smith sign the book if he came in, right?" There was no way Smith was getting past this guy without signing a book, but maybe a bribe to the other guard would keep him off the books.

"Well…maybe not. He was supposed to, but I wasn't here, so I don't know." Marvin avoided eye contact like the plague, so I thought I might be on to something.

"Does the night guy ever bend the rules for Agent Smith or other people?" I asked. I had to keep the pressure on if we were going to find Smith, and the clock was ticking.

"Sometimes he does favors for people. He says it's not really against the rules if the people are allowed to be here anyway, and Gerald is real smart, so I try to do what he says." Marvin was getting a little overwrought, so I nodded to Flynn.

She leaned her elbows onto the raised front of the desk. "It's okay, Marvin, you aren't going to get into trouble. We just need to see if Agent Smith is in the condo. But we don't have a key. Can you take us up there and show us the condo? Agent Smith or the man with him might be in trouble, and we need to get into that condo."

"I'm sorry, ma'am, I can't open the condo for anyone but Agent Smith."

I held out my badge. "Marvin, we work with Agent Smith. He may be hurt and need help. Or the man he brought here might be hurt. You need to take us to that condo, and you need to do it right now." I put on my sternest voice, and Marvin responded to the authority I pretended to have. Good thing, too. My next step was going to be knocking him right the fuck out and stealing his keys. This was easier on Marvin's head and easier on my fist.

Marvin nodded, and I led him to the elevator. We rode up six floors then followed Marvin to the door of the condo. He looked back at me, his eyes a little wide. I gave him a reassuring nod, and he swiped a keycard through the door.

I smelled it the second the door cracked. "Stay here, Marvin. Do not let anyone come into this room, no matter who, unless one of us tells you. Okay?"

Marvin stood ramrod straight and snapped off a rough salute. "Yes, sir!" I knew that nothing was getting through that door unless it killed Marvin, so I'd at least have a few seconds' warning. I motioned for Flynn to follow me, and I drew my pistol.

I slammed the door open and ran through in a crouch, sweeping the gun barrel from side to side as I went in, checking the room for threats. When the mundane world appeared secure, I opened my Sight and checked the Otherworld. Nothing.

Nothing except the fading golden wings around the body of our witness, who sat tied to a chair in the middle of the den, his throat cut from ear to ear. The smell of death was heavy, but it was all blood and bodily fluids, no ripe smell of decomposition. I walked over to the body and felt his forehead.

"He's cold. Been dead a couple hours at least." It was obvious that he was our last Nephilim sacrifice, even without my Sight. His throat was cut almost to the bone, but there wasn't nearly enough blood on the carpet to match up to the severity of the crime.

"But not more than that. It's only been five hours since we left Smith at the church."

"Yeah, I figure he brought this guy here right away, made him comfortable, and then killed him."

"There was no making this guy comfortable, Harker. He knew Smith was the killer. Remember at the church? As soon as Smith opened his mouth, this poor bastard pissed himself, then passed out in fear. He knew what was up, and we were just too stupid to see it."

She was right. Too stupid, too slow, too whatever. Just never quite good enough. Not for Becks' dad, not for Bolton, not for this poor son of a bitch. Well, that shit was about to be over. Once and for all. But we had to move, and now. Smith now had all the angel blood he needed to complete the ritual, so once he found a human to murder and just a tiny bit of Cambion blood, which he could supply in spades, the entire Queen City was in deep shit.

I shook myself out of my little pity party and turned to Flynn. "Okay, how do we find him?"

"What?" She looked at me, confused.

"You're a detective. This is your part. My part comes when we find him, and I send him to Hell to meet his daddy."

Flynn stared at me for a second, then nodded. "Okay, yeah. Let me think… he was in a Homeland Security Suburban when he left the crime scene. If it's still here, we can trace it."

"Parking deck," I said, already moving for the door. "Call this in. But let's find some way to keep it locked down as much as we can. If Smith is our Cambion, he might not be the only one in Homeland."

Rebecca froze in mid-stride at that, then I saw the logic of it flicker across her face. "Fuck."

"Yeah, exactly."

We headed for the elevator, leaving Marvin behind to stand guard until Paul and his crew arrived. The parking garage was a small thing, underneath the condos. It would have been very difficult for a Suburban to navigate, so we checked the oversize vehicle area first.

My shoulders sagged when I saw the black behemoth with government plates sitting astride two parking spaces like it owned the building. "Goddammit," I swore. "We needed a break."

"Be chill, Harker. I got this," Flynn said, moving to the car. She drew her pistol as she approached. *There's somebody behind the wheel. Looks too big to be Smith*, I heard in my head.

I drew my Glock and moved to the opposite side of the SUV. *I see him. You cover him, I'll yank open the door.* I did just that, pulling the door almost off the hinges as Flynn moved into position opposite me. The man in the car didn't budge, probably because he was dead. He wasn't a sacrifice, but he was just as dead. He was a big man, about the size of one of Smith's Homeland Security driver-goons, wearing what looked like an expensive track suit. His neck was broken, and his head twisted all the way around so he was staring at the back of the vehicle.

"You better keep an eye out behind you, motherfucker," I muttered at the absent Smith. I slammed the car door. "*Fuck!*" I punched the side of the Suburban, leaving a dent.

"Feel better?" Flynn asked.

"No. Now I'm pissed off and my hand hurts."

"Well, I got nothing for the hand, but I might be able to help with the other." I walked around the car to where she stood with the driver's door open. "What's the story?"

She held up a wallet. "Our victim is one Timothy Lang. He lived upstairs."

"And?" I asked.

"And…that means he was probably on his way to his car when Smith ran into him. I'm guessing Smith took Mr. Lang's car so we couldn't just track the Suburban, and then killed him because he's a dick."

"Yeah, no reason to kill this guy," I agreed.

"Except that Smith's a demon."

"Half-demon."

"Whatever. Anyway, now we just need a little old-fashioned police work and a little bit of luck. Okay, a lot of luck, but it's about all we've got right now." She pressed a button on her phone, then another one to turn it on speaker.

"CMPD technical operations, what can I do for you, Detective?" Nobody *ever* answers the phone that happy to hear from me. Just shows how much nicer Becks is than me, I guess.

"Mandy, I need a favor," Flynn said.

"Anything you need, Detective." Jesus, maybe I should try this whole "being nice to people shit sometime." Nah.

"I need to know vehicle registration info for a Timothy Lang. He lives in The Arlington."

"Is that the big ugly pink building?"

"Yeah, that's the one."

"Okay, I have a Cadillac Escalade registered to that name and that address."

"Perfect. Can you activate the onboard assistance on that car?"

"I need to know what it's for, Detective. We can, but we're only supposed to—"

"Timothy Lang has been murdered and stuffed in the car used by a suspect in two murders at St. Peter's last night. If we can locate Lang's vehicle, we can probably close three or more murders before lunch." That's another part of the whole "being nice" thing that just never occurred to me—explaining yourself. I would have just yelled at the poor woman on the other end of the phone until she did what I wanted. Becks' explanation took about the same amount of time, and people are easier to understand when they aren't sobbing into the telephone. I really might have to give this whole "being nice" thing a try.

"No problem, Detective. Okay, I've got it."

I opened my phone, ready to input the address. Turns out I didn't need to. I knew how to get to that house from anywhere in the city. Flynn and I exchanged a look, then hauled ass to her car as she hung up with the tech. We slammed the doors shut and Flynn peeled out onto South Boulevard, heading for the one place Smith could go to hit me in the gut the hardest.

His GPS placed his car parked right outside my Uncle Luke's house.

Chapter Sixteen

WE GOT THERE IN LESS THAN FIFTEEN MINUTES, BUT WE WERE STILL running late. We pulled up in front of Luke's house to find a half dozen thugs in cheap suits standing in front of the house.

"Stay here until I clear a path," I said to Flynn.

"I'll cover you," she replied, slewing the car sideways to put the driver's door away from the house.

I got out and started moving toward the door. Two no-necks closed ranks, and I moved them, forcibly and with extreme prejudice. They landed hard on the front lawn, and four more came at me.

"*Incendiare!*" I said, and a nimbus of fire engulfed my fists. "Come get some, fucktards."

They did. Two of them drew collapsible batons from their belts and went for my legs, while one took a step back and drew a gun. The last one just tried to bull-rush me, but I braced myself and dumped him on his ass with a picture-perfect hip toss. Thirty years of judo classes and pro wrestling videos and I might have picked up a few things.

Flynn put down the guy with the gun, drilling him right between the eyes with her Smith & Wesson .40 service pistol. I caught one baton in my right hand, the other in my left, and channeled my will to send heat down the metal rods. The fire vanished from my hands as the radiant energy poured into the sticks, and the thugs screamed as their weapons suddenly burned the fuck out of their palms. Getting burned is no fun, as I recalled from recent unpleasant experience.

I dropped the baton in my left hand, flipped the right-hand baton around so I held it by the grip, and, insulated from my own heat by magic, I knocked both goons out cold with shots to the head. I didn't give a shit if they were unconscious or dead. They were between me and my uncle, and that was not where they wanted to be. I looked around, saw no more bad guys, and stepped up onto the porch.

Only to get knocked back a good ten feet onto my ass when Orobas stepped *through* the door. And when I say stepped through the door, I mean he put a foot into the door, kicked it to splinters, and stepped through the door. He almost stepped through me as well, but I wasn't as well anchored to the porch, so I just sprawled on the grass instead.

Orobas stood in the doorway grinning down at me. His demon form was pretty unnerving, since he looked like every damn picture of a demon I'd ever seen, what with the red skin, goat legs, bat wings, and big fucking fangs and all. "I've missed you, Quincy Harker. It will feel good to rend your flesh beneath my fingers and pick my teeth with your shinbones."

"I'm glad you're so concerned with oral hygiene these days, Orobas. From what I remember of our last little argument, your breath smelled like you'd been brushing with a giraffe dick and rinsing with raw sewage." I drew my Glock and squeezed off a dozen rounds. Flynn took my shooting as a sign to do the same, and she put ten bullets in the center of Orobas' chest.

It didn't do shit. He jerked back with each impact, but just barely. The distraction was all I needed, though. I got to my feet and charged Orobas. I caught him around the waist in a perfect tackle that took both of us to the ground. I pushed off with my feet and arms and flipped right through the tackle and back up onto my feet, pulling some real *Matrix* shit that normal people just can't do.

Orobas cleaned my clock and embarrassed me the last time we scrapped, but I learned a few things since then. I reached into a coat pocket and grabbed a small box, then slipped on the rings inside. One plain silver band on each middle finger, no adornment, no jewels, just a plain band of silver metal. That happened to be blessed by the Pope and the Dalai Lama. There aren't a whole lot of things those guys agree on, but the concept that demons on Earth is a bad thing is one everybody can get behind.

Then I reached behind my back and unclipped a black cylinder from my belt. I brought it around in front of me and focused my will on the tube. A brilliant white beam of light extended from the hilt with a thrumming sound.

"A lightsaber, Harker?" Orobas said with a smirk. "I don't think Obi Wan Kenobi can save you this time."

"How about a soulsaber, dickhead?" I asked, advancing on him, my blade of concentrated mystical energy weaving patterns of pure magic in the air before me.

"How did a two-bit hack like you learn to conjure a soul blade? That magic has been lost to men since…that fucking winged bitch!"

"That's Miz Winged Bitch to you, fangboy." Glory descended behind me in a shaft of light whiter and brighter than even my soulsaber. Which wasn't all that surprising when you consider that her light was a conduit to the divine, and my light was generated by my admittedly spotty soul. She was a gleaming vision of righteous fury in chain mail and swinging a sword of fire.

"Kill them!" Orobas screamed. "No one enters the house until the ritual is complete!" *Fuck.* That meant the ritual had already begun. We needed to end this shit, and now. Orobas waved a hand, and a blade of pure darkness appeared in his hand. The demon charged Glory, and they came together with a concussion like a dozen mortars all landing at once. Then the rest of Orobas' minions charged me, and it was on.

Only thing between me and the front door of Uncle Luke's house was half a dozen goons with bats and knives. No problem, right? Usually not, but these goons were also Cambion that had fully embraced their demon side and taken on exceptional strength and agility in exchange for the human half of their souls. They weren't full-on demons, but they weren't normal men, either.

I ducked under a wild swing by the first goon, only to find my jaw directly in the path of the second asshole's bat. I spun to one side, lashing out with my magical blade. I heard a scream as the first demonspawn vanished in a flash of light, then got stood up by a kick to the shoulder from the first goon.

I heard the flat *crack-crack* of a semiautomatic pistol and knew that Rebecca had joined the fight. A splash of blood across my face was the only warning I got when she shot a giant thug about to crush my head with a pool cue, but as soon as he dropped, another one took his place. I winnowed the cadre of asshole demon helpers down to a pair of the smartest ones before they managed to crack a bat down on my right wrist and disarm me. I knelt on the ground in front of the Cambion and closed my eyes against the home run I knew he was about to swing at my temple, but the blow never landed.

Instead there was a screech of brakes, then a crash of crumpling metal as a black Hummer pulled up beside Flynn and a giant black Adonis kicked the driver's side door out. The door flew almost ten feet, and a figure stepped out of the truck with a football in his hands. He hurled the football at the head of the goon nearest me, and the half-demon went down, knocked completely unconscious. In all my days, I never, ever expected to be rescued by a hitchhiker demon riding the body of a franchise quarterback. But that's exactly what happened. He reached back into the truck and hauled out football after football, flinging each one at a Cambion and either knocking it out or killing it outright.

"*WHERE IS SHE, YOU SON OF A BITCH!*" Mort yelled, and I worried for the QB's ability to call signals in the next game.

Orobas turned to Mort and smiled. "Mortivoid, my dear boy, whoever do you mean?"

Mort in the football player's body covered the distance to Orobas in about five seconds, and he leveled the demon with an uppercut that would have killed a human. As it was, Orobas flew back several feet and crashed into the steps of Luke's porch.

"Where is she, you fire-sucking son of a spite demon!" Mort stalked over to where Orobas lay on the steps and stood over him, fists clenching and unclenching with every furious breath.

"She's inside, Mortivoid. What's left of her, that is," Orobas said, looking up at Mort with a smile. "I mentioned that you would regret siding with this piece of human excrement, didn't I? It took me almost seven years to find the relationship, but once I began to suspect, it was obvious."

"Get her out here. Now."

"Of course. Anything for such an old friend." Orobas stood, and Mort took a step back.

Glory stepped forward, her sword raised, but Mort raised a hand. "Not now, Glory. Not until he gives me my…until he gives me Christy."

"Motherfucker," I whispered. I looked at Mort. "She's your daughter. Oh, fuck. That means…"

"Yes, Quincy, it means she is a Cambion, and one of the final components for the spell," Orobas said with a smile. He waved his hands, and Christy appeared, standing in front of Mort.

"Oh, baby, I was so worried about you…" Mort's voice trailed off as he saw it. We all saw it at the same time. Christy stood there in front of us, held in place by Orobas' hand on her shoulder. But nothing held her head as it slowly tipped forward to land on the ground at Mort's feet.

The lifeless eyes of the Cambion that I almost considered a friend stared sightlessly up at me, and I tore my eyes away from her to glare at Orobas. He stood behind Christy's headless body, grinning at me over her neck like some perverted carnival cutout picture booth.

"You son of a *bitch*!" I screamed and raised my soulsaber. Orobas knocked me flat with a casual swipe of his hand, then shoved Christy's body at Mort. The demon riding inside the quarterback dropped to his knees, sobbing like a man who's lost the only thing on any plane of existence he ever cared about. Which he probably had.

Glory went at Orobas, her sword flaming again. She crashed into the demon and turned her head to me. "Harker, get in there! You have to stop Smith before he finishes the ritual, or everything we've ever done was for nothing."

I looked back at Flynn to tell her to cover the door and saw her sitting on the ground with one last Cambion goon standing over her. He held a knife in one hand, and I saw the blood drip from the blade onto the ground.

"Becca!" I screamed, and ran for her. The Cambion turned toward me, a nasty smile on his face, and I shouted "*Separato!*" without breaking stride. He kinda exploded. It looked a lot like he was drawn and quartered, only there were no horses, and he fell into a lot more parts.

I got to Flynn's side and knelt there, patting her face and sobbing. "Becks, Becca, baby, please no. I can't lose you, too. I can't. I don't know what I'll do. I swear to God if you die, I'll fucking kill everything. Oh fuck, Rebecca, please don't die…"

"Don't be such a fucking pussy, Harker, it's just a flesh wound." Flynn's voice snapped me out of my hysteria like a splash of cold water.

"But I…I couldn't feel you in my head."

"That's because he knocked me the fuck out. He slammed me into the car before he tried to stab me. My vest isn't great against knives, but it turned the blade enough that all he did was cut me. He didn't get in very deep."

"Are you sure? Let me see." I reached for her stomach, but she slapped me away. "Harker!"

I snapped my head up. Flynn looked dead into my eyes. "I'm. Fine. Now would you please go kill that motherfucker Smith and keep him from summoning more demons?"

I kissed her on the forehead and turned to the house, charging into a heap of shit one more time, just to save the world.

Chapter Seventeen

THERE WASN'T EVEN ENOUGH DOOR LEFT TO SLOW ME DOWN, SO I JUST barreled into the foyer and whipped my head from side to side looking for Smith. I closed my eyes and strained to hear inside noises over the sounds of a shrieking Mort and the tumult of Glory and Orobas throwing down. Either Luke had some oblivious neighbors, or he had someone cast a hellacious masking spell on this place.

I heard chanting to my right, so I sprinted in that direction, taking the library doors right off the hinges. I walked into something out of a horror movie, complete with asshole bad guy in robes and a no-shit goat mask. Smith had a casting circle drawn on the floor, and he had a large pentagram scribed inside it. At the five points of the star sat five jars full of blood, and I knew exactly where those came from. Staked to the floor with the same nails he'd used on the kid at the church, naked as the day he was born with Enochian sigils drawn all over his body in blood, lay Renfield. I couldn't tell if he was unconscious or dead, the magic of the circle screwed with my vision just enough.

"Oh, you are so fucked now, Smitty," I said as I stopped just outside the circle. I couldn't get in to kill him myself; the circle protected him. I'd have to find some way to take down the circle to stop the casting. "Luke's going to rip your head off and shit down your neck when he hears about this."

"Then it's good for me that I'm planning on burning this house down to the earth when I leave, isn't it?" He gestured toward the desk, and I noticed for the first time the pair of gallon jugs with a digital clock attached to them. The readout displayed eleven fifty-seven, and somehow I just knew that the big boom was planned for noon.

"It's not nearly as good as midnight, but really, there is a lovely symmetry to it, isn't there?" Smith looked at me and grinned. "You truly are a stupid bastard, aren't you, Harker?"

"You've been working for Orobas all along, haven't you?"

"I've been working for Uncle Oro my whole life. You could say I'm just carrying on a family tradition."

"What kind of shit are you spewing, Smitty? Am I supposed to believe you're related to Sponholz?"

"I don't care what you believe, Harker. In three minutes, you'll be dead, and I'll be the new ruler of this plane. It's too bad my little brother's dead. This could be just one more thing I beat him at."

Brothers? It made a kind of sense, but I'd never heard of any woman bearing a demonspawn and living through the trauma. "Wait a second...*Uncle Oro?* He's not your father?"

"No. Little Richie thought he was, but that's just because Mom and I never bothered to tell him any different. It served her purposes for him to think she was the only human in history ever to birth a Cambion and live, and I just didn't care enough to tell him."

"Your mother was a succubus. She was the demon half, and you had a human father."

"Fathers, actually. Mating with a succubus can be a...*draining* affair for many humans. Dear old Daddy didn't have quite enough stamina to keep up with Mummy's appetite."

I was a little nauseated by the conversation, but the longer I kept him talking, the less incantationizing he was doing. He finally stopped walking his circles and looked at me. "Huh. I'm monologuing, aren't I? Isn't that what we used to laugh about when we talked about stupid things the bad guys do? I should probably stop." He stepped to Renfield's head and nudged the manservant with one foot. Ren stirred and looked around, dazed.

"Good morning, Renfield. Time to die." Smith dropped to one knee, picked up a ceremonial dagger lying in the pentagram, and stabbed Renfield in the chest.

"NO!" I screamed, drawing my soulsaber and charging the circle. I slammed the blade of pure energy into Smith's magical barrier, hard. And again, and again, and again, until the hilt tumbled from my numbed fingers. The hilt tumbled to the floor, the mystical blade winking out of existence as soon as I was no longer holding it, and I slammed into the magical barrier of the circle.

Smith just laughed from inside his safe haven. "You can't break my circle, Harker. You're not strong enough to break one demonblood circle, let alone two." I looked down and saw what he meant. Two lines of dried brown blood twined around each other like snakes, making two tangled and interwoven circles. I opened my Sight and saw the magical energy braided together, making something much stronger than the sum of its parts. There was no way I was ever going to BS my way through that thing.

Smith knelt by Renfield's body, cutting open his chest and pulling out his heart to drip blood into a bowl by the topmost point of the star. He reached to one side and picked up another bowl of blood that I assumed came from Christy. He began to chant as he poured a small amount of the Cambion blood into the bowl of Renfield's, and I felt the pressure of a great magical working taking place near me.

I studied the woven circles in front of me, tracing the paths of their power, and realized the flaw in Smith's plan. One casting circle, formed properly and invoked by a strong wizard, could probably keep me out. Two circles, one inside the other, would be an even bigger deterrent. But two circles woven together? That formed a stronger whole, a circle completely impervious to brute force.

But not to penetration.

I straightened my hands into knife edges, then focused my will on my fingers, extending my personal energy outward into a narrow tip extending out from each hand like a needle. Then I inserted the needle into the woven energy, just like splicing a rope.

Or like stabbing through a bulletproof vest. I shook my head, throwing aside all thoughts of Becks and her injuries for the moment, because if I couldn't focus right now, there was no question she was going to die. If I could get this right, then I could see if she was lying about her wound or if she was really fine. But right now, I had to *focus*.

I pushed, and the hole in the circle grew wider. Smith looked at me, and his eyes went wide, but he didn't falter in his incantation. I got both hands into the circle's barrier up to the palms, and rotated my arms until my palms faced away from each other. I flexed my shoulders and pulled the magic of the circle away from itself, spreading the woven fibers of magic apart to make a six-inch hole that could only be seen in the Otherworld.

"Hey Smitty," I said. He looked into my eyes, and I said, "That was my friend, you son of a bitch."

Then I drew my Glock, jammed the barrel through the magical circle, and put fifteen nine-millimeter bullets into that traitorous half-demon motherfucker. I shot him full of holes from his guts to his eyeballs, and he slammed backward into the wall of his circle, shattering the casting, shattering the circle, and shattering the remains of his worthless skull when he hit the floor. I felt the magic dissipate, the casting broken, and the portal to Hell remained unopened, at the cost of one of my few friends. Again. I was really starting to want to kill Orobas.

I took one step toward Renfield, then looked again at the huge vault door that led to Luke's private sleeping chambers. It looked intact, but scarred, which was a pretty good way to describe me right about that moment. I holstered my gun and knelt by Renfield's side. I closed his eyes, pulled out my handkerchief, and wiped the worst of the blood off his face.

Then the timer on the gallon jugs of gasoline reached triple zeroes, and for the second time in as many days, I was burned to a goddamn crisp.

Epilogue

I STUMBLED INTO THE CHURCH SMELLING LIKE SMOKE AND DEATH. I HIT my knees in the center aisle and just stayed there for a long moment, gasping for breath. I looked up, and the famous fresco that once made up the entire back wall of the sanctuary looked down on me, its scenes of love and redemption looking empty to my eyes. The last time I prayed was the night my father died, the night that unbeknownst to me, to all of us, first tied me to Quincy Harker and set in motion the string of events that led to me kneeling soot-smeared and bloodstained on the stone floors of St. Peter's.

I looked at the fresco, looked around at all the trappings of faith, and felt something well up inside me. It bubbled up from deep within me, something I didn't know I still had. I dragged myself to my feet, using the pews for support. I stood, feet spread wide and weaving in the aisle. I looked at the altar, looked at the stained glass and polished wood. I looked around at all the little reminders of God and all His glory, and I screamed. I screamed with a rage that flowed out of every atom of my being. I railed at God, cursed Him and His inattention, cursed His willingness to let good men die and monsters live, and poured out all my fury in my words.

I shrieked and cursed for a good five minutes before I ran out of words. I collapsed onto a nearby pew and sat panting, bent over with my head on the pew in front of me. I had no tears. I hadn't cried since I watched the other policemen pull my father's casket out of the hearse. All I had was rage. Rage, and pain, and more rage.

"You feel better?" I knew Glory's voice. She manifested herself to me more than once, just so I wouldn't think Harker was crazy.

"No. And fuck off."

"I don't think so."

"No really, fuck off."

"Can't. You're my problem now. I just got a new assignment, and you're it. Seems like somebody thinks you're important enough for your very own guardian angel."

"For all the good it did the last guy."

"That's cold, Rebecca. I know you're angry, but I didn't make Q go after Smith alone."

"But you didn't stop Smith, either."

"I couldn't. I can't interfere with any malevolent creatures that Harker might piss off. Same goes for you now."

"Is he dead?"

"Which one?"

"Harker. I don't give a fuck about that lying asshole Smith."

"You'd better. Because Harker's alive, and Smith isn't. And it would probably be easier for everyone involved if it were the other way around."

"He's alive?" My rage pulled back a tiny bit. Just an iota, but enough that I could look up at Glory without wanting to strangle her.

"He's alive. He's running like the hounds of Hell are on his trail, but he's alive."

It felt like my heart started beating again. I reached out through our link, and she was right. I could feel him. It was faint, like he was weak and far away, but he was alive. That was the first moment I had felt his presence since the explosion. Harker, or my own fear of what I would feel, had been keeping our connection severed until then.

I let out a sigh. "Good. If he killed Smith, he's got to get out of here. Homeland Security will come down on him like an avalanche of assholes. Even the goons Smith hired were Homeland agents."

"That's what he said. And he told me to give you this." The angel held out her hand. Dangling from it was a small black box. A jewelry box.

"Oh, hell no. If he wants to pull some shit like that, it's going to have to be in person. No way is he getting you to do his dirty work. If he's giving me a ring, he's gonna sack up, get down on one knee, and ask me like a man."

Glory laughed. "That's almost exactly what I told him."

"I bet you didn't say sack up."

"You're right, I didn't."

"Is he going to be okay?" I asked.

"I don't know, Rebecca. I don't know if any of us are going to be okay by the time this thing ends."

I stared at the angel for a second, then we stood up and turned to the door. I had just stepped into the aisle when the door exploded off its hinges. In the doorway, smoke wafting from his once-immaculate suit, stood the man Harker introduced to me as his Uncle Luke.

Except the urbane businessman I knew was nowhere to be seen. This wasn't a multi-millionaire with an extensive jazz collection, legendary wine cellar, and deep knowledge of European history. This was a pissed off vampire with half a millennium of killing under his belt, and a lust for vengeance in his eye.

He stalked down the aisle to me, stopping just out of arms' reach. "Is he alive?"

"Harker? Yeah, he's alive. He killed the Cambion, who also happened to be our boss, but then he had to get out of town."

"Smith is the one that murdered Renfield?"

My mind flashed back to the remains of Renfield's burned and tormented body, and I closed my eyes. He was one of the few good ones, and now he was gone, just so a half-demon asshole could prove a point. If Smith wasn't already dead, I'd have shot him.

"Yes. From what Smith's surviving goons told us, Ren wouldn't give him the combination to your vault door. He knew he was going to be used for the sacrifice, so he took your secret to the grave."

Dracula closed his eyes for a moment, then let out a long sigh. "He was loyal. He was a good man. Very good. And he has been avenged."

"To some degree," I said.

"What do you mean?" The full attention of the King of the Vampires was on me, and I could almost *feel* his mind pressing against me.

"I mean that there's no way Smith was working alone. Smith was a Homeland Security Supervisory Agent. He ran the entire Charlotte Field Office. Every one of the Cambion we fought tonight was an agent. This shit is not just one guy, Luke. I have no idea how high up in the government this goes, but just because Harker killed Smith doesn't mean that Orobas' plan is done. I bet that demonic motherfucker is off somewhere working on his Plan B. We need to find him, and all his fucking minions, and finish this once and for all. And we have to make it look like they were all corrupt because that's the only way Harker can ever come home."

"We're going to need help. And I'm going to need a place to stay. My house seems to have come down with a bad case of the inferno."

I tossed him my key to Harker's place. I figured he wouldn't mind. He pulled out a cell phone and started tapping at the screen. "Who are you calling?"

"Reinforcements," he said. "This is too big for just the two of us. I should have done this seven years ago, but Quincy talked me out of it. I'm calling in the Shadow Council."

ONLY THE BEGINNING

Heaven Help Us

Chapter One

"WELCOME TO THE BREAKFAST DISH, I'M ALMA. WHAT CAN I GET you, stranger?" The hefty woman with a graying bun smiled at me and her voice cut through the chatter of the diner as the bell over the door announced my entrance.

"Two eggs, fried, bacon, toast, and enough coffee so I don't sleep for a week," I said from the door.

"Good enough," she said with a smile. "Sit anywhere you like and I'll bring it right out to you. You heard the man, Jarrod, get them eggs cracking!"

I crossed the scuffed tile floor to sit at the counter. The cracked red vinyl seat groaned under my weight and spun a little as I settled onto it. I nodded to the man sitting at the corner and pulled a folded newspaper out of my back pocket.

I spent a quiet few minutes reading the box scores, listening to the reed-thin man, who the waitress called Herman, pontificate to anyone who would listen, and anyone who wouldn't, about how miserable the Reds' pitching was this year, then turned to the classified ads. I had a fleeting thought about trying to pick up a used washer and dryer, then decided that I didn't plan on staying in Lockton that long. Just that morning I had secured a small apartment over one of the shops on Main Street on a month-to-month agreement. I flipped to the job listings and gave a quick scan, more to kill time than anything else. I hoped I wouldn't be there long enough to need the second month, and I certainly didn't plan on getting a day job at this point in my long life.

"Anything interesting in there, stranger?" Jarrod asked from the grill.

"Not so you'd notice, friend," I replied, folding the paper and putting it back in my pocket as Jarrod scooped a pair of fried eggs onto a plate, slapped a couple of strips of perfectly crispy bacon down beside them, and slid the plate under my nose. The smell of fresh breakfast cleared the last of the cobwebs from my brain and I dug in.

"So what brings you to Lockton, buddy? We don't get too many strangers around here." The man called Herman turned his attention to me.

"I'm a software developer working on a new mobile app for off-interstate travel, highlighting local eateries and points of interest off the beaten path. I'm here taking some photos and working on the graphical user interface. The first draft of the software is in beta right now. Once that gets all the testing completed, we'll work on the micro-payment side of things, then we'll get the launch site optimized and be good to go. Maybe another four months, maybe six, and we'll be out for sale." Herman's eyes glazed over after the second disconnected buzzword, and I called it a job well done. I pretty much had no idea what I'd just said, but I figured Herm didn't either, so my cover was going to survive at least through breakfast.

I finished my eggs and bacon in peace, having successfully bored Herman. The food was delicious, but the lights were a little too bright and my shoes pinched. The bright red Flash t-shirt was so not my style, but I was trying to be inconspicuous, so my usual black leather coat and Doc Martens were out of the question for now.

I dropped a ten on the counter and turned to leave, then froze as a big wall of trouble strolled in. The man was tall, broad, and thickly muscled, and he sniffed the air as he stepped into the diner. The bell over the door *dinged* his arrival, and all heads turned to him. He preened a little, enjoying the attention. I stood motionless as the newcomer paused in the doorway, looking around the room.

"Mornin' hon," Alma called out, her voice cheerful. "Just sit anywhere you like."

His eyes scanned the room, then landed on me. One eyebrows went up, and I almost *felt* the challenge in his gaze. His eyes were brown, with flecks of gold that I could see from across the room. He could look me in the eye, as tall as me, but much broader, with a thick beard trimmed close and wiry dark hair covering his arms. He rolled his shoulders and cocked his head to one side, taking me in with a glance. My t-shirt, jeans, and sneakers weren't exactly made for intimidation, but he recognized another predator as quickly as I had. Great, not forty-eight hours out of one frying pan, and here I am right back into the fire.

Werewolf. The word came into my head without any prompting, and the second I had the thought, I knew it was correct. Everything I'd ever known about werewolves fell into place at once, and it all made sense. Big, dark, hairy, arrogant as fuck—he looked every bit the alpha dog. That meant there was a pack in Lockton. No rogue wolf carried himself with that kind of confidence. They always had an air of whipped cur about them, like they were expecting somebody to come around and kick the shit of them. Which usually happened sooner rather than later.

The big wolf looked me up and down, then locked eyes with me again. He nodded, and I nodded back. A pair of predators acknowledging each other, and then moving on. I didn't feel the need to piss on my territory, and I hoped he wouldn't either. I'd been in enough fights in the last week, and I needed time to heal, recharge, and let the world forget about Quincy Harker for a little while. I was very happy hiding out in a small town in the guise of Harold Quinn for as long as I needed to, or at least until Flynn and Luke could clear my name.

I walked to the door, and the werewolf slid out of my way, allowing me to pass without ceding the appearance of dominance. I stepped out into the street, knowing that my time in Lockton just got a lot more complicated.

I walked down the sidewalk, my Sight open to overlay the Otherworld onto my view of the ordinary world. Nothing looked out of place, but that didn't mean anything. I'd made a couple of quick laps through the town before I rented my stay-by-the-month apartment and didn't see any monsters, magicians, or werewolves then. But they were there, and now I had to deal with them.

I turned right past Lucky's Pawn Shop and walked down the narrow alley. I stepped into the back parking lot, then walked up the stairs to the studio "loft" above, really just a big room with a small bathroom hastily built out in a corner. I unlocked the door, then drew a pair of runes in the air along the doorjamb at eye level. The wards I had protecting the apartment dropped, and I turned the knob.

"Be pretty damned embarrassing to get dropped by my own magic," I muttered as I closed the door behind me and re-activated the protections spells. I didn't take down the wards when I left that morning, just opened a portal in them to let me or any visitors through. Except I didn't expect to have any visitors. Not here, not in this life.

I opened the fridge, took out a Stella Artois, popped the top off with a thumb, and drained half the beer in one long draught.

"Fuck," I muttered. "That's all I need. Goddamn werewolves."

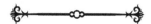

I slipped out into the night, muttering an incantation of cloaking then resetting the wards on the door. It wouldn't make me invisible, but it would help me blend into the shadows and disguise my features from a distance. Anyone looking at me from more than ten feet away or so would only remember a tall guy in a long coat. A little dab of vinegar behind each ear to hide my scent, and I was ready to hunt some wolves.

In my pocket I carried a folded printout of home sales within the past five years, with two houses circled. The wolf was young, so I assumed the pack had moved in fairly recently, but everyone seemed to know him when he walked in, so he wasn't a complete stranger. I didn't remember hearing a car door slam before he came in, and the engines in the parking lot were all stone-cold when I left the diner, so I assumed he lived within walking distance. That helped narrow my search. I headed east to the first house on my list, dodging the very few streetlights and keeping out of sight the best I could without looking like a burglar.

A tricycle on the lawn of the first place pretty much marked it off my list, but I walked around the side of the house and hopped the fence regardless. A backyard full of toys and little piles of dog poop confirmed that this was a were-free zone. Werewolves don't like their domesticated cousins, especially the yippy little variety, so the dachshund going apeshit through the sliding glass door at me would have been a snack if there were any bipedal furballs hanging around.

Back on the sidewalk, I revisited my poor life choices while I walked across town. It's not that big of a town, so I didn't get very far. I basically only made it through the past few days, where I landed in Lockton, Ohio, after killing a federal agent who happened to be a half-demon serial murderer trying to open a portal to Hell in North Carolina. It's not the first time I've had to stop that sort of thing, but it is the first time I had to go on the lam afterwards.

The second house on my list was at a cul-de-sac with open lots on either side of it and a patch of woods behind it. In other words, exactly the kind of place you would expect to find a pack of werewolves. Dogs aren't terribly creative, and they don't get any better just because they walk on two legs some of the time.

I didn't even have to sneak around to confirm my suspicions; there was a wolf on the front porch smoking a cigarette. He wasn't one of the guys from the diner, but his thick chest and shoulders, his posture, and the aura around him all cried "wolf!"

Sticking to the shadows, I slipped between two houses about fifty yards out from the wolf den and slipped through the woods to reach the back of the house in question. The yard dropped off in a steep incline in back, and a big wooden deck stuck out over the grass. I crept under the deck, keeping an ear out for feet or paws around me, but the place seemed silent.

I stepped out into the yard, bunched my legs, and jumped ten feet to vault over the railing and land on the deck. It's really handy sometimes to have Dracula's DNA mixed up in yours. Other times it's a huge pain in the ass, but at that particular moment, it was a bonus. I crouched on the deck and peeked into a nearby window, the shadows and my spell masking me from the occupants.

The lights from the living room blazed out onto the porch, and three werewolves sat around the screen, pointing and laughing. All the laughing stopped when I tapped on their sliding glass door. The biggest wolf, the one I'd seen in the diner that morning, walked over to the sliding glass door and opened it. He stepped out onto the deck, then slid the door closed behind him.

"I figured I'd be seeing you sometime," he drawled. "You wanna fight, or you wanna talk?"

"I guess that's your call, isn't it?" I asked. I held my hands out to my sides and summoned glowing orbs of energy to float above the palms. "Are you sure I'm somebody you want to throw down with?"

"I don't want to throw down with anybody, wizard, but I also don't like people skulking around my property in the middle of the night."

"I'm too tall to skulk. Sneak maybe, but not skulk."

"Whatever. You want to talk, come on in and grab a beer. You want to fight, throw those little glowballs at my ass and we'll throw down. But I'm going back inside. *Arrow* is on and I haven't seen this one."

Chapter Two

"**I** DON'T GIVE A SHIT WHAT YOU HAVE TO SAY, DETECTIVE. NOW WHAT do you have to say for yourself?" The red-faced pudgy man bellowed in my face. Again. He'd been alternating between screaming at me and cajoling me for two hours, playing both sides of the Good Cop/Bad Cop routine, and it was starting to wear very thin.

I was tired of this shit. I'd been dealing with all goddamn night, and I was over it. My partner/maybe fiancée/wizard/demon hunter/whatever else he was, Quincy Harker, was MIA. My immediate supervisor within Homeland Security was dead at Harker's hand. I had a pissed-off Lord of the Vampires to deal with, and I was really jonesing for a decent cup of coffee. Not to mention I needed to use the bathroom. I decided to lead with the easy one.

"I have to pee."

Homeland Security Deputy Director, Southeastern Region, Peter Buprof backed up a little. That was a bonus. The look on his face was priceless, too. It was kinda like you'd expect a dog to look when it finally caught the car it had chased for years. He looked so confused it was all I could do not to giggle, which I felt would be highly inappropriate, given the circumstances. Not to mention the evening's body count.

"What the fucking fuck did you say, Flynn?"

I stood up and walked to the door. "I said, I have to pee. And I'm going to go pee. Then I'm going to go to my office, and I'm going to fire up the very nice Keurig single-cup coffee maker that my Uncle Morris gave me for Christmas last year, and I'm going to make myself some real coffee, not like the shit they keep in the squad room. I'd offer you some, but you're being a dick, so drink the swill. Then I'll come back, and you can keep asking me the same questions you've been asking me for the past two hours."

Buprof moved to get between me and the door. "The fuck you will. You aren't going anywhere until I say you are."

"Am I under arrest, Deputy Director Buprof?"

His eyes got wide at my formal tone. "What?"

"I'm sorry, did I suddenly develop a stutter, or have you lost your comprehension of English since you've been yelling at me in mostly monosyllables and profanity since we got here? I asked if I was under arrest. Should I repeat the question? In Spanish? How about French? My Mandarin isn't very good, but I've got a pretty functional grasp of Farsi, if that works better for you."

He looked at the floor, his nostrils flaring as his forehead flushed an even deeper crimson. The way the vein in his left temple was throbbing, I was afraid he might stroke out right there in the interview room. Then I'd be blamed for two Homeland Security deaths in one week. And this one wouldn't be a half-demon serial murderer, so I might even feel bad about it.

After a solid fifteen seconds of staring at the floor, Buprof raised his bloodshot eyes to mine. "No, you are not under arrest, Detective. You are answering my questions completely voluntarily."

"Then I am voluntarily going to the bathroom and to get a cup of coffee. I'll be back in ten minutes or so. Why don't you take a minute to go wash your face? You're looking a little flushed." I reached past the Director and pulled the door open.

I stepped out into the hall and walked to the ladies' room, ignoring the stares from the squad room and the offices around the floor as I passed. I walked into the stall farthest from the door, sat down, and buried my head in my hands, thinking back to the events of the past few days, including being betrayed by someone I trusted, getting stabbed, and finding out a friend died at the hands of my ex-boss. This wasn't the worst week of my life, that was reserved for the time right after my dad died, but this was definitely number two with a bullet.

I felt something pull in my side, then something warm on my belly, and yanked off my jacket. I probed my black t-shirt and felt dampness under my fingers. "Fucking hell," I muttered, standing up and taking the shirt off. The small dressing I had taped over my belly wound was soaked through with blood, and now was nothing more than a sopping red square on my torso. I peeled the tape from around the gauze and stepped out of the stall.

A patrolwoman stood at the sink washing her hands. She looked up as I stepped out, starting to give me that little smile that women give one another when they find someone else working in the boys' club, kind of a solidarity thing that we can only express when no guys are around to see it and get threatened. But the smile faded as she recognized me, then her eyes widened as she saw the knife wound on my belly. The staples in my belly weren't going to do me any favors in bikini season, but that wouldn't matter much if I didn't figure out how to stop the world from ending before it got warm again.

"Detective, are you..." She was torn. I could see it on her face. Part of her wanted to shun the accused cop-killer, or girlfriend of a cop-killer, or agent-killer, or whatever Harker was supposed to be. But part of her was still a cop, and we protect and serve, and I was standing in front of her bleeding. And another part of her was a female cop, and there aren't many of us, and we try to look out for one another.

I gave her a little smile. "It's just a flesh wound, Santos. You don't need to bandage me up. I just need to wash the wound a little and dry it before I put my shirt back on and get back to my interrogation."

"I hate to...I mean, is it...I mean...Never mind, Detective. I'm sorry, I'll go."

I stepped in front of her. "Don't apologize. You're better than that. Ask me what you want to ask."

She straightened up and nodded. She looked me in the eye and asked, "Is it true? Are you dating Harker? And did he kill Agent Smith?"

"Yeah to both," I said. "But here's the other part. The part that hasn't gotten out in the whisper-mill yet. Smith was dirty. He was the serial killer we were chasing, and Harker and I knew it. But most of the evidence burned up along with Smith's body in that fire, so it's gonna be a bitch to prove it. So yeah, I'm dating Harker. And yeah, he killed Smith. But he saved a lot more lives in the process, and the real bad guy is dead, so now I have to patch up my shit and get back to proving his innocence."

Officer Santos looked me up and down, then nodded. "Detective, I don't know if I could stand in the middle of a public bathroom with no shirt on and blood running down my stomach and defend my *husband* that well, much less a boyfriend. So if you need any help, you let me know. I got you."

"Thanks, Santos. I appreciate it."

"No problem, Detective. Now get that stomach cleaned up. There's a first aid kit in the supply closet right behind the door there." I looked where she was pointing, and sure enough, there was a door I'd never paid attention to marked "Maintenance" right behind me. I nodded my thanks to Santos again and looked in the supply closet.

Fifteen minutes later, I was back in Interview Room One sitting across from Deputy Director Buprof holding a steaming cup of hazelnut blend and wearing a clean shirt I kept in my office. I felt more in control of myself with a fresh dressing on my stab wound and some caffeine coursing through my system. I was ready to take on anything that Buprof could throw at me.

He sat across the table from me with a digital recorder. He pressed a button on the recorder and pointed a remote at the two-way mirror behind him. I knew that turned on the video camera on the other side of the glass, so everything I said from here on out would be recorded in two locations. At least. God only knew how many other recording devices were set up on the other side of the mirror.

"Now, Detective, please recount for me the events of this evening, starting from the moment you arrived at Mr. Card's home."

I'd already been through this a dozen times in the hours since all the shit went down, but Buprof was a relatively new addition. He'd arrived from Washington on a Department of Homeland Security jet just a few hours ago, all hellfire and brimstone to root out the corruption in the Charlotte office and bring me and Harker to justice. I knew the drill. Get the suspect to repeat herself, hoping that she'll make a mistake, trip herself up in some way. I was telling the truth, so there was nothing to trip up. Harker and I had been investigating a series of murders similar to a set of killings he investigated seven years ago.

In both cases, Nephilim, or half-angels, were being murdered and their blood harvested to open a gate to Hell for the demon Orobas to bring a bunch of his nasty siblings and pals through to our world. Both times, the culprit was a Cambion, an offspring of a demon, in this case Orobas, and a human woman. They hid their identities from Harker by smearing Nephilim blood on themselves, which masked their supernatural nature. Both times Harker stopped the Cambion, who was a member of law enforcement. The first time, he did it by casting the bad guy into his own portal to Hell. This time he shot the bad guy, our supervisory agent with Homeland Security, in the face. A lot.

It would have been a lot cleaner for everybody involved if he'd sent Agent Smith to Hell, but that wasn't how things went down. And now Harker was on the run, and I was getting ready to repeat my story for a camera and a very upset Homeland Security middle manager.

Until the door opened into Interview One and a thirty-something man with an expensive suit, a slight limp, and a neatly trimmed dark brown beard stepped into the room.

"What the ever-loving fuck do you think you're doing?" Buprof said, standing up from the table. There went that vein again. I made a mental note to tell the good Director to go see a doctor when we were done here. If he decided against sending me to Gitmo, or Area 51, or wherever Homeland sent people they considered to be rogue members of their version of the X-Files.

"I think I'm stopping this bleeding circus right here," the newcomer said, putting a hand on my shoulder. "My client is going home. She is a sworn officer of the law, she has given her statement at least ten times already by this point, and while her incompetent excuse for a union representative may have allowed this sideshow to continue, I have no intention of doing so. I think it's time we ended this charade and all went home, don't you?" The trim man spoke with a cultured British accent, and when I gawked up at him with my confusion written all over my face, he looked down at me with deep brown eyes and gave me a conspiratorial wink.

"She's not—"

I stood up. "We've covered this already, Director. I've given a statement. I'm not under arrest. I'm going home." I spoke a little louder. "Captain, could you come in here?"

I heard a door slam, then the door into the interrogation room opened and my boss, Captain Benjamin Herr, stepped in. He didn't look happy, but he didn't look like he wanted to shoot me, either.

"Captain, am I on administrative leave pending an investigation? I need to know if I should plan to come back to work as soon as my side heals, or start looking for a new job." I figured I may as well cut straight to the chase and find out where I really stood with my department. I was pretty sure most of the Charlotte-Mecklenburg Police Department wasn't in league with a demon, but I had my doubts about Homeland Security.

Captain Herr thought about it, then shook his head. "No, Flynn. Your story matches what we saw from the dash cam of your department car, and it fits with the evidence. As far as I'm concerned, you're good. I'm going to put you on desk duty for another week or so until you heal up, and you'll have to be cleared by the department psychologist before you're back on active duty, but you're not suspended."

"I have some vacation and sick time coming, could I—" I started, but Captain Herr held up a hand.

"Take it. Get some rest, find out if your asshole boyfriend is okay, and make sure he knows that CMPD has no intention of building a case against him."

"Thank you, sir," I said, standing.

"Hold on a minute, Detective," Buprof said. "Just because your little band of blue brothers isn't going after your murdering sack of shit boyfriend doesn't mean Homeland Security won't. As of right now, you are officially suspended from the Department of Homeland Security. You are to surrender your credentials immediately."

I reached into the inside pocket of my jacket and took out my badge holder. I flipped it open to my Homeland credentials, took them out of the holder, and put the laminated ID card on the table. I held up the wallet holding my gold shield and Charlotte-Mecklenburg Police Department ID at Captain Herr. "You want this, Captain?"

"Did I stutter, Detective?" Captain Herr turned my own smartass comment back on me. "I said you're in the clear. That means you're in the clear. If Homeland doesn't want you anymore, CMPD will be glad to have you back with us full time."

"Thank you sir," I said. I slid my badge back in my pocket and stood up.

"Where the hell do you think you're going?" Buprof asked. "We're not done here."

"I believe that I clearly stated the opposite of that, Deputy Director," my newfound attorney said. He didn't raise his voice, didn't even hint at needing to raise his voice, but he spoke with such quiet assurance and carried himself with such calm strength that Buprof was forced to turn his attention to him.

"And who the fuck are you, exactly?" Buprof asked.

"Watson," the tall man replied. "Dr. Jack Watson, Esquire. I am Detective Flynn's attorney." He produced a business card from his jacket pocket and passed it over to the confused Homeland Security Director. "My contact information is on that card. All inquiries concerning my client should be addressed to me from this moment forward. Now, if you gentlemen will excuse us?" He nodded to Buprof and Herr and steered me out into the hall.

I leaned in to him. "Who are you again?"

He held out a hand. "Jack Watson. Now please let's not tarry. While I am an attorney, and I do have my J.D., I'm not what most Americans think of as a doctor, and I am not exactly licensed to practice law on this side of the pond, unless our mutual friend Mister Card has made some very effective telephone calls very quickly."

"Watson?" I asked, thinking to myself, *there's no friggin' way.* "Not...?"

"Yes, actually," he replied. "Doctor John Watson was my great-great-grandfather. So yes, *that* Watson."

It appeared the Shadow Council had arrived.

Chapter Three

I STOOD ON THE PORCH FOR A MINUTE STARING AFTER THE BACK OF THE retreating Alpha, then shook my head and went inside, dissipating my balls of glowing purple energy as I went. I was a tiny bit bummed that I didn't get to throw those at anybody. I didn't design them to kill anything, but they were gonna look *really* cool.

This was a new one on me. Walking into a werewolf's den didn't usually involve IKEA furniture in my experience, but this place was furnished in early 21st century modern craptastic sofas and bookshelves. The Alpha was sprawled in a recliner sipping a Coors Light while two other werewolves sat on the sofa watching television. Sure enough, there was Oliver Queen climbing a salmon ladder, all abs and attitude.

"Beer in the fridge?" I asked, pulling the sliding glass door closed behind me. If I needed to get out of there in a hurry, a pane of glass wasn't going to slow me down very much. Hell, if the wolves decided to evict me with extreme prejudice, the walls wouldn't slow me down much, either.

"Yeah," Alpha replied. "Grab me another Coors while you're at it."

I paused for a second, wondering if it was a test or some kind of macho dominance thing. Then I decided I didn't care, and I grabbed a Coors Light for the wolf and a Heineken for myself. I popped the top off the bottle with my thumb and handed the can to the were.

"Thanks."

"No problem."

"You know we got a bottle opener, right?" He pointed to my thumb, which bled a little from the edge of the bottle-cap.

"I heal fast," I replied, then held up my thumb. The tiny cut stitched itself shut in seconds, another of the useful abilities my vampire-enhanced blood granted me.

"That's handy," said the Alpha.

"You got a name?" I asked.

204 | Heaven Help Us

"I think I get to be the one asking questions," he replied. "You know, my house and all." He didn't raise his voice, didn't even take a stern tone, but it was pretty clear from the attention the wolves on the sofa paid to every syllable that this was not the dude to fuck with.

I shrugged and stepped over to in front of his chair. "Quincy Harker." I held out a hand.

"So not Harold Quinn?" he asked, taking my hand. His grip was firm, but not overly strong. He had nothing to prove, so he didn't bother to try. We shook, and I stepped over to a chair at the end of the couch. This put a coffee table between me and all three werewolves, space that I was going to need desperately if things got noisy.

"Nope," I said. I didn't bother explaining to him about my undercover status. I figured a werewolf might understand all about keeping his identity masked. I also didn't ask how he got my name, assuming he either asked the waitress or had some way to scan recent property rentals. He was the local Alpha, after all. If he didn't have the town pretty well wired, then he wasn't much of a pack leader.

"Fair enough. I'm Drew Semper. I'm the Alpha around these parts. The one by you is Billy, and the big dumb one is Rocco." He pointed at the two couch-surfing weres in turn, and they nodded to me. I nodded back.

"How long have you guys been in town?"

"About three years, maybe four." I appreciated the fact that he didn't lie to me, either. I knew from my hour on the computer that afternoon that the house was rented on an annual lease to a Luna Holdings, LLC, out of New Jersey, and had been rented to the same company for a little over three years.

"What are y'all doing here?"

"Why do you care?" Drew shot back. The wolf called Rocco started to growl low in his throat, and Drew and I both gave him a sharp look. "Be nice, Rocco. Our guest here might be nosy, but he hasn't threatened anybody yet."

After being around a fair number of people who thought I was threatening them just by walking into a room, I found Drew's self-confidence refreshing. "I care because I'm here trying to keep a low profile, and if you guys are running some kind of small-town protection racket, or redneck meth lab, or undercover gambling ring, or anything that might bring down federal attention on this town, then we're going to have a problem."

Drew put the footrest of his recliner down and leaned forward. "Are we? Are we going to have a problem, Mr. Harker?"

"Only if you want to, Mr. Semper."

"What if I told you we already had a problem?" *Oh shit. Wolf politics.*

"I'd tell you if it was going to put more eyes on this town, then that would be an issue for me."

"What are you hiding from, Quincy?"

"I don't think that's any of your business, Drew." I followed his move into first-name territory, unwilling to yield to his Alpha games. He stood up and stepped toward me, sliding the coffee table out of the way. I stood up to meet him.

We just looked at each other for a long moment, passing a whole lot of communication between us without ever saying a word. Finally, Drew turned and walked into the kitchen.

"Another beer?" he called over one shoulder.

"I wouldn't say no." I sat back down in my chair, then leaned forward and tugged the coffee table back into place. Drew came back with three Coors Lights and an opened Heineken for me. "Thanks," I said, draining off the last of my first beer and setting it on an end table beside the sofa.

"Coaster," the wolf identified as Billy said, pointing to a rack on the table. I nodded at him and got a coaster. No point in fucking up a guy's furniture.

"Now, Mr. Harker, what brings you to Lockton?" Drew asked once he was settled back into his chair.

"Not so much being *in* Lockton as being *out* of Charlotte."

"Charlotte's a nice town. What's that in, North Carolina?"

"Yeah," I said. No real surprise that a werewolf in Ohio didn't know much about Charlotte.

"Why'd you leave Charlotte?"

"I had a disagreement with my boss at Homeland Security."

"There's a wizard working for Homeland Security?"

"Until about two nights ago, there was a half-demon called a Cambion working as a supervisor for Homeland Security."

"What happened two nights ago?"

"He and I had that disagreement I mentioned."

"And this disagreement didn't go well for him, I take it."

"And thus I am in Lockton, Ohio, home of the World's Largest Nothing. Not a tourist trap for miles, no traffic cams, and no reason for anyone to visit."

"The perfect place for a man on the run."

"I'm not on the run," I protested. "I'd just rather not deal with the consequences of my actions right now."

"Story of my life," Drew said, holding up his beer. I saluted with my bottle, and we drank deeply.

We finished our beers in a relatively comfortable silence. As comfortable as you can be when in the literal den, fireplace and all, of a bunch of werewolves who could probably tear you limb from limb quicker than you could kill more than two of them. Right now, we were operating on manners and the threat of mutually assured destruction. I knew that if I tried anything, I wouldn't make it out of the house alive, and they knew that if they jumped me, at least one of them would be dead on the floor in seconds. Nobody wanted to take the chance that they would be the lucky winner, so we were at a stalemate.

Drew stood up, flowing to his feet in that liquid movement that true predators have. He looked down at me, and I focused my will on my fists. I didn't bother with the glowing light this time. If shit was about to get real, I wasn't going to need pyrotechnics, just firepower.

"Our pack has been in this part of the world for a long time, Harker, and we can stay here and in the towns around here because we don't start shit with anybody. We know the drill. We hunt animals, not people, and we don't let anything else hunt people in our territory. If you're cool with that, you can stay. But if you've got ideas about summoning anything nasty, starting some kind of coven, or otherwise fucking with the people of Lockton, then we're going to have a problem."

I didn't so much let my will dissipate as it popped like a soap bubble. "What?"

"You heard me. We look after these people. So if that's a problem, you need to move on to greener pastures. We don't know shit about you, except for some rumors Billy picked up on the BlackNet. And that shit is too farfetched even for me to believe, and I'm a friggin' Ohio werewolf, for fuck's sake."

"Yeah, that's probably the true stuff. If it sounds just cosmically fucked up, I'd believe it." I turned to Billy, who showed me the BlackNet version of my Wikipedia page on a tablet. "Yup, all that's pretty much true. Except that thing about Zaire. Never been there."

"You're saying you're really Dracula's nephew and you're over a hundred years old?" Billy asked.

"Nephew is just how we describe it. There's no real blood relation." I didn't bother trying to explain the whole thing about him nibbling on my mom before she and Dad were married, and I sure as fuck wasn't going into Dad's time with Uncle Luke's "wives." I didn't know the whole story there, and didn't want to. If they wanted to read about that part of my origin, they could read the book. Or watch one of the countless nearly unwatchable movies.

"So he's real?" Drew asked, his voice a little hushed.

"The werewolf is asking the wizard if Dracula is real?" I raised an eyebrow.

"Fair enough." Drew walked to the fridge and grabbed another round for everyone. I wasn't finished with the last one yet, but I didn't want to be rude.

He sat down and leaned forward, looking hard at me. "So what's it going to be, wizard? Are you going to move on, are we going to throw down, or are we going to try to be good neighbors?"

I took a long pull off my beer. Whatever I said next was not just going to impact the direction my evening was to take, but was going to have a big impact on how long my life in Lockton was to be. Even if I fought these guys and won, that would bring a lot more attention down on this little town than I wanted. The Lockton police department was two guys, one receptionist, and one cell, usually reserved for a pair of drunks on Friday or Saturday night. A trio of bodies would draw attention at the state level and maybe higher, and certainly make the papers. That was attention I couldn't afford. And that was if I won the fight, which wasn't a lock by any stretch. Werewolves are tough, fast, and resistant to a lot of the magic I used against creatures like demons, by virtue of the fact that they actually *belong* on this plane of existence.

"I think that as long as you guys have all your shots and nobody tries to hump my leg, we oughta be able to get along fine. I don't have a problem with lycanthropes as a rule, I just get nervous when any supernatural critter shows up that I didn't know about," I said. I took another drink of my beer, so I wouldn't waste too much if I had to smash the bottle across somebody's head.

The big one they called Rocco growled at me again, but Drew waved a hand at him. Drew stood up and stuck out his hand. I got out of my chair and shook it, feeling the power in his grip that he wasn't even trying to impress me with. That's what was impressive about it, that he wasn't trying.

"Welcome to Lockton, Mr. Harker. I hope we don't ever have to find out the answer."

I didn't ask the question. We both knew what the other one was thinking, and I was glad I wouldn't have to find out who was the bigger badass tonight.

"Now, since you're here..."

Oh shit, here it comes. I knew it the second he opened his mouth.

"There's something we could use your help with."

Yup. Right into the shit again. I will never fucking learn.

Chapter Four

I WALKED THROUGH THE DOOR OF HARKER'S CONDO, EXPECTING HIM to pop out from behind a door and tell me that it was all some kind of joke, some magical illusion bullshit of his and we could go back to the way things were a few days ago. Before we found out that Agent Smith was a half-demon serial killer, before Smith murdered Renfield, before Harker put a bullet in Smith's face and had to go on the lam.

But no, nobody jumped out from behind a door. There were a lot of people in Harker's living room, though, and I only recognized two of them. Luke was there, which made sense since his house was currently a pile of rubble. The other one had me draw my sidearm and level the Sig Sauer .40 pistol right at her face.

"What the fuck are you doing here, Van Helsing?"

Gabby Van Helsing was good in a fight, but she wasn't one of my favorite people. The first time we met, she almost killed Harker, then drew down on Luke. Now she was sitting in Quincy's living room, drinking his beer, and chatting with Luke like they were old friends.

Gabby stood and held her hands up. "I'm unarmed, Detective. Please don't shoot me."

"I don't believe you. No way do you sit in an unfamiliar room without a weapon or three somewhere around you."

An athletic black woman laughed from the couch. "She knows you, Gabs. Might as well come clean."

Van Helsing shrugged. "There is a pistol in an ankle holster, a pair of knives in the back of my belt, and four small stakes strapped to my forearms. I'll strip down if you really want me to, but I've got to let you know, I'm not into chicks."

Luke stood up and put himself between my gun and Van Helsing. "Detective... Rebecca, please put away the gun." Luke looked like hammered shit, and that was even taking into account that he was buried alive just the night before. His eyes were sunken into his skull, his cheeks were drawn, and he was pale, even for a guy that hadn't seen the sun since well before the American Revolution. He looked around the room, took a deep breath, and continued. "Gabriella is one of us. She is here to help clear Quincy's name and bring the real perpetrator to justice."

I raised an eyebrow at the Vampire Lord. "The real perpetrator was brought to justice, Luke. Harker killed him. That's why he had to run, remember?"

Watson slipped past me into the apartment and walked over to the kitchen area. "We believe that your Agent Smith was merely one cog in the machine, Detective. He had resources significantly beyond his normal capacity either as an agent of Homeland Security or a Cambion, and we feel that the conspiracy must go higher within the government."

I looked at the trim British dude who stood at Harker's kitchen counter pouring a drink. "Are you serious? You're talking to me about some kind of Illuminati shit?"

"We are a secret organization of powerful beings hidden from society for over a hundred years. It only stands to reason that there might be another one or two out there," Watson said, his voice mild, but his eyes serious. "Drink?"

"I'll take a Coke. Harker keeps them in the door of the fridge."

"He's out," the woman on the couch called from the den. I looked at her and she raised a familiar red-and-white striped can at me with a smile.

"And who the hell are you, lady? Besides the bitch who drank the last Coke, that is."

She laughed again, a bright, tinkling sound that felt somehow out of place in this room full of grim faces and serious demeanors. I liked her in spite of myself, and in spite of her drinking the last soda.

"I'm Jo," she said, and walked over to me, her hand out. We shook, and her grip was very strong. This was a woman who'd seen hard work and wasn't afraid of it. She was short and stocky, with broad shoulders and the no-bullshit stride of an athletic woman. Her hair was cropped short, and her brown eyes sparkled with amusement. "This is some fucked-up shit, right?"

"You can say that again," I muttered.

"Oh, please don't," Watson sighed, walking behind me to head to the living room and sit on the arm of the couch. "Let's move forward into the problem at hand. Countless rehashing of how 'fucked up' the situation is moves us no closer to a resolution."

"Well, can I at least get a handle on who everyone is before I dive right into hunting down a demon boss?" I asked, poking my head into the fridge. Empty. These fuckers had devoured the normally meager stores in Harker's refrigerator.

I took a glass down from the cabinet and poured water from the tap over some ice cubes, then went into the living room with everyone else. I grabbed a chair and sat between Harker's two sofas facing the door.

I looked around the room. Luke was there, looking like ten miles of bad road. Watson sat on the couch next to him, all perfect posture, trimmed beard and piercing intellect burning behind his eyes. Gabby sat across from him, keeping one eye on me and the other on Luke. Apparently there was still a little distrust there. The black woman sat beside Gabby, looking around the gathered people and giving me the occasional small smile.

"So who the fuck are you people? Luke I know, and Gabby I've met, but this dude walks into police headquarters introducing himself as Dr. Watson's great-great-grandson, and I've got no idea who you are, lady. No offense."

"None taken," the unidentified woman said. "I'm Jo. For the purposes of this gathering, Jo Henry. It's actually Jo Marinton, but it's easier to remember why I'm involved in all this mess if I just go by Granddaddy's name."

"Your grandfather's name was Henry?" I asked, starting to put things together in my head but not sure I was going in the right direction.

"Yup," she confirmed. "John Henry. Steel-driving man, hero of the battle of the railroad man versus the steam engine, all that. That was Granddaddy. Great-great-granddaddy, technically, but I figure we can let that slide."

"I thought he died after that whole thing with the steam engine." I was pretty impressed that I managed to dredge that little bit of history up on demand.

"Nah. He had a heart attack, and he almost died, but he really was as strong as the legends say. Old man was way harder to kill than anyone should have been back then. He lived to be almost eighty, even after that whole mess with the steam engine when he was a young man."

"Impressive. So what do you do?" I asked.

"For the Council, or for a living?"

"I dunno, whichever. Does working for the Council not pay much?"

She laughed, a musical sound that made me smile. Out of all these weirdos, she seemed the most *real*, like somebody I could have a beer and talk politics with, or sports, or just hang out. The rest of them were either a little terrifying, like Luke; a little psychotic, like Gabby; or a little too *British*, like Jack. But Jo seemed fun. I was relaxing a little around her, which was nice. There hadn't been a lot of relaxation in my life the past few days.

"Working for the Council doesn't pay shit," Jo said. "Like, literally, it's a volunteer gig. Some of us come from money, or are at least old enough to have some stashed, like Luke here." The Lord of the Vampires tipped an imaginary hat. "Or we kill things that are old and have a lot of money stashed, like Gabby."

"They don't need money after I burn them to ash." The sweet smile she gave me when she said that definitely pushed the needle on her well into "psycho" territory.

"Or they get royalty money off books written by and about their family." Jo pointed at Jack, who held up a glass of whiskey.

"I am also an attorney, and a rather good one at that," he offered up in a token protest. "But the fact that Old Doyle promised half the revenue from the Holmes character to my father doesn't hurt."

"Yeah, helped you afford that posh Oxford education, right old chap?" Gabby needled him in a terrible Cockney accent.

"Cambridge, thank you very much, and yes, it was very posh, and yes, Doyle's money definitely paid for it. Too bad I didn't go there straight out of high school, instead of spending a few years in the Army first." He reached down and knocked on his left leg, which gave off an odd metallic sound. I just looked at him, and he raised the hem of his pants to show a prosthetic leg. "Courtesy of an IED outside Kabul. I'm accustomed to it now, but it does cause certain challenges with airport security here in the States."

"So I'm one of the few members of the Council that actually has a day job. I'm a freelance editor, mostly nonfiction books. Self-help books, career guides, that kind of thing. It gives me the freedom I need to drop everything and come running whenever these guys call."

"And how many of these guys are there? Is this everybody? Or are there more Shadow People that I'll run into later?"

You know that feeling when a room gets uncomfortably quiet, like when the awkward guy from work tells a racist joke that he thinks will be funny and it's anything but funny? Yeah, that happened. Everybody kinda looked at each other, or their drinks, or the carpet, or basically anywhere but at me.

After giving the pause long enough to become truly uncomfortable, I clapped my hands. "Okay, that's fine. You can't tell me anything about the Council because I'm not on the Council. That's cool. I get operational security and partitioning information. I've done my fair share of interagency partnerships in my time. So

I guess all I need to know this—are there any more Council members here, and do I need to know anything else before we get to work?"

"No," Luke said, standing up and walking over to me. "To both of those things. We are the sum total of the Council that is currently here and working on this problem. There are more Councilors, but they are handling other issues at the moment."

"Okay, so what's the plan?" I asked, finishing up my water and walking over to the liquor cabinet. Harker always kept at least one bottle of Macallan tucked away behind the swill of a tequila selection in the bar, so I fished around behind bottles until I found the good stuff. Only a third of the bottle remained, but it was enough. I poured myself a generous slug and left the bottle out where the others could see it. I returned to my seat and looked around the room.

"What? There's no plan?" I asked.

"We just got here, Detective," Jo protested.

"Call me Flynn, or I suppose Rebecca if you have to," I replied. "Alright, since we don't have a plan, I guess that's Step One—make a plan."

"We need to figure out how high this problem goes within Homeland Security," Watson said. "Right now we aren't sure if Smith was an isolated mole, or if there's a widespread conspiracy."

"Assume he wasn't working alone," I said.

"Why's that?" Gabby asked. "You need to make some justification for your boyfriend shooting a federal agent in the face?"

"Not that one," I said. "He deserved everything he got and then some. But no way was he acting alone. He had organization, and he managed to kill four people right under our noses and get away with it. That takes help, and a ton of resources."

"So do you think his accomplice is someone inside Homeland Security?" Jo asked.

"Worse," I said. "I'm pretty sure that someone inside Homeland Security is his boss."

Chapter Five

"**T**ELL ME AGAIN HOW WE'RE NOT GOING TO JAIL FOR THIS? I DID mention that little disagreement with Homeland Security, right?" I whispered to Drew the next night as we stepped into the deserted hallway of Lockton High School. It smelled of disinfectant layered over years of teen spirit, that miasma of body odor, gym shoes, and hormones that just rolls off teenagers like cheap perfume off a stripper's ass.

"Rocco is the strength and conditioning coach for the football team. He gave me the keys," Drew said in a normal voice.

"And that gets us out of jail how exactly?" I didn't bother hiding my "I'm not convinced" voice.

"Because Billy is a dispatcher for the county 911 service and he's on duty tonight. So nothing about this is going to get reported. So as long as Chief Clark doesn't happen to ride by the school, we're good. And Chief Clark hasn't been out of the house after ten o'clock without a good reason for at least two years."

I couldn't argue with the man. He knew his town, after all. "Fine, then what are we looking for?"

"I don't want to influence your impressions. Just tell me what you sense, or however you do that shit."

I opened my Sight and almost fell down as I was overwhelmed by the magic thrown around in that hallway. I quickly shifted back to the mundane spectrum and turned on Drew. "What the ever-loving fuck was that?"

He held up both hands and took a step back, then seemed to catch himself and stepped back up to meet me. "That's what I wanted to know. What did you see?"

"I saw so much shit I could barely sort it all out. You seriously need to warn a motherfucker before you pull something like that. It's like if I shoved smelling salts and cayenne pepper right up your super-sniffer, Lassie."

He bristled at the dog joke, but didn't push it. "Alright, sorry. I didn't know it would be that bad. But you'll agree there's something fucked up going on around here?"

"That's putting it mildly. There is serious demonic influence all over this place. It's like somebody has been...oh no."

"Oh no, what?"

"Somebody's been playing with demons here, haven't they?" I should have known. It's not like they call me Quincy Harker, driveway repairman. Anytime somebody wants me to take a good look at something, odds are there's a demon involved.

"We think so. I told you Rocco is an assistant football coach, right?" Drew started walking down the hall without bothering to turn on a light or his flashlight. Not being a werewolf, I called up a floating ball of light and set it over my shoulder so I didn't trip over anything left in the hall by a lazy janitor or asshole teenager.

"Yeah. What about it?"

"Well, the team is really good this year. They haven't lost a game."

"Good for them," I said. I didn't hear a problem yet.

"Yeah, it's great. School spirit is up, the town is behind the team, there are even talks about forming a booster club for the first time in years."

"So what's the problem?"

We turned down another hallway, this one marked "Gym." "The problem is, they shouldn't be."

"Shouldn't be what?"

"Good," Drew said. "They didn't lose very many players to graduation, so most of the players from last year are back. And they weren't very good last year. Rocco's been amazed at the gains they've made in the weight room—he says that you can't make gains like that even with steroids. He's talking about some kids packing on twenty or thirty pounds of muscle just since school started."

"That's only been a couple of months," I pointed out.

"That's what I'm saying," Drew agreed. "Rocco says that there's something funky with these kids, and they don't play like normal, either. They run their routes perfectly, make throws like Tom Brady. It's like all of a sudden they're the Green Bay Packers instead of the Lockton Lions."

"Are you sure all this is legit? I mean, no offense to Rocco, but..."

"I know, he doesn't look like the brightest bulb in the box, but he knows football, and he knows jocks. So if he says this shit ain't natural, then it ain't natural. And now you're telling me there's a demon running around the school, too."

"Yeah, there's definitely something here. Let me take another look." I opened my Sight again, this time shielding myself a little instead of throwing my supernatural vision wide open. The athletic wing was even more covered in demonic essence than the first hallway we were in, so whatever was hanging around the school, it was more active down there. I looked past the glare of the demon taint but couldn't get any real hints on what type of hellspawn we were dealing with from the trail of badness it left in its wake. But there was a door on the far left side of the hallway that radiated evil like a homing beacon.

I motioned to Drew. "If you can do that half-way change thing where you get really big and scary, this might be a good time to do it." I pointed to the door. "There's something behind that door, and it's not very nice at all."

"I can do that." Drew started stripping down in the hallway. I gaped at him. "What? You think my clothes just magically disappear? I've ruined more jeans trying to transform while wearing clothes than I care to count. And I really like these shoes." I looked at his feet. They were nice hiking boots, so I kinda understood him. He got naked, then shifted into his half-wolf form.

If you've never seen a human turn into a werewolf, then good for you. It's not pretty and usually incredibly painful. The benefit to having an Alpha wolf with you is he's way too macho to scream as his bones realign themselves and his body miraculously packs on another fifty percent of its muscle mass.

I asked Luke once where the extra matter came from, because laws of nature and all that. His response—"it's magic, you idiot." I shut up at that point. No point debating physics with a guy who lives on human blood with no working digestive system. Especially coming from a wizard who makes fireballs with his mind and throws them at people.

After a few seconds of what must have been excruciating pain, Wolf-Drew stood in front of me, seven feet of hair, muscle, and teeth that didn't really get hurt by anything but fire and silver. And magic, but I didn't plan on throwing any bolts of pure energy at my partner for the evening. He shook himself all over and nodded at me. Verbal communication was pretty much out until he shifted back since I didn't speak Wolf and his jaw was now shaped all wrong for forming words. Didn't matter. Whatever I sensed behind that door was very unlikely to be big on conversation.

Drew and I crept across the hall and I pressed my ear to the door. I heard a soft *huff-huff* of breath behind me and turned to Drew. He tapped himself on the chest and gently nudged me out of the way. He had a point. My hearing is better than a normal human's, but I've got nothing on a werewolf, even one half-transformed. He put his head to the door and held up two fingers.

"There are two of them?" I asked.

He nodded, then waved his hand in the air to indicate one was close to the door and one across the room. At least, that's what I thought it meant. I nodded back at him, and he moved to the other side of the door. I drew in my will and whispered "*Fiero*" under my breath. A six-inch sphere of flame appeared floating over my outstretched palm, and I flung open the door. I lobbed the magical fire grenade into the room and was greeted by a very satisfying *WHOOSH* as it exploded inside the room. The contained space gave the fireball a little extra oomph, a fact I learned both in the real world and playing way too much *Dungeons & Dragons* in the 80s.

I gave the fire a couple of seconds to die down, then stepped into the open doorway. I stood there for a minute, letting the smoke billow around my boots and long coat, casting what I thought should be an appropriately badass image for a demon-hunting wizard, only to find a pair of imps standing in the room grinning at me.

"Got any more of those, human? That tickled," the first imp said, then launched himself at me from twenty feet away. His wings unfurled and he flew at me like a clawed lawn dart. I dove to the right, drawing my Glock as I hit the ground on my side.

Drew stepped into the doorway as soon as I moved, no doubt chomping at the bit after my failed theatrics. He reached out one hand and swatted the imp to the ground, his reflexes and strength a match for a minor demon any day. The only problem was that speed and power were not the only weapons imps came equipped with.

"Drew, watch the tail!" I yelled, hauling myself to my feet.

Drew either heard me or he'd dealt with imps before, because he dodged to one side as the little bastard's spiked tail came up over its shoulder and jabbed at his leg. The six-inch spike buried itself in the drywall beside the door, and Drew stomped on the demon's back. I heard the monster scream in pain and turned to find the other one.

I was a little late, since it was almost on me already. I threw myself flat on my back as the imp leapt at me. It flew harmlessly over me, then snapped its wings out in a heartbeat and whirled around to dive-bomb me where I lay on the floor. I squeezed off three quick shots with my pistol, then rolled out of the way. I kept rolling after it smacked into the floor, the nasty tail jabbing into the tile beside me. The razor-sharp point penetrated into the floor easily, leaving me to think unpleasant thoughts about what it would do to my chest.

I scrambled to my feet as the imp got to its wobbly feet. I shot it twice in the face, which knocked it back onto its ass, but had no other real effect. I didn't expect it to, I just needed a little separation.

"*Frigidos!*" I shouted, holstering my Glock and thrusting both palms out at the imp. Daggers of ice materialized and flew toward the demon, tearing holes through its wings and drawing blood from its face and torso. *So my magic can hurt it. Good to know.*

I spared a glance for Drew, who was methodically stomping the head of the imp he was battling. It wasn't dying and wasn't going to from that kind of damage, but it also wasn't getting up, so he was in pretty good shape.

"Fuzzy!" I shouted. Drew's head snapped up with a snarl, and I tossed a vial from my coat underhand to him. "Catch!"

He caught it and cocked his head at me. "Pour it on the demon," I shouted. "It's holy water!"

Drew did as I said, and the demon shrieked in agony. Apparently Drew had opened enough of a cut on the imp's skin for the holy water to touch its blood, and the little bastard melted away to nothing as Drew was in mid-stomp.

I turned to the remaining imp and held up a second vial of holy water. "Plenty more where that came from, asshole. Now you can go back to Hell, or I can vaporize your ass right now, and you won't just be dead on this plane, but you'll be forever-dead. Your call." I cocked my arm back to throw, but the imp wrapped its wings around itself and popped out of existence. Seems like even demons have a sense of self-preservation.

"What the fuck did you do that for?" I turned to see a human and very naked Drew standing in the room bitching at me. "That thing can come back and hurt more people, and you'll be the reason. Everything it does from here on out is on you, Harker. We had a chance to destroy that thing, and you didn't take it."

"I try not to destroy things that are the pets of bigger and badder things if I can help it," I said. "That imp can't come back across the plane unless someone or something summons it," I explained. "And whatever summoned it is the real problem, not some shitty little pitchfork monkey from the First Circle. You killed one—that sends enough of a message. Being able to kill this one and choosing not to sends an even stronger one. It says we don't give a fuck what this guy calls up from the Pits, we can handle it."

"Why don't we just see if that's true," came a new voice from the doorway. I hate surprises. They never end up being a pony, or even a stripper. It's always a pair of socks for Christmas, or another fucking demon.

Chapter Six

THE ROOM ERUPTED IN CHAOS AS I MADE MY PRONOUNCEMENT ABOUT Smith. I stood there watching the train wreck of conversation until they all ran out of steam and stared at me.

"Are y'all quite finished?" I asked.

Jack nodded at me. "Please proceed, Detective. What makes you think that Agent Smith's actions are not simply those of a deranged monster infiltrating a major governmental agency?"

"Have you ever used one word when three would do?" I asked. Watson gave me a flat stare, so I just went on, making a mental note that this dude had *zero* sense of humor. "Smith couldn't have been working alone. He did too much with little or no oversight, and there's no way some government functionary wouldn't have been looming over his shoulder every time we tried to do something. Ergo, we have at least one more Cambion to find inside Homeland Security."

"An organization that has currently suspended you," Watson pointed out.

"True enough," I said. "But now that I have the whole Justice League behind me, I'm sure one of you is a super-hacker or something."

"Or something," Jo said. "I wouldn't even call myself a mediocre hacker, but I know my way around a secure server. I'll see what I can dig up about Homeland's Paranormal Division and see if there's anything suspicious about any of their people." She pulled a laptop out of a bag and walked over to Harker's kitchen bar area. "Does this place have Wi-Fi?"

"No idea," I said. "I've never seen Harker touch a computer except to throw it out a window."

"Which he does with a frequency that is both disturbing and expensive," Luke said. He walked into Harker's bedroom and came out with a sleek MacBook. "I believe this should have all the information you need within its files. The password is 'Lucy&Mina.' Don't forget the ampersand."

"Thanks, Luke." Jo opened Harker's laptop, then her own. "You folks work on how to get into Homeland and deal with the boss. I'll message Sparkles and see what we can come up with."

"Sparkles?" I repeated.

Jo grinned at me. "Now *he's* a hacker. This guy can break into any system anywhere. And he's one hundred percent loyal to the Council. If there's a Big Bad, Sparkles will find him."

"Sure, but…Sparkles?"

"Long story." Jo smiled at me again and turned to her computers.

"So what's our play?" I asked the group.

"We wait until Jo finds the bad guy, then we deal with him," Watson replied. He had a dark look in his eyes that belied his oh-so-proper diction. This was a man that had seen some shit, and wasn't afraid to go back there.

"With extreme prejudice," Gabby added. Every word that came out of that girl's mouth reinforced my mental image of her wearing Hannibal Lecter headgear, I swear.

"Well until she's done, I'm going to go do what I do—detect things," I said, turning to go.

Luke intercepted me before I had done more than turn around. "You can't," he said, giving me a stern look. "It's not safe out there for you until we know more about what we're facing."

"Don't get in my way, Luke. I will not be fucked with on this. I don't know what Harker is to me yet, but I know he's important, and I know that whatever asshole was pulling Smith's strings won't quit just because we killed his puppet. So I'm going to go out there and do what I can to find him."

"And do what, exactly?" Luke asked. I looked at him. There was no malice there, no teasing or taunting, just an honest question. And I had to pause because I hadn't exactly given that part a whole lot of thought.

"I don't know yet, but I'll figure it out when I get there."

"That's a pretty solid symptom of Harker exposure," Jo said from behind Luke.

"Kiss my ass," I snarled. But she was right.

"Sorry," she said. Her words made it clear that she was anything but sorry, but I didn't feel like getting into a fight with her over it. "I just meant that Harker could go off half-cocked like that, but it doesn't work that way for people like us."

People like us? Did she mean cops? Vampires? Wannabe superheroes? I gave her a quizzical look, and she laughed.

"No offense, Detective. I mean normal human beings. Harker got away without making a plan because he had magic and superpowers. We aren't wizards, and we can't shrug off knife wounds and bullets."

"Speak for yourself, mortal," Luke said.

"Fair enough," Jo ceded. "Most of us can't shrug off knife wounds and bullets. We have to plan before we go running in after the monsters."

Just then my cell phone buzzed in my pocket. I pulled it out and tapped the screen. "Fuck."

"What's wrong, Detective?" Luke asked.

"There's a disturbance call. The captain asked for me by name."

"Isn't that a little out of your normal bailiwick, Detective?" Watson asked.

"Do you really talk like that or are you just screwing with me?" I asked, completely honest.

"I'm sure I have no idea what you're talking about," was the very stiff upper lip reply.

"He really talks like that," Jo said. "But his point is valid. Why are you going to a domestic disturbance call? Especially when you're supposed to be on leave?"

"This isn't an ordinary disturbance call, and it's not a domestic disturbance. It's at a bar."

"Doesn't make it any less not your problem."

"Still true. Except my captain knows this bar is a supernatural hot spot," I clarified.

"Mortivoid's pub?" Luke asked.

"Yep, there's some kind of shitstorm going down at Mort's, and I'm the lucky one who gets to go check it out." I started for the door, only to be cut off by Luke. Again. "That's starting to get old, Luke."

"My apologies, Detective." He sounded somewhat less than completely sincere. Like not at all. "I feel that I would be remiss in my duties as your protector if I allowed you to go unescorted to this 'disturbance.'"

"Thanks, Luke, but I got this...wait a minute, my *what?*"

Luke at least had the courtesy to look embarrassed. "Quincy made it very clear on several occasions that if he was not able to, in his words, look after you, that I was to fulfill his self-appointed duties in that regard. I think this situation qualifies."

"Ignoring the absolute chauvinistic bullshit inherent in that statement and accepting that there are a lot of things running around Mort's that I probably can't handle without a little help, what exactly are you going to do about it? It's less than an hour until sunrise. We can get there in twenty minutes, but then you're stuck in Mort's place all day. And that's ignoring the whole sleeping all day thing."

"I can go without sleep if the situation warrants, but you are correct that my aversion to sunlight makes me an untenable choice for your companion. I was going to suggest Gabriella serve as your partner for this excursion. She is very capable and has experience dealing with several different types of supernatural creatures."

"I got this," I repeated, and reached for the doorknob.

"I'm afraid I insist." I looked into his eyes and saw the implacable stare of a man who has seen the absolute worst humanity has to offer and has walked through those fires for a long time. There was not a word in the dictionary that was going to make him change his mind.

"If I try to ditch her, you'll just send a car, won't you?" I felt bad almost immediately.

"I would, but I have no cars, and no one left to send in one." The bleak look on his face reminded me of everything Luke had lost in a few short hours. All of the man's possessions were now just so much ash, and so was his manservant and companion Renfield. Smith paid for that, but we needed to figure out who was pulling his strings and extract a little payment from that asshole, too.

"I'll just take an Uber if you try to escape. Let's go, cop-lady. We got bad guys to shoot and monsters to maim." Gabby breezed past me and Luke and opened the door with a grand flourish. I shook my head and walked through. Me and the psychopath, just like I liked it. Not.

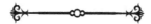

Mort's looked quiet from the outside, which was to be expected since it was almost dawn. I was dead tired and fresh out of patience for monsters and their bullshit, so I didn't bother with any of the normal pleasantries at the door. I just banged on it until the little green door-goblin opened up, then I stuck my Sig in his face.

"Open the goddamn door," I growled.

"Regular bullets won't kill me, you know. I'm technically a member of the Fae, so only cold iron—"

"Have you ever been shot in the eyeball?"

He gulped a little. "No."

"Do you think it's likely going to feel good?"

Another gulp. "Probably not."

"Is it going to make it hurt any less that you know it won't kill you?"

"Almost certainly not."

"Then open the goddamn door and get out of my goddamn way."

He did exactly what I asked, keeping the thick metal door between us as Gabby and I walked into Mort's anteroom. I kept my gun drawn, and Gabby spun a silver stake around in her hand like it was a toy.

"That was nice," my nutjob partner said. "I almost thought you would have really shot him."

"That's because I would have," I replied.

"Really?" Her voice was light, teasing.

Mine was not. "Really."

"I don't believe you."

"I don't give a shit what you believe. You weren't the one holding the door. It only matters what I believe, and what that little snotball believed. Now I've had a really fucked up couple of days, and I don't expect it to unfuck itself anytime soon. So if you'll excuse me, let's go see what passes for a disturbance in a demon bar."

I pushed open the door into the main bar and saw...nothing. Not a single monster at any of the tables, no one behind the bar, nothing. There were no customers, no employees, and no Mort. Nothing looked out of place, no overturned tables, no toppled chairs, no broken glasses or bottles. In short, it looked more placid than I'd ever seen it. Of course, I usually only came to Mort's with Harker, the one-man chaos vortex, so "placid" went out the window a few seconds after we arrived usually. But not this time. Everything looked calm. The only difference between this visit and every other trip I'd made to Mort's was that the wooden sign proclaiming "Sanctuary" was missing from over the bar.

Which wasn't anywhere on the list of things I'd consider a good sign.

I kept my pistol out as I made my way to the door at the end of the bar. It led to Mort's back room, where the hitchhiker demon usually stayed out of the public eye. I listened at the door for a moment, but heard nothing. I turned the knob, stepped through, and found the source of the "disturbance."

Mort sat alone in an empty bar, but it looked nothing like the 20th century dive bar Mort's was made out to be. This looked like a pub from Europe sometime between the Dark Ages and last week, all carved wooden furniture, candles, and pewter tankards. It had a weighty feeling about the room, like we were underground, or in a building set into a hill.

Even in the dim light from the wall sconces, Mort was easy enough to spot. Especially since he was the only person there. He had apparently returned the body of the NFL quarterback he'd been wearing when I saw him the day before, and now he was dressed in the skin suit of a thirtysomething white guy with a ponytail and goatee. He was big, too, with raw muscle bulging under his t-shirt.

"Hi Mort," I said, walking over to his table and pulling out a chair. I holstered my pistol and sat down. Gabby stood behind my left shoulder and a few feet back, close enough to be useful but not so close as to screw with my draw if I needed to reach my gun. She might be a psycho, but she knew her way around a fight. I looked Mort up and down. "Borrow a biker?"

Mort glanced up at me, his face solemn. "Murderer," he replied. "I thought I might want a body that deserved whatever punishment the authorities assign to it."

My hand drifted to the butt of my gun. "Punishment?" I asked. "Punishment for what?"

"I find it likely that we may break a few mortal laws in our quest, Detective. If the body I inhabit is already someone that you think should spend the rest of its life imprisoned, then I can do so with relative impunity."

"*Our* quest?" I asked, thinking there was no way he was saying what I think he was saying.

"Yes, our quest. Orobas killed someone very near and dear to me. He must pay for that. As must his master and all of his many minions. It is entirely possible that the streets of this city may run red with blood before my thirst for vengeance is slaked."

Yup, he was saying *exactly* what I thought he was saying. Mort, the demon bar proprietor, just volunteered to join the Super-Friends. Fuck me running.

"I like this guy," Gabby said from behind me. "He's got my kind of style."

Of course she likes him. He makes her look sane.

Chapter Seven

I TURNED TO THE DOOR, AND THERE STOOD THE STEREOTYPICAL HIGH school football coach. About six feet tall and two-twenty, with a little bit of a gut, brown mullet going gray at the temples, and a hell of a farmer's tan. He was even wearing the tall white socks, short shorts, and polo shirt version of the uniform, complete with a whistle around his neck.

"Who the fuck are you supposed to be, Varsity Football Barbie?" I asked, drawing in my will and starting to mutter an incantation under my breath.

"My name is immaterial, mortal. All that should concern you is my displeasure, which is great. You have banished or destroyed two of my favorite minions, and that has made me wroth."

I ignored his stupid archaic language, focusing on finishing the ritual of banishment I'd begun. I shouted "Amen!" and flung a ball of energy at him, only to watch in dismay as he held up a hand and caught my spell in midair. I didn't know that could happen. It's not that I couldn't do it, I literally had never heard of anyone even attempting it.

The demon coach turned the glowing orb of light over and over in his hands, looking at it with a little smile playing across his lips. He looked up at me and clapped his hands together, dispersing the spell in a flash of light. A wave of magical backlash blew through me and dropped me on my ass, leaving me with a sore butt and ringing ears.

I shook my head to clear the sparkles from my eyes and heard a tremendous roar from the far side of the room. I pulled myself upright and saw Drew, transformed again into his giant half-wolf form, slam into the coach from the side and send him clattering through a row of desks, ending up under the blackboard in a heap of fur, flesh, and twisted metal.

My Glock was going to be no use against that thing, and the one vial of holy water I had left felt pretty inadequate as well. I took a quick inventory of what I had on me and found my arsenal very wanting in the demon-slaying equipment department. I had a couple of silver-edged daggers on my belt and a pouch full of wolfsbane, since I expected to tussle with werewolves. I even had a couple of flash-bangs loaded with powdered silver nitrate, great for immobilizing weres and completely fucking useless against a demon. All I had was my wits, my magic, and a big goddamn werewolf for a partner. Nothing about this screamed "easy" to me.

Drew and the demon were going toe to toe, throwing haymakers and generally knocking the ever-loving shit out of each other. While the bad guy was occupied, at least for a few seconds, I looked around for anything in this classroom that might be useful. My eyes landed on an overturned desk, with one leg bent at an odd angle, and I got an idea.

I ripped the leg off the desk and swung it through the air a couple of times, testing it for balance and heft. It was just a two-and-a-half-foot aluminum tube, so it wasn't going to be worth a shit as a club, but I only needed it to work for a few seconds. I focused my will on the desk leg, imagining it in my head to be the flaming sword of the archangel Uriel, who stood guard at the gates of the Garden of Eden after Adam and Eve were kicked out.

"*Apparatio*," I whispered, letting my will flow into the aluminum in a slow trickle. As the spell took hold, the makeshift club began to shimmer in my hand, transforming into a flaming three-foot blade.

I turned toward the scuffle and shouted, "Hey, dickhead!"

The demon turned to me and jerked backward at the sight of the flaming sword. "Where did you get that?" it hissed.

"I called in a favor with an archangel," I said, charging the demon with the flaming sword. "Uriel sends his regards!" I swung the flaming blade at the demon's head, and when it brought its hands up to block the strike, I popped the cap off the vial of holy water concealed in my left hand and splashed it all over the demon's face. It screamed as the sanctified liquid burned its eyes and clapped its palms over its face.

"Begone, unclean thing!" I shouted. "In the name of the Father, I banish thee! In the name of the Son, I banish thee! In the name of the Spirit, I banish thee!" I threw as much will as I could muster quickly into the incantation and ripped open a small Gate behind the demon. I dropped the chair leg and the empty vial and shoved the demon into the Gate. It plunged through the rip in dimensions, and I pulled all my power back out of the rift, sealing it shut before anything on the ugly side of the universe noticed it and came through to our side.

The illusion I cast on the desk leg vanished the second I let go of it, and it clattered to the floor, just another piece of scrap metal. I dropped to my knees, every ounce of energy gone, and pulled the teacher's wastebasket over to me. I puked into the trash can for several moments, and after the second round of revisiting breakfast, Drew padded out into the hall and came back human and dressed again.

He sat on the teacher's desk while I vomited up my last month's worth of meals and looked down at me with curiosity written all over his face. Finally empty, I just lay flat on my back on the floor, the cool tile feeling good against my sweat-soaked head.

"That seems to have sucked," he said after a minute or two, apparently deciding that I was done.

I waited a few seconds to make sure he was right before I answered. "Yeah, that wasn't the best."

"What the fuck happened? You had a sword, then it was a piece of scrap. Then we were fighting a demon, then the demon was gone. Did I miss something?"

"I cast an illusion on the leg of the desk to make it look like something a demon would be afraid of—an archangel's sword. Then I opened a portal to Hell, shoved the demon through it, and closed the door on it."

"That sounds like a really good thing."

"It's about as good an outcome as I could have hoped for."

"Then why the puking?"

"There are two ways that I know of to open a Gate. One involves a protective circle, an involved ritual, a safe space, and about four hours of spellcasting. It's extremely difficult, but if you follow all the steps and take the time to create a circle within a circle to contain whatever you summon through the Gate, then you can perform the spell without any real danger to yourself or the rest of the world."

"That's not what you did here."

"The other," I went on, "involves basically taking all of my personal stores of magical energy and a decent chunk of my physical energy, and using those to rip a hole in the universe. It's exceedingly dangerous, borderline suicidal, and frankly completely fucking stupid. It leaves you drained of all magical energy, and you feel like you've got been run over by a truck for about a week. Not to mention the fact that you have a completely unprotected doorway between Earth and Hell for the time that the Gate is open."

"And that's what you just did."

"It seemed like a good idea at the time," I said, then promptly passed out.

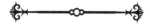

The next day about noon, after half a dozen Advil and three bottles of the red Gatorade, I stepped through the doors of Lockton High. Only this time, I went in through the front door like I belonged there. Because I did. Or at least the persona I wore belonged there. I followed the signs to the main office and stepped into the barely-controlled chaos that is a high school office half an hour before school starts in the morning.

"Can I help you?" The harried woman behind the desk barely looked up from her computer as she held up a finger to the student she was talking to.

"I'm Harold Quinn. I'm the emergency substitute for Mr...." I let my words trail off like I forgot the name of who I was supposed to be subbing for. I remembered, but I remembered him more as Ashkaranoth, the demon I sent back to Hell less than twelve hours before. A couple hours of research between bouts of the chills and more vomiting turned up his name, but not really anything else about him. He was a low-level lieutenant, traded back and forth between higher level demons depending on mood and who lost at cards that week or whatever gambling games demons played. He didn't have the power or the brains to get himself to this plane, and he didn't have anywhere near the juice to corrupt the school to the degree that I felt while walking the halls.

So now I was wearing fake glasses, khaki pants, and a polo shirt, working for seventy-five bucks a day as a substitute Social Studies teacher for a bunch of middle America teenagers who cared less about Social Studies than I did, if that was possible. Rocco got me in as the sub for the banished coach/teacher, proving once again that he was more than just an empty head on top of a pile of muscles, but I had to figure out exactly what constituted "Social Studies" on my own. Education in England in the beginning of the twentieth century was a little different than Ohio in the early twenty-first, but as far as I could tell, it was kinda like world history mixed with civics.

I stepped into the room and the noise level didn't just increase, it *blossomed.*

"We got a sub!" one kid yelled.

"Fresh meat!" bellowed another.

"Where'd they find this asshole, working the express lane at Walmart?" a girl in the front row muttered to her neighbor.

I held up a hand and stood in the front of the room, waiting for silence. After a couple of minutes of shouts and muttered aspersions toward my manhood and my ability to control the horde, the class quieted down. I figured they would. I could afford to play the long game—I wasn't going to age, and they weren't going to leave unless I let them. And if it really got ugly, I'd just turn one or two of them into toads.

"My name is Mr. Quinn. I will be your substitute teacher today, and for the rest of this week. Coach Karan had an emergency and had to leave town unexpectedly." *And this plane of existence*, I didn't add. "He didn't leave any lesson plans for me to follow, so we'll be making this up as we go along. As long as you treat me and your classmates with the respect we all deserve, we'll get along fine. And who knows, you might even learn something."

"Fuck this noise, I'm going to the weight room."

I was expecting this. In any group, there's always one person that has to push the envelope, has to determine exactly who's going to be the lead dog. I know, because it's usually me. This time it was a meathead sophomore with more muscle than brains. He had a Mohawk haircut that looked like something out of a bad 80s movie, a sprinkling of zits across his cheeks, and a sneer on his face that told me he was probably a big deal jock at this school. The black and red letter jacket helped with that, too. He started for the door, and I stepped in front of him.

"Get out of my way," he snarled.

He was almost tall enough to look me in the eye and outweighed me by a good thirty or forty pounds, all of it muscle and bad attitude. If I was a normal human, he would have worried me a little. I've never been accused of being normal.

"Get back to your desk," I said. I looked down the couple of inches at him and kept my voice very even. No point in my getting angry, I was going to win this debate no matter how poorly it went.

"I don't think so, pencil-neck. I can go lift any time I want." He pulled a crinkled piece of paper out of his pocket and shoved it into my chest.

I took the piece of paper, looked at it, then folded it into neat quarters and handed it back to him. "This says you have permission to be in the weight room during lunch, before and after school, during study hall, and during any class where the teacher excuses you from class."

"Yeah, that's right. So *excuse* me." He gave me the nasty grin of a shitty kid who's used to getting his way from all the adults in his life. I never liked those kids.

"You're not excused. Go sit down."

"I don't want to."

"I don't give a shit."

"You can't cuss at me. You're a teacher!" The outrage in his eyes made it clear that he didn't expect anyone to ever turn any tables on him and treat him like he treated other people.

I reached down with one hand and grabbed his belt buckle. I held onto the lapels of his jacket with the other to steady him, and I picked him up until he was directly at my eye level. His eyes widened, and I heard a gasp or two from the other students in the class.

"Listen here, shitball. I'm not a teacher. I'm a *substitute*. I didn't go to college for this crap. I don't want to make a career out of pretending to care whether or not you ever turn into anything more than a used car salesman at your daddy's Chevy dealership on the outskirts of town. I don't even want to be in this fucking town, so if you think you can intimidate me by threatening the seventy-five dollar a day gig I've got babysitting you fuckwits, you've got another think coming. Now you have two choices. You can go sit down and pretend not to be a total goddamn douchenozzle, or you can keep pushing me and find out how close to the principal's office I can get when I throw your ass down the hallway face-first."

I set him back down on his feet and took my hands off of him. "What's it gonna be, pal? You want to sit down and pretend to learn something, or you want to dance?"

He looked around like he was waiting for a buddy to step up and back his play, but everybody else wearing a letter jacket was very conspicuously staring at their textbooks. He gave me one last glaring squint that probably intimidated a lot of freshmen and middle school kids, then stomped back to his seat and dragged a book out of his backpack.

I turned to the rest of the class. "Now, what chapter were you on?"

Chapter Eight

THE PARKING LOT OF HARKER'S BUILDING WAS FULL OF MOVING VANS and contractor trucks when we got back there, me in my car and Mort a little wobbly on his body's Harley. I will admit that he looked pretty intimidating walking through the marble lobby with his engineer boots clumping across the polished floors. We got out of the elevator on the top floor, and I stopped dead in my tracks. The once-quiet top floor of Harker's building was bustling with activity, as his full-floor apartment was turned into a construction site. Hammering and the sounds of machinery echoed through the halls. Workmen hurried every which way, weaving around each other as they carried toolboxes and paint cans through doorways.

Mort, Gabby, and I slipped into the main living room and closed the door behind us, cutting the noise down to an almost bearable level.

"What the hell is going on out there?" I asked.

"Renovations," Watson replied from one of the sofas. "Once Luke realized exactly how many of us were likely to be working out of this space for the foreseeable future, he took a few steps to guarantee a little more space and privacy for all of us."

"In other words, he's building out some extra bedrooms so we don't all have to cuddle in Harker's bed or bunk with him in a light-tight safe room," Jo said from the table. She sat behind her laptop, hair pulled back in a ponytail. "What's with the demon?" she added.

At the word "demon" the room exploded into activity. Watson rolled off the couch and sprang to his feet, drawing a pistol from somewhere as he stood. The door to the bedroom flew open, and Luke dashed into the room, only to stop short when he saw it was Mort standing in the living room.

"Oh," the vampire said. "Hello, Mortivoid."

"Hello, Vlad," Mort replied with a nod of his head. "Would you please tell your minion to lower his weapon? I just got this suit, and I don't want to have to go search for another one."

Luke turned to Watson and motioned for him to put the gun away. Watson gave Mort a skeptical eyeball but tucked the gun into the back of his pants and sat down on the arm of the couch. "Mort, I must offer condolences on Christy's death. She was a fine woman and a very capable bartender. Her Bloody Mary was a true work of art. She shall be missed."

"Thank you, Vlad. I appreciate the sentiment."

I looked from Mort to Luke and back again. I didn't know if Luke knew that Christy was Mort's half-human daughter, and I sure as hell wasn't going to bring it up. I remembered the look on Mort's face when he rolled up on Orobas during the fracas at Luke's place, and it scared me. I didn't need to see that again anytime soon. I had a bad feeling I'd be seeing it in my dreams regardless.

"Now what are you doing here, Mortivoid? We have an arrangement. I don't eat your customers, and you don't stick your nose in my business."

"Your business became my business when Orobas killed my daughter. I want his head for a soup tureen. I want to send his soul back to Hell a torn and shredded thing, a scrap of consciousness so wisp-thin that demons will use him for toilet paper. I want to—"

"We get it. You're pissed. Moving right along." Gabby shouldered her way past Mort and I *en route* to the fridge. She opened the door and stuck her head inside. "Did nobody go grocery shopping? We're out of beer."

"Can we not freeload on all of Harker's food and drinks and instead figure out how we're going to clear his name and get him back to Charlotte?"

"Missing your half-vamp booty call, Detective?" Gabby asked as she walked past me to the liquor cabinet with a glass of soda water over ice. I watched as she poured the last of Harker's vodka into her drink and sat down on the sofa next to Watson.

"One, he's not half-vampire," I said as I walked over to where Gabby sat. I leaned over and plucked the vodka and soda from her hand. "Two, he's my fiancée, not my booty call. And three, if you think I'm going to sit here and let you insult Harker while you drink his booze in his living room and I won't slap the taste out of your mouth, you've got another think coming." I took a step back and handed the drink to Mort. "Hold this."

Gabby stood up and got in my face. "You wanna go, Miss Cop? We can go. I don't know what your problem is with me, but we can solve it right now if you want to."

"My problem with you is that I think you're a goddamn psychopath, and I can't handle any more crazy in my life right now. So if you're determined to keep being part of the problem, then would you please get the fuck out of my city before I shoot you right between the fucking eyes? Or if you want to be part of the solution, then please stop being such a pain in my ass!"

Gabby stared up at me for a long moment, her dark eyes boring into mine. "I like you, cop. You got stones. But you ever touch my drink again, we're going to have problems." She reached around me and reclaimed her drink from Mort. "And I'm a sociopath, not a psychopath," she said, sitting back down on the sofa.

A knock on the door ended any further explorations into Gabby's twisted psyche. I looked around, but everyone had that edgy look that said they were not at all expecting a pizza, so I put a hand on my pistol as I went to the door. Mort stepped back into the kitchen, and Gabby set her drink down on the coffee table. I didn't see her or Watson's hands, so I figured they had me covered if whatever was on the other side of the door wasn't friendly.

I put my eye to peephole and instantly relaxed. I turned back to the room and motioned for them to be calm, then opened the door wide enough for Officer Santos to come in. "Santos, what brings you out here? And how did you find me, anyway?"

"I looked up Harker's address. I just figured you'd be here." She looked past me into the room. "Oh, I'm sorry. I didn't know you were having guests..."

"No, it's fine," I said, moving her into the room and closing the door. "It's fine. These are some friends of Harker's. We're working on a way to clear his name."

"Oh yeah, that's your lawyer guy from this morning." Santos pointed at Watson, who nodded.

"And I am Lucas Card; I am Quincy's uncle," Luke said, extending a hand. They shook, and I suppressed a smile as Santos rubbed her hand after. Luke's hands are *cold*.

"Pleased to meet you," Santos said. "Detective Flynn, can I speak to you for a moment?"

I motioned her into Harker's bedroom. "Sorry, there's not really anyplace else to speak without the group," I said, leaning against the dresser. I didn't bother telling her that Luke could hear us talk through the closed door, and probably through the solid floor if he wanted to.

"What's up, Santos?"

"I just wanted you to know that Director Buprof took over the search at the scene this morning and kicked all our crime scene guys off."

"The scene? You mean Mr. Card's house?"

"Yeah," Santos said. "I'm probably not supposed to say anything, but it seemed really strange to me."

"Strange doesn't even begin to describe it. How long have they been there?" I asked, moving to the door and opening it.

"Only a couple of hours. I came over here as soon as my shift ended."

"Thanks, Santos. We'll head over there now and see what's going on. I appreciate you keeping an eye out for me."

"No problem, Detective. If you need anything, just let me know." She left, and I turned to see Watson standing up and grabbing his suit coat.

"Where do you think you're going, Watson?" I asked.

"Well, since you are almost certainly going to Mr. Card's residence, and he is unable to accompany you thanks to the daytime hour, a fact that your Mr. Buprof is almost certainly aware of, you will need someone with solid legal footing to accompany you. I am that someone."

"What in the world makes you that someone?" I asked.

"I am Mr. Card's legal counsel; therefore, I am his legal proxy in all instances where Mr. Card is unable to attend to his affairs himself, especially when he is indisposed due to a medical condition, such as his extreme reaction to ultraviolet light."

"So since he can't go out in daytime, you get to ride along," I translated.

"Exactly what I said." I was almost starting to like the smug bastard. Almost.

"Fine, come on," I said, turning to the door.

"I'm going, too," Mort said. "But this time I'd like to ride in the car. I don't like motorcycles."

"Maybe you should have thought about that before you hitchhiked into a biker. And no, you're not coming."

He got in front of me. That shit was really getting old. "Yes, I am. If Orobas is there, he'll just kill you. And if this Buprof is a Cambion, he'll probably kill you. If any of the Homeland Security agents are working for Orobas, *they'll* kill you. Get the picture?"

"Why won't they kill you?" I asked.

"They could try." Mort gave me a look and my blood ran cold. I decided I didn't want to fuck with the scary-looking biker demon, especially since he was more unhinged than normal after losing someone he actually gave a shit about.

"Fine, come on. But you two ride in the car," I said, picking up the helmet and keys Mort put on the table when he walked in. "I'm borrowing your Harley."

Chapter Nine

THERE ARE A LOT OF THINGS THAT MY CHILDHOOD AND EARLY LIFE provided. I had loving parents, wonderful brothers, a very bizarre surrogate grandfather who rambled a lot about monsters and killing them, and eventually a caring albeit equally bizarre uncle. I also had a certain level of celebrity and prosperity unknown to most people, thanks to the events of a certain book about my parents and Uncle Luke.

What I did not have, and had never experienced before, was Friday night high school football. Frankly, I didn't have football at all until well into adulthood and didn't start paying attention to it until I was over ninety years old. When you don't really age, you get to take your time exploring hobbies, and I had a lot going throughout most of the twentieth century.

So when I stepped out of my pickup in the Lockton High School parking lot the next night, I was completely unprepared for what I found. There were tents, vans, grills, the whole nine yards. It looked more like what I'd seen on TV of a college tailgate than a clash of high school athletes. There were banners pledging allegiance to one player or another, signs proclaiming what the Lions should do to the Ravens, the mascot of the rival du jour Warren G. Harding High School.

My head was on a swivel as I walked through the promenade of insanity, looking not just at the spectacle of teen sports, but also keeping an eye out for any sign of supernatural influence. I couldn't just wander around with my Sight active, because it blurred my normal vision and there was too much going on for me to be distracted and stay safe, so I cast a minor detection spell on myself before I entered the throng, hoping that anything hinky I encountered wouldn't be immediately malevolent.

I made my way to the concession stand without incident, grabbed a jumbo soda and a popcorn, then made my way to a seat in the home grandstand. I settled in behind an African-American family decked out in red and black with lion paws painted on their faces and a giant red foam finger on the hand of an octogenarian matriarch. I assumed they were there supporting #5, the starting quarterback, mostly because the parent-aged man and woman wore jerseys with the number on them. I figured they would be enthusiastic enough to hide my lack of jumping up and down.

The game started, and I saw what Rocco was worried about. The Lions looked like they were matched up against the other school's junior varsity team. Actually, it looked more like a college team playing against middle schoolers, the strength and speed levels were so disparate. After a perfect forty-yard pass for the third touchdown of the first quarter, I leaned down to the proud father in front of me.

"Your son?" I asked, pointed to the number on his jersey.

"Yeah, that's my boy, Javon Henderson. Remember that name, mister. You're gonna hear it on TV some Sunday."

"If he keeps playing like that, I believe it," I agreed. "How long has he been a starter here?"

"This is his first year," his dad said. "He's just a sophomore, and we've already got scouts calling from Ohio State, Miami of Ohio, Penn State, and Notre Dame. Just think about, buddy. My boy might play quarterback for Notre Dame."

I didn't bother telling him that Notre Dame was also the training ground for all the exorcists in North America. That wasn't on the list of things he needed to worry about. "That's great. He's got a ton of talent." I patted the man on the shoulder and leaned back. I wasn't joking. The kid had talent. The kind of talent that gets college graduates drafted in the first round into the NFL. Not the kind of talent that a fifteen-year-old kid from Ohio shows off in his first year of varsity ball. I didn't have to grow up with football to see that something was making these kids better than they had any right to be. Something that in all likelihood had a much darker side.

It was late in the third quarter, with the third string offense on the field and a three-touchdown lead for the Lions, when I felt it. Something was probing me. Something magical. I looked around but didn't see anything that looked out of the ordinary. The Lockton third-string running back broke loose and headed for the end zone, bringing the whole stadium to its feet. I used the confusion to mask me opening my Sight and sweeping the crowd for my magical Peeping Tom.

With the Otherworld laid over the mundane world, active or latent magic lit up like a miniature sun to me. With no surprise at all, I saw that three quarters of the football team glowed like sparklers on the Fourth of July, as did almost the entire coaching staff. As I kept looking around the stadium, there were two surprises to my magical vision. First, the quarterback didn't exhibit any signs of magical ability or tampering. He was just that damn good. And second, there was a woman in the stands giving off enough magical energy to power Cleveland. And of course, she was staring right at me.

My cover blown, I slipped out of the crush of humanity with as little fuss as possible, managing to only kick over one oversized soda on my way to the aisle. I hustled up the stands to the exit and through the gate into the parking lot without incident and thought I was at least close to home free when I felt a pulse of energy whizz by me and saw the tire of a battered Ford Focus to my left melt under the assault of a walnut-sized fireball.

"Goddamn it, just one time I want to have shit work out the way I plan," I muttered and turned around. There was nothing surprising in what I saw—the woman I saw in the stands glowing like a Christmas tree was standing in the parking lot glaring at me. She was a pretty woman, mid-twenties with long dreadlocks pulled back into a ponytail, jeans, a cream-colored sweater with a purple scarf, and hiking boots. If she didn't open conversations by hurling balls of fire at me, she looked like somebody I might enjoy talking books with. Except that all my reading lately had been on the summoning or banishing of demons, so my literary conversation game was kinda lacking.

"Can I help you?" I called out. She was still about fifty feet away, and I was okay with that. I didn't want to blow my cover and get into a big magical duel with a thousand or more townsfolk just a couple hundred yards away.

"What are you doing?" she asked. She started walking toward me, and I started walking backward, keeping the distance between us the same.

"I'm walking away so you don't blow up any of these cars if you miss again."

"I didn't miss. Consider that a warning shot." She reared back and flung another mini-fireball at me. The burning projectile zipped at me with a lot more velocity than my bigger fireballs, making me scramble to throw up a shield and deflect the burning orb into the ground. It exploded with a huge flash, and I blinked to clear the glare from my eyes.

When I could see again, the woman was right in front of me, a glowing sword of energy emanating from each fist. I pulled my shield in from a big curved tower in front of me into a more traditional buckler radiating out from my forearm and blocked her first slash easily. It turned out to be a distraction, though, and I barely avoided the stabbing thrust from her other hand.

"You're good at this," I said with a grunt, wrapping both of my arms in auras of energy and using them to slap her strikes away. I didn't want to hurt her until I knew she was evil. After all, an inappropriate body count was one of the reasons I was stuck in Lockton in the first place. I mean, Smitty definitely needed killing, but in hindsight I might have been just a little too public with the whole shooting a federal agent in the face thing. I was determined not to kill anyone in Lockton unless I knew for sure they were evil. And hopefully not well-connected.

"I've killed a lot of demons, asshole," the woman replied, shooting out a kick at my left knee. I checked the kick, but took a stinging shot to my shin as a result. She was too good for me to keep pulling my punches. If I didn't cut loose soon, she was going to get a shot through my defenses, and that would be bad. But if I did cut loose, I'd probably kill her, which might be worse.

I went very low to get under a head strike, then dropped her to her butt with a leg sweep. She went down with a *whoof*, and I had the time I needed.

"*Silencio!*" I said, dropping my shields and tossing tendrils of power out at her like Spider-Man's webbing. Strands of magical power flowed from my fingertips and wrapped around her face, tying her mouth closed.

"*Restrictus,*" I said, aiming the flow of my power down her body. More tendrils of energy flowed out of me, wrapping her entire body in glowing ropes of power. Trussed up like a turkey, my mystery attacker struggled against her bonds, but spinning the bonds out of my own energy instead of the life-force of people or things around me gave me two advantages.

One, I wasn't draining anyone of the energy of their life and soul. That wasn't my thing, if I could help it. Two, if she fought against the bonds, I could just throw more power at them and keep her tied up as long as I had the reserves. Which wasn't going to be long, given my current energy levels. I still wasn't anywhere close to recovered from opening the Gate, and I could feel the toll this little duel was taking on my magical energy.

I bent over, hoisted my attacker up across my shoulders in a fireman's carry, and started walking up the hill to the school. I saw a security guard heading our way about a hundred yards away, and whispered "*inconspicuous*" under my breath. I let out a little more power into a little "ignore me" cloud around me, encouraging anyone who saw me to see exactly what they expected to see and not to take notice of anything I did. It wasn't a foolproof spell by any stretch;

anyone with no real preconceived notions of what is "normal" wouldn't be affected, but I figured it would be good enough to fool a busy security guard at a distance.

I was right. The guard turned around and went back to the game, convinced that we were nothing he was interested in. I used the copy of Rocco's key I'd made just for tonight's adventures, and a couple of minutes later, I deposited my bundle of pissed-off witch onto the floor of "my" classroom.

I looked down at the scowling woman. "I'm going to let you go now, but I want to make a couple of things clear first. I am not the bad guy, so if you think I'm a demon, then you're barking up the wrong tree. I'm here to help. Also, there aren't any innocents around now, so I'm not going to pull any more punches. You try to throw another fireball at me, I'll shove it so far up your ass light will shine out of your ears. You get me?"

She nodded, and I released the magic binding her. She instantly scrambled to her feet and backed up, putting most of the classroom between us, then muttered a brief incantation and surrounded herself with a shield of power, ostensibly keeping me from putting any magical bonds on her again. She didn't have to worry about that. If this conversation didn't go well, I didn't have enough energy left to tie her up magically, I was just going to shoot her.

Chapter Ten

WE ROLLED UP TO LUKE'S HOUSE ABOUT TEN MINUTES LATER, AND it looked even worse after I'd had a little time away from it. The place was crawling with men and women in Homeland Security windbreakers and stupid dress shoes that should never be worn to muck around explosion sites. I put down the kickstand on Mort's motorcycle and two agents were on me like bodyguards on paparazzi.

"You can't be here, ma'am," the first no-neck agent said.

"Get back on your bike, Detective. This is a Homeland Security matter now," the second one followed.

"This is so far from a Homeland Security matter it's funny," I said. "Get me Buprof."

"The director isn't available right now, ma'am," No Neck One said.

"Get in the vehicle, Detective," No Neck Two said, putting his right hand on my shoulder. That was a bad idea. I grabbed his wrist in my right hand, ducked under his arm and twisted it around behind him in a hammerlock. I pushed down on the back of his head with my left hand and slammed his face into the roof of my car. His knees buckled and he went down.

I whipped out my handcuffs and had him bound in three more seconds, then I stood up, my Sig in my hand. "The next motherfucker that decides assaulting a police officer is a good idea is going to have a much worse day than this jackass. Are we clear?"

The three agents approaching my car immediately stopped and put their hands up. I nodded and holstered my weapon. I looked down at No Neck Two and asked, "Are you going to behave, or do I have to leave you like that?"

He glared at me but didn't say anything. "Fine," I said. "See if you can convince one of your pals to uncuff you." I stomped off toward the wreckage with Mort and Watson in tow, only to see a highly agitated Deputy Director Buprof moving in my direction, all red-faced and blustery. I steeled myself for the inevitable confrontation, and he didn't disappoint.

"What the ever-loving fuck do you think you're doing here, Detective? You're suspended! Hell with suspended, you're fucking fired! And you sure as fuck need to get the fuck out of my crime scene. You've got no legal right to be here, so get your little friends here and go." He stood there tapping his foot, arms folded across his belly, barely holding in his dress shirt from the strain.

"While you are partially correct, Director, you are, like so many Americans, rushing to judgement. As Mr. Card's counsel and his legal proxy, I am certainly within my rights to be here, accompanied by whatever assistants I require to complete my assessment of the damages to his property as I deem necessary." Watson stepped forward, a business card in his outstretched hand. "Watson, as I'm sure you'll recall. Jack Watson. I am the solicitor on retainer for Mr. Card and his enterprises."

Buprof looked at the card in his hand, then at Watson, then at Mort. "The fuck you think this is, some kind of a joke?"

"I assure you, Director, I am deadly serious. We are here to conduct a thorough inspection of Mr. Card's property for the purposes of his insurance coverage and would appreciate it if you and your people would vacate the premises while we did so."

"Yeah, like that's going to happen. Fuck off, you gimpy little prick," Buprof said, giving Watson a shove on one shoulder. He took a step backward, his foot came down on a piece of rubble, and his lost his footing with his prosthetic leg. He went down to one knee, catching himself with one hand before he went sprawling. My hand drifted to the butt of my pistol, but I didn't draw. Yet.

"See," Buprof said, "it's not safe around here. You should go." He glared down at Watson, and I would have sworn I saw a yellow gleam in his eyes. Was *everybody* in Homeland Security a demon? I could believe it about the TSA, but this was more than I was expecting.

Watson didn't bite. He didn't lose his cool, although anger flashed across his face so fast I almost didn't believe I saw it. He simply stood up, dusted off his pants, and looked at Buprof with the disappointed gaze of someone dealing with a particularly stubborn child. I knew that look well. After all, I was dating Quincy Harker.

"I'm not leaving. In fact, you are," Watson said, stepping up to just inside the boundaries of polite distance from Buprof. "We have a right to be here, and you are outside your jurisdiction. We have clearance from Captain Herr to look over the wreckage and remove anything of value before it is stolen, so long as Detective Flynn ensures that we do not compromise the police department's evidence gathering. Here is the notice to that effect." He reached into his jacket and pulled out a folded piece of paper.

Buprof glared at him, then held out his hand. Watson handed him the paper, Buprof read it over once, then passed it back to him. "Fine, but be quick about it. I'll give my team their lunch break, but you'd better be gone by the time they get back. And I'll be watching you personally."

"So long as you watch us from the seat of your vehicle, that will be fine," Watson said, tucking the paper back into his coat.

Buprof stomped off, yelling at his team to clear out for thirty minutes. Watson turned to me. "Do you have any idea what they would be looking for?" he asked. His eyes were a little wild and there was a hint of sweat on his upper lip. He looked decidedly un-British.

"No clue. Good thing we've got some time," I replied.

"We probably don't have that much time," Watson said.

"Why not?"

"That letter was somewhat less than genuine," he said. "I might have printed it at Harker's condominium and signed your captain's name myself."

"You forged my boss's signature? On a document you gave to a Deputy Director of Homeland Security?" I shook my head. "You're all insane. Every single one of you. It's not just Gabby and Harker, you're all nuts. What does it say for your organization when the *vampire* is the least crazy one of you?"

"That we picked the right vampire?" Watson gave me a rakish grin. "Now, about that searching..."

"I'll take care of that," Mort said. "Whatever that little piece of Pit trash was looking for, I should be able to sense it as easily as he could." Mort started walking toward the rubble, but I grabbed his arm.

"Slow down, there, Speed Racer," I said. "At least keep your eyes open. Luke didn't have any real idea what Buprof was looking for, but that doesn't mean it's not hidden in some trapped chest or something."

"What do you think this is, Detective? A computer game? Most magical artifacts require activation. It's unlikely that the Count ever realized the true power of the item he possessed, since he has no magical affinity. I would expect it to be something triggered or activated by the ritual that Agent Smith was trying to complete before our dear Mr. Harker interrupted him."

"Then it would be over there." I pointed in the general direction of the front rooms of the house. I didn't know exactly where in Luke's place the ritual had happened, but I knew roughly where the explosion emanated from. I followed Mort to the piles of debris that used to make up Luke's house, picking my way through the still-smoking wreckage.

Mort motioned me back, and I stopped at the edge of what used to be the house. Mort walked farther, stopping every now and again to kick aside a chunk of rock, or to lift a section of wall and peer beneath it. He always put everything back exactly where he found it, taking a lot of photos with his phone, furthering our ruse of documenting all this rubble for insurance.

After several long minutes, Mort stopped and turned to me. "You should come over here, Detective."

I did, trying not to turn an ankle and bust my ass on the treacherous footing. "What is it, Mort?"

"I believe this to be either your friend or the former Agent Smith." He pointed to a large slab of wood that looked like the underside of Luke's gargantuan dining room table. I could just see what looked like a finger sticking out from under it. "I wished to give you the opportunity to say goodbye if that is something you desire. I understand that is something that humans do."

"Thanks, Mort." I didn't want to see Renfield's body under that table, and didn't know if I wanted to see Smith's either. I wasn't sure if I would spit on him or kick his corpse, and just thinking about poor Ren made me well up a little. "I think I probably shouldn't disturb the body, though," I said, stepping back.

Mort looked at me, momentarily puzzled, then nodded. "As you wish, Detective." His oddly formal cadence was somehow reassuring. I think it would have bothered me if he just behaved like everything was normal. This proper speech pattern, while unusual, gave me something else to focus on instead of what might be my dead friend's body beneath a few inches of oak.

He leaned over and picked up the table, swinging it up on one end with no apparent effort, even though I knew that table weighed several hundred pounds. I couldn't help myself, I looked at the body beneath it.

It was Renfield. He was face down, thankfully, but I recognized his trim form instantly. He still wore his black dress pants and the burgundy cardigan that was his favorite item of clothing for relaxing after work, protected from the worst of the fire by the heavy table, which was too thick and treated to burn easily. One bedroom slipper hung from his left foot, with only a tattered sock on his right. I had a sudden urge to find his other shoe and put it on him. It just seemed too un-Renfield to be seen with only one shoe, even in death. I blinked back tears, then started as Mort pushed the table away to crash amidst the rubble.

"What the hell, Mort?" I exclaimed, almost falling but catching myself on a jagged chunk of wall that still stood.

"I believe this is what your Director Buprof was looking for, Detective." He bent over and pulled a sword in a battered scabbard from underneath Ren's body. It looked old, and dirty as hell, with some scorch marks, but since everything I knew about swords began and ended with "put the pointy end in the bad guy," that was all I could see.

"What is it?" I asked.

"It is a sword, Detective. They are implements of war, used in combat since time immemorial."

"I know it's a sword, Mort. What I don't know is why Buprof would want it."

"And you don't need to know, Flynn. All you need to know is that you're lucky I don't have you fucking sent to Gitmo after the stunt you and your limey bastard lawyer just pulled. This letter is a fake as his leg, you traitorous bitch. How dare you come in here and interrupt my investigation into the murder of a federal agent. John Smith was my friend, he was a loyal agent, and he was—"

"He was a demon, you pitchfork slinging pit monkey," said Glory, who appeared out of nowhere at my left elbow and stepped between me and Buprof. "I know what you are, and I know you're out of your depth here. You don't have any real juice, imp. You're just making this all up as you go along. Well, you stepped in it now because the Host knows what you're trying to pull, and they aren't happy. Now why don't you crawl back into whatever burning craphole you slithered out of and leave Detective Flynn alone?"

I shrank back in horror as Buprof underwent a complete transformation before my eyes. The portly, tight-assed Deputy Director and shrieking functionary vanished as a nasty smile crept across his face. Buprof's face reddened even further, until his skin was a dark crimson, and his eyes went yellow, with vertical slits for pupils. He opened his mouth in a wide grin, and I saw a double row of pointed teeth in his now fully revealed demonic face. He held the grin and let his true face shine through for a few interminable seconds, then slammed his disguise back into place before he spoke.

"The Host? You think I'm afraid of the Host? You're more even more deluded than you are sanctimonious, you bitch. The Host aren't going to stop us, the Host..." He cut himself off short, then gave Glory a sneer promising a host of terrible things.

"Never mind the Host. They aren't a problem. You are. You're not just pissing me off, you're interfering with a federal investigation, and I want you to get the fuck out of here before I throw every last one of you under the nearest jail." Buprof was back in bureaucrat mode, and I think I liked the demon more.

"Try it." Mort's voice was cold, and my hand dropped back to the butt of my gun. I felt goosebumps crawl up my arms, and I suddenly wanted to be anywhere else in the absolute worst way.

"Mortivoid, how absolutely fucking typical," Buprof said with a wide smile, turning his attention to Mort for the first time since we arrived. "How's the family?"

Mort shoved me to the side as he went at Buprof, and it was only Glory's quick reflexes that kept me from crashing to the ground. I guess there's some value in having a guardian angel after all. Tossing the sword aside, Mort tackled the burly agent around the midsection and drove him to the ground. The two rolled around in the dirt and wreckage for a few seconds before I drew my Sig and fired a single round into the dirt beside the two wrestling demons. Mort and Buprof separated, both clambering to their feet to stare at me.

"Cut the shit, you two, unless you want the only real human Homeland agent in the state to wonder why you two are rolling around in the dirt like pissed-off kindergarteners." Buprof threw a nervous glance at one of the nearby Suburbans, confirming that not every Homeland Security agent in the state was an escaped demon.

The Deputy Director Demon got up and dusted himself off, then stepped up to Mort again. "I will give you but one warning, Mortivoid. Leave. This does not concern you. The Legions have ignored your dalliances with mortals for far too long, and they are no longer inclined to do so. Interference with our plans here will not be looked upon favorably."

"Murdering my daughter is not looked upon favorably either, Burferon. So tell your superior, whoever he is, that he has made a powerful enemy. I will see someone suffer for what happened to Christy, and I spent enough time in the Pits to know suffering. Intimately." Mort picked up the discarded sword from the rubble and wrapped his hand around the scabbard, preparing to draw it.

Buprof's face went ghost-white as his eyes locked on the weapon in Mort's hand, and his bottom lip started to quiver.

"Count yourselves fortunate. I have to go. There's...something I must attend to." He turned around and hurried off, looking for all the world like something scared the crap out of him, rather than him being scariest thing in the area. Within half a minute, he was tearing away from the house in a black Suburban with a dozen agents loading all their gear into matching SUVs and rolling in his wake.

"What the hell was that all about?" I turned to Glory, who shrugged.

"Can't say," the angel replied.

"Can't, or won't?" I asked. I was still pissed at her for holding back information that might have wrapped up our investigation earlier, and maybe kept Renfield alive, and here she was doing it again.

"Does it matter, Detective? If I can't, I won't. And if I won't, I won't. So the two words are interchangeable in this case, aren't they?" If all angels were like this, I was beginning to understand why Harker enjoyed being a sinner so much.

"Whatever." I turned to Watson and Mort. "Judging from his hasty retreat, that might be exactly what he was looking for." I pointed at the sword in Mort's hand.

"I knew that from the moment I picked it up. Now please take this blessed thing." He held the sword out to me.

I stared at it, not terribly interested in holding something that made Mort nervous and sent Buprof running for the hills. "Why me?"

"It doesn't have to be you. It can be the angel, it can be the cripple, I don't care," Mort said, and his voice crept high with pain. "But I have to put this piece of hallowed tin down before it sets me alight like a candle!"

I took the sword. I didn't feel anything weird about it, but the way Mort sighed with relief, you would have thought he was sunburned and I just dropped him in a vat of aloe. "What's wrong with you, Mort?" I asked.

"The sword," he grumbled, rubbing one hand with the other as if to restore feeling in it. "It burns me. It must be blessed or divine in some way. It hurts to touch it."

"You didn't appear to be in any pain when you were confronting Director Buprof," Watson said, stepping up beside Mort, gingerly picking his way across the rubble.

"I was raised in the Pits, Mr. Watson. You learn at a very young age to hide pain. Or not. If you choose not, you don't get to an old age. So I didn't let on that I was being cooked from the inside out."

"Probably a good idea," I said. "Glory, you want to shed any light on the origin of this little pigsticker?"

The angel looked at me, then shook her head. "I'd love to, Rebecca, but..."

"You can't," I finished the sentence for her.

"Exactly."

"Some help you are."

"We all have rules, Detective. Even angels."

"I don't," Mort said.

"Say that in the presence of the Morningstar," Glory countered.

"If it's all the same to you, I'd rather not," Mort demurred.

I sighed. "If you two are done debating theology, can we get back to the house and see if anyone knows anything about this damn sword?"

"A lovely idea, Detective. Shall I drive?" Watson asked.

"Do what you like, I'm not riding with you," I said, striding back to Mort's Harley. "You still haven't figured out which side of the road you want to play on!"

Chapter Eleven

"**W**HO THE FUCK ARE YOU AND WHAT THE FUCK ARE YOU DOING HERE?**"** spat the woman standing in "my" classroom at nine o'clock on a crisp fall Friday night. I decided that I liked her, despite her alarming tendency to throw fireballs first and ask questions later. Throw enough f-bombs around, and I'll probably get on board with what you're saying. What can I say? I appreciate a good poetic rhythm to swearing.

"I'm Quincy Harker. I hunt demons. I'm here because somebody is calling up nasty shit around here and turning it loose on kids. That's not cool." It was more the summoning demons thing and less the siccing demons on teenagers thing that had me concerned. I think most teenagers are assholes that would benefit from a little up-close time with a good old-fashioned Pit Lord or even a run of the mill Torment Demon.

"You're a demon hunter?" She looked dubious.

"Yup." I honestly didn't give a fuck if she believed me or not. I just didn't want to kill her if she turned out to be one of the good guys. My soul had enough black marks on it already.

"Prove it." She wasn't throwing fireballs anymore, which was good. She was just standing in the fourth row of desks staring at me with her arms folded across her chest.

"No." I stopped proving shit to people after World War II. If there's one thing I picked up from Luke, and frankly there are many, it's that being the oldest person in your zip code means you don't have to answer to anybody.

"Why not?"

"It's not a fucking parlor trick, lady. It's what I do. Take it or leave it, it's the truth. You don't believe it, I don't care. But you start flinging those little fireballs at me again, I'm going to blast a hole in your ass big enough to drive a truck through, and fuck the cleanup crew."

I could almost see the wheels turning behind her eyes. She looked me up and down a couple of times, then finally nodded at me. "Don't you want to know who I am and what I'm doing here?"

I cocked my head to the side. It looked like she'd come to a decision, but I wanted to confirm it before we moved into the "getting to know you" part of the evening. "Are we gonna fight some more?"

"I'm not planning on it."

"Then sure, go ahead." If I didn't have to kill her, then I didn't mind learning who she was. If I was just gonna have to hide the body, then it didn't matter.

"I'm a witch."

"No shit, Sherlock." I got to know Holmes briefly before he died. Fun guy, but he fucking *hated* that phrase. So, of course, I used it every chance I got around him. Made me almost misty-eyed thinking about it now. Nah, not really.

She held up a hand at me, so I held off on any more smartass comments. "Let me try that again. My name is Beth Kirkland. I teach English here. And I'm a witch."

"Good to meet you, Ms. Kirkland. At least while I'm here, I'm Harold Quinn. I'm filling in for Coach Karan, who is unexpectedly absent for an unspecified time."

"And I suppose you know nothing about that?" She gave me one of those looks that says "fill in the blanks."

I was feeling charitable, so I figured I'd give her a little more rope to hang me with. "I don't know anything about Coach Karan actually being a demon and getting tossed back into Hell, that's correct."

"I never liked that son of a bitch."

"Me neither." I don't like demons as a rule, and I certainly don't like the ones that try to kill me.

"But if Karan was the demon, why are you still here, Mr. Demon Hunter?"

"I said he was a demon. I never said he was *the* demon, Ms. English Teacher. He wasn't strong enough to juice up a whole football team, even if everyone on the coaching staff was a demonic minion. Which they aren't, by the way."

"I know. I cast a divining spell on them during last week's game. Only some of the coaches are demons. There are a few that are completely human, except for one latent wizard and one werewolf."

"Rocco," I said.

"Yes," she agreed. "A perfect job for a wolf, a strength coach for a high school. Lets him get his natural aggression out lifting weights all the time, and gives him another pack to be part of."

"You teach sociology, too?"

"Minored in anthropology. I spent a lot of time focusing on Xeno-Anthropology at Notre Dame."

Now it was my turn to fold my arms over my chest and raise an eyebrow. "Exorcist?"

"No, nothing like that. But I grew up in a family of witches, so I wanted to go somewhere that had some coursework in nontraditional religious topics, and I got a scholarship to Notre Dame. It was either there or Cambridge. Those were the only places I could find with any real opportunity to study demonology and spell craft."

"Yeah, Hogwarts has been closed to new students for a while now," I quipped. I knew of at least half a dozen other places someone could go to study about witchcraft and spell-slinging, but they all worked very hard to keep themselves hidden. I was glad to see their efforts were working, it made me feel like I had a shot at staying off the radar myself.

"So what's the play?" Beth asked.

"Well, I was kinda planning on hanging around the school long enough to see who the demon is, maybe figure out what it wants, and then send it home with extreme prejudice."

"You're not going to kill it?" she asked.

"I thought you said you'd fought demons before," I said, folding my arms over my chest. My bullshit detector was going off like a Geiger counter at Chernobyl. You don't kill demons. At least not easily, and certainly not demons with the kind of power this one was throwing around. A lot of times the best you can hope for is to send it back to Hell and hope it doesn't find a way out anytime soon.

"It's been a while." She didn't meet my eyes when she said it. Because of course she didn't.

"Yeah, like your whole life? Look, sweetheart, this isn't fucking playtime. This isn't a goddamn movie or some kind of bullshit academic lecture under your pretty little golden dome. This is real life, and real people are going to get real hurt. And I don't have time to waste on a fucking amateur ghostbuster who watched too many *Paranormal State* reruns and now thinks she's a goddamn expert on all things supernatural."

She looked me in the eye, then, and she was *pissed*. "Okay, Mr. Big-time Demon Hunter, here's the deal. My kid brother is missing, probably dead, and I think it's got something to do with whatever is going on here. He was a sophomore here last semester, and when I came home for fall break, he was missing. The police said he ran away, but the more I talked to his friends and poked around the school, the surer I became that something fucked up was going on. So I got a job as a perma-sub for an English teacher on maternity leave and started looking for the source of the magic."

"What made suspicious of the school? The winning football team?"

"That was part of it. The Lions have always sucked. There just aren't enough people in town to build from. The school's too small. But now they're rolling over bigger schools like they're the friggin' Steelers, and it's the same kids that got their asses kicked nine games out of ten last season. So something's definitely going on there. But that's not all."

"It never is," I grumbled.

"What?"

"Demons never just fuck with one thing. They're total shit-stirrers, so with most demons, if they're doing one thing, they're doing a bunch of things. They might all feed into the same big plan, but it might just be more opportunities to fuck with humans."

"Or kill them."

"Or kill them," I agreed.

"I think that's what's happening here. I think someone is killing any students with any magical or psychic Talent." Most normal people don't have shit for magical Talent. A little bit of *deja vú*, a tiny precognitive moment once in a blue moon, that's about all most folks get in their lives. Then there are the folks with Talent. They're rare, but not as rare as most folks think.

"What makes you think something is taking kids with Talent?"

"I checked the school records. Since the beginning of this school year, there have been a record number of transfers, relocations, runaways, and kids just up and vanishing. In some cases, the whole family is gone without a trace."

"So you're saying you think students with Talent are being targeted?"

"I'm saying that there are eight hundred kids across four grades in this school. You'd expect seventy-five or eighty of them to have a bit of talent, right?"

She had a point. A good ten percent of all people have some latent magical power. Those are the people who might never use it for anything, might not even know they have it, but they've got a really green thumb, or a really lucky streak that lasts for years, or maybe they just know who's going to call before the phone rings. Those people could develop some power with the right catalyst and the right training, but most of them live out their lives never knowing it.

So yeah, with the number of kids in the school, eighty or so kids should have at least some Talent. "Sure, something like that," I agreed.

"I know of three. And they're all major Talents."

"Three?" I looked at her, and I'm sure she could read doubt all across my features because that number was way off, even by my most conservative estimates. There should have been a lot more people with some ability, and realistically, there should have been *fewer* major Talents, as she described them.

Those major Talents—people like me, and apparently Beth and her whole family, the people with significant power, are really rare. It's even more rare to find someone with power and an environment that believes in it and nurtures it. Even most people with a lot of natural Talent don't ever do anything with it.

And to do anything significant with it took years of training. Most humans die before they master any part of spell casting. Maybe Beth couldn't see latent ability in people as well as she thought she could. Some witches could sense Talent in others better than others.

She let out a sigh that said she knew she wasn't convincing me, then said, "I cast a spell during the pep rally this morning. Three students lit up to my Second Sight like beacons. As did you, Coach Rocco, and Coach Balomb."

"Those are the only coaches that you found?" Now I knew her spell was bullshit. Since half the football coaches were demons, if she couldn't see them, then she was way off base.

"I wasn't looking for demons. I cast the spell specifically to find Talented or magic-touched humans. Or at least mostly humans."

I wasn't sure if she meant me or Coach Werewolf with that and decided not to ask. "Okay, that explains why the rest of the football coaches didn't light you up, but are you sure the spell reached the entire gym? Maybe you missed them."

"I cast it on the doors. Anyone using any type of magic who passed through was dusted with magic that would show up in my Second Sight. It had no effect on normal humans or other-dimensional beings. And I cast it at lunch, so everyone who came through the doors of the gym all afternoon was dusted. I didn't miss anyone. I didn't cast it wrong. I didn't fuck up the spell. I know what I'm doing, and I'm right. There are no Talents left in this school."

If she was right, then I was pretty sure I knew what was going on. "We've got a problem."

"No shit, Sherlock." Now I saw why Holmes didn't like that phrase. It was really fucking irritating when it got turned back on you.

She sat on the top of a desk and stared at me. "Well?"

"Well, what?" I asked, looking at her and trying to figure out how she managed to sit on the desk like that. If I tried that shit, I'd be flat on my ass in a heartbeat.

"Well, what's the problem?"

"Oh, yeah, that. Sorry. Yeah, there's a problem. If the whole football team is hyped up on magical super-juice, and the school only has three kids left with any magical ability, where do you think the demons are getting the mojo?"

Her eyes went wide and the color drained from her face. "Oh, no."

"Oh, yeah."

"You mean...?"

"Yeah," I said with a sigh. "I hate to tell you this, but it's looking very much like your brother and the other missing students were killed for their magical energy, and that energy was pumped into the football team like some kind of mystical steroids."

Chapter Twelve

"WHAT, THAT THING? NO, THERE'S NOTHING SPECIAL ABOUT IT. OTHER than fond memories, of course," Luke said when I showed him the sword.

"What kind of memories?" I asked.

"Oh, you know, the normal thing. I remember the look on the face of its previous owner when I ripped his heart out through his chest, the feel of his blood splashing across my face, that sort of thing." He waved a hand in the air like he was talking about the weather, and I was reminded once again just how bizarre my life had become.

I was sitting in my boyfriend's living room with Dracula and descendants of Dr. Watson, John Henry, and Abraham Van Helsing plotting to hunt down and fight a demon before he opened the gates of Hell, with my guardian angel, who, by the way, borrowed her name from a *Buffy the Vampire Slayer* villain, watching over the proceedings. This was not something that I expected when I graduated from the police academy.

"Who was the previous owner, Luke?" Watson asked.

"An SS lieutenant, I believe, or perhaps a colonel. They do all blur together after a certain number, you know. It was in France, I believe...yes, Northern France in about 1943. It would have to be late 1942 or 1943 because I was following Quincy through Europe cleaning up some of his messes and trying to keep attention off the two of us. Yes, it was early 1943, there was still snow on the ground.

"I don't remember the name of the town, but it wasn't a large town. Just one of those typical French towns in the middle of the countryside with a collection of homes, shops, and the occasional farm. The Nazis had taken over some time before, and the population was fairly well quelled. The colonel—I remember now, he was a colonel—had taken over the biggest home in town. It sat atop a hill which once was in the middle of a quaint little forest, but the Germans had cut all the trees down and set up a few small barracks buildings surrounding the mansion. I suppose the colonel wasn't feeling all that secure in his position. It turns out that was a good idea.

"Quincy was in a very bad place, emotionally. His love, Anna, had been murdered by a Nazi less than six months before, and the severing of his bond with her drove him to savagery the likes of which I haven't seen...well, since my own losses drove me to certain unpleasant excesses some many years ago." Luke paused, and you could hear a pin drop.

I had certainly never heard him mention his life before becoming Dracula, back when he was Vlad Tepes, ruler of Wallachia. I'd read some of the stories before meeting him, and after I learned that not only was he real, he was in my city, I consumed every piece of Dracula and vampire lore I could. And there's a lot, not all of it good. Some guy even wrote a book about a vampire accountant, if you can believe that crap. But I never mentioned any of that to Luke. It seemed rude, somehow, like I was trying to pry into something that was none of my business. But here he was, talking about it, despite the obvious cost to himself.

He took a deep breath, seeming to push away memories that still pained him over about six centuries and continued. "Regardless, I was following Quincy's trail of Nazi corpses through Europe when I came upon him in France. He was in the living room of the mansion, surrounded by dead soldiers, battling the colonel. He was obviously tired because the colonel was actually doing him harm. Quincy was staggering, bleeding from several cuts along his arms and legs. Both his and the Nazi's guns lay on the ground out of reach, and it looked as though their battle would quickly become one of attrition, where whoever could withstand the most punishment would be the survivor. While I had faith in Quincy's abilities, I did not think it wise to leave anything to chance given his current mental state."

"You thought he was out of his head enough to let the Nazi kill him?" I asked.

Luke gave me a long look. "Anna was the first woman he ever shared his blood, his essence with. Her death would have devastated him had it happened under normal circumstances. When she was murdered in front of him, he went completely insane. His rampage was terrifying to watch, and I am not a man who is unaccustomed to the sight of carnage." I looked into his cold eyes and remembered that this was the man they dubbed "The Impaler" because of his ferocity in battle and his treatment of captured foes. Carnage was his milieu, so if whatever Quincy was doing scared him, then it was seriously awful.

He continued. "I stepped into the room behind the colonel and pulled out his heart. I drank my fill of his blood from the still-beating reservoir, then dropped it at Quincy's feet. I still remember the words I said to him that day as I dropped the drained heart at his feet. 'Eat it,' I said. 'If you're going to behave like a beast, you may as well go the whole way.' Then I plucked the sword from the dead man's hands as a trophy, turned on my heel, and walked out. I didn't see Quincy again for nearly seven years, until he met up with us in America near the beginning of 1950."

He clapped his hands, breaking the spell he'd held us all in with his words. "And that's the story of how I came to possess that sword. It is also all I know about the blade. I have never sensed anything supernatural about it in all the time it has been in my possession, although I can tell you from the manufacture that it was made around the time of my mortal life."

"What was that, the early fifteenth century?" I asked, more to confirm than anything.

"Yes," Luke said. "I was born around 1430. Records in that time were a little sparse, and I was ill-equipped to write down the date myself."

"Fair enough. So the sword was in France in the 1940s, and it originates from some time in the fifteenth century, that's all we know?" I asked the group.

"And it resonates to those with the ability to sense magical items, and Orobas wants to get his hands on it," Jo added.

"Then all we care about is that the demon doesn't have it, right?" Gabby asked. "Good deal. Demon doesn't have it. What's next?"

"It is important to understand why our adversary is interested in the weapon, Gabriella," Watson said.

"But she's right, isn't she?" I asked. "It's nice to know the provenance of the weapon, but if none of us have any magical ability, then all we care about is that we kept it out of the hands of the guy who wants to destroy the world, right? Or did you graduate from Hogwarts when I wasn't looking?"

Watson held up his hands in mock surrender. "Fine, fine, Detective. Far be it from me to want to know as much information as possible about the tools we have on hand before rushing into a fight. I'm sure that the American method of rushing in guns blazing will sort everything out just fine."

"Worked okay in Yorktown," I said, leaving the word "prick" unsaid, but heavily implied. I turned to Luke. "What's the plan? What's our next step?"

"I suppose it isn't any different than it was before we found the sword. We find Orobas, and we put a stop to his plans. Along the way, we should probably clear Quincy's name and think about finding a way to send Orobas back to Hell."

"All admirable goals, Luke, but do you have an actual plan to accomplish any of them?" Watson asked.

"Well, I could sit around the apartment staring at a sword, or I could start punching all the members of the local supernatural community. While diametrically opposed, I think that both methods would meet with a similar lack of success." Luke didn't look offended at Watson's snottiness. I guess when you've been around for a few centuries, a snotty Englishman isn't a big deal.

"There's always Option C," Jo said from her computer. All eyes turned to her as she stood up and grabbed a jacket from the back of her chair. She slipped on the leather jacket, then reached under the table and picked up a big maul with a long handle and hefted it over her shoulder. "I just got an email from Sparkles. He found Mort."

"Why was he looking for Mort? I mean, wasn't he just going back to the bar after we left Luke's place?" I looked over at Watson, who shrugged.

"That's what he said he was doing, but what's to say he wasn't lying? He's a demon. Who knows what he had in mind?" he replied.

"I can't argue with that," I said. "But that doesn't answer the question. Why was Sparkles looking for Mort? And am I ever going to meet this Sparkles person?" Who the hell even answers to a nickname like Sparkles? Was this an out-of-work stripper moonlighting for the Shadow Council?

"Probably not," Jo said. "And I had Sparkles put a trace on Mort's phone when he was with you two. He seemed pretty motivated to find Orobas, and he has connections that none of us have, so I figured if we all kept in contact, and I had a way to track Mort, then all our bases were covered."

"Seems good," I said. I grabbed my jacket and car keys. "What's with the hammer?"

"It's a family heirloom," Jo replied. "Besides, I don't like shooting people."

"You should really give it a try," Gabby chimed in, strapping a pair of nickel-plated Colt 1911 pistols to her hips. "It's a lot of fun. Especially arterial spray. That's my fave."

I sighed, then looked at Watson and Luke. "You two coming?"

Luke gestured to the window. "Still daylight. I think I shall continue my long-standing tradition of not bursting into flames for a little longer, for all the good it does me." I stared at Luke, and saw, not for the first time in the past few days, a level of melancholy and loneliness haunting his eyes. This was a man that was accustomed to people dying around him, often at his hands, but losing Renfield was different somehow. There was something cracked inside Luke, and it would take a long time to heal, if it ever did.

"I suppose I may as well," Watson said. He walked to the end of the sofa and picked up a bowler hat, trench coat, and a cane topped with a wolf's head.

"What the hell are you supposed to be? A parody of an urban fantasy novel cover? Do you come with your own smoke machine and creepy soundtrack?" I managed not to laugh at Watson, but only just.

"I think we'll find that my cane serves multiple purposes, and the coat is a type of tightly-woven fabric that is similar to Kevlar, but more puncture-resistant and is completely flame retardant." He huffed. He walked past me to the door of the apartment and held it open. "Shall we?"

"That depends. Jo, where are we going?" I asked.

"I have an address on Brookshire Boulevard. It's someplace called Coyote Joe's?" She looked at me with an eyebrow up.

"I know where it is, but I don't know why in the hell Mort would be there, unless he's looking for cheap beer and loud music," I said.

"So you can get us there? Good," Watson said.

"I can get us there, but why in the world is a demon in a biker suit in the city's largest country music bar?"

"Wet t-shirt contest?" Gabby asked.

"He's a fan of terrible music?" Watson offered.

"He wants to drown his sorrows over his daughter's death and he's already drank all the booze in his own bar?" Jo suggested.

"I don't know, but something tells me that the answer is going to be even stranger than any of those ideas," I said as we trooped out into the afternoon light to hunt down a demon in a giant country bar.

Chapter Thirteen

"**N**OTHING ABOUT THIS SEEMS LIKE A GOOD IDEA TO ME," BETH SAID to my back.

"You just described most of my life, particularly any of the parts of it I spent in Rio," I whispered. "Now shut up. I'd really rather not get caught here. I think it would end up on my permanent record."

"Oh, you're a regular comedian, Harker," she muttered.

"Laughter is not typically the response I look to elicit in women," I replied, and immediately thought of Becks. That was a mistake. My chest got tight, and my focus on the task at hand was completely gone for a moment as I sent feelers down the invisible connection tying me back to Rebecca, hundreds of miles away in North Carolina working to clear my name and find out how high in Homeland Security our problem went.

I couldn't see through her eyes, or even contact her with coherent thoughts, the physical distance was just too great. But I could feel her, and as my consciousness brushed hers, I felt a whirl of feelings pass through me, not all of them mine. Fear, anger, stress, worry, love, more anger tied really closely to that love, and pain both physical and emotional. All that coursed through me in half a second as my steps faltered and I went to one knee.

"Are you okay, Harker?" Beth's voice brought me back to the present, to Lockton, Ohio, and to the task at hand. Said task was breaking into the main office to steal Coach Durham Balomb's personnel file so we could go to his house and try to deal with Lockton High's demon infestation once and for all.

I shook my head to clear it, then nodded to Beth. "I'm fine. Just a little wave of psychic impression. Let's go."

"Are you sure you can do this?" she asked, pointing to the door to the main office.

"It's a door. With a standard cylinder lock. I've been magicking these things open since before you were born," I replied. I didn't mention that I'd been magicking them open since before her parents were born, too. So far, Beth

Kirkland hadn't asked any questions about my origin, and I wasn't looking to talk about it right now.

People tend to look at you strangely when they find out that the "Uncle Luke" you mention from time to time is actually Dracula, Lord of the Vampires, Vlad the Impaler, source of dozens of movies good and godawful, and arguably the most famous monster in history. Needless to say, I'd whammied my fair share of locks all over the world in the century and change I'd been around, so I wasn't really worried about popping open the door to a high school principal's office in the middle of nowhere Ohio.

I walked down the hall, sticking to the shadows and avoiding the few security cameras running on a Friday night. I stepped up to the door and put my hand on the lock. I focused my will on the tumblers inside, whispered "*Sesame,*" and turned the knob. The door clicked open, and Beth and I slipped inside.

"Sesame?" she asked.

"What?" I said. "It's just something to focus my will on the doorknob. I could have said 'cheeseburger,' as long as I believed it would work."

"You didn't have to cast a ritual, or beseech the Goddess for help, or ask the blessings of the Four Winds, or anything?"

"Neither do you," I said. "Magic doesn't really work like that. It doesn't come from some divine place. At least, not the magic I do. It's energy, and if you know how manipulate that energy, then you can do it. Simple as that."

"So you're not a believer?"

"Darlin', I've seen so much shit in my life, I believe in just about everything. But I don't mix my magic and my religion. Except when I need to send some demonic douchebag back to Hell. Which is what we need to do here, so point me to where the employee records are kept and let's go show Coach Balomb the way to go home."

"In that room next to Principal Nettles' office." She pointed, and I walked over and put the whammy on that lock, too. We stepped into the file room and started looking through cabinets. It only took a few seconds to find the right drawer, and Beth pulled out her cell phone as I grabbed the right folder.

"I don't think this is the time to take a selfie," I said as I saw her open the camera app on her phone.

"No, but I thought I'd take a picture of his address so we can put the file back and maybe still have an element of surprise."

"That's fine, but you don't really think our little expedition is going to be discovered in the time it takes us to drive from the school to the coach's house, do you?"

"We're going after him tonight?" She looked at me like I was crazy. I probably am, but I didn't think it had anything to do with Coach Balomb.

"No time like the present, right? Why wouldn't we?"

"I don't know, I thought maybe we'd take time to research him, find a weakness, get some help, that kind of thing."

I snorted. "Nah, that kind of planning works great if you're Giles or Willow, but I'm way more of a kick down the door and beat the shit out of everything in the room kind of guy." I handed her the folder. "Now let's go. You're navigating."

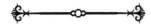

I hate it when demons invade the suburbs. It fucks with my sense of the universe. Demons belong in cities, in abandoned sewers, nasty-ass empty factories, or even creepy old houses tucked away in old neighborhoods. Demons don't belong in ranch houses with two-car garages. But that's where Coach Balomb lived. Not even at the end of a cul-de-sac, right in the middle of the damn street like he was some kind of insurance adjuster or something like that.

"What do you know about the coach?" I asked as I pulled my pickup onto a side street two blocks past the address on the file and turned off the lights.

"I don't know much," Beth replied. "He started here last year as an assistant coach and economics teacher. When Coach Pate had a heart attack last June, they promoted Coach Balomb to Head Coach, and he brought in some old friends from the last school where he taught. I don't know where, just that it's somewhere down south, apparently."

"I think he's from a little further south than anybody suspects. Sounds like he engineered the old coach's heart attack and has brought in his buddies from the Pits to serve him here in Lockton."

"Yeah, that's what I figured," Beth agreed.

"But why?" I asked. "Lockton isn't big enough to be a real target, and there's no magical ley lines that run through the place, nothing special about this town whatsoever."

"Just a town willing to sell its soul for a winning football team and a bunch of missing Talented kids." Beth opened her door, and I slapped my hand over the dome light to hide its glow.

"*Eclipso*," I whispered, and a small cloud of absolute darkness enveloped the bulb. I took my hand off the light and got out of the truck.

"Now you're just showing off," she said, closing the door and walking around the front of the truck to join me. "What's the plan?"

"Well, we can either knock on the door and try to bullshit our way inside, then try to fight our way out..."

"Which sounds like a recipe for certain death."

"Or we can blast through the front of the house and the back door at the same time, kill anything we encounter, and hope the element of surprise can buy us enough time to take out Balomb before he gets his shit together enough to fight back."

"Do you have any plans that don't involve our almost certain death in an exceptionally bloody fashion?"

"Not really, no."

"Goddess only knows how you've lived this long."

"If you only knew," I quipped.

Beth sighed. "Let's go with the two-pronged attack, then. I certainly don't trust you to be able to bluff your way through the door, so this way we at least have the potential to take a few of those assholes with us when we go."

"That's what I love in a sidekick, Kirkland—positive thinking. You take the back; I'll take the front."

"How will I know when to go?"

"You'll see the signal."

"What's the signal?"

"I'll figure it out when I send it. But you'll know it. I promise." She shook her head at me and peeled off toward the back of the house.

I walked up the sidewalk to the front of the coach's house and checked the ammunition in my Glock. The front door looked pretty easy to fortify, with a small porch that glowed like Christmas in my Sight. That wasn't going to work as an entrance. I scanned the front of the house and spotted a picture window with no magical enhancements on it.

"Bingo," I muttered. "This oughta serve as a pretty good signal." I pulled in my will, focusing my magical energy over my left hand, then drew my pistol. I put three rounds through the big window and flung a fireball through the shattered glass. It exploded with a massive *BOOM*, and I sprinted across the lawn to leap through the hole in the wall where a window used to be.

I heard a muffled *crump* from the back of the house, followed by a string of small explosions like firecrackers. Sounded like Kirkland blew in the back door, then flung a fistful of those mini-fireballs into the house. Between us, we had the place burning pretty good, which might not have been our best move as the humans surrounded by denizens of Hell. They were a lot more resistant to fire than we were, but I had enough protections woven around me to keep me alive for a couple minutes at least.

Which might be more time than I had, given the fact that I had four demons staring at me from the living room and the door to what looked like the kitchen. None of them wore their human suits, but when wearing their natural forms, they didn't look that far removed from people. Just a little taller, way skinnier, with red skin, yellow eyes, and porcupine spikes instead of hair. Oh yeah, and preternaturally long arms, double-jointed knees, and three-inch curved talons on the ends of each of their six fingers.

So maybe they didn't really look anything like people, except for being bipedal and having roughly human faces, only more angular and sporting curved fangs. So they were nasty little bastards, but these were definitely low-level demons. The ones staring back at me now weren't even as strong as the one I'd banished a couple nights before, so I was only a little bit convinced that I was about to die.

They were way more confident in their ability to kill me than I was because they all charged me at once. I flung up a shield of force with my left hand, effectively blocking the three coming at me from the den. The one rushing me from the kitchen required a different approach, since I still held my gun in that hand. So I shot him. In the face. Four times. He dropped, but not fast enough to actually stop moving, so his momentum drove him right into me, which drove me hard into the other three with my shield, sending me and all four demons tumbling ass over teakettle to the floor.

I dropped my pistol, but held my shield, and wriggled out from under the dead demon that sprawled across my legs. The other three writhed on the ground, scratching, clawing, and biting at each other trying to get to their feet.

"*Electro!*" I shouted, reaching my hand in the air and pointing my index finger toward the ceiling light. Electricity flickered from the light fixture to gather around my fist, and I flung a ball of lightning at the squirming mass of demon dickheads on the floor. I've smelled a lot of nasty shit in my life, but nothing quite so foul as fried demon on old shag carpet. I'm not sure if it was the sulfurous stench of demon flesh or the horrific stink of polyester fibers, but that was the grossest thing I've ever smelled.

Beth came into the front room, covered in soot and demon blood. She leaned against the door into the den and looked at me. "Maybe next time we can try *not* to burn the house down before we run into it?"

"Maybe next time we don't have a next time?" I asked, then looked around. "Did you put the fire out?"

"Yeah. I called to it and channeled it into the ground outside. Scorched some grass and turned the dirt to glass, but at least we aren't going to die."

"You won't die from the fire, witchy-witch, but you will most certainly die tonight." I didn't even turn around. I didn't have to. Whenever somebody shows up and makes a pithy comment at what I really wanted to be the end of a fight, it's usually something bigger and badder than whatever I just fought. So I knew Coach Balomb had decided to join the fight, and shit was about to get real.

Chapter Fourteen

IT ALL MADE SENSE TO ME WHEN I PULLED INTO THE EMPTY PARKING lot. Mort was a demon, and country music bars are a special kind of Hell, so it only made sense that he wanted to be there. His motorcycle was parked in the portico by the front door, and the door hung from broken hinges. We were in the right place.

I parked right behind Mort's bike and killed the engine. The four of us got out and made a quick check of our weapons. I ejected the magazine from my Sig and replaced it with bullets dipped in holy water and blessed by a Catholic priest who did things for Harker like bless bullets. Apparently in his line of work, it's a good idea to have people around for stuff like that. Life was so much less complicated when all I had to do was solve murders by humans.

The noise coming from inside told me that someone objected to Mort's presence and was doing something about it, with extreme prejudice. The sound of shattering glass and splintering wood rang through the parking lot. I drew my sidearm and waved the others in around me.

"Okay," I said, "when we get in there, let me take the lead. Mort's familiar with me, so I might be able to talk him down a little, and I am still a cop, so that gives me some authority with whoever else is in there. Watson, you go around and see if there's a back or side door. I don't want any of these guys getting away—"

"Is this because of my leg? Because I assure you, I can hold up my end of a fight." He scowled at me, and I looked down at his leg.

"Shit, sorry, I forgot. Is it better for you to come in the front with me, so you don't have to walk as far?"

The scowl changed to confusion as he tried to process what I was asking. "No, I simply meant that I am capable of handling a frontal assault, that my leg will not prove a liability in the fight."

"Oh," I said. "Sorry, didn't think about that. No, I just need somebody to cover the door, and you're the most lightly armed, so I wanted to put you out of the line of direct fire. But if you—"

"No, that's fine. Thank you, Detective."

"Thank me if we all get out of this alive. Jo, you and Gabby are with me. I'll lead, and you two fan out...god*dammit.*" I swore as I heard loud reports from inside and noticed that Gabby was nowhere in our little huddle. "Fuck it, let's go!" I ran into the building where Gabby was laying down a pretty serious field of fire with her two .45 semiautomatics. That's a big bullet, and she was a decent shot, so everything she hit was on its ass seconds later.

The problem was that everything she shot was a demon, and bullets aren't very effective against a lot of Hellspawn. So while Gabby was knocking them down, they were getting right back up again. A few of them stayed down after headshots, so a change in tactics was obviously required.

"Headshots, Gabby!" I shouted. She nodded, then holstered one pistol and switched to a two-handed grip to give herself better control for the difficult task of shooting a moving target in the face before said target kills you. Nothing's ever as easy as it looks on *NCIS.*

I scanned the room for Mort, but all I saw was a shit-ton of demons. Red demons, black demons, demons still in human form, whatever you wanted, apparently they were all redneck day drinkers because this bar was full of them. I heard the scrabble of claws above me and looked up just in time to see a little green bastard with talons on all four limbs and a long tail with a scorpion spike on the end of it drop to the ground right in front of me.

"Duck and roll!" I heard from behind me, and I did just as I was told, diving to my right into an awkward roll that would probably result in some bruises in the morning. If I kept this shit up, I was definitely going back to *krav maga class.* I spun back to the demon just in time to get splashed with black blood and little bits of demon skull as Jo swung that nine-pound hammer like she was Babe Ruth. The demon's head disintegrated into the world's nastiest oatmeal, and she reached out a hand.

"Good reflexes," she said.

"I date Harker," I replied. "Fireballs are a thing that happens in my life," I said by way of explanation. There was a brief moment when nothing was immediately charging us, so I took the opportunity to shout for our quarry.

"MORT!" I yelled. "Cut this shit out and come talk to me!"

"Not until he tells me where to find that murdering son of a sulfur-sucking pitworm!" A voice from the center of a writhing cluster of demonic bodies on the floor bellowed back.

I looked at the others and nodded. "Let's get him out of there." Gabby, Jo, and I walked toward a pile of a dozen demons all struggling and scrambling to get a grip on a piece of Mort's new body and rip it off. It looked like a pileup on the football field, only with more claws and fangs, and about ten percent fewer tattoos.

We got to within a few feet of the squirming mass of demons and raised our weapons. "Get off the interloper, assholes," I said over the barrel of my pistol.

A seven-foot demon with stubby little horns and a tail that looked like the one you get in the naughty devil costumes at Halloween got to his feet and glared down at me. "And what if we don't want to, human?"

"I don't waste much time on what a demon does or doesn't want, fucktard," I said, then I shot him. In the groin. He dropped to his knees, making him a much more reasonably sized foe, and I stepped to the left. Jo took one long stride forward and came around with her great-great-grandfather's hammer again. The rectangular head of the hammer caught the demon right on the hinge of its jaw and knocked its head clean off.

The pile of demons froze, and the room fell silent as the *thump, thump, thump* of the head bouncing along the bar's hardwood floors reached everyone's ears. The body made a wet *thwap* sound as it fell over, and the entire mass of a dozen or more demons separated and came to its feet almost in unison. I took a step back as the three of us stared down at least twelve or fifteen monsters straight out of humanity's worst nightmares.

"Ummm, Mort?" I said. "A little help here?"

Mort's voice, when it came to me from the floor, was weak and thready. "I'm not sure how much help I shall be, Detective. I seem to have more than one dislocated limb."

"Well, shit," I said. I looked at the nearest demon, a skinny little monster with four arms and three-inch claws on the end of four fingers on each hand. He grinned up at me and showed off a pair of fangs that dripped with green ichor. I grinned right back and put two .40 rounds from my Sig into his forehead.

"Who's next?" I looked around at the assembled demons and heard Gabby draw and cock one of her pistols. "We probably can't send you all back to Hell, but which one wants to go first?"

"I would suggest that you believe the human," Mort said as he staggered to his feet. I looked past the mob in front of me to see how he was doing, and he was in surprisingly good shape for a guy who was under a pile of demons less than a minute before.

"You okay, Mort?" I asked.

"I have certainly seen better days, but my need for a new meat-suit is not immediate. I do appreciate your concern, but your coming here was mostly unwarranted. I was merely allowing these boys to vent some of their frustrations before moving on to the real reason for my visit."

"Which is?" Jo asked. She stepped forward to stand at my left elbow, her hammer slung across both shoulders and her hands draped over the handle.

"I need information, and I am of the opinion that Terry has it."

"Who's Terry?" Gabby asked, stepping up on the other side of me.

"I'm Terry," said an Asian man in an expensive suit seated at one of the tables near the stage. I hadn't noticed him before on account of he wasn't immediately trying to eat my spleen, but he certainly had my attention now. He stood up and buttoned his jacket, his long fingers delicate as they handled the sleek fabric. "Ter'i'math," he said, extending a hand to Gabby, then me, then Jo.

We each shook hands with him. I was surprised to feel the strength in his grip, given his slight frame. He was built more like a fencer than a monster, with neat, close-cropped hair, no facial hair, and dark brown eyes. He stepped back to stand between us and Mort.

"What can I do for you, Mort? It's been far too long since I've seen you in my establishment. Would you like a drink?"

"No thank you, Terry. I'm here on business."

"And from the looks of my staff, it might be unpleasant business indeed." He gestured at the gathered demons, most of whom were bleeding from split lips, had eyes swelling shut, and generally looked like they'd been through a war. At least one of the bigger ones was missing an ear, and a solid half dozen of them were not getting up from the floor.

"Sorry about that," Mort said. His tone made it clear that he wasn't the least bit sorry about anything. "I told them I was here to see you, and they said you weren't here. I explained to them that I could see you sitting right there, and I was not leaving until we concluded our business, and things may have become heated from that point." Mort looked a tiny bit chagrined. "I did hope that you would make things easy and simply provide me with the information I desire."

"Which is?" Terry asked.

"The whereabouts of Orobas." If Terry had any reaction to Mort's desire, he didn't show it.

"And why do you need to find Orobas?" Terry asked. I held my breath for the answer. My Sig was still in my hand, and I flexed my fingers on the butt of the gun.

"To kill him. He murdered someone I care about, or his minion did, and since the minion is dead, my vengeance must be visited upon Orobas, and anyone who shelters him." I didn't miss the thinly veiled threat in Mort's words, and neither did Terry. But his only response was slightly raised eyebrows and a mild smile.

"I'm afraid I can't give you that information, Mort. Orobas works for me occasionally, and it would be poor form to just hand him over freely. It also would hinder my operations here."

"What operations are those?" I asked. Terry's gaze swung to me, and we locked eyes. I'd stared down junkies, murderers, gangbangers, vampires, and demons, but something in Terry was just *different*. It was like a whole universe floated behind his eyes, a depth of knowledge and power very different from anything I'd ever gazed upon before.

"And what the hell *are* you?" I asked in a whisper.

"I am an Agent of Chaos," he replied, addressing the last question.

"A what?" Jo asked.

"I care not for good or evil, as those are purely mortal terms, and subjective ones at that. After all, you cannot think that the Morningstar considers himself evil, can you? He certainly has all the characteristics of a hero. A failed relationship with his father, a long trip from home, a valiant failed effort to return home in spectacular fashion, extended torment far from the home he loves, then the inevitable attempt to return home again. Sounds just like a movie, doesn't it? It just needs more Jedi to make a franchise."

"So you don't buy into the whole good and evil thing, I get it. But what is this whole Agent of Chaos thing?" Gabby asked, her eyes flicking from Terry to the demons surrounding us, then back again. She had that look on her face that said she really wanted to get back to shooting things, and I really didn't want to deal with that at the moment.

"I work to upend the status quo, regardless of what it is. If there is peace, I work for war. If there is war, I work for peace. Stasis is death, and boring besides. I am change, I am randomness, I am..."

"You are droning on, Terry," Mort interrupted. I couldn't hide the chuckle, just like Terry couldn't hide the scowl that crossed his face for the briefest of seconds before flashing away.

"My apologies, Mort. As I was saying, I can't give you Orobas's whereabouts so you can kill him because he is useful to me alive. Have a nice day." He turned to walk back to his table, apparently done with us.

He stopped short at the sight of a slim man in a trench coat sitting at his table sipping a beer. "Sorry about the drink, friend. Proselytizing makes me thirsty," Watson said as he stood up. "But you can have your chair." He waved to the seat with a little bow.

"You come into my place of business uninvited and drink my beer? You are a brazen one, human. Tell me, how would you like to learn to walk with *two* metal limbs?" Terry's hands were glowing with power, and I could hear the fury in his voice even if his back was to me.

I raised my pistol and pointed it at the back of his head. Gabby did the same. "That would be a mistake, friend. Two rounds in the back of your head might not kill you, but it would fuck up that snazzy haircut you're sporting," I said as I pulled back the hammer on my Sig.

Terry raised his hands and turned back to me. The purple glow around his hands was matched by one coming from his eyes, and the anger on his face was unmistakable. I had pissed off an Agent of Chaos in his living room. I used to think being around Harker made my life more dangerous. Now I was seeing the kind of trouble I could get into when he was gone.

Chapter Fifteen

I DIDN'T TURN AROUND. I DIDN'T NEED TO. AFTER ENOUGH DECADES, AND enough fights, it just wasn't necessary anymore. "Coach Balomb, I presume?" I asked, still looking at the remains of the electrocuted demons on the living room floor. If this place was a rental, nobody was getting a security deposit back after tonight.

"And you are Harold Quinn, or should I just call you Quincy Harker? Would you prefer Reaper? I hear that's something you've answered to in the past."

Now I turned around. I was incognito, or at least I was supposed to be. So how did this fuckwad of a life-sucking demon in Dipshit, Ohio, know who I was? I looked him up and down. He wasn't anyone I'd fought before, at least not in his natural form.

Human suits were apparently optional at Casa Balomb because this assclown wasn't doing anything to hide his demonic nature, either. He stood a little over six feet tall, with six-inch curved horns protruding from his gleaming crimson skull. His face was shaped more like a human than the other demons, but his lower jaw stuck out, and a pair of wicked tusks protruded up and rested against his cheeks.

His torso was covered in black and red scales, making a shimmering suit of armor that I was glad I wouldn't have to try to stick a sword through, but which certainly made my pistol useless. He wore jeans, but no shoes, and his feet had the cloven hooves of the upper-level demonic horde. He wasn't an Archduke or anything like that, I would have felt the power in him then, but he wasn't going to go down to a lightning bolt, either.

"You have me at a disadvantage, then, demon. You know who I really am, but I have no idea of your name." I kept it cool, drawing in my will so I would have enough power at the ready to react to whatever he threw at me.

"You may call me Balomik. I am Ruler of the Second Circle, Master of Lust and Tempter of Mortals." He threw his arms open wide and black bat wings sprouted from his back, filling the room and knocking over a chair.

"Really?" I asked, folding my arms over my chest. "Does Asmodeus know about this? I doubt he'd take the demotion kindly."

Balomik looked startled, like I'd called him out on something huge. Which I had. Kings of Hell don't take lightly to lower-rung demons laying claim to their territory, and Asmodeus was a particularly jealous dude. Probably had something to do with being the *actual* King of the Second Circle and the Master of Lust. Kinda goes hand-in-hand with jealousy.

"I mean, if you think he wouldn't mind, we can call him up. I'm sure if you're really the boss, you wouldn't have any trouble controlling a wimpy little piece of shit like Asmodeus." I whipped out my pocketknife and sliced open my thumb, then used the blood to draw a hasty, but slightly incomplete, circle around myself. Then I called up my will and started the ritual to summon a demon.

Balomik's eyes went wide before the third word of Latin passed my lips, and he charged me. I sidestepped his bull-rush, then pressed my thumb to the floor as he crossed the line of my circle. I poured my will into the ring of my blood, snapping the containment spell into being and trapping the demon inside.

"You bastard!" Balomik shrieked as his head crashed into the magical barrier. "Set me free this instant or I will tear your soul to shreds!"

"I think that might be a bad idea for me, Bally. I'd probably be in way better shape if I just kept you trapped in this circle until Beth here calls the local Catholic priest and he jumps on his hotline to the Vatican and we get a fuckton of exorcists down here. How long do you think it will take them to get here? Six hours? Maybe four if they've got a helicopter nearby. And I bet they *always* have a helicopter nearby. You know The Church, they always have the coolest toys."

"What do you want, Harker?"

"What's the most valuable thing in the world, Bally? I want information."

"Nothing's free, Harker. I'll tell you anything you want to know, but I'm going to want my freedom in exchange."

"Not a problem," I said, ignoring the bulging eyes on my current partner.

"What the hell are you saying, Harker?" Beth yelled. "There is no way I'm letting you set this demon loose! He killed my brother, and he's going back to Hell for it."

"We don't know that," I said.

"Oh, no, she's right," Balomik interjected. "I killed her brother. Freddy Kirkland, right? He was good. A lot of power in that little warlock. Tasty morsel. I skimmed a little cream off the top before I distilled his essence into the 'supplements' we gave the football team. Yummy."

"Yeah, what's that all about?" I asked. "I get killing Talents, and I even understand sucking the magic from their souls and selling it, or using it to power up your meat-suits, or whatever. But making the high school football team better? That seems a little altruistic for your kind."

"Let's not be speciesist, Quincy. I can call you Quincy, can't I? After all, we're buds now, right?"

"I don't give a shit what you call me, assclown. Just answer all my questions and I'll think about not telling Asmodeus that you've been claiming his crown."

"Fine," he grumped. I was afraid for a minute that he was going to sulk and I wouldn't get anything else out of him. But he went on. "Jazzing up the football team wasn't my idea. I was just going to kill the Talents, bottle their essence, and sell it on the black market. I know a guy in Cincinnati that moves a lot of that type of product."

"But..." I prodded.

"But when I called up Jerry over there—" He pointed to one of the charred demons lying on the floor. "His name is Jeraxil, by the way. In case you care about the names of the men and women you sent fleeing back to Hell in unspeakable agony."

"I don't." I didn't. Really. Couldn't possibly give less fucks about the well-being of any of the demons I've banished, battered, mutilated, or actually destroyed over the years. I feel more remorse about killing a black widow in Luke's garage. The spider at least isn't malevolent; it's just hanging around spinning webs in the wrong places. Demons are universally bad motherfuckers at heart, and every one of them would rather fuck you over than look at you.

"I didn't expect you to," Bally continued. "So Jerry comes up with the idea of using a winning football team to rouse school spirit and get people distracted from the missing kids. He's a Demi-lord of Deception, really good at that kind of thing. So I went with it, and we started giving the team 'nutritional supplements.' All the kids that took them turned into super-athletes almost overnight. And suddenly nobody was paying attention to a bunch of missing nerds and malcontents."

"My brother wasn't a malcontent!" Beth snarled.

"No, that one was a huge nerd. Right down to his Deadpool boxers, sweetie. But he had a ton of magical energy. He singlehandedly won us that game against Martin Luther King Jr. High."

"What's the end game?" I asked.

"Don't have one, really," Bally said with a shrug. I gave him a sharp look, and he raised his hands in protest. "I'm a *demon*, you dipshit. I saw a chance to fuck with some humans, and I took it. One day I was in Hell, working like a dog, then this portal opens up and it's all blue skies and buckeyes, so I stepped through. And here I am. Look, all I know is I'm not in Hell poking some cheating husband in the balls with a pitchfork, and I don't plan to go back. So let me out of here and I'll vanish into the wilds of America. I hear Nebraska is nice this time of year."

Whatever. This asshole was never going to get near a cornfield if I had anything to say about it, and I did. While it's not a good idea to lie to monsters as a general rule, you could bend the fuck out of that rule if you planned on killing or banishing the monster in the immediate future. And since I really hoped I wouldn't run into Bally after I died, all I needed to do was get him off this plane of existence to take care of him.

"So you just wandered into town with a plan to kill off all the Talented humans?"

"Not exactly. I wandered into town and decided to kill *all* the humans. But Jerry got here before I did, and he spotted all the Talents in town. When me and the rest of the boys showed up, Jerry came up with the plan."

"And you just did what Jerry said without caring who was in charge?" That didn't fit with the hierarchy-obsessed demons I'd known in the past.

"I didn't care who was the boss then and don't care now. Jerry and me got along good, and he let me be the human with the whistle. He got to make his nasty little plans, and I got to eat humans. Where I come from, we call that a win-win."

Time for the million-dollar question. "Okay, asshat. One more bit of information, and you can get out of that circle. Who sent you here?"

"No idea." I stared at him, not believing a word of it. "Look, somebody opened a door out of Hell, and I took a fucking stroll, alright? I don't know why, and I don't know who. And frankly, I don't give a fuck."

"So all this shit has nothing to do with what's been going on in Charlotte? Or Orobas?" On the one hand, it meant that not every demon in the world was looking for me. On the other hand, it meant that somebody was just randomly setting demons loose on Earth. The bad in that scenario far outweighed the good.

"Not everything revolves around you, Quincy my boy," the smug prick said with a grin.

"No, sometimes things are all about other people. And this is all about my baby brother, you fucking asshole." Beth's voice came from right behind my left elbow, and I turned to her just in time to watch her throw a fistful of something white at Bally.

Salt. *Fuck.* Nothing disrupts magic like salt. This was gonna hurt.

My mouth fell open as the magical barrier I had trapped the demon in flashed into view for a second, then popped like a soap bubble. I turned back when I felt something scrabbling at my jacket and stepped back as Beth reached under my arm and yanked my pistol free.

"What the fuck are you doing?" I asked, my head swiveling from a suddenly free demon to an enraged English teacher.

"What you obviously don't have the balls to do. I'm killing this son of a bitch." She raised my Glock in a two-handed grip and squeezed off six rounds at Balomik. The shots rang out, making my ears ring in the enclosed space, and three holes appeared in the demon's chest.

But that's all. Just three little holes, roughly nine millimeters in diameter. No blood, no falling down, and certainly no dead demon on the floor. Balomik looked down at his chest, then looked back at Beth and grinned.

"Ouch," he said, then took two steps forward and plunged his hand into the woman's chest. Her eyes went wide as the demon turned his hand sideways, then yanked it back out, taking three ribs, a huge chunk of flesh, and Beth Kirkland's heart with it. The demon looked me in the eye, brought the still-beating heart to its mouth, and bit a chunk out of the muscle, letting Beth's lifeblood pour down his chin and drip onto the floor.

"Delicious," the demon said with a smile as Beth collapsed to the floor, dead before she even started to fall. "I love it when the meat is fresh."

"*In the name of*—" My incantation was cut off short as Balomik backhanded me into a china cabinet. Dishes and silverware clattered to the floor around me as I slid down in a heap of shattered glass and stoneware.

Balomik stood over me, munching on the dead teacher's heart like he was eating an apple. I shook my head to clear the stars from my vision and tried to rise, only to find a cloven hoof planted square in the center of my chest.

"Stay," the demon said. "Let me be very clear, Quincy Harker. I know you planned to double-cross me and send me back to the Pits. But I left something out of my little origin story. When I first got to Lockton, I got a message. It showed up on my doorstep one day. Just a plain white envelope with a typed letter inside. The letter said, 'No one touches the Reaper.' I don't know who sent it, but they had enough juice to let me out of Hell and keep tabs on me through my best magical disguises.

"So you get to live, Quincy Harker. But so do I. And I don't just get to live in Hell, I get to live right here on Earth. You can chase me, and you can maybe even catch me. But you can't chase me and hunt down your old pal Orobas, who I hear has something big planned *in Atlanta* in a couple weeks. So you make the call, Reaper. Let a low-level demon loose on Middle America, or let Orobas do whatever he wants in the biggest city in the Southeast. Take your time. Think it over."

I didn't miss the clue. Orobas was in Atlanta, or he would be soon. I looked up at the demon, weighing my options. I had time. He was going to terrorize Middle America for a while, but I'd eventually chase him down. After all, I'm Quincy Harker, it's what I do.

I nodded at him. "You've got a deal, dickhead. You get away, today. But I'll find you again. And when that happens, it'll be your heart served for dinner." I didn't know who in the world would eat a demon's heart, but it was still a good line.

Balomik smiled down at me. "I look forward to our next meeting, Quincy Harker." Then he pulled his cloven foot off my chest and snapped a kick upward into my chin, slamming my head into the remains of the wooden cabinet I was tangled in. My vision went all starry, and the last thing I heard before I passed out was the clip-clop of hooves on the front sidewalk and the taunting laugh of a very self-satisfied demon.

Chapter Sixteen

So there I was, in the middle of a country bar, staring down an Agent of Chaos, whatever that really was, with a gun pointed at his head to keep him from de-limbing my newfound partner in the magical Super Friends.

Some days I really hate my life.

Terry, the neatly groomed aforementioned Agent of Chaos, stared at me for an interminable moment, then broke out into a laugh. I had a lot of ideas in my head about the way I was going to die, most of them involving alternately a junkie in a liquor store holdup or a nursing home out of my mind with dementia, but none of them ever included a magical Asian man in an expensive suit laughing in my face as he killed me.

"You are one hilarious human," Terry said.

"I'm glad I amuse you," I said, working to keep my gun steady. Holding a gun on somebody looks really easy in the movies, but after the first minute, keeping your arms extended with a couple of pounds of plastic, metal, and ammunition in your hands is exhausting.

The purple glow around his hands winked out and Terry glanced over his shoulder at Watson. "You should thank your friend, Dr. Watson. She just saved your life."

"So you're not going to kill Watson," I said. "That's good. I don't know how to kill Chaos Agents, or whatever you call yourself, but if you'd made meat out of my lawyer, I would have been honor-bound to try."

"Well, good," Terry replied. "That saves all of us disappointment and annoyance. You would have been disappointed because I can't be killed, and I would have been annoyed because getting blood out of hardwoods is annoying."

I looked over at the splattered brains of the demon I'd shot in the face earlier. "Sorry about that, then."

"Well, we all have our off days, Detective. Now would you all please leave so I can clean my club before we have to open?"

"No," Mort said. "I'm not leaving without Oro's location. I'm sorry, Terry, but he has to pay for what he did to me."

"And I'm sorry, Mort, but Orobas is too useful to me. He sows chaos in his wake like a little demonic Johnny Appleseed, and that's very valuable to me. Unless…" Terry's face took on a thoughtful expression. "No, you wouldn't do that. Not even for revenge."

"Do what?" Mort asked. "I'm willing to do almost anything."

"But only almost," Terry said.

"Well, even demons have our limits. What did you have in mind?" Mort asked.

"Take Orobas's place."

"What?"

"Become my new agent. Work for Chaos. Sow discord, foment revolution, spread disinformation, convince terrible candidates to run for high elected office, that kind of thing." Terry walked back over to his table and took a sip from his drink. The same one Watson had been drinking from a few minutes before. I guess if you can't die to a bullet in the brain, germs aren't exactly a concern either. He smiled at Mort. "Come on, Mortivoid. It'll be fun. It'll at least be interesting."

"What would the Morningstar have to say about that?" Mort asked. "I'm intrigued, but Lucifer still scares the shit out of me."

"As well he should," Terry said. "But we have an arrangement. As long as you don't start rescuing kittens from trees, Lucifer is fine with his people working for me. After all, you lot are the original unruly children, aren't you?"

Mort fell silent for a moment, seeming to consider the idea before finally nodding. "You're not wrong, Terry. We did sort of invent the rebellious teenager stereotype. Fine, give me Oro's location, and as soon as I have things sorted with that bastard to my satisfaction, I'll add sower of chaos to my list of duties and accomplishments."

Terry stepped closer to Mort and held his hand out, pressing it to his borrowed forehead. "Mortivoid, demon of the Pit, do you so solemnly swear to sow discord where there is none, bring war to the peaceful, peace to the contentious, and become the true random element in every situation?"

"Fuck you, I do what I want," Mort replied, and instead of a refusal, that seemed to be the acceptance of the pledge to chaos because the demon's body was bathed in that same purple light, only this time it strobed with random intensity and time, pulsing crazily as it washed over Mort, eventually spilling out his eyes, nose, and ears like chaos was simply pouring out of him.

"Your term of employment begins once you have extracted your revenge from Orobas. Until then, you are still wholly Lucifer's man. Once you come into my employ, however, the Dawnbringer shall have to share dominion over your wretched soul," Terry said. The purple lightshow went dark, and I blinked to get the afterimage out of my vision. I felt like I'd been to a Prince concert, without the amazing guitar solos.

Mort looked at his new boss and said, "Okay, now that's done. Where's the bastard that killed my daughter?"

"Oh, that," Terry said. "Oro is at the airport. He's flying out of here in an hour. Said something about Charlotte losing its luster." Mort didn't say a word, just turned and hauled ass out of the bar. Seconds later, I heard his motorcycle roar to life.

I sighed. "Great, now we get to chase a demon and probably a bunch of hellspawn Homeland Security agents through airport security. I'm totally going to end up on a no-fly list after this."

On the way to the door, I called Captain Herr to fill him in on what was up. "Captain, I've got a lead on—"

He cut me off. "Bad news, Flynn."

"What?"

"You need to come in to the station."

"Captain, I've got a hot lead on the asshole that's behind—"

"Did I stutter, Detective?" He cut me off again.

"No sir, but...sir, what's going on?"

"I will discuss this with you *back at the station, where you are coming right now. I will expect you to wrap up that arrest and be back here within the hour.* Is that understood, Detective?" I got it. There was someone there with him, and if I showed my face at the station, I was screwed. He was probably under orders from someone to take my badge and gun. But I had an hour, maybe two if he could stall, before they put out an APB for me and considered me a fugitive.

"Yes, sir. I understand. I'm all the way down in Pineville near the mall, and you know what 485 is like in the afternoon, so it might be more like an hour and a half or two hours before I get there."

"Fine, two hours," he said. "But if you aren't here by shift change, Detective, it'll be your ass." He hung up, and I walked faster.

"What was that all about?" Jo asked.

"Somebody's pressuring my captain to get me off the case, or arrest me, or suspend me, or something. I have two hours before I'm out of any kind of official juice. Good thing the airport's just a couple minutes from here because I'm now on a serious clock."

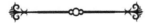

I pulled into the airport and glanced over at Jo, who was staring at her cell. "Any idea where we're going?"

"Just got a text from Sparkles. Looks like Buprof used his Homeland credentials to request special clearance for a flight from Charlotte to Atlanta on a private jet. The hangar is over by the aviation museum."

"I got it," I said, turning right and heading that way. "How are we going to know when we find the right place?"

"I think the sight of burning automobiles may be a sign that demons are trying to cover their tracks," Watson said from the back seat.

I looked around and saw pillars of smoke off to the left. "Nobody likes a smartass, Watson," I said, turning the car in the direction of the smoke. We pulled up in front of Mona Lisa Air, a small charter jet company. A small Lear Jet was pulling out of the hangar as I parked the car and jumped out.

"Watson, go to the office and tell the tower there's a terrorist on that plane and he's going to fly it into the White House!" I sprinted in the direction of the plane, but the whine of a bullet and the flat crack of a revolver sent me diving behind the nearest car. Watson peeled out toward the tower in my car, and I heard a couple of bullets smack into the pavement behind him as he went.

"Hello, Detective," Buprof's voice rang out across the tarmac. "You should have run with your boyfriend. Now you're going to die, just like he will when I catch up to him."

"I'm not dead yet, you hellspawn son of a bitch!" I yelled back at him. I looked over at my car, where Gabby and Jo were hiding behind the engine block. Jo's hammer wasn't going to do much good at a distance, but I had high hopes for Gabby's marksmanship. She crawled on the ground along the side of the car to the back, then took up a position by the back wheel on her belly, giving her a decent vantage point to light up Buprof. All I had to do was get him to poke his head up.

So I stood up, hoping my battered Kevlar vest still had plenty of stopping power, and that Buprof wasn't going to try to manage a headshot from fifty yards. He popped up from behind a toolbox in the hangar, and sure enough, the bastard squeezed off three rounds, all of them *spang*-ing off the car in front of me. He was trying for body shots, good. I could probably live through one of those.

Gabby opened up on Buprof the second he was visible, but all her shots either went wide or ricocheted off the toolbox. So much for counting on the sniper skills of a psychopath. Out of the corner of my eye, I saw Jo running in a crouch from her car toward the hangar, weaving from car to fuel truck to a random prop plane to a black SUV near the hangar doors.

I stuck my head out from the front bumper and let loose a few more random shots at the last place I saw Buprof. There was no return fire, just a high-pitched whine of a jet engine spinning up. *Fuck.*

"The plane just started up!" I yelled to Gabby.

"What do you want me to do about that?" she asked.

"I don't know, shoot something!" I poked my head back up above the hood, only to be met with a hail of bullets. I dove for cover, then peeked around a tire to see if I could spot where he was shooting from.

"He's at your ten o'clock," Gabby said from my shoulder. "And moving left. He's trying to get enough of an angle on us to shoot around the car."

"We should make sure that doesn't happen," I said. "Any ideas?"

"I thought you said I was a psycho."

"I did. Still think you're nuts. But right now, you're the psycho that's been in more shootouts than me."

"Good point. Okay, when I give the signal, run like hell away from the car."

"Which direction?" I asked.

"It won't matter." Gabby smiled at me, and I felt strangely like I just had a bonding moment with Charles Manson. She laid down on the asphalt and slid under the car for a few seconds, then scooted back out, trailing a small plastic battery holder with two wires running from it. She pulled a battery out of her pocket and pressed one end of it into the holder, making very sure not to let the other end touch the other contact and complete the circuit.

"Gabby, are you going to blow up this car?" I asked.

"I sure hope so," she said. "Now shut up and let me listen." She didn't have to listen for long. I popped up into Buprof's view, then dropped straight down again. He fired half a dozen shots at where my head was, but I was long gone.

"Run!" Gabby said, then slammed the battery home. A loud beep came from under the car, and we sprinted away from the vehicle, trying to use the car to shield us from Buprof's view. That part didn't work for shit because he opened up on us before I took my second step.

Gabby's bomb, however, worked just fine. We each covered about twenty yards before a loud *WHOMP* came from under the car, and it flew several feet into the air before crashing to the ground engulfed in flames. The burning wreckage gave us a few seconds of distraction to find cover, and I even had a couple seconds to look for Buprof and put a few ounces of lead in his general direction. Nothing hit the asshole, of course, but I reminded him that I was there.

Until the plane pulled out of the hangar and made all of us completely irrelevant. The sleek little private jet rolled onto the tarmac, and priorities shifted in a big way. The door to the plane was still open, and I caught glimpses of motion inside, then Mort's body came flying out to crash onto the asphalt. He rolled over two or three times, then came to his knees, beating at the pavement with his fists.

"OROBAS!" Mort screamed, and the pain and fury in his voice was terrible to behold.

"Sorry to shoot and run, Flynn, but dear old dad and I have somewhere much more interesting to be," Buprof shouted. He darted out from behind the sedan he was hiding behind and hauled ass toward the accelerating aircraft. He made it to within about ten yards of the plane before something whirled out at him from his right, hit him around the knees, and he went down like a sack of really ugly potatoes.

Jo ran to the downed Deputy Director's side, and brass knuckles flashed in the sun as she knocked him unconscious. Gabby and I ran over to her, our pistols trained on the fallen Cambion. There was no point; he was out cold. I holstered my weapon and looked over at Jo, who had retrieved her hammer and stood over Buprof with a little smile on her face.

"Fond memories?" I asked.

Jo looked up at me and a shadow flickered over her face. "Not really. Okay, not at all. I hate demons, and all demonspawn. It's a long story." I decided it was definitely one I wanted to hear, but this wasn't the time.

We turned and watched as the plane taxied onto the runway and took off, with Orobas and our best lead to the investigation locked safely aboard. I heard a car pull up behind us and turned to see Watson stepping out of my car.

"I couldn't stop the plane, I'm sorry." He sounded about as beaten down as I felt.

"You tried. We couldn't stop him, either. But we got a consolation prize." I pointed down at the unconscious demonspawn. "Maybe he can tell us where the plane was going."

"Oh, I can tell you that," Watson said. "I couldn't stop it from taking off, but I got the flight manifest and the owner of record from the airport. The plane belongs to one Reginald Barton, a tech billionaire and art speculator from Atlanta. It's headed home."

"So Orobas is headed to Atlanta?" I asked.

"It certainly appears so," Watson concurred.

"Well done, old chap!" I said in my worst British accent. He actually winced.

"Please don't ever call me that again," Watson said, but there was a little smile on his face that belied his grumpy tone.

"So we're going to Atlanta to stop Orobas once and for all?" Gabby said. "Good deal. I love Atlanta. Great food, good shopping, plenty of nasty things to shoot. It's my kind of town."

I looked at her. "Have you ever considered therapy? Like, lots of it?"

"Nah. I'm crazy, but it's a really fun crazy. Kinda like Harley Quinn, without the abusive relationship. So when do we leave? I'm ready to head to the ATL and kick some demon ass!"

A groggy Buprof chuckled from the ground at our feet. "Foolish bitch, Daddy dearest will eat your soul for breakfast, then he will take dominion over this worthless plane of existence!"

"Oops, sorry about that," Jo said, standing above Buprof at his ribcage.

"Sorry about what, you worthless piece of human waste."

"This," Jo said, then dropped her hammer squarely on the half-demon's crotch. He doubled over and rolled around on the pavement in agony, spewing out a steady stream of profanity as Watson zip-tied his wrists together and dumped him into the trunk of my car.

"Now what?" Jo asked. "It's a good four hours to Atlanta, and we can't leave until it gets dark. So what do we do until then?"

"We take Director Buprof back to the condos and let Mort and Luke take turns ripping off limps. Sound like a plan?" I looked at the others.

"At least a decent way to waste a couple hours," Gabby said, then hopped into the back seat.

We gathered up Mort and drove off into the welcome sunset, with a half-demon in the trunk and a loose idea of a destination in mind. This was going to be the strangest road trip in history.

Epilogue

"**H**ARKER, YOU SURE KNOW HOW TO MAKE A GODDAMN MESS." THE voice was low, gravelly, and familiar. Way too familiar. And nothing like what I imagined either Rebecca Romijn or Heidi Klum sounded like, so I guess my very pleasant dream of pillow fights and back rubs was over.

I didn't open my eyes. My head felt like someone had pried the top off, dropped a grenade inside, and slammed the lid shut again. "Hello, Adam. What are you doing here?"

"Fetching you. It's time to come in."

"Is the heat off already? It's only been a few days."

"Nah, you're still radioactive as hell. But Luke needs you more than you need to lay low. It's time to roll out and end this shit. And for that, they need their big guns."

Adam wasn't kidding when he referred to himself as one of the big guns. He was honestly one of the biggest dudes I'd ever seen, and was as strong as a bull elephant besides. "Sounds good. The boss got away, but he told me where Orobas was headed. Balomik has his own shit to answer for, but that's going to have to wait for another day."

"Shit to answer for? Like the pretty woman with her heart ripped out lying on the scorched carpet surrounded by demon carcasses?"

"Well, when you put it like that..." I said. Adam looked around, and I heard the sirens. "Fuck. We gotta go." I struggled to my feet, not helped by the mountain of ugly china and dishwater scattered around me. I kept sliding on plates and Adam finally had to pick me up and deposit me on my feet beside him.

The giant bent over, then straightened up and handed me my pistol. Apparently I'd dropped it when I got my ass beat by the demon. "Yeah, wouldn't do to have you involved in *two* mysterious murders and destroyed crime scenes, would it?"

"You're a regular laugh riot, Adam."

"Thanks, I've been working on new material." Part of the problem in dealing with someone who isn't exactly human is that you never know when they're joking or not. Some of the wiring is just off enough that their sense of humor doesn't exactly match the norm.

"You got a car?" I asked. My pickup was parked a few blocks away, and walking even that far with my swimming head and the police presence that was about to be swarming this place was right out.

"Yeah."

"Good. The demon told me before he knocked me out that Orobas is in Atlanta, or he will be soon."

"That fits with what I've got. Luke called me a couple hours ago to come get you. They lost Orobas at the airport, but he's on a charter to Atlanta right now. They're already on their way down there."

"Sounds good. Let's roll." We picked our way through the wreckage of the house out to a massive Hummer idling by the street.

"This thing's your ride?" I asked. "Could you maybe have gone for the inconspicuous option?"

"Harker, you might have missed the fact that I'm over seven feet tall and am carrying more muscle mass than the Bengals' offensive line. Inconspicuous is not a word that is often associated with me."

"Good point. I suppose you're driving?"

"You're damn skippy I'm driving. I've ridden with you before, Harker. I'm not in a hurry to take my life in my hands again."

"That's something I've always meant to ask you. Can you die?"

"Haven't found anything that can kill me yet. Bullets won't do it, old age won't do it, knives won't do it. And as a bunch of peasants learned to their despair a long damn time ago, fire and pitchforks sure as hell won't do it. Now let's go meet up with the rest of the crew and kill this fucking demon."

"Sounds good, pal." I followed the giant out to the Hummer and me and Frankenstein's monster rode off to Atlanta on a demon hunt.

Heaven Can Wait

Chapter One

"Get out, I have to go find a parking spot." Adam's gravelly voice shook me from my doze as he pulled into the packed parking lot in Little Five Points. I looked out the window, erasing the fog from my brain as I processed that we had made it to Atlanta intact.

"Where the hell do you think you're going to find a place to put this thing in Little Five in the middle of the afternoon?" I asked, rubbing sleep from my eyes. The parking lot had a few spaces, but they looked tight for normal cars, much less Adam's Hummer.

"I know a guy. I'll meet you inside in ten minutes. They've got a big table. I told Jack to save us seats." I never heard him make a call. I must have been out cold. But that made sense. We'd been driving all night, leaving Lockton, Ohio, a little before midnight. With stops for gas and bathrooms, and one longer break at a truck stop where I showered off the worst of the blood and smoke covering me from my fight with a band of demons masquerading as high school football coaches, it took the better part of twelve hours to get to the middle of Atlanta.

I made it almost to Knoxville before I crashed hard, the last remaining bits of energy, excitement, and abject horror from the night's festivities running out of me about an hour after sunup. I finally gave in to my exhaustion, leaned the seat back, and slept for a few hours. I wasn't too worried about Adam falling asleep at the wheel, since I'd never known him to sleep. I'd never asked, it seemed rude somehow, but I honestly didn't know if the big man *could* sleep. There were a lot of things I didn't really know about Adam, despite having known him for as long as I could remember.

Adam had been a fixture in my life since my childhood, attending a few family functions now and then with Luke. My uncle often referred to Adam as my "cousin," but it didn't take me too long to realize that he was no more my cousin than Luke was my "uncle."

But when your parents are Jonathan Harker and Mina Murray, you don't question the vagaries of your family tree. You just say hi to whatever strange "uncle" or "cousin" might be visiting and get on about your business.

So, I commenced to getting on about my business. I restored the passenger seat to its upright and locked position, opened the door, and slid down from the giant vehicle onto the damp asphalt. It was a cool, drizzly afternoon, and Atlanta's artsy district seemed to be just waking up. The bookstore and drug store both looked almost deserted from where I stood, but if there's going to be one place in Little Five Points that will always be hopping, it's The Vortex.

The Vortex is a local landmark, the kind of place that a city's residents talk about with pride no matter if they've ever darkened the doors or not. Starting out in the 90s, the bar and burger joint boasts good food, cold beer, funky-ass wait staff, and serious attitude. In other words, it was my kind of joint. I walked through the giant skull façade over the front door and stepped into the dimly-lit joint. Music blared, rock and roll posters covered every surface, and the smells coming from the kitchen reminded me that Adam doesn't eat, and doesn't let anybody else eat in his car, so the food options on our trip had been limited to whatever I could shovel into my face while he was refueling his battle wagon.

A tiny hostess with more tattoos than I had teeth stood by the door. She wore a laughing skull t-shirt, a pair of cut-off jeans, and black Chuck Taylor high-tops. A silver ring winked at me from one eyebrow, and she looked me up and down, appraising the new arrival, before finally speaking.

"You must be the guy they're waiting on," she said after a few seconds. "Where's your friend?"

"Parking the car," I replied. "And what do you mean I must be the guy?"

"Your friends are over there." She jerked a thumb over one shoulder to a long table where Detective Rebecca Gail Flynn, Gabby Van Helsing, and a bunch of people I'd never met face-to-face sat around a laptop. "They told me to be on the lookout for a giant and a dude that looked like a mass murderer. You're nowhere close to being a giant, but I wouldn't be surprised if you left a pretty high body count in your wake." She gave me a grin and reached under the hostess stand for a couple menus and some rolled silverware.

"Follow me." She turned and walked toward the table.

I did, thinking she was way more accurate than she wanted to know. There was a trail of bodies behind me a mile long and twice as wide, and I felt pretty sure that trail was going to get nothing but longer before I was through with Atlanta.

You gonna stare at that screen or you gonna get up and give me a hug? I asked across the mental link I shared with Flynn. I saw her straighten up in her chair, then stand up like a shot and turn around, her head whipping side to side, tossing brown curls around her face as she looked for me.

I stood ten feet away, drinking in the sight of her. It had only been a few weeks since we were last together, but it felt like ten years. The bond we shared was more than just partners, or boyfriend/girlfriend, or whatever we were. When I shared my blood with her to save her life a year ago, she got inside my head. Literally. Distance weakened the connection, so when I was in Ohio and she was in North Carolina, it felt like a part of myself was missing. A part that just came rushing back all at once when our eyes met.

She was gorgeous, there was no question about that. This woman, who I had looked out for since she was a little girl, had grown into a beauty. And that beautiful woman took three steps across the restaurant floor, wrapped her arms around my neck, and kissed me like I haven't been kissed in a very long time. I kissed her back with everything I had and wrapped my hands around her trim waist. I felt her suck in a breath, and I pulled back.

Her dark brown eyes squinted in pain, and her mocha skin was suddenly a little pale.

"What's wrong?" I asked, then I remembered. Her side. That fucking demon back in Charlotte stabbed her while I was inside dealing with Smith. "Shit, I'm sorry. Are you okay?"

"I'm good, I'm good." She smiled up at me. "No, seriously, I'm good. You just pulled me in when you kissed me and my side pressed up against... what the hell is that, anyway?" She pointed at my side with a little grin.

I looked down at the offending hardware, a short gladius I had hanging from my belt. I'd picked it up from a stash of weapons in Adam's car when a couple of bikers got a little more interested in the Hummer at a gas station than I was comfortable with, then forgot to take it off.

"Sorry, I must have poked you with my giant rigid sword," I said with a lopsided grin.

"In your dreams, Romeo," Flynn said, slapping me on the chest. "It's good to see you again, Harker."

"Good to be seen, Detective." We were both using that formal tone that lovers use when they're teasing each other in front of people. It's really cute to the lovers, but often less so to the spectators.

"Oh for God's sake, do you two need a moment? I'm sure it won't be the first time the lavatories in this place have been used for purposes God never intended, but you're putting the rest of us off our lunch," a skinny British guy at the end of the table protested.

"Shut up, Jack, you're just mad nobody's ever greeted you with that much enthusiasm," said the woman next to him. She was an athletic woman in a leather jacket with an easy grin and black hair pulled back into a tight ponytail.

I walked over to the table and pulled out one of the empty chairs. I looked around the table and gave a little wave. "So… I'm Quincy Harker. I guess you all know that. Who is everybody? Everybody that I haven't either fought beside or against, that is. I assume you're Jack Watson?" I said to the British guy.

"What gave it away? My dashing good looks, the obvious intellectual superiority to everyone in the room—"

"The fact that you're the only guy at the table he didn't grow up with?" the mystery woman said. She leaned over the table and extended a hand. "Ignore Jack, we all do. I'm Jo Henry. I hit things."

"With a big damn hammer," Gabriella Van Helsing added. My first meeting with Gabby wasn't the most festive occasion I'd ever experienced, but we settled into a tentative truce by the time that case finished up. I hadn't known Luke recruited her into the Shadow Council until I found out she was in Charlotte while I was on the run. I still wasn't sure how I felt about her. Our last meeting had left me thinking she might be a little more insane than my normal partners.

"Good to meet you, Jo. And Jack. And good to see you again, Gabriella," I said. "I assume Luke is stashed somewhere lightproof?"

"I am indeed safely ensconced in a room at the Westin downtown. While blacking out the windows was an unusual request, I doubt it was the strangest thing the hotel has been asked to do for a guest." Luke's voice came from the speakers on the laptop. Video conferencing and ubiquitous Wi-Fi made it a lot easier to keep a vampire in the loop in the modern era.

Luke peered around me. "Where is Adam?"

"Looking for parking," I replied. "Kind of an Olympic sport in Atlanta."

"It wasn't really a problem," Adam's rumbling voice came from behind me. I looked up, a little surprised that someone that damn big could move that quietly.

"Good to see you, Adam," Luke said with a nod. "I believe you know Mr. Watson, and this is Gabby Van Helsing." Luke waved his hands around the screen, and Adam nodded to the new players in turn. Apparently, he knew the Brit, but I knew he spent a lot of time in Europe.

Adam stretched out a hand to Gabriella. "I knew your grandfather," he said. "He was a good man."

Gabby looked confused. "Is there anyone who didn't know Grandpa Abe? Because I'm starting to think I'm the only one on this team with a normal human lifespan."

"I'm one hundred percent human, Gabs, no need to worry about that," Jo said, standing up. She shook hands with Adam. "Joanna Henry. Call me Jo."

"I've heard of your great-grandfather, but we never met. He was reputed to be a man of great character. As was yours, Mr. Watson," he said to Jack.

"Thank you, Mr.… I'm sorry, I don't believe I caught your last name?" Watson said.

Adam looked at me, and I shrugged. If the folks around the table hadn't figured it out yet, it wasn't on me to tell tales. He turned his gaze to Luke, who, likewise, gave him no help. "Franks is the name I have used most often in this country recently. That will suffice, I believe."

Watson knit his brow, and I could see Flynn's shoulders shaking as she stifled laughter. She knew exactly what was going on, of course, thanks to our restored mental connection. Jo leaned over and whispered something into Watson's ear, and his head whipped around and up to look back at Adam.

"You're…you're really…*really?*"

"He says while he sits eating wings and Skyping with friggin' Dracula," I said, waving a waitress over. "Adam, grab a seat. I'm gonna get some lunch and maybe a few beers and we can get this party started. Can I get a Laughing Skull and a dozen wings, crispy, with the hottest sauce you've got on the side?" The waitress walked off, and I turned to the table.

"Okay, what's the deal?" I asked. I guess it was mostly directed at Luke, but it was Becks everyone looked to for the answer.

"Alright, I'll start. Orobas is here in Atlanta. Some bajillionaire named Reginald Barton flew him down here on a private jet. We don't know what he's up to, or how he's tied to Barton, but Orobas with a bankroll can't be good. What was going on in Kentucky?" She looked at me with a little grin. She knew damn well I hate Kentucky thanks to some bourbon-induced bad decisions in the 90s.

"Ohio, but close," I replied. "There were demons, and the one in charge knew about Orobas, but from what he said, it sounded like Oro wasn't the lead dog in the team. So, we need to figure out who's pulling the strings and what their endgame is."

"According to Sparkles, Barton is a collector of antiquities, with a specific taste for artifacts thought to have some mystical properties," Jo said, looking up from her phone.

"Sparkles texts now?" I asked.

"I think he does whatever he wants with anything connected to the internet," she replied with a nod.

"Yeah, probably so," I agreed.

"Who is this mysterious Sparkles, and am I ever going to meet him?" Flynn asked.

"Almost certainly not," Luke said, then smoothly changed the subject. "Well, it seems that Barton's taste for magical items explains his interest in this." He picked up a sword and held it up in view of the camera.

"Since when did you get all Ren Faire on us, Luke?" I asked.

"As it appears this sword was what Orobas wanted from the wreckage of my home. I felt that leaving it in the car would be ill-advised," Luke replied.

"I thought Smith was trying to open a portal to Hell to bring all his buddies across and invade the world?" I asked. "I mean, I'm just the dude that shot him in the face, but that's sure what it looked like he was doing from where I was standing."

"That may well have been Agent Smith's goal, but once you thwarted that attempt, it seems that Orobas turned his attention to acquiring this weapon."

"Why?" I asked. "I mean, swords are great if you need to cut off an arm or make a hole in somebody, but I haven't found one that can open a doorway to Hell."

"That doesn't mean there's not one out there, just that we have yet to encounter it," Adam chimed in.

"Aren't you just a ray of fucking sunshine?" I grumbled.

"I am typically considered somewhat dry and sardonic, so no, I would assume that I am not, in fact, a ray of sunshine," Adam replied. I looked over at him, but his face betrayed nothing. I'd worked with Adam for decades, and I could never tell if he was fucking with me or not. Either he had the greatest sense of humor in the world, or absolutely none.

I gave my head a shake and went on. "Okay, so we have the sword, and we know who's partnered up with Orobas down here. How do we plan to fuck up his plans and save the world?" I asked.

"This week," Flynn added.

I looked at her, questioning.

"You left out a bit. It's supposed to be 'how do we save the world *this week?*'"

Luke's face blurred on the laptop, and suddenly we had a split image, with Luke on half the screen and a unicorn head on the other. The unicorn's mouth started to move as we all stared at the computer.

"Well, you might want to start by killing the demons that are currently climbing the Ferris Wheel outside Centennial Park," the unicorn said.

"Goddammit, Sparkles," I said. "Why can't you just say hello like a normal person?"

Chapter Two

I THREW AN AMERICAN EXPRESS BLACK CARD AT THE WAITRESS AND TOLD her I'd be back for it later. Then we hauled ass out of the restaurant. Flynn and I sprinted down the sidewalk after Adam toward a small hidden parking lot where he'd stashed the Hummer while the others jumped into what looked an awful lot like Flynn's unmarked police car.

"Did you just give two people you barely know and a psychotic the keys to your cop car?" I asked after I got into the passenger seat and clicked my seat belt on.

"Yeah, kinda," Flynn replied. "I'm not a hundred percent sure it's going to be my cop car when I get back to Charlotte, so I only kinda give a shit. Besides, Jo's an excellent driver."

"Gabby is driving," Adam said, looking in the rearview mirror.

"Goddammit," Becks replied. I couldn't help but laugh.

I pulled out my phone and fired up a Skype link to Sparkles. "What do we know, pal?" I asked.

Sparkles popped up on my phone screen and the computer screen built into the dash. "Hang on, let me loop the other car in." The unicorn head vanished, then reappeared with a smaller inset image of Gabby, Watson, and Jo.

"Someday I'm going to learn how you do that shit," Jo said.

"I don't think you will, Jo, but you're welcome to try," said the unicorn.

"Give us the skinny, horn-boy," I said.

"What do you want to know, Harker? There are demons climbing the outside of the Ferris Wheel and eating people. Here, watch the video."

The image on the screen switched from a unicorn head to a live security cam feed. Sure enough, there were demons on the Ferris Wheel. I was pretty sure that shit wasn't included in the price of admission. A pair of the nasty bastards, mid-level Torment Demons from the looks of them, had the wheel stopped and were calmly climbing the center chords, then walking out onto the supports, ripping the door off its hinges, and swinging in. Once inside, the demons vanished from the camera shot, but after a few seconds, a head flew out the door.

"Oh, that's nasty," I said.

"They're discarding the bits they can't eat," Adam said. "No meat or muscle on a skull, except the jaw. Nothing worth consuming, unless you're a big fan of tongue."

I gave him a sharp look, but he just shrugged. "I don't eat anything, Harker. You don't have to worry about me turning cannibal on you."

If that was supposed to reassure me, it didn't work. The video switched back to Sparkles and the occupants of the other car.

"Okay," I said. "The good news is that Torment Demons are fairly run-of-the-mill bad guys. They're big, strong, and very hard to hurt, but they don't have any magic. They have to get their hands on you to do any harm. They're not any faster than normal humans, but they do have seriously sharp claws, teeth than can chew through chain, and very tough skin. Normal blades probably won't do anything. We'll need magic, blessed weapons, or something crazy sharp to make an impression. But if there are only two of them, we should be in pretty good shape. I've dealt with two on my own before. It sucked, and I almost died, but I did it."

"Yeah… about that," Sparkles said.

"What about it, bud?" I asked.

"There's a half a dozen Reavers running around on the ground."

"Fuck," I said.

"What's a Reaver?" Flynn asked.

"Yeah, clue us in, Harker," Jo agreed. "We don't all hunt demons that often."

"Reavers are nasty little bastards," I said. "They're like overgrown imps, only instead of being mischievous, they're just fucking mean. They're about five feet tall, skinny little fuckers, with extra-long arms, razor-sharp talons on the ends of their fingers, and elongated jaws with a shit ton of pointy little teeth. All Reavers do is eat, fight, and fuck, and you don't really want to be part of any of the three. I know I don't. A pair of hungry Reavers can strip an elephant to bone in five minutes, and they're always hungry."

"So how do we kill them?" Gabby asked.

"Reavers go down easier," I replied. "That's about the only good news. They can be hurt with normal weapons. They heal fast, but not so fast that you can't take them out of a fight. The only way to kill one is to behead it, and even then, you probably need someone to consecrate the body to make sure it's really dead."

"And even that doesn't really kill it, does it?" Becks asked from the back seat. I turned to look at her, and she went on. "That just sends it back to Hell, right?"

"Most of the time, yes. There are weapons that can actually kill a demon, but not many, and I sure as shit don't have one. But sending it back to Hell is good enough for our purposes because that makes them stop killing people, and that's about all we can ask for on short notice. So, when we get there, I want to put you, Jo, Gabby, and Watson on the Reavers, working in pairs back-to-back. These fuckers are *fast*, so you need somebody to watch your six. Adam and I will work on taking out the Torment Demons."

"How exactly do you plan to do that without blessed weapons? You just going to throw fireballs at them and hope they don't kill you too quickly?"

"Nah, I'm going to shoot them off the Ferris Wheel with a high-powered rifle and ask friggin' Frankenstein to rip them limb from limb. Once they're torn apart, I'll figure out a way to kill them."

"You know I don't like being called that. My father's name was Dr. Frankenstein. My name is Adam."

"I know, pal, but it's the twenty-first century in America, and that's what everybody knows you as over here. Sorry, but it's just a lot faster this way."

Becks just sat in the back seat muttering about the level of surreal in her life since she'd met me. If she only knew what was coming, she would have known everything until then had just been a warmup.

Adam didn't bother trying to find a parking space this time; he just ran his Hummer up onto the sidewalk and pulled up close to the Ferris Wheel. That also happened to put him right on top of a Reaver demon, which I'm sure was no accident. I stepped on an arm as I got out of the truck and almost busted my ass, but I managed to catch myself.

A cop ran over to us, sidearm out and a wild look in his eyes. "You can't be here! This is dangerous, you people have to—"

I held up my Homeland Security badge. "We'll take it from here, officer. This is a National Security matter. Please tell your men to focus on setting up a perimeter and getting the wounded to safety. We'll handle the terrorists." My badge wasn't worth the metal it was stamped out of since my consultant status with Homeland was revoked a few seconds after I shot my Supervisory Agent in the face, but this beat cop didn't know that. All he saw was somebody who wasn't shit-scared, had a badge, and was giving orders.

He nodded and grabbed his radio, relaying my message to the rest of the locals.

"Terrorists?" Flynn asked, sliding out of the back seat to stand beside me.

"Yep. These guys will be a lot more likely to accept any mundane explanation, no matter how stupid, than they will a supernatural one. In their world, demons are something in comic books and movies, but terrorists are hiding behind every trash can."

Flynn nodded. "If they only knew that the real threat from illegal aliens came from other dimensions instead of other continents."

Just then the others ran up behind us, Watson coming to a limping stop behind the two women. "You alright, Jack?" I asked.

"The leg makes it a little difficult in a sprint, friend. I walk fine, but running is right out except in most extreme cases." He pulled up his pants leg a little to show me a steel rod where his leg used to be.

"Shit, man, I'm sorry, I didn't know. Maybe you should—" I started, but he held up a hand to stop me.

"Oh sod off, mate. I can do anything except run and the high hurdles. Now what's the plan?" He drew a small pistol from under his jacket and chambered a round. I noticed Gabby had strapped on her guns as well, and Jo carried a gigantic friggin' hammer. I looked at her, then at the hammer.

"I don't like guns. And anything a bullet can stop, a damn nine-pound hammer can stop, too. Plus, one head is silvered, and the other head is cold iron, so it's good against most things. And in a pinch, I can do this." She gave the end of the handle a twist and a yank, and it came off into a wooden stake.

"Nice. You four are on Reaver duty. Adam and I will work on the... fuck, let's go." I gave up on the instructions as the body of a fifty-something woman slammed into the bricks a dozen paces from where we were standing. I looked up to see a Torment Demon holding a teen boy out of a gondola by his hoodie. The fabric started to rip, and even from a couple hundred feet away, I watched the demon's smile get wider and wider and the boy struggled to grab hold of something to save himself.

"Adam, can you try to catch him?" I asked. "I don't know what that kind of impact will do..."

"It won't matter, Quincy," Adam said, his deep voice quiet. "Even if I caught him, the impact with my arms would shatter his bones. And probably tear my arms off, which would render me useless for a time."

"For a time?" Flynn started to ask, then her mouth closed with a *click*. "My life is so fucking weird. Come on, y'all. Let's go kill some demons." With the wave of an arm, her team moved off into the park, hunting Reavers and helping the cops get the civilians out of the way.

The kid was dead. I had to let that one go. It sucked, and it pissed me off, but that's all I could let it do. I walked around to the back of the Hummer and opened the tailgate. I popped open a compartment in the floor and pulled out a Remington 700 rifle with a scope and bipod. I picked up a pair of three-round magazines from a slot labeled "Holy Water" and slapped one into the rifle.

Walking around the front of the Hummer, I flipped down the bipod and found I couldn't get the angle right to steady the gun on the hood of the truck. I was too tall to shoot up at that kind of angle. So, I put the bipod up and steadied my elbows on the hood, sighting through the scope until the view was full of demon chest. No point in trying to get fancy, I just needed to hit the bastard and make him fall. No headshots here, not that I had too much faith in my ability to make one.

I let out my breath and squeezed the trigger. The big rifle bucked, and I saw the bullet spark off the metal frame of the gondola. The demon spun around, looking for me, and my second shot didn't miss. Quite. I was a little low, but hitting the nasty bastard in the knee had the desired effect. The demon's leg went out from under it, and he tumbled to the ground, slamming into the bricks with a sickening *thwap*. The worst part about that sound was that I knew it wasn't enough. The demon would be out of the fight for maybe a full minute, but unless we banished it, it would heal, even from that fall, in not near enough time.

"My turn," Adam said, running toward the downed demon while I swung the rifle around to find the next target. This one was smarter, of course, because he knew I was coming. He had a woman acting as a human shield, and there was no way I was sniper enough to shoot the demon without killing the woman.

"Fuck," I muttered, trying to think of another option.

"Leave us alone, Reaper!" the demon shouted. "This is our city, and before long it will be our world!"

"Fuck you, asshole!" I yelled back, because I'm witty like that.

"What are you going to do, shoot me? You can't hit me unless you're willing to kill this human, too. And then what? You going to raise this sweet little girl she's got up here?"

Fuck me, she's got her kid with her. "Why don't you come on down here and show me just how much this is your city, dickweed?" I yelled up at the demon.

"After I'm done with the bitch, maybe I will!" It shouted, then pulled back from the door into the gondola. I cursed whoever decided that Ferris Wheels should advance from the old bench seats into having big people-cages because I had no shot at the demon.

But I guess I didn't need to since I saw a dark form swing over from the main body of the wheel onto the spoke where the carriage swung. Adam hadn't stopped to fight the first demon after all; he'd apparently just scrambled up the Ferris Wheel like a really ugly Spider-Man and was now on top of the cage carrying the demon, mother, and child. He swung into the gondola, and the tinted windows blocked my view. The thing rocked wildly, and I wondered how anybody managed to stay inside through all that. Then someone didn't.

Two someones, actually. Two giant forms tumbled out the door and plummeted to the brick below, turning over and over and scrabbling at each other the whole way down. Adam and the demon landed with a mighty *THUD*, and I sprinted over to see what was left of them.

Not much left of the demon, as Adam managed to land on top. He rolled over, sprawled on his back looking up at me.

"Ouch."

"You're not dead? I think that fall might have even killed Luke," I said, absolutely baffled by how he was able to speak.

"I don't know how I'm alive, Quincy, and I don't know that I can be killed. But I know we need to banish these things before they reconstitute themselves. And I know that both my legs are very severely broken, so could you please carry me somewhere that I will not be lying in demon entrails? They smell horrible."

He wasn't lying. The scattered demon guts gave off a wretched odor, like three-day-old gamer funk mixed with rotted asshole. I leaned over and hoisted Adam over my shoulders in a fireman's carry, then deposited him into the grass a couple dozen feet away.

"Before you begin the ritual of banishment, could you take a moment to set the bones in my arms and legs? They will heal quickly, and I would prefer that everything line up correctly when they do."

I looked at the twisted mass of bones that were Adam's extremities, and an involuntary shudder ran through me. Any human would have died instantly, and even if they didn't, the pain from those injuries would have put them into shock. But Adam wasn't even as close to human as I was, so he just sat there stoically as I set his arms and legs.

"Lay there, and don't move," I said. "I'll deal with these fuckers, then we'll... son of a *bitch!*" I cut myself off as I looked over and saw the first demon getting to his feet. He was *not* supposed to heal that fast. Bastard was messing with my timetable.

Oh well, stuck fighting an unkillable demon with my backup sidelined by injury. Story of my stupid life.

Chapter Three

THE TORMENT DEMON WASN'T ANYWHERE NEAR FULL STRENGTH YET, and I could only hope that was going to be enough to let me trap it and banish it before it killed anymore people. Notably me. The rifle was still up at the Hummer, so all I had on me was my Glock and the short sword I'd strapped to my waist hours before. This was about to suck.

The demon hadn't turned his attention to me yet, mostly because it was currently regrowing an arm, but I figured I didn't have a lot of time. I drew my sword and dashed in behind the big bastard, slashing down to hamstring him. Which was a great idea, except that my gladius was in no way consecrated, or blessed, or holy, or magical. So, it hit the demon's skin and bounced off, sending vibrations up my arm and making my fingers tingle with the impact.

That got the demon's attention. Just what I always wanted—the undivided attention of a pissed off, invulnerable, seven-foot tall monster with a mouth full of razor-sharp fangs and claws that could rip me from nuts to nose in half a second. It spun around and backhanded me with its one good arm, sending me sprawling to the ground a good four feet from where I started. I rolled to my feet and drew in my will, coalescing energy into a glowing sphere three inches in diameter above my outstretched hand.

I flung the ball of purple light at the demon and smacked it right in the chest. It had part of the desired effect, smacking into the creature and leaving a burned mark on its chest, but not the rest of it, which was to knock it down or maybe make it give a shit about the damage in some way. No, it just grinned at me and stalked forward, not even bothering to charge me.

I fired energy ball after energy ball at the creature, backing up at about the same pace that it was moving forward, but it was a losing proposition. I was running out of energy at about the same rate the demon was healing, and that was going to put me staring down a fully-healed Torment Demon sooner rather than later.

"Adam, a little help!" I shouted over my shoulder.

"Busy right now, Quincy," came the reply. I spared a glance and saw he wasn't joking. He was standing toe to toe with the other demon, trading punches that would have caved in the skull on a normal man. Every once in a while, he darted forward to pull the demon's leg out from under it, but the beast was quick to spring back up. I turned my attention back to the problem at hand, racking my brain for anything I could come up with on destroying tormentors. Nothing came to me, so I just kept flinging fireballs at the demon until I backpedaled off the sidewalk and tripped over a discarded bicycle.

I flopped down on my ass atop somebody's mountain bike and looked up at a grinning Torment Demon. There are a lot of things I don't mind looking up to: mountains, stars, even a full moon, but a happy demon is never something I want to see looming over me.

Fortunately, the demon's smile faded abruptly as a gleaming blade sliced through its neck. The head toppled to the ground, and both segments of the dead thing dissolved in a cloud of sulfur, sent back to Hell where it belonged.

I stared up at a much more welcome sight, a blonde woman resplendent in silver chain mail with wings and a shiny gold-rimmed helmet. "Hi Glory," I said. "I was really hoping you'd show up."

My guardian angel just shook her head at me. "You know that's not supposed to be how this works, right? You aren't supposed to just randomly jump into lethal situations counting on me to save you. I'm supposed to be here for the unplanned things that could kill you."

"In my defense, I didn't plan on demons attacking a Ferris Wheel today," I countered.

"You're a dick, Q. A real dick." Glory turned and unfurled her wings, flying across the grass and finishing off the demon Adam was ripping apart. Then she took out the last of the Reavers, and we all gathered back at the Hummer.

"Did you just call me a dick?" I asked the angel.

"If the shoe fits," Adam muttered.

"Screw you, golem," I said, an old crack that never failed to get under his skin. He hated being called a golem more than Luke hated being asked if he sparkled. I turned my attention back to Glory. "Did you call me a dick? I didn't think angels could curse."

"Swearing isn't a sin, Q. Lying is a sin, but since you really are a dick, I get to say that as much as I want."

"She's not wrong about that part, is she, pal?" Watson asked with a grin. I just glared at him, and he took a step back. I didn't dislike the Brit, but I didn't want him getting the opinion that since we were on the same side, that we were friends or anything like that.

I glanced around the park at the carnage the demons wrought. There were bodies and body parts scattered across the whole area beneath the Ferris Wheel, and a veritable army of cop cars and ambulances were lined up just outside the perimeter the first cops had established.

I pulled out my cell phone. "Sparkles," I said to the blank device. "Can you do something about the curious locals?"

"Already on it," said the unicorn that popped up on my screen. "The officer in charge just had a video conference with the head of the local FBI office, who had never met, about the 'terrorist incident' in the park today. And all the video shot by those news vans will find itself mysteriously erased."

"Thanks, man. Any live feeds get out?" I asked.

"I'm almost insulted that you felt you had to ask. But no, you're good. But you've only got maybe two minutes before the crowd grows past the size I can manage. After that, you're gonna be all over YouTube."

"Got it," I said. I slipped the phone into my pocket and looked around. "Let's get out of here, kids."

"Just a second," Flynn said. "Glory, who called these bastards? And what did they want?"

"I would assume that Orobas summoned them," the angel replied. "But I have no idea why."

"Is nobody else going to maybe remark on the fact that we are standing in the middle of a park in Georgia chatting with an angel like we're talking about the weather?" Jo asked. I noticed that while her jacket was torn and there was blood running down one arm, the head of her hammer was streaked with gore and what looked like little flecks of Reaver skull. She had obviously given as good as she'd gotten.

I took a second then to give her, and the others, a once-over. Flynn was untouched, but I wasn't surprised by that. She'd been through enough shit with me to know when it's best to fight from a distance. Watson was similarly unscathed, but Gabby. Well, Gabby looked like she'd taken time off from shooting a Manson family biopic to remake *American Psycho*. She was covered in blood from her knees to the top of her head, and gore streaked her arms like she'd been kneading bread made with blood and entrails.

"What the fuck happened to you?" I asked. "I thought you had guns."

"I did," she said with a grin. Her white teeth shining through a mask of blood across her face was truly unnerving. "But then I had to get up close and personal with a couple of the Reavers. It didn't go well for them." She drew a pair of foot-long daggers from somewhere behind her back and twirled them around, all the while keeping that godawful grin plastered across her face.

"Has anybody ever told you about the message of our Lord and Savior Hannibal frickin' Lecter?" Flynn asked, taking a big step sideways to create some separation with Gabby.

"Don't worry, Detective. I still mostly like you," Gabby said, putting her knives away.

I shook my head, trying to focus on the questions at hand more than the mental wellness, or lack thereof, of my partners. "Okay, let's focus for just a minute, people. It makes sense that Orobas called these bastards, but why? Was there something here worth going after? Have there been any other incidents around the city? Why right here, right now?"

"I'll go ask the constables," Watson said, and walked off to the nearest pair of cops.

"I don't know of anything spiritually or mystically significant about this park," Jo said. "But I'll jump online and see what I can grab real quick." She walked over to a park bench and sat, pulling a tablet out of her jacket pocket and tapping away.

"She kept her iPad from getting busted while fighting demons? Maybe she does have super-powers," I said.

"Glory, can you make a quick lap around the city and make sure this was the only demon summoning on the calendar for this afternoon? I'd hate to think we missed an important engagement," Flynn asked.

"I can do that." Glory gave me a stern look. "Try not to do anything suicidal in the next hour." Then she vanished.

I looked at Gabby, standing there covered in gore like an extra in a community theatre *Titus Andronicus*. "Why don't you go run through the fountain or something?"

"It's cold," she grumbled.

"Unless you're planning on walking back to the hotel, which probably won't let you in looking like Carrie, you should at least rinse off," I replied. She scowled at me, then handed her gun belt to Flynn and stomped off toward the Olympic Ring-shaped fountain.

Becks watched her go, then looked at me. "Sometimes I think you're one hundred percent batshit crazy, Harker. Then I spend time around some of your friends."

"She raises a valid point, Quincy," Adam said. "I believe I shall also go rinse off the worst of the gore before I have to drive to the hotel. I do not relish getting blood out of my upholstery. Again." He gave me a sharp look before following Gabby to the fountain.

"Sorry!" I called after him. "Demons," I explained to Flynn. We stood there, alone for the first time since I'd joined them, and of course, things got awkward.

"Umm," I started, not really sure what I wanted to follow that brilliant opener with. "Did you get the... box I left for you with Glory?"

"I did." Her voice was cold, and she didn't look at me.

"And?" I asked. I could outwait her. I was over a hundred years old. I had the long game down.

"And I'm not going to respond."

"Why not? Are you not interested? Because I thought we..." I could feel a lot of things bouncing through our link, but they were all jumbled up. At the root of it all, I could feel interest, along with fear, anger, worry, and a host of less fun things.

"Oh, we definitely did. But if we're going to take that kind of step, and I'm not saying we should, but if we are, I sure as hell am not going to be proposed to by a proxy, even if she is an angel. Let's get through this whole end of the world thing, make sure neither one of us comes down with a bad case of the deads, and then talk about maybe going on a date.

"Harker, I'm nowhere near ready to get married. Two years ago, I thought you were just a conman fleecing people out of cash by spinning horror stories, and now I'm fighting demons in a park with Frankenstein, and I've got Dracula on speed dial.

"My life has gone from zero to a monster movie in eighteen months, and I don't even know if I'm still going to have a *job* when I get back to Charlotte, much less know if I want to marry you. And *then* there's the whole thing where I get old and you don't, and I've seen *Highlander*, and I know how well that turns out, so... we've got a lot of shit to figure out before I put that ring on my finger."

I looked down into her brown eyes and saw the emotion welling up, right behind the tears that threatened to spill down her caramel-colored cheeks. I gave her a little smile, sending emotion across our link to make sure she understood that I meant what I said. "You're right, Becks. I was scared when I sent that ring with Glory, and it was dumb to put you in that position. I'll slow down a little. But make no mistake about one thing, Rebecca Gail Flynn—I love you, and I will tear down the Gates of Heaven itself to make sure we are never separated again."

She smiled up at me, then threw her arms around my neck and kissed me, jamming her lips to mine with a ferocity that reminded me I was with a warrior woman. She pulled back and looked me in the eye. "Nicely said. Sometimes I forget that you weren't raised by wolves, but that was actually poetic."

"Live long enough and you read a lot. Even poetry. I'm partial to Billy Collins, myself," I said.

"I hate to interrupt your little *tete-a-tete*, but I think I know why the demons attacked here," Jo said, walking up with her iPad in hand.

"What's up?" I asked.

"There was a some kind of strange disturbance up at Stone Mountain about an hour ago, just about the time the demons hit the first gondola. Lots of flashing lights in the sky were reported, and the rangers that went to check it out are now being called in as missing, their vehicles abandoned."

"Shit," I said. "There was something there, and Orobas went after it."

"And got it, from what these reports sound like," Jo agreed. She handed me the tablet, and I read a string of messages from Sparkles. Everything was just like she said—rangers missing, lights over the mountain, and a big hole in the ground at the summit. Whatever was there, it was gone now.

"Fucking hell," I grumbled. "Alright, we still have to check it out, just to see if we can pick up any clue as to what was there. Jo, you and the others go circle back to Luke and see if Sparkles has found out anything about Barton. Flynn and I will ride up to Stone Mountain with Adam and poke around. We still have our Homeland credentials, even if we're fired."

"*So* fired," Flynn agreed.

"Adam!" I yelled. "Get your big ass over here! We gotta go hunt demons in the woods."

"Again?" he called back. "Must be Tuesday."

Chapter Four

WE TOOK THE BACK ROAD UP TO THE TOP OF STONE MOUNTAIN AND pulled off to the side behind half a dozen cop cars and one lost-looking UPS driver. Adam and Flynn followed me as I badged us past the uniformed cop on crowd control duty, and we started to look around for any traces of Orobas or anything magical.

"I guess that's what we came here for," Flynn said, pointing at a smoking crater in the rock some ten feet in diameter.

"And that's why she's the detective, ladies and gentlemen," I replied. We walked over to the hole, which looked just like any other big hole in a big rock. There was smoke, there was rock blasted to pebbles, and there was one really shaken college kid in khakis and a polo shirt talking to a cop. The kid was tall and so terrified his man-bun was shaking as I walked over to eavesdrop.

"I dunno, dude," the kid was saying as I walked up. "It's like I said, man, one minute he was a normal dude, and the next he was a friggin' monster. He was like ten feet tall, with six arms and gigantic teeth. Scared the shit out of me, so I hid, man."

More like seven feet tall with two arms and a shitload of attitude most likely, but I didn't need to correct the kid. He'd just survived his first demon encounter; he could see as many arms as he wanted. "So you didn't see anything after the dude turned into a monster?" I asked.

The kid looked at me like I was his best friend just for even thinking that I believed him, but the cop he was talking to was way less enthused. He was the kind of guy who looked like he broke a sweat just walking up from his car, and he certainly didn't need any interlopers in his case. He was in his fifties with a belly that stuck out so far I wonder if he just took it for granted that he still had feet and a scowl on his red face that looked permanent.

"And who the hell do you think you are, mister? And how the hell did you get past Gerald?"

"Quincy Harker, Homeland Security," I said, flashing my badge. He wasn't as inclined to just automatically yield the floor as his younger buddy down by the crime scene tape line, so I passed over my wallet when he held out his pudgy little hand.

He squinted at the picture, then at me, then passed it back over. "Who're they?"

"They're with me," I said.

"I didn't ask who they were with, smartass, I asked who they were. You want to stay on my crime scene, son, you better—"

I stepped forward and picked him up by the front of his shirt. I lifted him up about two inches off the ground so we could look eye to eye. "Look here, Deputy Fuckwit. This shit is so far out of your jurisdiction it might not have even come from the same galaxy. You're so far in over your head you can't even see the sun, and you don't even know it yet. There are things out there that your little pea brain can't handle. That's what I'm here for. I handle the shit you only see in your nightmares, and that's what shit we're dealing with here. Now unless you can come up with some normal criminal that can carve a ten-foot hole in solid fucking granite in a matter of seconds, you need to get out of my way and let me do my job. You got me?"

He nodded, silently, and I put him down. I gave him a steady look and said, "Now fuck off out of here while the adults deal with the bad things." He hustled back down the hill toward his car, and I turned my attention to the kid.

"Don't kill me, man," the kid said, shrinking back a little closer to the edge of the hole than was probably safe. I reached out and grabbed his shirt, too, but only to pull him back before he fell in the crater and smashed his skull in. "I'm not gonna kill you, kid. I just want to know what you saw."

"Like I said, man. There was a dude, then he was a monster. He made some kind of weird light show with his hands, and then the ground blew up. A chunk of rock whizzed by my head, and I screamed a little. That's when it came at me. But I fought it off." He puffed up at that last bit, proud of himself for standing up to the monster. Too bad it was a load of shit.

"You fought it off?" Flynn asked, incredulous.

"Yeah, man. It came after me, but I judo-chopped it right in the nose, and it flew off out of here, man."

"Is that why you pissed yourself?" I asked. "Because you were so damn proud of the way you judo-chopped a demon? A demon that would have ripped off your arm and beaten you to a bloody pulp with it had you even so much as looked crosswise at it."

His long face fell, and I felt like I just nut-shotted Shaggy from the Scooby-Doo cartoons. "It's okay, kid," I said. "You can tell all the girls that you fought the thing off. I just need to know what it got out of the hole."

"The hole?" the kid asked, and I revised my opinion on the harmlessness of marijuana. This kid had definitely smoked his last brain cell.

"Yes, dumbass, the hole! The great big fucking hole in the rock that you almost fell into ten seconds ago!" This time I yelled. It had been a long couple of weeks. I think I was allowed a little yelling.

"Oh, yeah. Sorry, man. I didn't see what it took out of the hole. I was kinda hiding."

I took a deep breath because the more deep breaths I took, the less likely I was to throw this idiot kid off the mountain. "*Kinda* hiding?"

"Okay, I was totally hiding. In there." He pointed over to the snack bar beside the sky tram stop at the top of the mountain. "I pulled the drink machine out from the wall, and I hid behind it. Sorry, dude."

I looked at my feet, then up to Heaven, then back at the kid. Just as I opened my mouth to say something truly vicious, Flynn stepped in. She doesn't always play the peacemaker, but she's a hell of a lot better at it than I am, so I let her do the talking.

"Hey… Dave," she said, reading the kid's nametag. "Why don't you and I go into the office and look at the security camera footage. Maybe there's something useful there." She pointed up at a small camera mounted to an overhang on the roof of the tram stop. It pointed in the general direction of the hole.

That's why you're the detective, I thought to her.

Shut your pie-hole is what came back to me across our mental link, but I felt a little smile behind it.

"Yeah," Dave said. "I think there's a monitor in the electrical closet."

"I'll go with Dave, and we can take a look at the footage," Flynn said.

"We'll stay out here and in the crater, see if we can pick up any… forensic evidence." I went with that lame excuse to poke around the crater because saying "I'll open up my Second Sight and see what's going on in the metaphysical spectrum" always sounds so pretentious. And had the potential to get me put in a padded room.

Flynn and Dave headed off into the little snack shack, and I turned to Adam. "Watch my back for a minute."

"Story of my life, Quincy," he said, but I knew he'd cover me if there was anything dangerous in the mundane world while I was focused on the Otherworld. I didn't need to wonder long. The instant I opened my Sight, I found plenty of trace all over the mountaintop. There had definitely been a demon close by, and Stone Mountain wasn't going to be considered sanctified ground anytime soon, but there was also nothing useful. I saw where Orobas changed, because his taint on the rock got stronger, and I could see the trail he left going down into the crater. The crater itself literally glowed with dark purple magical residue, both from demon taint, which usually has a reddish tinge to it, and the destructive magic used to dig the crater.

I got closer to the edge of the crater, which really wasn't much more than a big hole about ten feet across and maybe five feet deep in the center. I scrambled down into it, kicking over the occasional rock to make sure I didn't miss any mystical trace that I could follow back to Oro, but the big bastard had covered his tracks pretty well. No blood, no hair, nothing I could really use in hunting him down in a city as sprawling and jammed with different energies as Atlanta.

There was a rectangular depression in the very bottom of the crater, so I got down on my hands and knees to examine it more closely. The stone was shaped here, not naturally formed or blasted away, so whatever had been down here had been here for a long time, and hidden by something powerful enough to make the very stones of the earth bend to its will.

The hole left by whatever it was measured about a foot-and-a-half by two feet and was about eight inches deep. I couldn't tell anything else about it, except there was a hint of pale blue energy glowing faintly in my Sight. Whatever was there, it was long gone, and it had enough power to tint the soul of the mountain.

I dropped my Sight and poked around the dirt a little, looking for actual physical clues, but there was nothing. The only hope I had was that Orobas left a fiber or something behind, but there was very little chance of that leading me to him, no matter how many episodes of *CSI* I watched. I clambered back out of the hole just as Flynn came back.

"No Dave?" I asked.

"He had to go call his boss. Something about a demon attack being a very good reason for shutting down the snack bar for the rest of the day," Flynn replied.

"Makes sense. Anything on the video?" Adam asked.

"Just a big damn demon hauling a box out of the ground. But he made that crater with a spell, Harker."

"Yeah?" I had kinda figured that much.

"Can you do that? I mean, look, I know you wizard types have a lot of juice, but that's a big damn hole."

"I don't know if I have that much power or not, Becks. Oro isn't just a Reaver or a Torment Demon like we fought this afternoon. He's a legitimate big deal in the Armies of Hell, and we've been lucky all the times we've dealt with him before not to have a lot higher body count." I remembered the last casualty of Orobas's plan to remake Charlotte into his own private Hell-condo. Renfield was more than just my uncle's butler; he was a friend, and I watched him die. It wasn't the first time that happened to me, and it wouldn't be the last, but that didn't make it any easier.

"I guess I didn't realize just how powerful he was," Flynn said, her face a little drawn.

"Would it have mattered?" Adam said. I looked up at him, but there was no sarcasm there, just acceptance of our place in the world. We stood between the bad things and the helpless, and sometimes the waves of shitty washed one of us away.

Flynn looked at him, then at me. Then she shrugged her shoulders, let out a sigh, and said, "No, it wouldn't. I picked up a badge to stop bad things from hurting good people, and this is just more of the same, only on a bigger scale."

"Ain't that the truth," I agreed. "Now let's get back into town and find this demonic fuckwit before he annexes all of Georgia into the Fifth Circle of Hell."

"If you think we're not already in Hell, Harker, then you've never driven through rush hour on I-285," Flynn said, walking off down the hill to the truck.

Chapter Five

Luke hadn't just rented a few rooms at the Westin Peachtree downtown. In his typical European royalty fashion, he'd rented the entire top floor. I walked into the room he and his band of merry people had converted into their war room, and I had to say, I was impressed. All the furniture was gone, and heavy blackout fabric masked all the windows. That left enough space in the center of the floor for a conference table with a bunch of decent desk chairs, no doubt carted in from the surrounding rooms.

The rest of the crew was already there, and Sparkles' face was up on the wall-mounted TV. I'll admit, even when you're as old as I am, there's something a little unnerving about walking into a room and seeing a giant unicorn staring at you from the television. I walked over to one end of the table and gave Luke a hug. He stiffened because we aren't usually the hugging type, but it had been a strange couple of weeks.

"How you doing, Luke?" I asked, pulling back. I kept my voice low. The room wasn't big enough to lose any of our words, but at least folks could pretend to let us have a moment.

"I have had better months, Quincy. My house was destroyed, my manservant slain, and now I am forced to reside in a hotel and dine upon supplies garnered from a local blood bank. It is altogether a barely tenable situation, and I sincerely desire to resolve this unpleasantness and return home as soon as possible."

"Yeah, I'm right there with you. Let's get these goofballs in line and save the world." I started to turn, but Luke put a hand on my arm. I turned back to him. "Yeah?"

"Did he suffer, Quincy?" Luke's voice was thick with emotion, and the look on his face would put the lie to all those years of people calling him "monster." This was not the King of the Vampires, the Impaler, the source of so many nightmares and horrific stories across the centuries. This was just a man who'd lost one of the very few people in the world he thought of as a friend, and he wanted some reassurance.

I remembered the scene. I remembered Smith grinning at me as I tried without success to break through his protective circles. I remembered the dazed look in Renfield's eyes as he came out of his drug-induced stupor. I remembered the knife in Smith's hand, then flashing down and burying itself in Ren's chest. I remembered the blood, the gore as Smith cut open my friend's chest in front of me and pulled out his heart, as if to prove to me that Renfield was really dead. I saw all of that in an instant while Luke stared back at me.

"No," I said. "It was quick. He didn't suffer." Neither did Smith, much to my chagrin. I shot him in the head, and he dropped like a stone. I wanted him to suffer, wanted him to feel a shred of the pain he inflicted on me, on Luke, on the families of the other men and women he murdered. But I didn't take him alive, or even torture him. I just dropped him in his tracks. I thought that was the end, but it turned out to be just the beginning.

I turned from Luke to look at the rest of the team. Adam and Becks had taken seats on one side of the table with Watson, Jo, and Gabby on the other. The foot of the table had no chair, presumably so we could all see and hear Sparkles. I took the empty seat next to Flynn, and Luke sat at the head of the table. I wanted to make some joke about carving the turkey, but between a couple of demon fights in one afternoon, plus reliving Renfield's last moments with Luke, my sense of humor was seriously lacking.

"What do we know?" I asked.

"We know the demons in the park were a distraction, that whatever Orobas was after, it was hidden at Stone Mountain," Watson said.

"Yeah, under ten feet of rock," Flynn added. "Solid rock, too. Orobas used a spell to blast the rock away and get to what he was after. That smacks of serious magic to me."

"You're not wrong," I said. "And not only was there some serious magic being thrown around up there, whatever was hidden there was pretty serious all on its own."

"What makes you say that?" Jo asked. I looked over at her, but there was no challenge in her eyes, only curiosity. I still wasn't sure where I stood with all these people, but she didn't look like she wanted to get into a pissing match. Which was good. I didn't know what exactly was going on in Atlanta, but it sure felt like we were going to be on a tight schedule.

"The magical blast had the force of several sticks of dynamite. For whatever was in the hole to survive that, it wasn't just a run of the mill magic wand," I replied.

"Is that even a thing, or are you just using magic wand as like an example," Gabby asked from her seat to my left. She leaned back, feet on the table and a beer in her hand.

I decided to make an example of my own. I stood up, using some of my enhanced speed to go faster than normal, and grabbed one of Gabby's feet. I pulled up, dumping her on her ass against the wall. "Pay attention, Gabby," I growled at her. "This isn't fucking playtime. Orobas is the real fucking deal, and we don't have any idea what he's up to yet. If we fuck this up, all of Atlanta could go up in smoke, so sit up straight, shut your mouth, and focus." I never raised my voice, but I didn't have to. Everybody could see where my head was.

"I don't think that's quite correct, Harker," Sparkles' voice came from the screen.

I sat down and turned to face him. "You know it's pretty hard to take you seriously when you're wearing that face."

The unicorn face frowned, which is even stranger than you would expect it to be, and the image on the screen shifted to a round-faced young man with short curly hair and freckles. "Is this better, asshole?" he asked.

"Much," I replied. "You want to introduce yourself to the nice people, or should I?"

"I got this," Sparkles said. "My real name is Dennis Bolton."

I heard Flynn gasp from beside me. Good to know she'd been listening when I told her about the first set of Orobas's sacrifices I encountered.

Dennis turned to look at her. "You've heard of me? Probably from your asshat boyfriend there. Well, it's all true. He got me killed. Well, mostly killed, but there was enough of me left to magically transfer my soul into the internet."

Flynn sat there, gaping. Jo leaned forward and said what I figure everyone else was thinking. "What the fuck?"

Dennis laughed. "Yeah, exactly. What. The. Fuck? So there I was, deader than shit on stage at the theatre, when Harker casts a binding spell to trap my soul."

"He stuck you back in your body?" Gabby asked.

Dennis laughed again. "Yah, not exactly. Orobas has a bad tendency to leave big holes in bodies when he's finished with them, so there wasn't enough of my body to hold the soul in. So Harker put me in the next best place. At least that's what he thought at the time."

"Where was that?" Flynn asked. I didn't answer. To be honest, it was a little embarrassing. I couldn't think of anything better at the time, but looking back on it, it wasn't my most shining magical moment.

"Come on, Quincy, spill it. Where did you put your fine horned friend?" Watson asked, and I could almost hear the ration of shit he was preparing to give me.

"I put him in my cell phone," I said.

"What?" "How the...?" "Where?" I let the explosion of questions go on for a few seconds until I raised my hand for quiet.

"I had a new phone with a big hard drive. I cast a binding spell to tie Dennis' soul to the phone, hoping it had enough memory to hold all of him."

"But he missed one small detail," Dennis added.

"I forgot that the phone was tied to the internet. So as soon as I put Dennis into the phone..."

"I left," the face on the screen said. "I got pulled into the phone, then dove right back out along the nation's most powerful wireless network, and suddenly I could hear *everything* now."

"I think that's two different commercials," Jo said.

"I'm allowed," Dennis replied.

"Fair enough," Jo said with a nod. "So then what?"

"Well," Dennis said. "I kinda surfed on the web for a little while, figuring out how to reconstitute myself, at least my consciousness, figured out how to interact with Harker via text message, then later on Skype, then FaceTime and other video chat apps. But I stay away from Chatroulette. That's some fucked up shit right there."

"So now you're alive on the internet?" Gabby asked.

"Let's not get out of hand with the whole 'alive' thing," Dennis said. "But I'm conscious at least."

"And very useful," I said.

"Don't patronize, Harker. I know I'm a badass cyber-ninja. You don't have to tell me." Dennis glared at me from the wall.

I held up both hands in surrender. "Okay, Bruce Lee, what do you have for us?"

"I think I know what Orobas is up to. At least what his eventual plan is. And I *think* I have an idea how he plans to do it, but it doesn't make a whole lot of sense."

"He's a demon, dude," Gabby said, leaning back in her chair again. She started to move her feet toward the table, but Jo reached out and smacked her knee. She gave me a guilty glance and sat up straight. "They don't make sense."

"That's where you are incorrect, Gabriella," Luke said. "There are certain aspects of a demon's personality that will always bleed through, no matter what type of disguise or subterfuge they attempt."

"So what is he up to?" I asked, looking at the screen.

"He wants to open a doorway to Hell," Sparkles said.

"We stopped that plan, bud," I replied.

"No, you stopped one version of that plan," my disembodied friend countered.

"What do you mean?" Flynn asked. "Harker killed Smith and disrupted the spell. They missed the date for the ritual. We should be good until the spring, at least."

"If I'm right, Orobas isn't planning a ritual. He's just planning to rip the fabric of the universe apart with brute force," Sparkles said.

You could have heard a pin drop on the carpet as everyone sat there trying to digest that little bombshell. After almost a full minute of silence, Watson looked at me, face pale and a little bead of sweat on his forehead and asked, "Can he do that?"

I thought about it for a second. Frankly, I'd been thinking about it ever since Dennis made his proclamation, but I didn't like the conclusion I kept coming to. "Yeah," I said. "Yeah, I think he probably can. It would take the release of an incredible amount of magical energy, and it would have to be concentrated in one spot, but I think it could be done."

"How?" Jo asked. "I mean, I know I'm the least magically inclined of anyone here, probably, but that just doesn't make any sense to me." There were nods and murmurs of agreement from around the table as everyone tried to wrap their heads around the concept.

"Okay." I stood up and held up my hands for quiet. "I'll try to explain it as best I can. Think of Earth, Heaven, and Hell not so much as up, down, and center, but more like just adjacent dimensions. There are a few more, as I understand it, but I don't have the ability or interest in trans-dimensional travel, so I haven't spent a lot of time studying it."

I started to pace, trying to put my thoughts into coherent sentences. Luke caught my eye and gave me a nod, so I just took a deep breath and pushed on. "The dimensions all touch each other, pretty much at all points, like a weird

Venn diagram. When someone summons a demon or an angel, or an angel travels to Earth, they basically use their magic to open a tiny hole between the dimensions, called a Gate. These Gates take a shitload of energy to open, and even more energy to hold open."

"That's why you always use a ritual for summoning, because you have to focus your energy more than with most of the magical shit you do?" Gabby asked. She was leaning forward on her elbows now, her pose of calculated indifference completely forgotten.

"Yeah, exactly. I also try to tap into a ley line if I can, kind of a network of magical energy that crisscrosses the world. Whenever I can draw from a line, it's less of my own energy I have to use. So, I can create manageable Gates for a limited time with just my own energy. If I have a group of people working together, lending me their energy, then I can open a bigger Gate, and for a longer time."

"That's what Smith was doing back in Charlotte," Flynn said, making the jump.

"Again, there's a reason you're the detective, Becks," I agreed. "Smith was doing exactly that. The only difference was that the people lending their energy to his ritual weren't willing participants, and he was using every drop of their life force so he didn't have to use any of his own."

"The bastard," Luke muttered. I didn't acknowledge him with words, just gave him a short nod.

"So, what is he saying about making a rip in the dimensional fabric?" Watson asked.

"A Gate is a managed portal between two places, and it takes a lot of power to keep it open for longer than a few seconds. The dimensions are always shifting, and the natural order of things is to keep them tangential but separate. So, a permanent Gate between Heaven and Earth, for example, would take such a constant stream of power as to be almost impossible to maintain," I said.

"So what's the problem?" Gabby asked. "If you can't keep it open, then we just kill anything that comes through, and when it closes, no problem, right?"

"I wish," Sparkles said. "That's true about a managed Gate between two places. But that's not what I think Orobas is trying to do."

"Oh fuck me sideways," I said as the full enormity of what he was saying hit me.

"Yup, you got it." Sparkles gave me a wry grin. "That's exactly what I'm thinking."

"Would you care to let us mere mortals in on the secret?" Watson asked, then glanced at Luke and Adam. "Mortals and et cetera, of course."

"He's not trying to just open a doorway between Earth and Hell anymore," I said. "He wants to blow open a hole in the fabric of every dimension that touches ours. A rip in the fabric of reality that wouldn't be a link between two specific places, but a hole that would stay open forever between Earth and every other realm of existence."

"But wouldn't that mean..." Flynn's voice trailed off as she tried to process it.

"Yeah," I said. "Not only could Orobas and all his demonic buddies take over the Earth, they could storm Heaven, too."

Chapter Six

"**T**WO QUESTIONS," FLYNN SAID, STANDING UP AND WAVING EVERYBODY silent. She was looking at Sparkles' image on the screen, but also around the table at me, Luke, and the rest of the team. "First, how does one go about tearing a hole between dimensions? And second, how do we stop him?"

"I think the idea is to destroy a bunch of magical artifacts at one time, releasing all their stored energy into one focused blast," Dennis said.

"That fits with what we've heard about the Barton character that rescued Orobas from Charlotte," Watson said. "He has a reputation as an avid collector of occult objects and magical instruments."

"That also explains why they were digging around Luke's place," Jo added. "There's something magical about the sword, we just don't know what it is. They wanted to add it to their mystical bonfire."

"More like mystical pipe bomb," Gabby said. "I like a good explosion as much as the next girl—"

"More," Flynn piped in. "For the record, Gabs, most 'next girls' don't actually like blowing things up."

"Their loss," Gabby said, then went on. "But even setting aside my love for things that go boom, blasting open a hole between Heaven and Hell sounds like a terrible idea. Most of the stuff in Hell is there because it doesn't deserve Heaven, right?"

"Or because they were there once and tried to take it over," Adam's rumbling voice chimed in.

"Even worse, there wouldn't be a direct link from Hell to Heaven," I said. "They'd have to pass through our dimension to get upstairs."

"And I'm guessing that most demons aren't the type to just casually pass through, leaving things unmolested," Watson said.

"Yeah, not so much," I agreed.

"So back to Question Number Two—how do we stop it?" Flynn spoke over the rest of us, and we settled down.

All eyes turned to the screen, and Dennis shifted his image back to the unicorn. "Sorry, kids, I have no fucking idea."

"Neither do I," Luke admitted with a rueful shake of his head. "Despite magic being the force that keeps me alive and sentient, I have very little experience with its actual performance."

"Well, I suppose that's my department," I said. "But I have no clue, either. I've never even heard of a ritual with this kind of power, much less any kind of counterspell or way to undo it."

"So what do we do? Just run like hell and hope that the demons leave something left of the world to live in?" Jo said. "Fuck that. There's got to be a way. There's *always* a way, if we just fight hard enough."

"Your namesake would be proud," Luke said, and I saw just the slightest blush on Jo's dark skin.

"She's right," I said. "There's got to be a way to stop, or worst case, reverse what Orobas is trying to do. I'll get to work researching the most powerful spells and artifacts I can find to see about coming up with a reversal or blocking spell."

"I'll help," Watson said. "I'm good with research. Got to put that posh Cambridge education to use, right?"

"Nightfall is still a few hours away, so I will assist the two of you until such a time as any of my contacts in the city will be available, then Adam and I will go have a few quiet meetings."

"I know a few people in town, too. I'll take Flynn with me to poke around the more interesting parts of Atlanta. Maybe we can dig up some dirt on our Mr. Barton," Gabby added.

"That leaves you and me digging through the interwebs again, buddy," Jo said to Sparkles.

"It's what I live for," he said with a whinny.

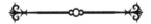

Six hours later, I drove back to the hotel with a disappointed Watson in the passenger's seat of my rental car, a stack of spellbooks in the trunk, a huge box of takeout from Fox Brothers' Barbecue in the backseat making me hungry, and bad attitude.

I carried the books up the elevator, and Watson handled the food. We walked into the "war room" to see Jo buried in her laptop and Becks sitting with her head down on the table, fast asleep. Jo made a shushing motion to me as the door opened, but Flynn sat up and rubbed her eyes, looking at me sleepily.

"Anything?" she asked, her voice thick with sleep.

"No," I said. "Looks like you had about the same luck."

"Yeah, Gabby punched a lot of people, but nobody could give us shit on Barton. It's like the dude is a ghost."

"A ghost with a hell of a bankroll," Sparkles said from the TV. He was wearing his Dennis face this time, and I reflected for just an instant on the cost of associating with me. Sure, maybe he would have ended up trapped in the internet like a modern-day Tron without my influence, but it's pretty damned unlikely. Anna, Flynn's dad, Dennis, now Renfield—I was starting to have the death of a lot of good people on my conscience. I looked around the room as I set my spellbooks down on the counter and wondered if any of these folks were going to get added to the list before we were done here.

"Penny for 'em," Flynn said.

"Huh?"

"You were a million miles away. What's up?"

I looked around the room. Sparkles and Watson were exchanging status reports, but Jo was looking right at us. *Not a lot getting past that one.* "Nothing," I lied. I could see in Flynn's face that she knew I was lying, and it didn't sit well with her. Hard to lie to someone who can see inside your head. But right at that moment, I didn't care. I couldn't stand in the middle of our war room, such as it was, and express my doubts that we'd be able to do this job, or get everybody out alive if we could. That wouldn't help anyone. I kept a tight rein on my emotions and my thoughts, sending a quick promise across our mental link to explain later, when we were alone.

"Nah, it's cool," I continued the lie. "I was just thinking about this one spell I heard a rumor about. It diverts energy from one place to another. Maybe we could use it to spread out the magical energy released from Orobas's plan to a bunch of places, so it couldn't open a permanent rift."

"But wouldn't that open a lot of small, temporary, rifts? That might be just as bad," Jo said. "Opening a dozen gateways to Hell all over the world, even for a little while until they closed on their own, seems like a recipe for a demonic invasion."

"And without having a team on the ground everywhere we diverted the energy to, who knows what kind of shitshow we'd be in for," I agreed. "Yeah, that's *no bueno*."

"Well, let's eat, then we can get back to it after dinner," Watson said, setting containers of food out on the table.

"Did somebody say food?" Gabby asked as she came in. She was in a tattered t-shirt, jeans, and no shoes, with a towel wrapped around her head.

I looked at her with one eyebrow raised.

"Had to shower," she said. "My clothes got a little blood on them."

"Some of the people we talked with weren't very cooperative," Flynn agreed.

"Funny, you're not covered in blood," I said. "Or did you already wash off the evidence?"

"No, I managed to stay out of the splash zone," she replied. "But trust me, interrogations with Little Miss Sunshine here are messier than a Blue Man Group show."

"Adam and Luke already head out?" I asked.

"Yeah, they're off looking for seedy underworld connections to cajole, bribe, or intimidate," Jo said.

"I wanted to go, but they said I would intimidate their contacts," Gabby whined. "Imagine that—Frankenstein's monster meets Dracula, and *I'm* the scary one?"

"I think that says something about your negotiation methods, Gabriella," Watson said, looking at the containers of food with a skeptical eye. "Is there anything in this assortment of, dare I call it, food that isn't fried?"

"The barbecue isn't fried, but the pickles are," I said, pulling a paper plate out of the box and piling it high with pulled pork, macaroni and cheese, and fried pickles. "I thought about getting Frito pie, but that would have taken way too long to explain to Captain Cambridge here." It was a statement of geographical prejudice that only Flynn smiled at my culinary humor.

"What's next?" Flynn asked as we all sat down to eat. Sparkles had vanished from the TV screen, not enjoying watching people eat.

"Oh yeah, that reminds me." I pulled a map of Atlanta out of my back pocket and tossed it into the middle of the table. "After we eat, I'm going to need everybody but Becks to clear out of here for an hour or so. I have a ritual that may let us locate the other major magical artifacts in the area, but I need quiet to perform it."

"So you're going to perform a 'ritual' with your girlfriend for about an hour that requires the conference table?" Gabby asked with a smirk. "You know, one of the bedrooms on the floor might be more comfortable for that."

"Blow me, Gabs. It's a geolocation spell, so I have to spread the map out. I'll use Rebecca as an anchor while I send my astral form out into the city, using the map as a guide. That should let me locate any hot spots of mystical energy a lot faster than driving all over town. Flynn will be my tether back to my body in case I get lost or run into anything with bad intentions. Any happy fun time will have to wait until Orobas is dealt with."

"Not that it's any of your business," Flynn added. Gabby put up her hands in mock surrender, but the little upturn at the corner of her mouth never vanished.

We plowed through healthy servings of barbecue and fried pseudo-vegetables in silence for a few minutes, then cleared the table. Jo, Gabby, and Watson retired to a nearby room with a stack of arcane books to scour for world-rending spells while I dug four big white pillar candles and a box of Morton's salt out of another bag Watson brought up with the food.

I spread the map out onto the table and held the corners down with the candles. I poured a circle of salt around the table, making sure there were no breaks in it, then had Flynn step over the line and sit at the foot of the table.

"You're going to be my anchor. All you have to do is keep our link open, and every once in a while, just throw a thought my way."

"Kinda like psychic radar? I just ping you every so often to make sure you can find your way back to me?"

"Exactly like that," I agreed. I sat in the chair at the head of the table and looked behind me to make sure the line of salt was still intact.

"What's the circle for?" Becks asked.

"It's just a little precaution," I replied. "I don't think anything is looking for me, and what I'm doing is unlikely to set off any defenses that local magicians have put on their stash of toys, but just in case, I want a little extra security around my physical form while I'm off dancing in the astral plane."

"Makes sense. But what if I need to bring the circle down for some reason?"

"Obviously, I hope you won't, but if something gets in here with us, and you need to bolt, just scrub the line of salt with your foot. Because we'll be linked when I invoke the circle, your essence will be tied to it as well as mine, and you can take it down just like I can. Sound good?"

"As good as anything."

"Okay, then. Let's go on a magical scavenger hunt."

Chapter Seven

I PUT MY HANDS ON THE TABLE, TOUCHING THE MAP, AND SENT A TENDRIL of my consciousness out to Flynn, strengthening the link that was always there, bolstering it with a mental image of steel cables wrapped around each other into a thick, sturdy rope of metal wire, tying us together.

Whoa, I "heard" in my head. *That's way tighter than we're usually linked.*

Yeah, I sent back. *Because I'm leaving my physical body, I needed to beef up the psychic tether so I'll have something to follow if I get lost or need to jump back in a hurry. You good? I'm about to start the spell.*

I'm good.

I closed my eyes and poured a little bit of my essence into the circle, invoking it. The rest of the hotel room fell away as a shimmering barrier of magical energy snapped into place around me, the conference table, and Becks. My circles are a little different from the old-school ones that people used in the days before electricity, indoor plumbing, and hotels. My "circle" was shaped more like a dome, a semi-circle of magical energy with a flat bottom under our feet. It took me about ten years to figure out how to shape the energy to flow in a dome over my head with a flat disk under me, but it became a necessary evil once the floor beneath me was pretty much guaranteed to have conduit and wires running through it. That kind of breach makes a typical circle, which is more like a sphere, very vulnerable, and is why a lot of practitioners only work outside nowadays. If you can get far enough into the woods, you know that the bottom part of your circle is only going through dirt and roots, and it's still intact beneath your feet.

That doesn't work for me. The demons I hunt are most often in buildings. Or in people who are in buildings. And after the first time an imp rode a water pipe through my circle and knocked the shit out of me, I learned that the old ways weren't very good anymore. But now my circle was secure from attacks from below and above, so I could start my ritual.

There wasn't a spell for what I was trying to do, so I was making it up as I went along. The story of my life. I focused my consciousness inward, concentrating on the core of *me*, those things that defined my very Quincy Harker-ness. Not my height, weight, hair color, or clothes. More my sense of being, my smart-ass personality, my slightly off-kilter moral compass, my friendships, my desires, my love for Rebecca, my regrets about Dennis and Anna… all the things that over a century of life built up to make me into the man I am. I took that essence of myself and separated it from my physical form, stepped outside myself, and with a slight tearing sensation, I was free.

I looked to my right, and there I sat. My hair needed a trim, I could use a shave, and I was a little too skinny. My jacket needed desperately to go to the cleaners, and my Doc Martens had seen better days. But my jeans were mostly clean, and my black button-down shirt still held a vestige of a crease here and there where it once saw the bottom of an iron. The bags under my eyes told the real story, though.

This was a man who needed about a week's worth of sleep, a month's worth of good meals, and if the beginnings of a spider web of broken blood vessels on my nose was any indication, a serious decrease in the alcohol intake.

I look like hell, I thought.

You've seen better days, Flynn agreed.

Why didn't anybody tell me?

I thought we'd save the world first, and if we didn't all die in the process, I'd bring up the idea of a vacation.

Makes sense.

Now go find us some magical trinkets so we can finish up the world-saving and move on the sunny beaches and umbrella drinks.

Yes, ma'am.

I turned to the map, spread out over the conference table. It was a lifeless thing, but I knew how to change that. This was sympathetic magic, where I wanted to use the map as a representation of the real city to show me the location of items. I focused myself on the map and poured energy into it, strengthening its representational link to Atlanta. As I did, I concentrated on the mystical ebb and flow of the area, the pulse of magic that breathes in the heart of everywhere people live.

The map started to glow in my Sight, a spider web of ley lines crisscrossing the surface as the natural pathways of magical energy materialized. Wherever they crossed, the light flared a little brighter, and where enough lines converged, a node appeared, a hub of magical focus where the power was closer to the surface, easier to access for practitioners and the mundane alike. Nodes began to flare into my view all over Atlanta: one in Centennial Park, one at the Fox Theatre, one right down the street at the Marriott Marquis hotel of all places. A smaller one at the Margaret Mitchell house, one at The Vortex, no surprise there. There were even a couple of churches built on nodes, a fact that would amuse the local witches and likely horrify some of the pastors.

I focused past the nodes to the less natural hot spots. Some places popped into view that were instantly recognizable to me. The Masquerade nightclub was a long-standing meeting place for supernatural types, so I disregarded that one. Anything near Little Five Points was going to be too popular with local weirdos and wannabes to house any artifacts of real use, but three places twinkled in my view. Sitting far from any ley lines, nodes, or known locations of magical practitioners, there was a house in Buckhead that shone like a beacon to my astral self. There was also a hot spot in Grant Park near Zoo Atlanta, and one more right on top of the CDC.

Great, do I want to go into the house of likely a powerful magician, go argue with a wild animal, or play with the plague? I'll start with the magician. Looks like I'm off to see a wizard.

I concentrated on the image of the house in Buckhead, focused my mental imagery on the map, the surrounding streets, fixed an image in my head of tree-lined avenues and ridiculously large homes, and stepped into the map.

I closed my eyes tight as I dove forward, half-expecting to run face-first into the walls of my own circle and get slammed back into my body and knocked silly with magical backlash, but the spell worked exactly how I wanted it to, and when I opened my eyes I was "standing" on a sidewalk in front of a two-story house on a tree-lined street in north Atlanta.

Well, that went better than expected. I reached out along my mental link to Flynn and felt her respond with a little tug. Good, my anchor line was holding. *So far, looks like everything's coming up Harker.*

I walked to the front door and stepped right through it into a grand foyer. The floors were marble, and a huge staircase curved up in front of me, banister gleaming in the light from a crystal chandelier above me. I was a little confused at the ease of my entry. This house was warded to high heaven, but only against physical threats. There was nothing in place to keep out spirits or astral projections, which seemed off to me. Why ward against one type of threat, but not the other?

"Probably because I am not afraid of ghosts or spirits," came a voice from my right. I turned to see a man standing there with a pair of long curved daggers in his hands. He was a big man, easily six-three and about two-fifty, and nothing about him looked soft. He wore his brown hair short, and he was dressed for bed, in a pair of pajama pants with no shirt and bare feet. He held the knives like he knew how to use them, and they glowed like a pair of miniature suns in my Sight. I knew right away that those blades could cut me to ribbons, even in my incorporeal state.

I knew that was too easy.

"Yes, you should have," the man replied.

I cocked my head sideways. *You can hear me?*

"Of course I can hear you. You are in my home, my domain. I am the master here, and I can do whatever I choose. I can hear the spirits, I can see ghosts, and I can send you back to the afterlife!"

I'm not a ghost! I'm an astral projection. I realized a little belatedly that admitting I was essentially a psychic cat burglar might not be any more endearing than being a ghost. My host apparently decided the same thing, since he charged me with those glowing knives aimed straight at my chest.

Chapter Eight

I FELT FOR THE TETHER TO FLYNN, LOOKING TO USE IT AS A QUICK ESCAPE, but it was gone. I had no connection to the outside world, nothing tying me to my body, and no good way to get out of this house before its owner skewered me with his glowing spirit blades.

I dodged left to avoid his first charge, my mind racing as I tried to come up with a plan. I couldn't fight him because I didn't have any mass or form. But he could hurt me with his magical blades. At least they certainly looked like they would hurt, and he was waving them around like they would hurt, so I figured it best not to take the chance.

He swiped at me with one hand, but I kept dancing back. I'd never fought anyone while incorporeal before, so I was at a disadvantage. Worse for me, my opponent moved like it wasn't his first ghost battle. I danced around the foyer until I got to the front door, then dove forward to get outside and start making my way back downtown to the hotel the best I could.

Except I couldn't get through the door. I smacked into the wood just like I was solid, crossing my eyes and sending stars shooting through my vision. *What the fuck?*

"By the way, revenant, my domicile is built as a spirit trap. Think of it as a roach motel for the supernatural—ghosts check in, but they don't check out." He laughed, an ugly thing that bubbled up from some dark place, and I started to wonder about his intentions in turning his home into a beacon of mystical energy, then setting a trap for anyone who decided to take a peek. This was not a dude who just stumbled onto an artifact. This guy knew what he was holding and how to use it.

And he wanted to use them on me, as evidenced by him charging me again. I was hamstrung without my connection to Becks, trapped in this house with a pissed off ghost hunter, but I was the furthest thing from helpless. As I leapt over his charge, I started to remember all the things I knew about astral projection and defending myself while spirit walking.

I couldn't kick his ass, but I could still touch magic. Hell, I pretty much was magic at that point. I sprinted up the stairs, and when he followed, I vaulted the railing down to the first floor to create some separation. He spun around and sprinted down the stairs after me, but I had the seconds I needed.

I drew in my will and muttered "*momentum torporos.*" I released the spell, and a ball of flickering blue-white energy shot toward the man. He intercepted the spell with one of his knives, slicing it out of midair.

I followed up with a bolt of pure energy, this one much more solid and red in color. He blocked the onslaught with his other blade, seeming to absorb it into himself.

"Is that all you've got, spirit!" He laughed, a big grin splitting his grim face. "That won't be enough to keep me from draining what remains of your life force!" He charged me again, twirling his blades around his hands like the star of a badly dubbed kung fu movie. I spun to the right and conjured a gleaming blade of pure power, a soul blade capable of carving this bastard to ribbons, even in my spirit form. I slashed at his hamstring, but there was no hamstring there. He stopped on a dime, gathered his legs under himself, and leapt backward over my head, landing about two feet in front of me.

He grinned at me as I stared at him, mouth hanging open, and thrust both daggers for my exposed midsection. "Die, you dead bastard!"

I didn't bother to point out to him just how odd that sounded. I was too busy knocking his blades aside and shoving one hand into his chest up to the wrist. I might be incorporeal, but that didn't mean I couldn't affect things in the material world. When my spirit hand closed around his heart, his eyes went wide with pain and shock.

My astral form was made of energy, so I couldn't really squeeze his heart until blood poured out of his eyeballs like I wanted to. But since I was currently made of energy, I *could* disrupt the normal rhythm of his heartbeat, leaving him feeling like someone was playing bongos inside his chest. It didn't look very pleasant, judging by how pale he went, and by how quickly he dropped both knives and clutched his chest.

I withdrew my hand and took a step back. "Can we talk like civilized people now, or am I going to have to do something rude to your bladder? You'd be amazed what organs are susceptible to low-grade electrical impulses."

He rubbed his chest and stepped farther back from me. He made no move to pick up his magical blades, so I didn't see a need to pursue him. "You speak?"

"Yeah, I speak. My girlfriend tells me I speak was too much, and my shrink says I don't ever really say anything, so the jury's still out on that bit. But I speak. For now, though, I'll let you have the floor. Who the fuck are you, pal, and how did you learn to use those pig-stickers?"

"You don't know who I am?" He looked confused, but at least he stopped darting glances at the knives on the floor like he was going to dive for them and start after me again any second.

"I have no fucking clue who you are, dude. All I know is there's some kind of serious magical mojo in this house, I'm guessing those knives, and that this place is built like a motherfucker of a ghost trap."

"So you're not here to punish me for neglecting my duty?"

"I'm not into that, man. I'm sure there are plenty of ladies in the ATL who'll cater to whatever fetish you're into. Or dudes. Whatever, it's none of my business. But no, that's not why I'm here. I'm here for the knives. Well, really to keep somebody else from getting the knives."

"Who would want my Spirit Blades?"

"Do you really call them that? A little pompous, don't you think?"

"What else would you call them? They're blades that can send ghosts to their final rest. They've been called The Spirit Blades of Callanwolde as long as I can remember. They are passed down to the firstborn of every generation for safekeeping, so when I came of age, my father bestowed them upon me and dubbed me the newest Knight of Callanwolde. It is our duty to defend the city against mystical threats and cleanse haunted locales of restless spirits."

"You talk like a guidebook entry," I said. "Who told you that bullshit?"

He looked offended. I guess I couldn't blame him, but I only have so much patience for people who try to stab me. It's a miracle I'm as chill around Gabby as I am, given the circumstances of our first meeting.

"That was the charge laid upon me when I came of age, to take up the mantle of the Callanwolde defenders and keep the civilians safe from vengeful spirits and evil specters. I have not fulfilled my obligations of late and am willing to accept whatever judgement the keepers of the spirit realm wish to lay upon me." Wow, this guy *really* took himself seriously.

"Look, I'm going to give you the benefit of the doubt because it sounds like somebody has fed you a line of crap, and it was probably somebody you trusted, like a parent or something. So, it's not really your fault you're an idiot, it was obviously drilled into you from a very early age. But let me make something clear—you are not Ghost Avenger Batman, I am not an evil spirit, and there is somebody very big and very bad coming for those knives, and if he gets them, you will be fucked beyond belief. And not in a good way."

He didn't look convinced, but I didn't have a chance to use my "pretty please" voice because just then the front door exploded inward, and a pair of demons stepped into the foyer.

"Fucking great," I muttered. "Party crashers." I turned to the superhero wannabe. "Run!"

He did. Except instead of running away like any sane person would when a pair of seven-foot dudes with crimson skin, goat legs, horns, yellow eyes, and fangs crash through their front door, Captain Stupid ran forward, scooped up his knives, and charged the demons.

It went almost as badly as I expected it to go. I got the hell out of his way, pushing off from the floor and sailing halfway up the staircase before turning to watch the carnage. The demons either couldn't see me or rightly didn't consider me a threat because they focused their attention on Sir Callanwolde, or whatever his name was.

He was fast, I had to give him that. That was about all he had going for him against a couple of heavily-muscled monsters that made Hulk Hogan look like Bill Gates. His initial charge took the demons off guard, and he actually scored a hit on the left-hand demon, carving a deep groove in its chest with his knife. The monster howled and lashed out with a wild looping punch that Callanwolde ducked effortlessly, then darted in to stab the demon under the armpit. It screeched in pain and dropped to one knee, rolling away from the crazy human with the glowing knives.

I had a moment of hope for the guy when it looked like he was holding his own and getting some good licks in. Then the second demon stepped in, and it all went to shit. While Callanwolde was focused on the first beastie, its partner clubbed him across the back of the neck with both fists. I heard the *crack* of bone all the way across the room, and the formerly courageous defender of Atlanta fell in a heap to the marble floor of his foyer.

I fired off a blast of pure power at the demon as it raised a foot to crush the downed man's skull. I caught it right on the side of the head, with all the effect of a fruit fly on a semi-truck. I think it might have noticed, but my energy was depleted from the fight, and some more powerful demons have certain types of magical resistance. Looks like I found one of the ones resistant to psychic blasts. Just my luck.

The demon's foot came down on the dark-haired man's skull, and the sound was like a melon dropped from a great height, a wet cracking sound followed by the *splat* of his brains squirting across the gleaming floor.

The second demon reached down and hauled the first one to its feet, then picked up the knives and tucked them into its belt. It looked up at me and smiled. "Normally I'd kill you for that cheap shot, Harker, but Orobas has something special planned for you. It's okay, though. He promised me I get to flay you for a century or two after you die, so we've both got that to look forward to."

The other demon grinned up at me, then said, "But don't worry. You won't have to wait long. Orobas is going to turn this shitheap dimension into a brand new Hell soon enough, then we can play with what's left of your tattered, pitiful soul. Bye for now." They turned and walked through the shattered door out into the night, unfurling their wings and leaping to the sky as soon as they were clear of the building.

I hurried after them, but they were out of sight before I cleared the front steps. *Becks, are you there?* I felt our connection as strong as ever, restored when the homeowner/magician died and his jamming spell was abruptly snuffed out.

Yeah, where the hell have you been?

Long story. Have somebody head over to this address with a body bag and a spatula. I'm coming back to you. I lost this one, but we've still got to try and keep the other artifacts out of Orobas's hands.

Chapter Nine

I BLINKED QUICKLY, ADJUSTING MY VISION TO THE PHYSICAL SPECTRUM and physical eyes. Flynn sat at the side of the table, her sidearm out and her chair positioned where she could see me and the door without moving.

"You're taking this whole bodyguard thing pretty literally, Detective," I said.

"You have a way of making people want to kill you, Harker," Becks replied with a sideways grin. "Even people who like you. So, I thought it might be a good idea to stay armed while I was watching over you."

"And here I expected to wake up with pictures of dicks drawn all over my face."

She grinned at me. "Who says you didn't?"

I laughed as I got up from my seat to go piss, then grabbed at the table for support as my rubbery legs almost gave out. Flynn stood up like a shot and got my arm over her shoulders, providing a stable base.

"Shit, sorry about that," I said. "I forget how draining astral travel can be."

"Not to mention astral demon-fighting," Flynn replied. I'd filled her in on the scrap at the magician's house on my way back.

"Yeah, that's not the best, either," I agreed. "I'm good now, just needed a second." I straightened up, but kept my arm around her, more for internal stability than physical this time.

"Look, Rebecca…" I started, but she put a finger to my lips.

"I know," she said, cutting me off. She looked up into my eyes, her brown pools deep with emotion. "We've got a lot of shit to sort out *when this is over.* But the key part of that is when this is over. We can't figure out what we're doing until we know there's going to be a world to do it in. So, let's put all kinds of talk about the future on the shelf until we kick Orobas's ass back to Hell and make sure we *have* a future. Then you can tell me how much you adore me, and we can talk about this ring." She pulled on a chain around her neck, and the diamond engagement ring I bought for her came into my view.

I looked at her, feeling a familiar jumble of emotions through our psychic link. She loved me, just like I loved her, and when we were this close, there was no chance of hiding that. But she was also scared. Scared of what it might mean to be with me, scared of the world I lived in, scared of losing me, and of losing herself in me.

I knew those feelings all too well because they rattled around in my head all the time. I felt all those things and more. I felt the fear of the inevitable pain of losing her, the pain of a man who's lived more than a century looking like he's thirty and knows that he has to watch his loved ones grow old and die while he just stays stuck in the same place forever.

We stood there, and the moment stretched out as we looked in each other's eyes, a lot of unspoken communication passing back and forth through our link without words. Just feelings flowing back and forth as I enjoyed the feeling of her in my arms.

But biology eventually won out. "I gotta piss," I said, breaking contact and heading the hotel room's surprisingly large bathroom. I looked in the mirror after washing my hands and decided she was right—I looked like refried shit.

"You're right, babe, I look like ten miles of bad road," I said, walking out into the war room. "As soon as we kill this motherfucker, we're going somewhere with white sand and umbrella drinks."

I cut off as I saw we weren't as alone as I thought. Watson, Gabby, and Jo sat around the table with Flynn. The map was rolled up at one end of the table, and Watson sat behind an open book with a grim look on his face.

"I'm guessing you don't look like you just ate a lemon raw just because I piss too loud," I said.

"No, and I wish I were only concerned with your bathroom habits," the slightly prissy British man said. It was a little hard to reconcile this slender man with a perfectly groomed beard and a limp with my memories of his portly ancestor. John Watson was a man with a ready smile and a peppermint in his pocket for the neighborhood children, his "Baker Street Irregulars" that served as his lookouts, his intelligence network, and his errand boys. I remembered him as an older man, but there was always steel beneath his love for fine Scotch and good meals. This new Watson hadn't shown me anything like that, but he acquitted himself well against the Reavers, and Becks trusted him, so he must not be a complete douche.

"Well, spill it, Doc," I said, pulling out a chair and leaning back with my arms across my chest. "What did you find out that's worse than knowing that Orobas plans to use a metric fuckton of magical artifacts to tear open a gaping doorway between Earth and Hell?"

"We found out what it takes to cast the spell in the first place," Watson said. His voice was somber without a hint of the pompous attitude he'd displayed ever since I first met him. I took a closer look at the man, taking in the dark look in his eyes, the pallor of his skin. He was shit-scared.

I took a deep breath. "What does it take, other than a metric fuckton of powerful magical artifacts?"

"Life," Watson said.

I let out the breath I was holding in almost a laugh. "Well, yeah! We knew that. I mean, shit, Watson, it took the combined life force of half a dozen people just to try and open the Gate Orobas wanted to open in Charlotte. I figured somebody would have to die to make this hole in the universe."

"Not somebody, Harker. A lot of somebodies," Jo said.

I looked at her. She looked just as rattled as Watson. "Am I missing something?" I asked. "How many people are we talking about?"

"The book doesn't say," Watson said, sliding a huge leather-bound tome across the table to me. "But it seems to indicate that the loss of life would be somewhere near double the population of Paris at the time the book was written."

I took a second to look at him, thinking about the French city I knew. "When was the book written?" I asked.

"The original text dates to the thirteenth century, give or take a few decades," he replied.

I shook my head. "I'm sorry, I'm not that old. Part of me really hates to ask, but how many people are we talking about?"

Watson just looked at me. It was Jo who answered. "It looks like the spell requires the energy of about a hundred thousand souls to fuel it."

"Holy fuck," I said.

"Yeah, pretty much." Gabby spoke for the first time. Even she looked rattled by the potential loss of life, and she was pretty much a psychopath.

"Where the fuck are they going to find that many people? And how are they going to harness that many souls at one time?" I asked.

"They're going after the Georgia Dome," Flynn said.

I turned to see her on her laptop. "What?" I asked.

"The Falcons have a playoff game tomorrow night, and there's a country concert at Philips Arena at the same time. Between those two events, you've got well over a hundred thousand people concentrated in a couple of blocks."

I stood up and slid the book back over to Watson. "Give me that map," I said to Jo, who handed me the rolled-up paper. I spread the map out, concentrating on the area around the Georgia World Congress Center and the Georgia Dome, just a few blocks from the building we were in. I poured a tendril of energy back into the map, reactivating the sympathetic spell I'd cast earlier, and opened my Sight. The lines of power flared into life all over the representation of Atlanta, with brighter points glimmering at the intersections.

"Looks like I remembered right," I said, pointing to the map.

"Remembered what?" Watson asked. "I can't see anything."

"Oh yeah, sorry," I shifted the spell slightly so that the lines showed up in the normal spectrum, and the others gasped.

"What is that?" Jo pointed at the lines and glowing dots.

"Those are ley lines," I said, giving them the condensed explanation of lines and nodes and how they moved magical energy around the world. "And that," I added, pointing to a spot near the Ferris Wheel attacks we'd foiled just the day before, "is a big-ass node right in the middle of the park."

"Just a block or two from the arena and the football stadium," Flynn said.

"Yep," I nodded. I released the spell, and the glow faded from the map. I sat down and looked around the table. "Orobas is going to try to open the rift in the middle of the park, probably under the Olympic Fountain. The summoning yesterday was probably just a test run to see how strong the node is and how active the lines in that part of town are."

"If the size of the monsters summoned is any indication, they are both strong and active," Watson said.

"Pretty much," I agreed.

"So he's going to destroy Philips Arena and the Georgia Dome to open a doorway to Hell in the middle of downtown Atlanta," Flynn said.

"And this time when we use the words Hell and Atlanta in the same sentence, we're not talking about changing planes at the airport," Gabby said.

We all sat silent for a long moment before Gabby spoke again. "Well, if nobody else is going to ask the hundred-thousand-dollar question, I will. What are we going to do about it?"

I looked around the table at a whole bunch of eyes staring back at me. Sometimes it really sucks being the oldest guy in the room. It means that everybody looks to you for answers, no matter how unqualified you might be. And this was a situation where I was starting to feel uniquely unqualified.

"I'll be honest with you, kids," I said. "I have no fucking idea."

Nobody spoke for several minutes after I admitted to having no clue how to stop the oncoming apocalypse. Finally, Watson pushed his chair away from the table and walked over to the small wet bar against one wall of the room. He poured himself a highball glass half full of amber liquid, then poured another one and brought it to me without a word.

"Sorry, ladies," he said. "I have no idea what you drink, but having seen Mr. Harker's home liquor stores when we were in Charlotte last week, I know him to be a man who appreciates a good whiskey. And barring the presence of that, this American swill shall have to do."

I nodded my thanks, ignoring for the moment that fact that he had been in my apartment more recently than I had.

Watson rolled up the map, pushed the books of magical history to the side, and leaned forward, his elbows on the polished wood of the conference table. His glass cradled between his hands, he looked across at me. "It seems to me we will have to deal with a three-pronged attack from our adversary. Orobas will be at or near the ley line node to cast the spell. Then there will be someone—"

"Or something," Gabby interjected.

"Thank you, Gabriella," Watson replied. "There will be a force of some sort at the football stadium, and another at the concert hall. We will need to eliminate all three forces in relatively short order to avoid giving away our foreknowledge of events and losing the element of surprise. Does that sound roughly accurate?"

Once he started talked tactics, I revised my opinion of Watson in an instant. "Where did you serve?" I asked.

He started a little. "Afghanistan. Why?"

"You don't talk like that unless you've been somewhere facing a determined and inventive opposition force."

"What they lacked in resources, they made up for in knowledge of the area, improvisational ability, and dedication to their cause. I lost a lot of good men thanks to IEDs over there."

"I'm sorry," I said. "I don't know exactly what that's like, but I've seen a few wars, and they don't get better as we get more efficient at killing each other, just bloodier."

"True words," Watson said with a little nod. "Now, back to the problem, or problems, at hand. We have an opposing force that will be entrenched in three positions, surrounded by civilians, and with weapons of nearly unimaginable power. And we need to dispatch all of them simultaneously without arousing undue suspicion from the local populace or constabulary."

"Just another day at the office," Jo said. "We do more impossible shit before nine a.m. than most people do in their entire lives."

Chapter Ten

"NOTHING HERE," WATSON SAID INTO HIS BLUETOOTH HEADSET. HE scanned the crowd below him through the scope pressed to his cheek. He wondered, not for the first time, why exactly Adam carried a hunting rifle with a scope in a hidden compartment in the back of his Hummer, but it seemed better not to ask. And it certainly came in handy in their current endeavor.

"Concourse looks clear, too," Jo replied.

"I've got nothing except a couple dozen horny stagehands back here," Gabby said from her position backstage.

"There's nothing on the cameras," Sparkles added.

"Hells," Watson muttered. "Do we have any idea when this massacre is supposed to take place?"

"Harker thought around nine p.m. made the most sense. The concert will be in full swing, and the game will still be early enough that even if the Falcons are getting killed, most folks won't want to leave yet," Jo replied.

"I'll never understand you Americans. Leaving a match before the last goal is scored. You call yourself fans?" Watson said. "Gabby, have you seen anything at all out of the ordinary?"

"Have you ever been backstage at a concert, Jack? Everybody back here looks out of the ordinary. I can't tell if I'm at a tattoo convention or a meetup for middle-aged men with beer guts and ponytails. Wait a second, there's something… never mind."

"What is it?" Watson asked.

"There was a dude who was way too young and pretty to be backstage, but then he picked up a guitar. He must be with the band. What are you seeing?"

Watson took his eye from the scope and gave the crowd a broad once-over. He knelt on the catwalk high above the scoreboard and peered over the thousands of t-shirt-clad people beneath him. "I see an outlandish number of John Deere hats, quite an obscene amount of flannel, and absolutely no one wearing pants that aren't at least a size too small. And that's just the women."

"Welcome to a pop country concert, Watson," Jo said, chuckling a little into her headset. "Wait a second, that's not right…"

"What is it?" Watson and Gabby asked simultaneously.

"There's a service door open," Jo replied. "I'm going to go check it out." She said nothing for a couple of tense moments, then came back on the line. "There's a stairwell going down behind this door. I'm going to head down and take a look."

"Wait for us," Watson said. "I can be to you in just a couple of minutes."

"Yeah, me too," Gabby added. "Don't think you're going to get to go kill stuff without me there."

"Okay, first, have you ever considered therapy? Like, a lot of it. And second, fine, I'll wait. I'm beside the restrooms at Section 114."

"On my way," Gabby said.

"There in a moment," Watson added. He made one more pass over the crowd through the rifle's high-powered scope; saw nothing more than excessive consumption of overpriced and watery beer, poor fashion decisions, and even more poorly thought-our hairstyles; and put the gun back in the soft case Adam supplied. He walked down the catwalk, tucked the gun and case behind a large breaker panel, and descended a short ladder to the spotlight booth. A befuddled stagehand looked up from his phone as Watson stepped into the small space.

"What are you doing up there, man? You're not supposed to be here…" The young man looked from Watson to his headset hanging on the safety rail several feet away. Watson pointed to his chest at "MAINTENANCE" embroidered there over the name "Steve" in script.

"There was a circuit breaker needed replaced. Lights flickering in the bathroom in one of the skyboxes. Sent me up here to take care of it. I been up there for like an hour messing with it." Watson's southern accent wasn't great, but it looked like it was going to be good enough to get past one bored stagehand.

"Oh, alright," the spotlight operator said. "Well, you better get down, then. My call light's blinking, so I guess the show's about to start." He picked up his headset, clicked a button on his belt pack, and said, "Spot 3 on headset."

Watson gave the man a little wave and slipped past him to the metal ladder that took him to the steady concrete of the last row of the upper level. He wasn't as fast on a ladder anymore—only having one foot that felt the rungs made him proceed with caution—but he managed.

Three minutes later, he joined Gabby and Jo beside the concession stand.

"You leave Adam's gun up in the rafters?" Gabby asked.

"Had to," he replied. "Couldn't exactly go carrying a hunting rifle through the concourse with twenty thousand people around, could I?"

"You obviously don't know the country music audience," Jo said. "That's the door." She pointed to a door across the wide expanse of tile and glass with "AUTHORIZED PERSONNEL ONLY" on it in big letters. The white letters on a red sign left absolutely zero doubt as to who they were directed at.

"You think our quarry might be down those stairs?" Watson asked.

"That's the best option I've found," Jo said.

"I think she's probably right," Sparkles said over their earpieces. "Those stairs lead down into the maintenance tunnels, and the only better place to plant a bomb for maximum carnage is underneath the stage."

"I checked there," Gabby said. "Nothing out of the ordinary." The others stared at her. "What?" she protested. "I made friends with one of the stagehands."

"Is he still alive?" Jo asked.

"Of course! I don't go around indiscriminately killing… Oh screw it, I can't even say that with a straight face. But yes, this one is alive." Gabby grinned, then continued. "Unconscious and tied up inside a wardrobe case that isn't slated to get opened until their next show in Baltimore, but alive."

"Why do I even ask?" Jo rolled her eyes. "Let's get down there and see if we can find this bomb."

"What makes you so sure it's a bomb?" Gabby asked.

"How else would you kill everyone in this arena?" Jo fired back.

"Acid in the sprinkler system would be a good start. Incendiary devices scattered throughout the seating area, then bar the doors. Wouldn't be as efficient, but could lead to more mayhem. I could also just release a couple dozen demons, or a couple of machine gun teams, although I think Jack would have seen those from the catwalk. A biological agent in the beer could take out a good half the crowd, and if we used a contact poison on the doors and seat arms, we could make sure we got everyone that way…"

"You're truly disturbed, did you know that?" Jo looked at her teammate with a look of mild horror on her face. "Do you sit around dreaming up ways to kill thousands of people in one shot?"

"Nah, but it's something to pass the time on the toilet. I got tired of Angry Birds. Let's go." Gabby walked across the crowded concourse, opened the door, and started down the stairs. A security guard spotted her and started in that direction, but Watson intercepted him.

"I got her, man," he said, pointing to his jacket. "She's a... new friend, if you get my drift." He put a lascivious waggle into his eyebrows. The guard laughed and slapped Watson on the back, then walked off.

Watson followed Gabby down the stairs, drawing his Glock as he did so. Jo slid into the stairwell last, shrugging out of her long duster and dropping it to the floor, then pulling her hammer from the ring on her belt.

"No more Wyatt Earp cosplay?" Gabby said with a smirk.

"You try carrying around a three-foot hammer and see what your wardrobe looks like," Jo grumbled.

"I'm good with my leather jacket," Gabby replied. "It hides the girls perfectly."

"The girls?" Jo asked. "I don't think that jacket does much to minimize your boobs."

Gabby reached under her arms and drew a pair of pistols from well-concealed shoulder holsters. "Yeah, but if people are looking at my boobs, they aren't looking at the girls." She turned the nickel-plated Colt 1911 pistols so they glinted in the light of the stairwell. "This is Thelma," she said, holding up the gun in her right hand. "And this is Louise." She gestured with the left-hand gun. "My new girls. I had a friend deliver them to the hotel this afternoon."

"You have a friend who runs a firearm delivery service?" Watson asked.

"You don't?" Gabby replied. "Let's go shoot something. I want to try these ladies out."

The trio descended the stairs into the basement of the building, then spread out in three directions as they entered the larger area below ground. The basement was a huge area directly under the basketball floor, with huge concrete pilings holding up the rest of the building and a network of pipes and electrical conduits snaking overhead.

"Dennis, can you hear me?" Watson whispered into his earpiece. There was no reply from the disembodied computer wizard. Watson pulled out his cell phone and saw NO SERVICE at the top of the screen. Swearing under his breath, he slid the phone back into his pocket.

He looked across the room at Jo, then over at Gabby, then focused his attention on the middle section of the room. He moved across the room, dodging behind pieces of equipment and pallets of program books and plastic beer cups in a crouch, a position made more difficult by the fit of his prosthetic. After all these years, Watson moved with barely a limp, but some positions were very painful to walk in, and stooping down to make a smaller silhouette was one that made his stump rub painfully and the straps bind in uncomfortable ways. He stopped, pressing his back to a pillar, and massaged his thigh. Not for the first time, he cursed the IED that took his leg below the knee and the lives of two of his squad mates.

Momentary pity party over, he took a deep breath and stepped around the concrete support. His eyes caught a flash of red up ahead and at his two o'clock, and he moved in that direction. He slid from shadow to shadow, ducking behind pillars to conceal his progress. Moving slowly cost him time, but he reached the pulsing red LED barely a minute later nonetheless.

"Fucking hell," he whispered, looking at a block of C4 the size of a loaf of bread sitting on the floor next to the central support pillar. Glancing around, Watson estimated them to be almost exactly at center court, where an explosion would take out most of the floor seats and weaken the entire structure considerably. The amount of explosive material staring at him would certainly bring down a good chunk of the floor above them, but it wasn't enough to destroy the building.

The device was an ugly thing, nothing like the elegant bombs on the television shows. There was no convenient countdown timer on the front of the device. Watson had no idea what was supposed to trigger the explosion, just that he had to stop it.

"This would be a lovely time to have studied munitions," he muttered to himself. "My uncanny skills at interpreting contract clauses are somewhat less than useful here."

"I've got something." Jo's whisper cut through the still air. Watson looked in her direction, then started running her way as he heard a muffled *oof* from his right. He looked back at the bomb, hoping that he could devise a way to stop it by the time he got back. Or he could just get killed by whatever Jo was fighting. That would save him a lot of headache.

Jo was trading kicks and hammer blows with a pair of six-foot demons. They were all teeth and claws, with no real strategy. Jo dodged, jabbing with her hammer and using the handle to block more than swinging it the traditional way.

Gabby stepped out from behind a pillar and fired off four quick shots into the backs of the demons. They went down in a heap, and Jo smashed their skulls to gravy with her hammer. Watson turned back to the bomb, ringing ears now adding to his distraction.

"What did you... oh, shit," Jo said as she came over to Watson's side.

"Oh shit, indeed," the Brit said as he knelt in front of the device, looking in vain for something as simple as an OFF switch.

"Do you know how to disarm that thing?" Jo asked.

"No bloody clue," Watson admitted.

"Then get out of the way and go find the other charges," Gabby said, putting a hand on his shoulder.

Watson looked up at her. "You know how to disarm a bomb?"

"I'm not just a pretty face, Jacky-boy. I spent a year doing underwater demolitions while I was looking for a sea serpent in the Gulf of Mexico."

"There are sea serpents in the Gulf of Mexico?" Jo asked.

"Not anymore" was Gabby's simple reply. She holstered her pistols, took Watson's spot in front of the device, and pulled a small multi-tool from her belt. "There are probably four more devices just like this, set to go off about thirty seconds after this one blows. That would pretty much guarantee the whole building comes down. There might be some perimeter bombs for the first responders, but I doubt it. Orobas wants to maximize death toll, not instill maximum long-term fear in the population." Watson looked down at the woman with new eyes. The wise-cracking Harley Quinn-inspired psychotic was gone, and in her place was a smart, capable woman who was an expert in her craft. The wild-eyed grin she usually wore plastered across her face was nowhere to be seen, replaced by a wry smirk.

"Yeah, I'm like an onion, Jackie-boy. I've got layers. Now go find those other bombs while I figure out whether it's the red wire or the blue wire."

Watson nodded to Jo, and they split up. Jack headed off to one side of the arena's underbelly, his pistol in one hand. It took only a few moments to locate the other devices, and by the time he returned to Gabby's side, she had removed the detonator and separated it from the plastic explosive.

Jo walked up just as Watson did. "I found two more bombs," she said.

"As did I," Jack replied.

"Okay," Gabby said, showing them the electronics in her hand. "Now, we'll split up and take them all out faster. All you need to do is cut the—" Her words died in her throat in a strangled gasp as she clutched her neck.

"What's wrong?" Jo asked as Gabby dropped to her knees.

Jack looked past the stricken woman to see a slight man holding his arm out toward Gabby, his hand in a choking motion. He drew his pistol, but a blur of black crashed into him, and he tumbled to the floor under a ball of hair and teeth. Jack let the gun fly, concentrating on the monster atop him.

He used his momentum to carry himself and his assailant over in a tumble, shoving against the thing's body to create some separation. Jack let out a yell as razor-sharp teeth clamped down on his arm, and their skid across the floor came to bone-jarring halt against a massive concrete support pillar. Watson stared at the thing chewing on his arm and saw it was some type of dog, or wolf, or wolf-demon. Whatever it was, it had his left arm in its mouth and was worrying it like a chew toy.

Jack swung around until he could get his right hand near the thing's head and started punching. He quickly abandoned that idea when he found the skull as hard as the concrete he was writhing on. Claws ripped at his chest and belly, and Jack was very glad he had kept his wool coat on when they descended into the basement; otherwise the creature would have disemboweled him. Blood ran freely from the creature's mouth, and blood and spit splattered Watson's face.

He finally contorted himself around enough to reach his pocketknife and flipped the small Gerber knife open. Jack jammed the knife into the dog-thing's eye, then withdrew the short blade and did it again. He repeated the process several times, feeling the jaws clamp down ever tighter on his forearm with every stroke, until finally, with one last great thrust, he heard a soft *crunch* as he pierced the beast's brainpan and drove the knife into its brain up to his fist.

The beast opened its maw wide in one final yelp of pain, and Jack drew his arm back. He heard an echo of the dog's yelp behind him, then another, louder *crunch*, followed by a muttered, "Take that, you low-rent Vader motherfucker" in Jo's voice.

"Is everyone alright back there?" he called.

"Yeah, we're good. Whatever you did to the dog hurt the magician, too, so he couldn't hold us anymore. Then I bashed his head in. You okay?" Jo asked.

"Been better. Been worse. How's Gabriella?"

"I'm fine," came a hoarse croak. "As long as that fucker's dead. I'm going to take the rest of the bombs. Jo's coming with to cover me. Quicker that way. We'll meet you at the stairs."

"Aces," Jack replied.

Watson gritted his teeth and looked at his arm. It wasn't completely ruined, but it would be useless for several weeks, if not months. The major veins seemed intact, and he could move all his fingers independently, if not with any strength. He slithered out of his coat and used the dark wool to wipe off as much blood as he could. Then he cut away the sleeve of his shirt at the shoulder and fashioned a crude bandage from his shirt sleeve and strips cut from his coat. By the time he was finished with his field dressing and made it back to the stairs, the women were waiting for him.

Gabby held five electronic devices in her hands, and Jo carried her hammer loose. "Wanna help?" Jo asked, hefting the hammer.

"No, be my guest," Watson replied.

"Fair enough." With a nod to Gabby, Jo hoisted the hammer. The dark-haired woman set the electronics on the ground, and Jo smashed them to tiny pieces. After a few quick hammer blows, the detonators were blissfully inert.

"What did you do with the plastic explosive?" Jack asked.

"I left it there," Jo said. "With no detonator, it's completely harmless, and we can send a bomb disposal unit in here if we manage to save the world tonight."

"And if we don't, nobody will care," Gabby added, the mad gleam returning to her eye. "Now let's go to the park and see if Harker found something else to shoot. You and Jo killed the bad guys this time, so I *really* want to shoot somebody." She spun around and took the stairs two at a time heading out into the night.

"Sometimes I wonder how much of that is an act..." Jo mused.

"Then you decide that if you knew the answer, it would terrify you?" Watson said.

"Yeah, exactly. How's the arm?"

"Well, I fear I will have to postpone my piano recital, but I think with work and good whiskey, I will manage to make a full recovery."

"Assuming we save the world in the next two hours," Jo said.

Jack nodded. "Because if we don't do that, I fear I shall have much more to worry about than an injured arm." He turned and followed Gabby up the stairs to the next impossible task.

Chapter Eleven

LUKE STEPPED ONTO THE CONCOURSE AT THE GEORGIA DOME, WINCING at the roar of the crowd as the Falcons' starting lineup took the field. "I can't believe I allowed myself to be talked into this," he muttered.

"Let's face it, Luke, you're a sucker for anything that kid asks you to do. You always have been." Adam's voice rumbled across into Luke's ear from the Bluetooth headset he wore.

"It's not so much the activity that I loathe as it is the disguise," the ancient vampire replied. "You do understand that I have the ability to cloud men's minds and make myself invisible to their perceptions, correct?"

"I remember," Adam said. "I also know that clouding seventy-five thousand minds at once is probably a stretch, even for the Lord of the Undead."

"You know I hate that name."

"I do," Adam admitted. "But not as much as you hate your disguise."

Luke looked down at himself and had to admit that his old friend was correct. He was currently decked out in blue jeans, sneakers, a Matt Ryan jersey purchased from the team store, and a black Falcons baseball cap. "I feel as though the only thing missing from this ludicrous ensemble is a giant foam finger," he muttered.

"You should have said something," Adam replied. "We could have gotten you one of those, too." Adam stepped up beside Luke, a giant cup of beer looking tiny in his massive hand. Adam wore his usual brown pants but added a bright red Falcons hoodie to his wardrobe. With the hood up to conceal his scars, he just looked like a very large fan walking around the concessions area.

"Where should we begin?" Luke asked. "I have only a limited familiarity with explosives. My methods of dispatching enemies are typically much more… immediate."

"I think we might need to look at a different idea than explosives," Sparkles said in Luke's ear. "I don't know how much C4 it would take to bring down an entire football stadium, but it's going to be much harder to kill all these people that way. The building is just way too spread out."

"That makes sense," Adam said, adjusting the Bluetooth device in his own ear. "Even if you collapse a whole end zone, you might leave half the people alive. So, what's the other idea? How do we kill a stadium full of people in one shot?"

"A small nuclear device would almost certainly do the job," Luke said, and both Adam and Sparkles fell silent as the truth of his words sunk in.

"Fuck me, Luke," Sparkles said. "I don't even have a body anymore, and I just got a chill down my spine."

"Am I incorrect, Dennis?" Luke asked.

"No, no," Sparkles said. "You're right, it's just… shit, a nuke?"

"It makes sense," Adam said. "It's about the only thing that could take down an entire stadium without having a plane to deliver the payload. And it's not like Orobas is going to give a shit about what happens with the fallout since he's trying to destroy the Earth anyway."

"It also explains why Quincy sent the two of us here to handle this site and sent the three humans to handle the arena," Luke said.

"Because you can bring down an arena with traditional explosives, and you guys wouldn't be harmed by any leaking radiation," Sparkles agreed. "Well, goddamn, boys, what do you want to do?"

Luke let out a deep breath, more for effect than any need. "Well, we were sent here to find and disable an explosive device. I suppose now it's more critical than ever that we do so."

"Agreed," Adam said. "Now where do you suppose one hides a nuclear bomb in a football stadium?"

"That's not something I've ever considered, Adam. As I mentioned, large-scale slaughter hasn't been my forte for quite some time," Luke replied.

"I have the plans called up," Dennis said over their link. "There is an access tunnel underneath the stadium that circles the field. I'd start down there."

"And how are we supposed to find this thing, Dennis?" Adam asked. "Do we just go around the underbelly of the stadium whistling and calling out 'here bomb, here bomb'?"

"I thought we'd be a little more scientific than that, but not too much," came the reply. "Let's start by looking for anything or anyone out of the ordinary. People that don't look like they belong at a football game. Or in this dimension."

"Oh, so look for people like us?" Adam asked.

"Pretty much," Dennis agreed.

The big man nodded and stepped over to a nearby service entrance. Finding it locked, he wrapped his huge hand around the knob and squeezed. The squeal of metal crushing in his grip was almost drowned out by the roar of the crowd as the opening kickoff spiraled into the air, but not quite. One particularly alert security guard walked over to the pair with one hand on his pistol and the other on his radio.

"What are you doing over here?" the rotund guard asked, his moustache quivering.

Luke turned to him and waved a hand in front of the man's face. "These are not the droids you are looking for."

The man's eyes glazed over in a blink. "These are not the droids I am looking for."

"Go on about your business."

"I will go on about my business." The guard turned around and walked off.

Adam looked down at Luke. "Did you really just Jedi mind trick that guard?"

"Whatever works, my giant friend. Whatever works."

The two descended the narrow stairwell into the bowels of the stadium, concrete pressing in on all sides. Luke opened his senses wide, listening for anything out of the ordinary, but the din of the crowd above and the bustle of an active stadium below were simply too much for him to sort anything out.

Adam pushed open the door into a wide curved hallway, big enough to drive team buses into. Several television trucks were parked in a loading area ahead of them with cables snaking across the floor to various ports and panels. People in headsets and baseball caps hustled to and fro, all at an almost-run.

"I think it's safe to say we're not going to find anything in all this chaos," Adam said, keeping his voice low.

"As loathe as I am to insert myself into that fray, my friend, I have to disagree. Were I to plant a bomb under a venue such as this, the place where the most people would be rushing by is exactly where I would do so."

"Because it would have the highest death toll?" Adam asked.

"No," Luke disagreed. "If we are indeed looking for a nuclear device, it will kill everyone in the building regardless. No, I would hide something here for the simple fact that the more people rushing through an area, the less likely it is that a disguised package would be noticed. As long as it isn't bright red with 'BOMB' on the outside in giant letters, a box could sit here for hours, and everyone would just assume that someone else put it there."

"That actually makes a lot of sense," Adam said.

"It's the same method I used to smuggle coffins on freighters," Luke said. "Just put one more box in a crowd of boxes and busy people, and no one ever noticed."

"And here I thought it was some kind of magic."

"Simply my near-mythic understanding of human nature, my oversized friend. Nothing more."

"Well, I suppose if you live through enough centuries, you're bound to pick up a thing or two. So, let's go check things out." The two stepped out of the stairwell and walked over to the nearest TV truck, striding across the concrete like they owned the place. Luke peeled off to the right and circled around the first truck while Adam turned left and walked to the back of the second. They met behind the trucks, and each shook their head.

"There's nothing lying around. Nothing bigger than a Cheetos bag, anyway," Adam said.

"I cannot smell any plastic explosive or dynamite," Luke added.

"You can smell explosives? What are you, a TSA dog?" Adam asked.

"I have been around enough war zones to know that explosives all have a distinct odor that cannot be effectively masked," Luke replied.

"I'm not picking anything up on any of the infrared scans or... wait... what the ever-loving fuck is *that*? You guys gotta move. I think I found what you're looking for, and it is most certainly *not* a nuke," Dennis said over their headsets.

"Where are we going?" Adam asked, already in motion toward the front of the trucks. He stripped off his hoodie as he went, getting rid of the too-small garment so his arms could move more freely. A man stepped out of the truck into his path, but Adam just swept the two-hundred-pound man aside as if he were a fly.

The man stared up from the ground as the scarred giant stepped over him. "I thought wrestling was in here tomorrow..."

"The thing you're after is about halfway around the walkway from where you are," Dennis said. "Go to the right and haul ass. If it's putting off anywhere near the light that it is heat, you won't be able to miss it." Luke and Adam did as they were told, sprinting down the corridor to confront whatever awaited.

Luke quickly outpaced his bulkier friend, pouring on his enhanced speed and moving far past any human pace. He rounded a bend in the hall and came up short, almost toppling over in his haste to stop. "Dennis…" Luke said into his Bluetooth.

"Yeah, Luke, did you find the thing?"

"Oh, I found it… I'm just not sure what you think I can do about it."

"What do you mean? You've got to kill it. Or destroy it, or something."

"I can't even get near it, Dennis. Remember? I'm invulnerable to many things. Garlic is a myth. I care nothing about running water. I don't stop to count grains of rice or salt. I am no more affected by holy water or religious iconography than a human, and driving a stake through my heart will only render me unconscious, not turn me to dust. But there are two things I cannot, under any circumstances, come into contact with. One of those is sunlight. The other is, if you'll recall…"

"Fire," Dennis finished the sentence.

"Yes, Dennis. Fire. Now given that knowledge, what in all the hells am I supposed to do with *that?*"

The "that" in question was a six-foot walking bonfire. A fire elemental. And it was walking straight toward Luke. Luke did something he hadn't done in a fight in literally centuries. He started backing away.

"Luke, what are you doing?" Dennis said over the comm. "I've hacked the security cameras, so I can see you. Don't back up, charge that thing!"

"I can't, Dennis. I'm hundreds of years old. I am the very definition of 'highly flammable.' If I get near that thing, I will burst into flames."

"If you don't do something, the whole place will burst into flames! That red pipe over your head, the one that makes a right turn into the room beside you?"

"Yes?" Luke said.

"That's the main gas line for the building! It branches out from that room to every skybox kitchen and every concession stand in the stadium. If the flame guy gets to that pipe, it could shoot fireballs out of every gas port in the place. The whole joint would go up in flames!"

"That doesn't sound good." Adam's rumbling voice came from both Luke's headset and his right ear as the giant man came to a halt right beside the vampire. "Dennis, can you tell from the video exactly what this thing is?"

"Not exactly, but I think it's a fire elemental. It's made entirely of flame, so there's not really anything to punch."

"That makes things a little more complicated," Adam said.

"And also simpler," Luke added.

The big man turned to him, a puzzled look on his scarred face. Luke continued. "If it's an elemental, then something summoned it. If I can find that something, or someone, and dispatch it, then the elemental should return to its own plane."

"Should?" Adam said.

"Nothing is definite, my large friend. Nothing except the fact that I cannot go near the creature, so I must render my assistance in another fashion." With that, Luke dashed off past the elemental, farther into the bowels of the stadium.

"I suppose that leaves me to wrestle the man made of fire," Adam said with a sigh.

"Bring back memories?" Dennis asked.

"Yes, and not good ones," Adam replied. His mind flashed back to a crowd of angry villagers, pitchforks, the supposed death of his "father," Victor, and a pretty blonde girl who died at the hands of a monster who didn't know his own strength. Adam had spent decades working to atone for that one accidental murder, and it seemed that now, after all these years, the fire had finally caught up with him.

He rolled his shoulders, turned his head side to side, and cracked his knuckles. "Any suggestions would be welcome right about now," he said.

"Sorry, big guy," came the voice in his ear. "I've got nothing. I'm working to hack the sprinkler system and at least douse him a little bit, but so far no good."

Dennis's words sparked something in Adam, a flicker of inspiration that the heat and situation fanned into a plan. He looked around the immediate area, and finding nothing that fit the bill, grabbed a golf cart and tossed it into the path of the oncoming elemental. The man of fire barely slowed, just flowing around the obstruction like it wasn't even there. Adam then grabbed a cart full of metal cylinders with soda company labels on them and shoved the cart at the monster.

The metal tubes exploded upon contact with the fire-beast, dousing the elemental in a spray of de-carbonated soda syrup. The monster shrank upon contact with the liquid, but slowed its approach only for a few seconds. Adam dashed a dozen yards back up the tunnel and smashed the glass cover of a nearby fire box. He pulled the fire extinguisher from the wall and marched into the path of the elemental, extinguisher in hand and a faint hope for survival in his heart. Whatever happened next, it was going to hurt.

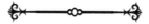

Luke sprinted along the tunnel, looking for anyone who looked deep in concentration and testing every doorknob he passed. He finally found an unlocked electrical room and ducked inside. This was as likely a place as any to hold a summoner, and he needed to find and dispatch this magician before Adam was burned to a crisp. Luke wasn't sure exactly how much flame his friend could endure before succumbing to the damage, but he was in no rush to find out.

His normally placid features split into a wide smile as he came upon a slender woman seated inside a protective circle, head bowed. She was obviously the summoner, and just as obviously vulnerable. Her magical circle would keep out any energy or mystical attacks, but it wouldn't stop Luke from simply stepping across the line and snapping her scrawny neck. He opened his mouth to warn the woman that this moment was going to be her last when something large and heavy crashed into him from the side.

Luke slammed into a breaker panel, his head smacking painfully into the metal cover. He turned to see his attacker and found himself face to face with a demon. This was a Reaver demon, one of the smaller creatures Quincy and his friends had faced the day before, but it was still a vicious close quarters opponent. Its overlong arms and wicked claws shredded Luke's overcoat but were unable to reach his flesh.

Luke smashed his right elbow down into the demon's grinning face, pulping its nose and eye socket, but it didn't release its grip. Luke wriggled his other arm free and rained fists down upon the demon's skull, to no avail. After almost a full minute of struggling in the monster's grip, Luke pushed off the wall with his left arm, ripped the cover off the breaker panel with his right, then reached into the electrical box, gripping one of the hot lugs with his left hand.

High-voltage electricity rocketed along every nerve ending, passing through his body into the demon. Luke's body went rigid; the demon's body began to convulse. As more and more power flowed through him, Luke noticed the unmistakable stench of burning hair—his own. Finally, the demon shook itself off Luke, who managed to pull his hand out of the panel and break the connection. He collapsed to one knee and looked over at the demon. Or rather, he looked as the scorched concrete where the demon last fell. There was no demon there, just the reek of sulfur and burned flesh.

Luke knew all too well that the burned flesh was his own, but there wasn't time to worry about that now. He took three long strides across the floor, stepped on the edge of the magician's magical circle, and kicked her under the chin. Even in his weakened state, Luke's power was more than strong enough to topple the woman backward, her head smacking into the concrete floor with the sound of a cantaloupe dropped from a great height.

Luke looked at the unconscious woman, then down at his smoldering flesh, and a small smile flitted across his features. "Dennis, did the elemental disappear when I rendered the spellcaster unconscious?"

"It did, Luke. I don't see anything else on the security cameras. I think you got the only one. And the arena team took out their bomb, so all that's left is to find Orobas and send that fucker back to Hell where he belongs."

"I concur. Please let Adam know that I will be with him momentarily. I feel a slight hunger that I must indulge before rejoining him." Luke clicked off his headset and put it in his pocket without waiting for an answer. He smiled down at the unconscious magician. "And you, my dear, can rest easy in the knowledge that your death will not be in vain. You may not have accomplished your initial goal, but healing me before I rend your employer limb from limb is a fate not without its merits."

He started toward the woman, fangs extended and a smile on his face that would have chilled the blood of anyone near enough to see it. "Just a little snack, and then we'll return to our regularly scheduled program of saving the world."

Chapter Twelve

Cᴇɴᴛᴇɴɴɪᴀʟ Oʟʏᴍᴘɪᴄ Pᴀʀᴋ ʟᴏᴏᴋᴇᴅ ʟɪᴋᴇ ᴛʜᴇ sᴇᴛ ᴏꜰ ᴀ ʜᴏʀʀᴏʀ ᴍᴏᴠɪᴇ when I walked up to the site of Orobas's planned ritual. I don't mean that there were dead bodies lying around and people covered in fake blood and effects makeup; I mean that it looked like someone was shooting a movie right in the middle of the Olympic Fountain. There was a crane with huge lights hanging from it, a team of gophers running around with clipboards and headsets, and a crowd of curious onlookers standing behind portable metal barricades.

I chuckled a little at the sheer balls of it all. Oro hadn't just found a way to hide his ritual from the authorities and people who might want to stop him, he'd found a disguise that would get him extra souls to destroy just off the bystanders and hopefuls looking for half a second of screen time. It would have been an incredibly elegant solution, except that I planned to spoil the whole damn party.

I walked up to the barricade with Flynn on my left side and a step behind to clear my hands in case I needed to fling a spell in that direction on short notice. I threw one leg over the barricade, and a minion rushed over to intercept me.

"Excuse me, sir," the minion said. She looked human, a short woman in a Walking Dead Crew t-shirt, jeans, hiking boots, and a Madea's Your Mama baseball cap with a long curly brown ponytail pulled through the back. She wore a radio on her belt and carried a clipboard, the uniform of production assistants the world over. "You can't come onto the set. We're going to start shooting in just a couple—"

I didn't slow down, just kept walking like she hadn't even spoken. I held up my Homeland Security badge and said, "Get the people out of here. A biological agent has been released in the Georgia Dome, and we need this area evacuated as quickly as possible." I pitched my voice loud enough that the nearest civilians also heard me. I saw out of the corner of my eye the nearest people turn to their neighbors and start to chatter. Good, I needed to sow a lot of confusion and more than a little panic if my sketch of a plan was going to work.

The PA got a confused look on her face, and she reached for her radio. "I need to check on that. But until I do, could you please step behind the barricade?"

"No, I can't," I said. "Detective, will you see that these people begin the evacuation quickly and efficiently?"

Becks' face flashed dark, and a hint of red appeared at the tips of her ears. She was pissed that I stuck her on crowd control, but I was not letting her go toe-to-toe with Orobas. That guy beat the shit out of me the first time we met; I was not about to let him get his hands on Flynn.

You're going to have some explaining to do about this bullshit when we get out of here, I "heard" across our mental link.

Deal, I replied. *Now let's focus on that whole "getting out of here" part*. I turned my attention back to the little PA who was frantically trying to convince me to stop marching onto the "set."

"Look, kid. I'm not stopping. And you're not going to wrestle me to the ground and sit on me, so why don't you go talk to my partner back there and start getting these people, and yourself, to safety?"

She looked at me like I was completely insane. It wasn't even close to the first time I'd gotten that look from a woman, so I knew it well. "Sir, I can't *leave*. That would be highly unprofessional, and I might never work in this town again."

I didn't bother telling her that if she didn't get as far away from this park as humanly possible, and in the next few minutes, she probably wasn't ever going to work again anywhere. I just shook my head. "Fine, lady. Do what you gotta do. But I'm going to go put a stop to this shitshow before anyone gets hurt or killed." *Preferably before I get hurt or killed.* I kept that thought to myself, though.

I shouldered past the woman and heard her radioing for security behind me. It only took a few more seconds for me to break through the next security barricade and see what Orobas had going on. It was an elaborate ritual, apparently, because there was a huge double circle drawn on the brick plaza at the park's fountain. There were people lying on their backs dressed in white robes at the cardinal points of the circle and a grinning Orobas in the center. The circle glowed with so much magical energy that its purple light was visible even without opening my Sight. Even the mundanes could see this thing, although they doubtless thought it was just a little bit of movie magic.

"Hello, Harker," the demon called to me. "I'm so glad you could make it to our little film shoot." He smiled even bigger, showing more teeth than I felt comfortable seeing, much less having aimed at me. His double circle was, at least, drawn in chalk, not blood, and the people positioned around his circle were alive, for the moment, but the Enochian scribblings in the space between the circles told a story of demons, dimensions, and doorways that I really didn't want to see come to pass.

"Hi, Oro. I think there are some folks in town that would like to have a word or two with you. Why don't you step out of that circle, and I'll see if Luke is free to say hi?"

"I'm just fine in here, thanks. But please pass along my condolences to your uncle. I know how fond he gets of his lackeys."

"And what about Mort? I think he's got a couple things he wants to say to you, too," I said, stepping close to the mystical barrier. The double circle was reinforced against both magical and physical attacks. If I was going to have any shot of stopping Orobas from completing his ritual, I had to get that circle down. I reached out to test the barrier, but drew my hand back before I actually touched the circle. The tingle in my fingertips told me all I needed to know— Oro's boundaries were strong, and I was not getting through to him easily.

I looked around, trying to find something to disrupt his circle, and my eyes landed on the people at the compass points of the circle. Each of them held an item on their chest, and all of them looked ancient. One held a book, another a dagger, then a helmet, and a folded bundle of fabric. At Oro's feet was another book, and this one was bigger and more ornate than the one held by his minion.

"What's with the toys, Oro?" I asked. "Planning a magical garage sale after your apocalypse?"

"You know full well what I intend to do with these artifacts, Quincy. It would have been much simpler with the sword of St. Joan, but she always was a contrary bitch, even in life."

"The sword of…" It took me a second, but I realized Orobas was talking about the blade we dug out of the rubble of Luke's house. Apparently, it was more than just a souvenir Luke took off a dead Nazi, but the sword worn by Joan of Arc, supposedly a gift to her from God himself when she took up arms as a man to go into battle.

I reached over my shoulder with my right hand and drew the sword. "You mean this old thing? I just grabbed it on my way out the door thinking if you wanted it, it must be important. Might even have a way to fuck up your little tea party here. So, what's the deal, Oro? Is this little pigsticker important?"

I answered my own question as I slowly extended the sword, point-first, toward Orobas in his circle. I expected nothing more than to get my arm halfway out and bump the blade into his magical barrier. But that's not what happened. Not even close. As the tip of the sword made contact with the circle, it collapsed. The glowing purple sphere blinked out of existence with an audible *pop*, and I saw Oro jerk within his inner circle as the power used to create it rushed back into him causing a painful magical backlash. I took two steps forward and jabbed the sword into the inner barricade, and it popped like a soap bubble, too, rocking Oro almost flat onto his back.

With his circle down and the mother of all backlash headaches, Oro looked up at me. "You will not thwart my plans again, Quincy Harker. I *will* open the Gates of Hell upon this miserable world, and I *will* storm Heaven itself, proving once and for all that it is Orobas, not that pitiful twat Morningstar, that is the true King of Hell. Mere moments from now, the power of a hundred thousand souls will flow into me, and I will be unstoppable!"

"Oh, are those the souls at the concert?" Jo asked, walking up beside me with her hammer in her hand. "They're a little drunk, and you'd have to be to listen to that godawful excuse for music, but they're fine. We defused your bombs. Because we're cool like that."

"Or did you mean the souls at the football game?" Luke asked, kicking over the metal barricade behind me. "Because they're all safe as well. We disposed of your little firebug, and now it's your turn."

Orobas stood, glaring at me and my friends. Then he raised his arms, and a half dozen demons flew in to stand beside him. Looks like I wasn't the only one who brought backup. These weren't anything special, just run-of-the-mill demonic soldiers. They each were basically human in size and shape, except for the crimson skin, bat wings, the hooves where feet should be, the barbed penises (shut up, they were impossible to miss), and the curved black horns.

"Is that all you've got, Harker? A monster, a bloodsucker, a half-vampire illusionist, and a few humans? I obviously brought far too many demons along." He snapped his fingers, and the demons charged us.

Or at least the demons tried to charge us. They took the first step, but then a blur of motion appeared from my left, and the demons suddenly fell to the ground, every one of them missing a head. I looked to my right, and standing there covered in gore with a pyramid of demon skulls at its feet was an eight-foot demon with obsidian skin, a four-foot curved blade, and a double row of teeth smiling at me from an elongated mouth that reminded me of an alligator with a bad attitude.

"You killed my daughter, you son of a pit imp." The voice that came out of the demon was something I've heard in my nightmares ever since. It was a low, rumbling, viscous sound, like boiling tar covering searing flesh. That voice held within it centuries of screams and millennia of torture, and every word came out of that double-razored mouth with a smile.

"Mort?" I asked, almost under my breath. I'd never seen Mort's true form since he was a passenger demon and preferred to possess others. Now that I saw his real body, and particularly his red, pupilless eyes, I understood why. Nothing he could ever possess would give me cause to almost piss myself just by having it turn its gaze on me.

But that's exactly what it did. It looked at me, and that awful voice spoke again. "Hello, Harker. Please do not interfere. This putrescent cock-boil is mine, and I will have his soul for breakfast."

"You can do what you like with his soul, Mortivoid," Luke said, stepping up beside me. "But I get to take a piece out of his flesh."

"Are you threatening me, Vlad?" Mort asked, reverting to Luke's birth name.

"Not at all," Luke replied. "Simply proposing an alliance. We kill him together, then you may have him for any length of time after that such as you desire."

"I may have something to say about that," Oro chimed in. All heads swiveled back to the demon, who stood in the center of his shattered circle with his hands pointed to the sky.

"Attack!" he screamed, and from the skies above Atlanta, it started to rain demons of all shapes and sizes.

I looked at my team, gathered around me looking terrified but determined. "Get as many humans to safety as you can, then start sending these bastards back to Hell!" They jumped into action, some drawing weapons and some moving toward the PA and the civilians clustered around her.

Orobas took advantage of my momentary distraction to leap from his circle and swat me to the ground, knocking the sword from my grip and cracking my head on the ground. I looked up at the monster, and not for the first time, thought, *I fucking hate demons.*

Chapter Thirteen

IT WAS RAINING DEMONS OVER ATLANTA; I WAS FLAT ON MY ASS IN FRONT of the monster responsible for the death of Renfield, Christy, and countless others; and Count Dracula was about to get into a pissing contest with a hitchhiker demon about who got to kill the bad guy first. And I dropped my sword and was pretty sure I had a slight concussion. My day was quickly approaching Defcon Fucked.

Orobas was distracted from his desire to rip my head off and shit down my neck by Luke crashing into him from the side and sending him ass over teakettle across the brick pavers around the Olympic Fountain. Mort followed a split second behind, his sword blurring through the air like a Cuisinart with more teeth. I almost felt bad for Orobas, until I remembered that he wanted to blow open the doors of Hell and relocate a couple million demons into my dimension.

Fuck, the demons. I looked up and saw a solid dozen Reavers scurrying across the park after any civilians who lingered outside the metal barricade protecting the "film set" of Oro's ritual. There were at least as many Torment Demons stalking the fleeing humans, and one twelve-foot demon of a kind I'd never encountered before. It was an ugly bastard, to be sure, with four legs, a spiked tail, and half a dozen arms. It looked like the uglier brother of a Kali statue mated with a tarantula, without any of the charm of that kind of pairing.

"Adam, go for the Torment Demons," I yelled. "Becks, Gabby, take out the Reavers. Watson, you and Jo cover the civilians." The four humans Oro used in his ritual were just red splotches on the ground, the first victims of the demons, but there were still plenty of people that needed help.

"What are you doing, Harker?" Flynn called back to me.

"I'm doing what I do, Becks," I shouted. "Sending the big nasty back to Hell." I took a deep breath, picked up my fallen magic sword, and charged the four-legged giant with a wordless bellow. *It's a good thing I'm a fast healer because this might hurt.*

The thing looked at me, its inhuman face splitting into a grin as I ran at it. It reached down with one clawed hand, but I'm a little quicker than the average bear, so I ducked under and opened a long gash in its forearm. The wound glowed with a blue-white light, and a smell like roasted assholes engulfed me. The demon jerked its hand back, and it reared up on its back pair of legs to strike at me again, this time much more seriously.

I guess it still thought I was human, though, because instead of trying to run or dodge, I did what no human should ever do when confronted with a demon—I leapt right at the thing. I vaulted into the air, my sword flashing down in an overhead strike worthy of its own Mortal Kombat move, and split the demon's head right down the middle.

My momentum crashed me into the thing's now-bleeding face, and we tumbled to the ground in a heap of blood, demon brain, and godawful funk. I've smelled some truly unholy things, and seen things no human should ever see, but when I stood up, one foot firmly planted in the skull of a dead demon, my stomach did barrel rolls at the stench.

But it was dead. With one shot I had killed the biggest damn demon I'd ever seen. And not just "sent it back to Hell" killed it, but "turning to slush on the ground" killed it. This thing was forever-dead, the kind of dead that's really hard to manage with extra-planar beings. I looked at the sword in my hand with a new appreciation. It didn't look any different, just a plain blade, about three feet long, with a glided cross guard and a leather-wrapped hilt.

"Good sword," I said, then turned to see who needed a hand. Adam was the nearest, and also the one in the deepest shit as three torment demons were pummeling the shit out of him. I figured he was probably fine as long as they didn't literally rip him limb from limb, but I still took a running start and chopped two of the demons down before they even turned to look at me. The third one got a single swipe at me with its claws, but I cut that hand off before I spun the sword around and opened the nasty fucker from his nuts to his nose. Demon guts spilled out onto the ground, and I whirled around in a lethal spin, taking the monster's head.

"Nice sword," Adam said, giving me a nod.

"Yeah," I said. "If I'd known it was a demon-slayer, I would have been carrying this thing for the last seventy years instead of letting it hang on the wall in Luke's study."

"But where's the challenge in that, right?" Adam asked, and for just a piece of a second, I thought I saw a smile flit across his face.

"I could use a few less challenges, old pal," I replied. "Now let's get rid of the rest of these bastards and see if Luke needs a hand."

"You take the last three Torment Demons," Adam said. "I'll go back up Flynn and the others."

As much as I wanted to be the knight charging to Becks' rescue, he was right. The Reavers were nasty little shits, but they could be killed with mundane weapons, or even Adam's bare hands. I had the only weapons we could really use against the Torment Demons, my magic and this shiny new toothpick in my hand. I nodded and set out to clear the plaza of demons while Frankenstein's monster rushed off to save my girlfriend.

My new weapon proved to be way more than Oro's army of dickheads could handle, and just minutes later, I joined Flynn, Gabby, Watson, Adam, and Jo as we converged on the scrap still taking place in the middle of the fountain where Orobas's circle used to be. His spellground was totally wrecked with ritual elements scattered all across the brick. Becks was covered in blood, but she assured me none of it was hers, and the team looked largely uninjured, with the exception of a growing shiner on Jo's left eye and blood dripping from Watson's knuckles.

Orobas had all he could handle with Luke and Mort both taking chunks out of his ass almost at will. Luke went high, and Oro threw up his arms to block the Vampire Lord from literally ripping his head off, and that left his gut open for Mort to slash across his belly with his sword. Then Oro doubled over to protect his midsection, but that left the back of his head exposed for Luke to rain down elbows on his exposed head that would make Royce Gracie proud.

"They're just playing with him," Jo said.

"This isn't a game," I replied. "They're going to torture him until he knows just what kind of pain they can inflict, then they're going to hurt him some more. Maybe sometime right before sunrise they'll kill him. But only if they get tired enough."

I stepped forward to end the scrap and put Orobas out of all our misery, but stopped at the sight of a man stepping into the far side of the fountain. He was a big man, at least six-and-a-half-feet tall, and thickly muscled, with close-cropped brown hair and a dark brown beard. He wore a tailored suit and shoes that looked more expensive than my car, although that set the bar pretty low.

I walked around the torture scene in the center of the fountain to meet the man. "Reginald Barton, I presume?"

"You do, indeed, Mr. Harker. You presume a great deal," the man said with a terse nod. He gestured to the destroyed ritual and demon bodies littering the landscape. "You presume to interfere with my plans yet again. You presume to massacre my minions, disrupt my ceremonies, and generally stick your nose in where it doesn't belong again and again. I begin to tire of your interference."

"Well I guess it's a good thing you're here, then. This way you can ask me nicely not to fuck up your plans to destroy the world, and I can tell you to your face to kiss my lily-white ass. Now, do you want to get back in your car and go back to playing Aleister Crowley in your McMansion on the hill, or would you rather I beat your ass a little first?" I sheathed my sword and summoned a trickle of energy from the nearby ley lines. Power flooded into me, and I channeled it into glowing balls of crimson energy floating above my readied fists.

"You think to threaten me, human?" Barton asked, an incredulous look passing over his face. "You must truly be the stupidest mortal this hunk of rock and celestial shit has ever produced." He raised his hands to the sky. "Look upon my true form, mortal, and kneel before your Lord and Master!"

White light poured from Barton's body, growing in intensity until it was painful even through my closed lids. My concentration shattered; my energy globes vanished with a crackling *pop*. I turned away and covered my face with my hands, only looking back when the light finally faded. Through the multicolored spots in my vision, I saw a tall figure, nearly seven feet in height, clothed head to toe in white robes, with a nimbus of light surrounding its head and giant wings of purest white peeking out over its shoulders.

Fuck me, it's a goddamn angel.

Chapter Fourteen

THE ANGEL FORMERLY KNOWN AS REGINALD BARTON SNEERED AT ME. "Now do you understand the heights of my superiority, mortal? I am not just an incredibly wealthy human. I am of the seraphim, placed in dominion over this world by God Himself, destined to rule over all of the inferior beings such as yourself."

I couldn't help it. I tried, I really tried not to be an asshole to the angel, but I couldn't stop myself. Not even Flynn in my head warning me to shut the fuck up could keep my mouth shut. "If you're so goddamn superior, show me your dick, you neutered assclown." Then I took two long steps forward and punched the angel right in the face.

I liked the angel a lot better when he was looking up at me from his now-soaked ass in the middle of the gorefest that was the Olympic Fountain. His robes looked a lot less impressive covered in water and demon blood, too. I knew the second I did it that it was a mistake, but it didn't matter. This celestial cocksucker was responsible for all the pain Orobas, and by extension Smith, had wrought, including Renfield, Christy, Dennis, and God Himself only knew how many others. If that didn't call for a good right cross, I didn't know what did.

Barton glared up at me from the ground, then quicker than my eye could follow, he stood before me again, this time clad in gleaming white armor. "You dare to lay hands on one of The Host, you sniveling worm?"

"I've been called a lot of things, pal, but sniveling has never been one of them."

"You have interfered with my plans for the last time, Quincy Harker," he said, reaching out and wrapping a hand around my throat. He didn't even seem to strain as he lifted me off my feet. I gasped in his grip, kicking my feet in futility.

"Don't bother to struggle. It will only make this hurt more." The angel grinned up at me, and spots started to dance around in my peripheral vision.

Then a shot rang out, and the angel dropped me to the ground. I slammed into the bricks in a heap, rolling to the right to create some space between me and the pissed-off celestial. The angel stood with a hand pressed to its back, a look of shock spreading across its face. Flynn stood about fifteen feet away, her service weapon in a standard grip leveled right at the angel.

"Don't move, asshole. I might not be Homeland Security anymore, but I will still put a dozen rounds in your ass if you touch Harker again." From the look on her face, I believed her.

The angel smiled, and my heart sank. He turned to Flynn, waved a hand, and she flew back into Adam, knocking him into Watson and making a huge pile of bowled-over Shadow Council scatter like tenpins. "Do not presume to assault your betters, mortal. Now all of you lay there and let the grownups talk."

He turned his attention back to me, which was marginally better than trying to kill my girlfriend, I guess. "All I wanted to do was open a little bitty doorway to Hell and take over Heaven. Is that so much to ask?"

"I don't give a shit what you do with Heaven and Hell, but when you use Earth as a landing zone, that's when I get a little grumpy. So why here? Why not just go straight from Hell to Heaven?" I thought if I could get him talking, I could maybe come up with an idea for how to beat up a celestial being before he got bored with monologuing and just crushed me like a gnat.

"Because what better way to get the attention of the Father than by destroying His favorite children?"

"Huh?" I was honestly confused. Of course, it's always been tough to keep track of who was God's chosen people at any given time.

"Man, you idiot. If I threaten the very existence of humanity, then God will *have* to take notice again," the angel replied. There was definitely some shit going on that was above my mystical pay grade, but I didn't care. All I cared about was keeping this fucker's attention while Mort and Luke crept up on him from behind.

"You mean God isn't paying attention to Earth anymore, and you want to… make Him?" I asked. My cavalry was almost within striking distance. I just needed a couple more seconds.

"I mean that no one has seen the Father since the end of the war on Heaven, you idiotic mortal! God, Lucifer, Michael, and the rest of the Archangels— they're all gone! They've been gone for millennia, and no one can find them. So if I kill enough of you fucking overgrown gorillas and let Orobas relocate a few million demons to right outside the Gates, He'll have to come back and take care of things again! I'm tired of cleaning up your fucking wars, and disease, and poverty, and… fucking filth! How are you all so *dirty*? It's truly disgusting.

And stop that." He waved a hand behind him, and Luke and Mort flew back, bowling over Adam, who had just made it to his feet. It was like slapstick comedy, only way more terrifying.

The angel stepped over to me, holding out his hand. A blade of pure white light materialized out of thin air, and he raised it high over his head. I reached over my shoulder and drew my own sword, barely getting it up in time to block his decapitating stroke.

Barton stepped back, shock written all over his face. I was pretty surprised, too, since I was staring up at him from behind a blade suddenly wrapped in flame. There was heat coming off the sword, but none of it hurt me. The hilt didn't get warm, the flames didn't scorch my eyebrows off, nothing like that. It just lined the edge of the blade in a bright red-yellow inferno. Sometimes I love magic.

"Where did you get that?" the angel gasped.

"Oh, this old thing?" I replied. "I took it off a Nazi in France a long time ago. Your pal Oro seemed to think it might be important. Looks like he was right."

"Important?" The angel's face was incredulous. "Oh, you ignorant ape. That is the sword of the Archangel, the blade that Michael wielded in the war with Lucifer. That sword is far too powerful and sacred to be sullied with your touch."

"Well, then you'd better back the fuck up, pal, because otherwise I'm gonna do a lot more than touch you with it. I'm gonna stick it so far up your ass fire shoots out your ears." I scrambled to my feet, sword in front of me.

Barton grinned. I hate it when the bad guys smile. It usually means that my life is going to get a lot more complicated. The grinning angel raised his blade of Heavenly light over his head and ran at me, raining blows down upon my head and shoulders. I parried the best I could, but I started to wear out in seconds. Swords are heavy, and angels are *fast*. I put all my power into one big block and shoved him back, then conjured a circular shield of force around my left forearm. Now I could deflect with my shield and strike back with my own sword.

I went after him, my own sword ready for battle, but quickly realized that fighting with a sword and shield is a lot harder than it looks in the movies. I got my feet tangled up in each other trying to move, swing, and defend all at the same time, and with a flick of his sword and a quick kick to my left knee, Barton toppled me to the ground, my sword again skittering across the ground. If I couldn't hold onto it any better than that, maybe the angel was right and I didn't deserve to wield the thing.

I looked up at the angel. He smiled down at me, a grim, tight smile that held no real mirth. "It's time for this to end, Harker. You have fought valiantly and well, for a human, but I marched across the plains of paradise to throw back Lucifer's horde. You could never stand against me in battle." He raised his blade over his head and brought it down to cleave my skull and end me once and for all.

I'm sorry. I love you, I thought to Flynn as the blade rushed down at my face. I closed my eyes, hoping that if there was someone upstairs taking notes, that my good deeds finally outweighed my sins.

Then there was a ringing crash, and the blade struck brick inches from my cheek. I opened my eyes, and there was a blade hovering six inches from my nose, but it wasn't the white-lined blade that Barton tried to kill me with. This was a sword outlined in brilliant blue light and held by decidedly feminine hand.

"Stop this, Barachiel. Your insanity ends now." I knew that voice, but not the tone. I followed the arm holding the blue-lit blade all the way up to the face of Glory, my guardian angel. She had been peculiarly absent through most of this endeavor, particularly to show up now, right before I was going to get my head split open. Of course, I guess that is what guardian angels do.

"You?!?" Barton, now Barachiel I guess, gasped. "Get away from here, cherub. You have your orders. You are not to interfere in my plans. You cannot disobey me. I outrank you."

"You do, and you are right. I cannot disobey an order or a duty. It is not possible. But I was also ordered to protect this man, and those orders were given long before you embarked on this mad attempt to recall the Father and the Archangels."

I rolled out from under Glory's sword and stepped behind her, stooping to pick up my sword as I went. I was no kind of match for Barachiel in a fair fight, but if I got lucky, maybe I could find a way to cheat.

"That's a loophole, cherub, and you know it. Now get out of my way and let me destroy this mortal," Barachiel said, raising his sword.

"I cannot," Glory replied, her face grim. "He is my charge, and I am his guardian. That is my role, to protect his line. I have done so for millennia and will not stop now just because it inconveniences you."

Millennia? Who the fuck are you, Harker? Flynn asked in my head.

Fucked if I know, apparently, I thought back. I leaned forward and whispered to Glory, "Can you take this guy?"

She didn't bother to lower her voice. "Not a chance. But I will defend you from all threats, or surrender myself in the attempt." With that, she raised her sword and charged Barachiel.

She made a better go of it than I did, but not very much. She immediately spread her wings and took to the air, but Barachiel responded in kind. They danced an aerial duet of blades and flame for almost a minute before Barachiel parried a thrust and responded with a long slice across Glory's belly. She doubled over, and the seraph's blade flashed across her back in a looping slash.

There was an explosion of white lights, and Glory crashed to the ground, crushing bricks to red powder and leaving a foot-deep crater with her impact. Barachiel floated down above her, his sword held high in his right hand, and in his left, dripping with glowing golden blood, he held Glory's wings. He stood over her, wings held high in one hand. While he spoke, the beautiful white feathered wings turned to ash and drifted off onto the wind. When the last of the wings had disintegrated, Barachiel opened his hand and let Glory's holy essence blow away into nothingness.

"Now you are not even a cherub. You aren't fit to soar across the heavens. You shall never again pass through the Gates. You are worse than a mortal. At least they live out their pitiful little powerless lives with the hope of getting into Heaven. But you? No, Glory. You will die here and your essence will be scattered across the ethereal plane. You are nothing, and to nothing you shall return."

"You talk too fucking much," I said, shoving my flaming sword through Barachiel's back. A foot and a half of fiery sword emerged from his chest, and he let out a howl like nothing I've heard even in my worst nightmare. Red-orange flame spread from his chest to engulf his entire form, from head to feet, and he erupted in a brilliant flash of purest white light.

I sprawled to the bricks, knocked loopy from the force of the explosion. I dimly noted that every bruise, scrape, cut, or torn muscle was instantly healed by the outpouring of divine energy. I raised myself up to my elbows, looked around the plaza at my friends and the bodies of dead demons, and managed to croak out, "Does that mean we won?"

Then I passed out.

Epilogue

THE SUN ROSE ON ATLANTA AGAIN, SOMETHING NONE OF US COULD HAVE guaranteed mere hours before, and we gathered in the war room for one last debrief before heading off to our various homes, or what remained of them in Luke's case.

Glory sat at the table with us, her face pale. She was dressed in a spare t-shirt of Flynn's, and it turned out she and Gabby were close enough in size for Glory to borrow pants and other clothes. She hadn't said much since the battle ended, and I was a little worried. Glory was usually pretty quick to let me know what was going on, usually in the snarkiest way possible.

"So is he dead?" Jo asked, grabbing a cruller from the middle of the table. Adam, being the most considerate among us even though he didn't eat or require caffeine, had made a coffee and donut run while the rest of the team showered and searched for unbloodied clothes.

"He is," Glory replied. "His essence will return to the fabric of Heaven, from which we all were formed."

"I don't know what all that means, but I'm good with it," Gabby said. An almost-solid line of powdered sugar rimmed her mouth, making her look somehow even more psychotic than usual.

"What about Orobas?" Adam asked. "He was the one that started this whole mess, after all."

"Well, sort of," I said. "It turns out, even Oro was a little bit of patsy in Barton... I mean Barachiel's plan."

"But is he a dead patsy?" Adam persisted.

"Not exactly," Luke said with a slight smile.

"What does that mean?" Watson asked.

"It means that Mort kept him alive and is taking him back to Charlotte to play with him some more," Luke replied.

"Isn't that a little dangerous?" Watson asked.

"More than a little. We did our best to make sure that he can do no harm, removing his appendages and cauterizing the stumps. Then Mort put him in a casket and is ferrying the torso back to his bar, where he plans a lengthy process of torment for the demon that dared harm his family. I have been invited to assist whenever I so desire." Luke smiled, and I got a little chill.

I'd been in the room in France when Luke had what he referred to as "an unpleasant conversation" with a Nazi spy. Every once in a while I still woke up with those images haunting my dreams. And that guy hadn't hurt anyone Luke actually knew personally. I didn't want to be in Oro's shoes. Not that he needed them anymore.

"What about the Chaos thing?" I asked.

"What Chaos thing?" Luke replied.

"Isn't Mort supposed to take Oro's place as an Agent of Chaos?"

"Yes," Luke said. "Once Orobas dies. That is another reason Mort is keeping Orobas alive." He gave me a smile. "He isn't breaking his word, or even amending his deal. He is simply shifting the timetable."

"Lesson number twelve," I said. "Don't make deals with demons."

Flynn leaned over to Glory. "What about you?"

Glory looked at her. "What about me?" Her voice was flat, lifeless, like someone had ripped away her very essence. Which he had.

"What are you going to do?"

"I don't know what I can do. Without my wings, I am merely a human. And the only one who can restore my wings is the Father Himself. And Barachiel was telling the truth—no one has seen Him since the Great War."

"Well, how do we find him?" I asked.

"How do you find God?" Glory asked. "You might be the last one of all of my charges I expected to ask that question." A little smile crept across her face as she started the long climb back out of the dark places inside herself. As an angel, Glory had never seen those dark places before. We were going to have to watch her as she got used to being human. Hopefully we could make it very temporary.

"Yeah," I said. "I guess it's high time I got a little religion."

"There are two theories on how to bring the Father back to his throne—"

"Is it really a throne?" Gabby asked. I glared at her, and she shrugged.

"Yes, it really is a throne," Glory said. "As you may imagine, the Father is somewhat old-fashioned. In fact, I believe He may be the very meaning of the word. Many feel as Barachiel did, that if humanity is placed in enough jeopardy, God will return to rescue His creation. But so far, despite the human race's best efforts, you have not managed to create enough carnage to get His attention."

"What's the other theory?" Jo asked.

"That if all the Archangels, including Lucifer Morningstar, were brought into one place and called for Him at once, that their collective voice would be enough to call Him."

"Well, okay then. We just need to hunt down some Archangels and get them to ring up old Dad on the phone and get Him to come home, and bring you a set of new wings while He's at it," I said.

"Too bad all the Archangels fled at the same time the Father did," Glory protested. "But…"

"Yes?" Watson prodded.

"You have Michael's sword." She pointed to it leaning in a corner of the room. "That implement is a part of his very being. With that, we may be able to call and bind Michael to one place."

"Okay, that's one," I said. "How many Archangels are there?"

"Seven," Glory said, "plus Lucifer, who was an Archangel before he was cast down."

"So we just need to find their favorite sword, or teddy bear, or whatever, call the Archangels, and by the way, *Satan*, into one place without starting another interdimensional war, then convince them to send God a telegram saying you need your wings back," I said.

"Pretty much," Glory said. She stood up and pushed her chair back from the table. "Thank you for the thought, but it's impossible. I should just get used to being human." She started walking to the door.

I cut her off, putting my hands on her shoulders. "Come on, G," I said. "Look around the room. Impossible is kinda our thing."

"But it will be incredibly dangerous, and quite likely deadly, to handle some of these artifacts. Not to mention the Archangels themselves."

Flynn stood up and moved next to me. "Yeah, dangerous, possibly suicidal? Sounds like every Tuesday. Glory, you saved us all out there. Not just Harker, but the rest of us, too. We had no chance at stopping that bastard until you showed up. We owe you for that. The human race owes you for that."

"And more than that, you're our friend," I said, "and we take care of our own."

"Damn straight," Jo said, standing.

"Absolutely." Watson rose from the table.

"I don't feel the need to stand to add my affirmative response," Adam said, still seated.

"Oh, come on, Frankenstein," Gabby said, tugging on the big man's arm. "We're having a Spartacus moment. And, of course, I'm in. It sounds like the kind of gig where I get to shoot stuff. A lot of stuff."

Adam rose and looked down at Gabby. "I do not like being referred to as Frankenstein. My father's name was Frankenstein."

"Nobody likes a grump, Franky," Gabby said with a smirk.

"So it looks like everybody's with you, G," I said, motioning around the table at the group, every one of them on their feet and looking at us. "Now let's go hunt down some angels and find God."

I looked around the room at my friends, my former guardian angel, and my... what was she now?

"So..." I said, turning to Flynn. "About that ring around your neck..."

She looked at me, that smartass smile on her face, the one that made me realize this was the woman for me in the first place. "What about it?"

"Can I have it back?" I kept my face completely calm and composed, despite the fact that my stomach was roiling.

Becks' face fell, but without a word, she reached around behind her head, unfastened the clasp of her necklace, and handed me the engagement ring I left for her with Glory. Flynn had made it very clear that a proposal via proxy was neither accepted, nor acceptable.

I took both her hands in mine and dropped to one knee. "Rebecca Gail Flynn, I am not a perfect man. A lot of times, I'm not even a good man. And I am so much too old for you that it's not even funny. I don't know where this next quest will take us, but I know this—I want you by my side for it. For this, and for everything that follows. Rebecca... Becks... will you marry me?"

She looked down at me, a pair of tears rolling down her cheeks, a smile that lit up even the darkest corners of my soul on her face, and nodded. "Yes."

I stood up and kissed her thoroughly, then pulled back to look her in the eye. "Then let's go storm the Gates of Heaven."

To Be Continued in Quincy Harker Year Three,

And

The Shadow Council Case Files, Volume One

The Quest for Glory
Begins in 2017

About the Author

John G. Hartness is a teller of tales, a righter of wrong, defender of ladies' virtues, and some people call him Maurice, for he speaks of the pompatus of love. He is also the best-selling author of EPIC-Award-winning series The Black Knight Chronicles from Bell Bridge Books, a comedic urban fantasy series that answers the eternal question "Why aren't there more fat vampires?" In July of 2016. John was honored with the Manly Wade Wellman Award by the NC Speculative Fiction Foundation for Best Novel by a North Carolina writer in 2015 for the first Quincy Harker novella, Raising Hell.

In 2016, John teamed up with a pair of other publishing industry ne'er-do-wells and founded Falstaff Books, a publishing company dedicated to pushing the boundaries of literature and entertainment.

In his copious free time John enjoys long walks on the beach, rescuing kittens from trees and getting caught in the rain. An avid Magic: the Gathering player, John is strong in his nerd-fu and has sometimes been referred to as "the Kevin Smith of Charlotte, NC." And not just for his girth.

Falstaff Books

Want to know what's new
And coming soon from
Falstaff Books?

Try This Free Ebook Sampler
http://bit.ly/falstaffsampler

Follow the link.
Download the file.
Transfer to your e-reader, phone, tablet, watch, computer, whatever.
Enjoy.